MW01119525

To Bruce,

Delighted to hear you are doing so well.

Best wishes for the future,

Jim Rogers

The Iboga Visions

Jim Macgregor

The Iboga

Visions

NGT
PUBLISHING

First published in Great Britain in 2009 by
NGT Publishing Limited,
7 Queens Gardens, Aberdeen, UK.

Copyright © Jim Macgregor 2009
The moral right of Jim Macgregor to be identified as the author of this work has been
asserted by him in accordance with the Copyright, Designs and Patents Act 1988.

ISBN 978 0 9554293 5 4

All rights reserved. No part of this publication may be reproduced,
stored in a retrieval system, or transmitted in any form or by any means,
electronic, mechanical, photocopying, recording, or otherwise, without the prior
permission of both the copyright owner and the above publisher of this book.

British Library Cataloguing-in-Publication Data
A catalogue record for this book is available from the British Library

All characters in this book are fictitious, and any resemblance
to actual persons living or dead is purely coincidental.

Typeset in Minion Pro and Gill by Gravemaker+Scott, tomscot@btinternet.com

Printed and bound by TJ International

www.ngtpublishing.co.uk

ACKNOWLEDGEMENTS

THANKS TO ALL WHO HELPED in the completion of *The Iboga Visions*. I would especially like to acknowledge: Tom Cahill of the U.S. Veterans against War movement for his tremendous encouragement over the years; Nicky Taylor for considerable help with the manuscript; Gerry Docherty for giving so generously and enthusiastically of his expertise and time; Katzel Henderson, Hamish Henderson's widow, and their daughters, Janet and Christine, for kind permission to include excerpts from the great man's *Lament for the Son* – perhaps the finest poem of the Second World War; Patrick Scott Hogg for permission to include lines from his epic, *Tony o'Blair*; Kate Blackadder for her superb editing and suggestions for improving the novel; Norman Thomson of NGT Publishing for his unfailing support; and lastly, but of course by no means least, my wonderful wife Maureen, for being so understanding and for being my wee pal.

PROLOGUE

Northern Mali, Africa.   October 31st 1847.

PRAISE BE TO THE ANCESTRAL spirits for yet another excellent crop of young males. Twenty-three fit and healthy boys had reached puberty and would, this very night, embark on an incredible journey back in time to visit their ancestors. They would return wiser, more aware of their tribal origins, and ready to take their place as men within the tribe.

Six district elders scraped bark from the roots of an iboga shrub and ground it in a large decorated mortar. Only when unanimous agreement on its strength and consistency was reached, would it be presented for the ritual. Dressed in his magnificent ceremonial leopard skins, Chief Liabubu kissed the sacred mortar and held it aloft in presentation to the several thousand gathered before him for the ancient sacramental rite-of-passage ceremony.

Faces laced with apprehension, parents of the initiates stepped forward with wooden bowls to accept equal measures of the iboga. Mothers finger-fed their sons the holy paste as they sat round the baobab by the river. When they began to retch and vomit, fathers took their hands and walked them slowly round the massive tree. When they became drowsy and began to stagger, the boys were taken down to a woman standing waist high in the river. Lindiwe, the most fertile Dogon woman with eighteen living children, passed each of them underwater between her legs. Following their symbolic re-birth, it was time for the journey.

Now virtually comatose, the boys were placed on their backs at a safe distance from a huge bonfire which lit the African night sky. Women with engorged breasts knelt to rub nipples on their lips and express milk into their mouths. A sudden thunderous beating of drums shattered the tranquility, and the communal celebration got underway with feverish singing and naked virgins dancing erotically over them. Apart from one, who appeared to be convulsing, none stirred.

The first of them roused before dawn. By nightfall, all but one had joined the land of the living as men. Though the celebrations continued, Bacari's parents carried him away. They wailed for three days by

7

a big boulder which marked out his grave among many in the children's cemetery. It was no consolation to know that from time to time the ancestors might persuade a boy to stay with them, often the best of the crop.

CHAPTER ONE

Western Desert, Iraq.   April 4th 2003.

THOUGH THERE HAD BEEN little traffic on the Baghdad-Amman road that morning, the Australian SAS soldiers manning the road-block were uncharacteristically quiet. With their long hair and beards, the men of Kilo 6 patrol usually appeared casual and relaxed, but today there was a palpable tension among them as oppressive as the blistering heat on this lonely stretch of desert track. Just the day before, a suicide bomber had loaded a car with explosives and blown himself up at a nearby US army check-point, taking three marines with him. The importance of remaining alert at all times was brought starkly and violently home to the men. Their lives depended on it.

It was four days after 'Shock and Awe'. Coalition troops had triumphantly entered Baghdad, and the Amman road had become a rat run for desperate men fleeing the capital. Several of Saddam Hussein's henchmen making for the border with Jordan had been captured by the Australians, but the big prize they were after was Saddam himself.

'Vehicle approaching at speed!' shouted one of the soldiers when a car appeared in the shimmering distance.

'Take your positions! I've got the road!' barked Sergeant Tom McCartney, resetting the sand-coloured beret on his blond hair. 'If there's the slightest whiff of danger, let the fucker have it!' His hands clenched with annoyance on his M4 machine-gun when the young rookie, Trooper Pete Presley, remained on the road beside him as if rooted to the spot. Not for the first time he wondered if Presley wasn't going to prove to be a liability. 'Elvis!' he yelled practically in his ear, 'move your arse, these motherfuckers are dangerous.' It had the desired effect. Presley started as though he'd been kicked, and ran to take up his position in a shallow ditch alongside the road.

Troopers Mark Binnie, aka Bins, and Mick Hare, known to everyone, even his girlfriend, as Bunny, jumped up onto the back of the long-range patrol vehicle. Bins swung the heavy machine gun round on its tripod to face the oncoming car while Bunny covered the road behind. Presley crouched in the ditch across from McCartney, his M4 at the ready. The other two members of Kilo 6, Bob Brannigan, known

9

as Shortarse because he towered over his mates at six foot six tall and nearly as wide, and the quiet but competent Joey Stevens, took up their stations at strategic points along the road in a state of readiness as the car approached, raising a cloud of dust on the dry desert road.

McCartney rooted his feet on the track and raised a forbidding outstretched palm, his authority underscored by the fire-power that surrounded him. This was always, for him, the tensest moment, but his demeanour didn't betray his relief when the car began to slow.

The middle-aged Iraqi driver was no novice at the games people played in his country – games that had to be played strictly by the rules for anyone to have a hope of survival. He did everything by the book, approaching the road-block slowly and pulling up at the precise point indicated by the soldier when he yelled: 'Get out of the car!' This was not an invitation.

The driver said some words to his three passengers as he slowly opened his door. No sudden movements to upset the man who stood in the road. Tom McCartney had the power to intimidate by his very presence, his supple yet well-muscled six-foot-three frame testament to the hours he spent jogging and working out. The M4 he held underlined the fact that this was a dangerous man to cross. The driver held his hands up, palms forward, when he got out of the ageing Peugeot.

As the driver walked forward and McCartney readied himself for a routine document check, the front passenger door opened and a woman stepped out. A yell came from the back of the car then all hell broke loose. What followed took place in less than five seconds, McCartney estimated later, far too short a time for anything other than instinct to play its part in the tragic chain of events.

In that instant McCartney's attention was diverted from the driver to the passenger, his body alert and ready to fire if need be. He was surprised to see a young woman dressed in western clothing. She walked quickly towards him, smiling as she reached inside her white canvas bag.

McCartney's entire body involuntarily tensed as Elvis screamed unintelligibly and pulled once on the trigger of his M4, firing three bullets into the woman's back. Just as her body hit the ground, a man leapt from the back of the car yelling and running towards McCartney. In immediate response, Trooper Binnie up on the patrol vehicle opened fire, the merciless blast of heavy machine gun fire wiping out the whole party instantly – the driver, the running man and the remaining back seat passenger – and reducing the car to no more than a pile of burning scrap.

The devastating noise and violence of those few seconds was succeeded by a strange moment of quiet and calm, with only the crackling of the burning car to disrupt it.

McCartney knelt over the woman, shaking with the adrenaline coursing round his body, to confirm a non-existent carotid pulse in her neck. His first thought, bizarrely, considering the wreck of a body that lay before him, was, 'young and pretty'. Her vivid blue eyes seemed to stare accusingly at him, as the blood congealed in her blonde hair. The sweet fragrance of her Chanel No 5 mingled with the noxious smell of burning human flesh and tyres that filled his nostrils.

Presley broke almost a minute of stunned silence. 'Fuckin weapon, she was reaching for a fuckin weapon!'

McCartney said nothing as he gently moved the woman's right arm, her lifeless hand stopped for ever as it reached in her canvas bag. He marvelled at how in those few seconds the bag's pristine whiteness had been dyed entirely red with not a speck of white showing through the rapidly drying blood. His stomach lurched when he recognized the passport clutched in her dead hand. 'Australian! Jesus Christ Almighty, she's fuckin Aussie.'

Within two hours, US troops had surrounded the area and senior military investigators were arriving by helicopter. News of another four dead Iraqis might earn a few inside lines in the following morning's newspapers, but three of the dead were Westerners. It was certain that the incident would make front page news across the world when it emerged that the dead Australian and her two travelling companions were opponents of the Iraq war and had been in the country as human shields. The Iraqi driver had been taking them from Baghdad to Amman on the first leg of their journey home via Jordan. It had all the ingredients of a media fuck-fest. Nothing was more certain to feed their frenzy, for the massacre of the innocents would make wonderful copy.

When Tom McCartney learned this, his first response was anger. The international group of peace activists, whose ultimate aim was to stop the war by 'shielding' strategic targets from possible US-UK attack simply by their presence on site, had been one extra and unquantifiable threat for the blokes on the ground. He believed the civilians were totally misguided, and didn't seem to comprehend that their very presence in areas of conflict was inevitably destined to put the troops in danger. And now, due to the foolhardy actions of a naïve and unthinking civilian who should never have been in the country in the first place, three other people lay dead.

When the implications became clear, Kilo 6 was ordered back to base. Given the circumstances, somebody would have to take responsibility for the killing of a group of unarmed civilians. McCartney knew that the officer who had thought it a sensible idea to post the untested Presley to such a volatile area would not be the one to take the blame.

Although not quite as young as his baby face and tendency to blush made him appear, Pete Presley had been worryingly inexperienced alongside the cynical and hardened troopers of the Special Air Service Regiment. He had been assigned to the regiment and Kilo 6 just days earlier to replace Matt Brownlow, who'd been wounded by a sniper's bullet.

Of course it wasn't Presley's fault, but the men had not found it easy to accept him in the place of the comrade who had been with them for the last eighteen months – it would be difficult for any man to fit seamlessly into a patrol which had been through so much together that each knew the others' responses instinctively. Presley had undergone some specialist SASR training but not yet passed the extremely testing selection course. Although he had proved himself a good soldier to get this far, he wasn't used to their oft-times unorthodox approach to the job compared with the regular army regiment from which he'd been drafted.

It was a subdued and strangely quiet group of men who were driven back to their camp at the huge Al Asad airbase, 180 kilometres west of Baghdad. The normal banter was absent and the nearest anyone got to humour was Bob Brannigan's comment as they set off: 'That's another fine mess you got us into, Stanley.'

'But I thought she was going for a gun,' Presley complained for the umpteenth time. In truth he was not the only one who had thought that.

'But I thought she was,' mimicked Brannigan.

'Easy on, Shortarse. Don't give the boy a hard time,' interrupted Joey, ever the peacemaker. 'He assessed the sheila was a threat, he neutralized the threat. End of story.'

'And the guy, acting like a fuckin dickhead. What did he expect us to do?' added Bins. 'Christ Almighty, fuckin peaceniks. They come out here thinking they're saving the fuckin world and they can't even keep their fuckin heads down.'

'Have a thought for the driver,' put in McCartney from the front. 'Poor bastard follows the rules, dead safe, no problem, and the numb-nut westerners get him shot to pieces.'

A silence settled over the vehicle as the six men pondered on the ironies of fate.

Bunny spoke for the first time. 'So Tom, what's the score? How d'ya reckon the brass will play it?'

'Like they always do. They'll either spin like fuck to deflect blame from us, from the army, or they'll fuck us good and proper. Hang us out to dry. It'll depend on the reaction and pressure from politicians and the media. If it gets too heavy they'll say we're a rogue element in an otherwise highly professional and disciplined coalition force; nothing more than a few rotten apples in the barrel. They'll announce they've removed us from the barrel and we'll be court martialled. I don't need to tell you they'll be instructed to play it in whatever way guarantees the best outcome for our political masters.' McCartney turned in the front passenger seat to eyeball each of his men sitting behind. 'Kilo 6 will play it by the book. The last time we had a minor fuck up it nearly turned into a major incident because I lied. We tell it like it happened, no spin, no bullshit. A split-second decision which proved to be the wrong one. Anyone got an argument with that?'

'No Sarge,' came the unanimous response.

Brannigan glanced at Presley and opened his mouth to speak. A frown from Joey and he closed it again. Nothing was going to be served by berating the lad for his lack of experience, but he knew his thoughts were echoed by the other four members of Kilo 6. If Matt Brownlow hadn't taken that sniper's bullet, it was a cast-iron certainty they wouldn't be at the centre of what was sure to become an international storm.

McCartney hardly spoke for the rest of the journey. As the patrol leader he knew he was likely to get it in the neck for the disaster. He went over it again and again in his mind, wondering if he could have acted any differently. Truth was, he was so stunned by Presley killing the woman that his normally calm and clear mind had frozen for those essential seconds when he maybe could have prevented the slaughter. But that was a big maybe. Once the second passenger jumped from the car screaming, Binnie's burst on the big machine gun was inevitable. All their training said if they believed they were under attack they must take out every potential threat. In fact – from a certain angle, they had played it by the fuckin book.

But for all his rationalizing, McCartney couldn't put the memory of those piercing blue eyes or her smile out of his mind. It was the genuine and friendly smile that had first relaxed his guard. She hadn't for one moment struck him as a threat. Looking back on it, he would describe it as a smile of recognition. The Aussie woman had obviously recognized their berets and Excalibur badges and was delighted to meet a group of fellow countrymen in the middle of a foreign desert. For that, they had gunned her down in cold blood.

Yet, at the same time as that huge sense of guilt, he also felt resentment towards them. He knew that his whole future career in the SAS Regiment, in the army, now hung in the balance. Who did they think they were? Fuckin amateurs playing at peace-making. Acting like they had a God-given right to question military authority. All his life so far had brought him to this point without deviation. And now he could lose it all for a moment's miscalculation caused by peacenik motherfuckin do-gooders.

McCartney had wanted to join the army since he was a child, forever playing at soldiers in the back yard of his grandparents' big old house in Melbourne. He had been brought up by them after his mother died when he was just four years old. As soon as his grandmother allowed, he had started taking regular camping trips alone in the outback, loving the challenge of surviving in the wilderness by using his own skills, even at that young age.

It was the same desire for physical challenge that led him to take up judo and karate, and go on to become the youngest ever in his home state awarded a black belt. Sure, on a couple of occasions he had lost control and damaged an opponent – but they were contact sports, for fucksake. He started competing in triathlons, still searching for the ultimate challenge.

McCartney had enlisted on the first day he was eligible, and applied to join the SASR very soon after. On completion of his initial six-year term, he had readily agreed to sign on for another three and was immediately promoted to Sergeant. During his service he had been involved in many highly dangerous reconnaissance and rescue missions in Afghanistan and elsewhere. If he had to be cruel and unforgiving to an enemy who would kill him, then so be it. He was a soldier.

Sergeant McCartney was proud to be playing his part in operation Iraqi Freedom and the campaign to install democracy in Iraq. It was, for him, a just war against the threat of weapons of mass destruction, terror and totalitarianism. His patrol was among the very first of the crack Australian troops sent into Iraq. Each man was highly trained, supremely fit, and chosen by McCartney himself. They had been parachuted into the Western Desert a full month before the war officially started, with a mission to gather intelligence deep behind enemy lines. They had been spectacularly successful, but their luck turned when Matt Brownlow, the oldest member of the unit, was wounded and evacuated. McCartney actually preferred a five-man patrol, and had been content to carry on as such, but pressure had been brought to bear on him to accept an untested replacement in the form of Pete Presley. The young soldier's SASR selection test had been postponed because resources were overstretched by the demand for troops in Iraq. McCartney had reluctantly agreed, but wished now he had stuck to his guns and refused. Christ, what value hindsight?

Throughout his service, McCartney had been a model soldier. As a sergeant in the elite Australian regiment, he was not a man to be crossed. He was nearing completion of three years as sergeant and intended signing on for yet another three. Now, as the truck lurched towards their destiny, he knew there was a very real chance of it all falling apart, his career reduced to no more than sand blowing off the barren desert.

They discovered the full extent of the media mayhem the following morning back at base. It seemed as though every television channel, every newspaper, and every news website in the world was covering the story. It was already common knowledge that the Australian woman was Donna Mulhearty, a journalist and one of the first human shields to arrive in Iraq. Her two companions in the car, also human shields, were Tom Cahill, an American Vietnam veteran turned peace activist, and Giuseppi Del Buon from Italy. The three were on their way home after US troops entered Baghdad. Fuck! How unlucky could he be? Add Hashim Abdallah, the unfortunate Iraqi driver, and they had managed to stir up righteous indignation on four continents at once. That had to be a world record!

The names of those killed seemed to be the only thing the media agreed on. Some reports suggested the Iraqi driver had fired on the soldiers first, while other stated that the patrol had opened fire after he ignored their instructions to stop. Reports from journalists embedded with the US military were riddled with contradictions in what appeared to be a deliberate attempt to sow confusion in the public's mind. The official version was modified numerous times to a definitive account: The vehicle approached the soldiers at an alarming speed, but eventually stopped. The woman jumped from the car and moved towards them in a threatening manner. They believed she was reaching for a weapon, or to detonate a suicide bomb. They responded to the perceived threat by shooting her. Likewise, others in the car were behaving erratically, considered a threat, and shot. Compared to earlier reports suggesting the driver had opened fire, it was closer to the truth – if such a concept can be permitted in matters political or military.

Sergeant McCartney and his men were subjected to repeated interviews, together and individually, with the three man team charged with the task of investigating the incident. SASR Captain, Roger Cooper, was the officer in charge. Captain Ben Jones was from the US military, who had insisted on having some input since the Australian troops in Iraq were working in conjunction with them. The final member of the team was Captain Steve Grey from the Australian Army Public Relations office, whose job it would be to sanitize and present the findings of the investigation for public consumption.

Captains Jones and Grey took Troopers Presley and Binnie away for individual interviews, while Captain Cooper asked McCartney to come with him. The other three members of Kilo 6 had to sit and stew in the waiting room until it was their turn to face the inquisition.

'Well, Tom,' said Cooper, once the two men were settled in the small interview room. 'I'm sorry to see you in this situation. An almighty cock-up out there, it seems?' It is always encouraging when the judge opens an enquiry with his complicit conclusion.

'I'd say it was an accident waiting to happen, sir.' Tom decided that this one he would have to play with a straight bat. He had known and worked with Roger for years, but this was no time for chumminess. He had important points to make. 'Once foreign civilian peace activists were allowed into the area, and once the decision was taken to assign an inexperienced trooper to the patrol, it was inevitable.'

'Can you explain a little more what you mean by that?' encouraged Roger.

'I mean that we had two unknown quantities here. The westerners were inexperienced in how to behave safely in the situation, and like any raw recruit might, Trooper Presley reacted precipitously in the circumstances. Sir.'

'But Trooper Presley was under your command, Tom. Do you take no responsibility for his error of judgement?'

'Of course, the ultimate responsibility is mine. I'm not denying that, no. I had stressed to him just prior to the fuck-up that our safety relied on following our training. However, sir, you know yourself that in the heat of any critical situation, training needs to be backed up by experience.'

Roger nodded, took some notes and seemed satisfied with Tom's stance. 'Moving on, then, to Trooper Binnie. In your report you say he immediately opened fire on the second civilian. Another error of judgement?'

'No sir. The man who jumped from the car appeared to Binnie to be acting in an erratic and unpredictable way. He was, he definitely was. Never seen anyone do anything so fuckin stupid as that, and it's the very behaviour we look for when assessing potential suicide bombers. From his position on the back of the LRPV, Binnie didn't have the same view of the woman as Presley. Once Presley opened fire, Binnie considered the patrol to be under attack and opened fire in turn.'

After some moments of silence, and for the first time since he had invited him into the room, Roger looked directly into McCartney's deep-set blue eyes. 'This is the six-million-dollar question, Tom. Why did you not order your men to cease fire once the woman was shot? An error of judgement on your part?'

'No sir.' McCartney looked back with eyes that bore no doubt, 'When the man jumped out of the car we had had no chance to find out whether or not the woman had been going for a weapon. It happened in an instant. Could easily have been a set-up. Once Presley opened fire, we were in automatic mode. There was no time to issue any order between Presley shooting the woman and Binnie opening fire from the LRPV. There was hardly time to think. We're trained to act and, I would stress this, I had no proof that the passengers in the car were not a threat. So even had there been time to order ceasefire, I might not have done. My priority has to be the safety of the patrol. Sir.'

Over the next week both McCartney and the other five men repeatedly gave their account of those few seconds when they were asked the same questions time after time by the officers: What did you see? Why did you open fire? Did all members of the patrol act correctly? Were you in the correct positions for such an operation? In hindsight would you have acted differently?

McCartney never wavered from his account: He and his men were properly positioned for the operation. The car was the only one on the road. Its driver was given ample warning to stop and did so appropriately. When the driver was instructed to get out, he emerged slowly, demonstrating that his hands were empty. Almost immediately, the woman opened the front passenger door and the man sitting directly behind shouted at her. She walked forward with a smile on her face whilst reaching inside her bag. At that instant, Trooper Presley yelled out and shot her. The back seat passenger, who had shouted at the woman, immediately threw open his door and leapt out. Trooper Binnie considered the patrol to be under attack and opened fire. The entire episode, from the driver getting out of the car to all four being killed, took about five seconds. Over and over again the story was agreed and repeated like a sacred mantra.

Asked if he considered himself culpable in any way, McCartney replied that he had, in hindsight, made an error in accepting Trooper Presley into his team. He added that he was not blaming Presley for shooting the woman. In the instant Presley had to react to what he believed was a serious threat to the patrol, he did exactly as he should have done and neutralized that threat. He made it clear that if blame had to be attached then it should lie with those who ordered Presley's transfer – and the politicians who appeased interfering peaceniks. This was not recorded.

Over the following weeks, the incident received less and less international attention as other major events unfolded in Iraq. Human shields were vilified by the American press as 'Saddam dupes and stooges' and 'terrorist supporters, morons and cowards'. The Republican Senator for

South Carolina labelled them 'treasonous for giving aid and comfort to US enemies'.

Australian newspapers quoted an Australian Defence spokesman: 'Tactical actions were reviewed after the incident and were determined to be in accordance with the rules of engagement. Some internal aspects of the patrol were investigated fully and appropriate action has been initiated. For the protection of our soldiers the Australian Defence Force does not normally publicly discuss the details of internal investigations and any disciplinary action taken. We treat these issues confidentially in order to allow correct and appropriate application of military law.'

Another Australian official stated: 'I don't find anything strange in this at all. I mean, when the military is in combat you expect quite confused situations. It's important for the SAS Regiment to be allowed to operate without excessive public scrutiny. People can't sit here in armchairs taking an antiseptic look at things. You really have to trust the decisions of the people on the ground when you put them in that type of combat situation. Believe me, we know how to deal with these things. We'd like to tell you more, but it's not in the national interest.'

Trooper Presley returned to Australia on 'extended leave' and was never to wear the SASR insignia nor, indeed, an army uniform again. Sergeant McCartney and Kilo 6 were cleared of responsibility for the deaths and sent back on duty as a five-man patrol. Lieutenant Colonel Gardiner, their commanding officer, offered words of support and quietly encouraged McCartney to keep his patrol out of the limelight. These things, and much worse, happen in war.

CHAPTER TWO

'AND SO, LADIES AND GENTLEMEN of the jury, examination of Miss Mulhearty's body will prove conclusively that Sergeant McCartney did not shoot her; will prove that my client is completely innocent of the charge of murder for which he stands before this court today.'

Sitting in the dock in full dress uniform, McCartney instinctively straightened as his Defence Counsel addressed the jury. After a pause the barrister added: 'Unfortunately the body is missing. We are confident this is merely an administrative oversight, and I shall be requesting an adjournment until such time as it is recovered.'

There was a ripple of movement through the members of the jury at this totally unexpected development. They turned to look at each other, some still clearly keen to see him proved not guilty, but the majority looked sceptical or downright disbelieving. McCartney knew that if he didn't speak up now, he might be spending the rest of his life in prison.

'Please your honour,' he said, addressing the judge who was dressed in full red velvet and ermine robes. 'I think I know where the body is. I can find it.'

The judge instructed both barristers to approach the bench and held a whispered conversation with them. He glowered down at McCartney, intoning: 'You have twenty-four hours to find the body of the deceased. Return at this time tomorrow.'

McCartney made his way alone to the basement of an ancient Mesopotamian building. It was dark and cold. Cold as the grave. A blast of air rushed past his face and the stench of death and decay almost overwhelmed him. Feeling rough stone walls beneath his hands, he took cautious steps forward. Underfoot the ground felt soft but uneven, and he appeared to be walking over something at one and the same time yielding and constricting. As he edged round a corner, a narrow shaft of sunlight revealed highly decorated coloured tiles and exotic carvings on the walls. He came to an abrupt halt. His heart began pounding wildly as he made sense of the horrific scene before him. He was standing at a junction in a maze of stone tunnels with recessed tombs in the walls. Shafts of daylight pierced the gloom at widely spaced intervals, and he could see that countless thousands of bodies had been laid out on the floors of the tunnels which branched off in all directions. Grotesquely, every corpse had been skinned so that the skull and protruding eyeballs made each look exactly the same as the next. The mutilated dead reminded him of the photographs of dissected bodies he had seen in an old anatomy book, photographs that had fascinated and terrified him when he was a youth.

Holding a hankerchief to his face he bent closer to investigate, reaching down with his hand. 'What the fuck?' he screamed as a hand grabbed hold of his. The cold, dead hand began pulling, pulling him down to join the morass of bodies which filled the tunnel. Dragging himself away, he looked around frantically and started to run.

'Vivid blue eyes, vivid blue eyes,' the mocking mantra repeated over and over with the rhythm of an express train, the blood pounding in his head as he ran searching for Donna Mulhearty's body in the endless tunnels of this stinking hell. It was the fragrance of Chanel No 5 that stopped him in his tracks at an arched doorway where ancient steps disappeared down into darkness. Guided by the light of a candle, he cautiously made his way down into a dungeon. More and yet more legions of skinned and rotting bodies lay in tangled heaps in every corner. A grieving mother could not have identified her own in this mass of intertwined arms and legs, but the hint of perfume drew him onwards.

Moving body parts with his foot, and leaning in for a closer inspection, he saw the unmistakable vivid blue eyes deep in the midst of the stinking pile. Those eyes that haunted his thoughts since he had first seen them, suddenly flickered and stared accusingly at him. He reeled back in horror when the Australian woman's skinned corpse raised an arm towards him, clutching her passport and pleading wordlessly that he save her.

'I'm sorry, so sorry' he cried, his breath constricting, making him choke.

He felt a hand on his shoulder and flinched away. 'Please forgive me. I should have,' he sobbed. The hand began to shake him insistently.

'Tom, you're doing it again,' said a familiar voice. 'Wake up, Tom, wake up!'

He opened his tear-filled eyes to see the concerned face of Joey Stevens peering over him where he lay in his sleeping bag under the camouflage net. 'It was the same nightmare again, Joey, exactly the same.'

Joey shook his head. 'You can't go on like this. You need to get yourself to the doc, Tom. This is doing none of us any good. None of us.'

Fully awake, Tom gathered his wits, embarrassed that one of his men had seen him in such a vulnerable state. 'I'll be all right,' he said. 'Now bugger off.'

'Please, Tom. You're making yourself ill.'

'You're such a fuckin old woman,' he snarled. 'Get your arse back out there.'

Joey shook his head and turned to go.

'And Joey' he grabbed his leg and forced him to turn back.

'What?'

'Don't breathe a fuckin word of this.'

Tom was fooling himself if he believed the others hadn't noticed the change in him since their return to duty. He was edgy and irritable and had withdrawn from the usual camaraderie of macho banter and calculated insult.

Despite his rejection of Joey's suggestion to see the medical officer, he had been close to doing just that several times, but was worried what the MO might discover. No, more than that, he was worried what the MO might do. Since the incident on the Amman road he had been suffering from insomnia. Each and every night, if he did eventually fall asleep, the horrific nightmare of the catacombs recurred. By day he was anxious and nervy, jumping at the slightest unexpected noise, paranoid and bristling at the personal comments routinely made by the rest of the men. One incident in particular had shaken all of them. They were on a rest period drinking in the bar at the airbase when Jim Tranter, sergeant of Kilo 5, spotted them sitting together in the corner. He headed straight over, calling out loud enough for all heads in the room to turn: 'Well, if it isn't the Trigger-Happy 6.'

The four privates returned the insult good-naturedly, with various hand gestures and comments about his parentage.

'On your own?' queried Brannigan. 'Where's your girl guides? Fucked off with some big boys?' he jeered good humouredly, referring pointedly to Kilo 5's widely known lack of positive results over the past couple of weeks.

'Well, at least we haven't killed any civilians recently,' retorted Tranter.

'Fuck you!' muttered Tom, draining his beer.

The others laughed. It was a kind of acceptance.

Tom leapt to his feet. 'Shut your fuckin mouths,' he yelled. 'The lot of you! I'm sick to death of the whole business. And as for you Tranter, what the fuck would you know about it?'

Tom's men looked at him uneasily. A few weeks ago, he would have been giving as good as he got and then some. 'Hey, hey, calm down, Tom, the man's offering his support,' said Joey, putting a restraining hand on his arm.

'I don't need fuckin support,' he growled, as he pushed Joey away and stomped off to the bar. 'I need another drink.'

When he returned a few minutes later carrying his stubby and a whisky, they were discussing the dead Australian woman. It was now common knowledge that the Mulhearty family and her boyfriend were creating a huge problem back home for the Australian Government. They had made clear in press and television interviews that they blamed the soldiers, and were demanding action be taken against them. Her father told the world's media he did not believe official accounts of her death and wanted the culprits brought face to face with the family to explain exactly what happened. The army had bluntly rejected the claims and demands.

'At the end of the day,' Bunny Hare was saying, 'we're blameless for the deaths. These things happen in war.'

'Aye,' agreed Bins. 'We've got a job to do.'

Jim Tranter nodded. 'It was just another bad day at the office.'

Tom, who had just taken a mouthful of beer from his stubby, physically recoiled when he heard this. Without warning he launched himself across the table, knocking drinks flying, and smashed the bottle over Tranter's head. 'You fuckin drongo. You stupid, fuckin drongo,' he screamed. Blood spurted from Tranter's head as the other men wrestled the broken bottle from Tom. When a semblance of order was restored, Bunny joined Tranter at the first-aid post for stitches to his hand. Shortarse Brannigan hustled Tom out of the bar. 'C'mon, you're sinkin too much piss, mate.'

Once outside, the fight went out of him and he allowed the huge soldier to take him quietly to his quarters.

'What the fuck was all that about?' asked Brannigan.

'Sorry, cobber. Lost it for a minute there.' He tried to pass it off with a laugh. 'Tell Tranter to be better prepared next time. Calls himself an expert in hand-to-hand?'

'You need to hit the sack, Tom. You're fucked letting all this get to you, mate.'

There was a silence of understanding between them. Words were not required. Brannigan headed back to the bar. Once the door closed behind him, Tom finally allowed himself to let go. He lay face down on the bed and wept.

Tom McCartney's mental turmoil rapidly worsened thereafter. His anxiety increased until he felt permanently strained when on duty, and it began to affect his confidence to make decisions. He had been renowned for his ability to offer sound operational judgements in an instant, but now found his mind clouded by indecision. The dreaded 'what if?' would present itself every time he was called on to make a snap decision. What if that car is full of civilians? What if it's a suicide bomber? What if one of the patrol makes the wrong decision? What if there's a sniper hiding in that ruined building? This one was a newly insistent worry. Snipers were certainly a regular threat, but once the niggling doubt had entered his mind, it rapidly leapt from possibility to probability. He permanently expected one of their number to be picked off each time they turned a corner or broke down a door.

It soon reached the stage where McCartney was finding it more and more difficult to walk or drive past any building. He was constantly scanning the area for real or imagined threats, to the point where the rest of the patrol lost confidence in him. He was so concerned with the tiny, minute details of whether that was a shadow in the rubble of a ruined building, or a movement in the shrubs and bushes nearby, that he stopped looking at the big picture and found himself unable to make operational decisions that shaped their days on duty. He ran the permutations of every decision through his head before giving an order, anxious that he was making the wrong call. Most worrying of all, he knew he was doing these destructive things, thinking these irrational thoughts, yet he couldn't stop himself. The excessive worry about snipers he traced back to the incident where Matt Brownlow was wounded. Although at the time he had treated it merely as bad luck, as had Matt and the rest of the guys, he now began to question his judgement in that situation. He blamed himself for allowing it to happen to his oldest and most trusted patrol member. The road-block disaster had merely reinforced his loss of confidence in his own judgement. Even worse, he recognized – whether rightly or not – that the nagging doubt about the soundness of his judgement had led him to handle that incident badly. He knew, his men knew, and he knew his men were starting to doubt him.

In addition to these constant worries and nightmares, McCartney was suffering from severe pounding headaches, poor concentration and flashbacks to the Amman road incident. It left him feeling persistently tired and drained and took a heavy toll on his relationship with his men. Part of the close bonding between the members of a small unit like theirs, so essential to keep them an effective, efficient and safe fighting force, was based on the fact that they socialized together, that they were genuinely friends. It was routine for them to drink together at the bar during their off-duty rest periods, and to share details of their family news when they received their weekly mail.

All this was now threatened. The troopers of Kilo 6 could see that he was having a hard time, but he wouldn't let any of them near enough to help him, or even to talk about his problems with them. Tom began isolating himself, fearing he was losing his sanity. Following the incident with Jim Tranter, he started drinking with US marines on the Al Asad base rather than with his Australian comrades. The Yanks were a sociable lot, and tended to gather together in a large noisy group in the bar, joking and laughing. Some nights they would get quite riotous, with singing or arguments developing depending on the way the mood turned. Tom felt he could be more anonymous among them, allowing the noise and convenient camaraderie to blank out the constant anxiety in his head. In an effort to stop the nightmares he was drinking heavily, but still the bad dreams recurred night after night.

Late one evening, as was becoming increasingly frequent, Tom was still in the bar after most of the others had drifted back to their rooms. In search of anything to put off the moment when he would have to head for his own bed, and endure the inevitable disturbed sleep and nightmares which waited for him there, he went over to where the last remaining marines, Dave Cartwright and Mike O'Brien, were sitting, head to head in a corner. Tom slumped down opposite them with the remains of his beer, as the barman pulled down the shutters over the bar and began wiping the tables. 'Hey guys, got no homes to go to?' he slurred. The two Americans looked up.

'Just seeing to a bit of business,' said Dave in a low voice, passing a small package to Mike.

'What's that, then?' Tom asked bluntly, his drunkenness masking the blindingly obvious.

'Keep your voice down, buddy,' said Dave.

'Something to help me sleep,' explained Mike, examining the plastic bag of small white tablets.

'Fuck sake, that's just what I need. Seriously, I've not slept well for months. The booze doesn't make any difference now.'

'Well, a couple of these before you turn in and you'll sleep like a baby,' said Mike.

'Can you get me some?' The desperation in his voice was obvious. 'If I don't get some decent kip soon, I'll go out my fuckin mind.'

'This guy,' said Mike, indicating Dave, 'Can get you anything. Tell you what, take a couple of these tonight, and see how you go.' He pressed two of the tablets into Tom's hand.

'I'll bring some more tomorrow night,' said Dave. 'Make sure you've got cash on you.'

'Sweet dreams,' said Mike as they parted.

'I hope so,' said Tom.

The diazepam knocked him out. Though still haunted by disturbing dreams he got a better night's sleep than for many a week. Most importantly, he was not visited once by the corpse of Donna Mulhearty. When he awoke, he found himself drowsy and unable to think clearly or function normally, but as the morning wore on his energy levels rose, and his mind cleared. The patrol noticed he was in a better humour, even cracking the occasional joke. Where once they would have groaned, they responded with far heartier laughs than were warranted.

Tom sought Dave Cartwright in the bar that evening and secured a fortnight's supply of the little white pills.

For the next few days Kilo 6 were carrying out surveillance of known trouble spots in the Baghdad area. Supported by his chemical props, Tom's anxiety levels were much lower, but within a week of starting the diazepam, he found himself back among the skinned and rotting corpses, searching for the vivid blue eyes of Donna Mulhearty. This time, however, when her hand reached out to grab him, the diazepam prevented him from waking properly and he was subjected to a horrifying, endless chase through the catacombs, running, always running to get away from the hordes of corpses which rose up and pursued him. He woke bathed in sweat, shaking and terrified.

Tom didn't dare take any diazepam for the next three nights. He tossed and turned, desperate for sleep, but at the same time afraid of falling back into the nightmare. During what snatched moments of sleep he got, the vivid blue eyes of the Australian peace activist were constantly following him, her finger pointing at him, her passport clutched in her skinned and bloody hand. Accusing and cursing him.

As soon as they returned to base, Tom went to see Dave Cartwright. 'Hey there,' the American greeted him. 'After more of the old knockout pills?'

Tom grimaced. 'Not so good at knocking me out as I hoped. But I suppose a bigger dosage might work?'

Dave looked at the Australian, noting the bags under his eyes and his increasingly haunted and haggard appearance. 'I've got something else that should do the trick,' he said. 'Come to my quarters this evening.'

When the rest of Kilo 6 left for the bar, Tom slipped out and headed for the American quarters. Following Dave's directions, he opened the door to a small four-bedded room where he found Dave, Mike O'Brien and another marine with a southern accent, who he knew from their bar-room sessions as Chuck, having a bit of a party. Beer cans and a half-drunk bottle of bourbon spilled onto the floor. There was an ashtray full of cigarette ends, and the air was thick with smoke, but the smell in the air wasn't tobacco.

Chuck waved languidly at him and Mike laughed in a lazy way. This was so unlike their usual hyped-up hail-fellow-well-met way in the bar. Only Dave seemed to be his normal, pretty serious, business-like self.

'Tom, good to see ya,' he said. 'Grab a beer.'

He cleared a space on the edge of one of the beds and sat down. Picking up a tinny from the floor, he popped it open and drank a long draught. 'So,' he said, feeling unaccountably nervous. 'Have you got something for me?'

'Have we got something for you!' said Mike conspiratorially, laughing foolishly and lying back on the bed opposite Tom.

'Sure,' said Dave. He tossed a sealed plastic bag onto his lap. Tom picked it up and inspected it, expecting to see tablets. He was surprised to see there was, instead, a small amount of a light brown powder in the bag.

'What's this then?' he asked suspiciously.

'Ah,' said Dave. 'A novice.'

'That, ol' buddy,' said Chuck, smiling knowingly, 'is the answer to a maiden's prayer.'

'It's heroin,' Dave finally came to the point. 'Heroin of the very best quality, hot from Afghanistan.'

A wave of anxiety overcame Tom and he licked his lips, his mouth suddenly dry. He took another long drink from his beer. 'You haven't got any other pills, then? This isn't my scene, mate.'

'Well,' said Dave slowly, 'I'm sure I could find you something. But nothing that'll hit the spot the way this does.'

'How d'ya know it's not your scene till you try it, buddy?' asked Chuck.

'Yeah,' agreed Mike. 'I was wary myself at first. But trust me, it makes all that crap out there' – he jerked his thumb towards the war zone outside – 'bearable.'

'I'm not injecting any shit into myself,' said Tom.

'No need for that,' said Dave. 'The thing to do is smoke it.'

'No evidence, see,' explained Chuck. 'No marks on the arms for the MO to find.'

'And,' added Mike, 'it's not addictive if you smoke it.'

'Really?' said Tom, dubiously.

'Really,' said Dave. 'Wanna try?'

Tom tussled with his conscience, with everything he had read, with his very upbringing. All of which told him heroin was a bad scene. 'Okay,' he said finally, in sheer desperation. Anything that might rid him of Donna Mulhearty's ghost would be worth it.

The marines demonstrated how to heat up a small amount of heroin on silver foil, then to inhale the smoke through a rolled-up piece of card. He sucked in the hot smoke and, to his surprise, found that he was almost instantly overtaken by a feeling of calm and relaxation as a pleasant warmth flooded his whole body. His worries became a distant memory. His brain stopped racing through the myriad of obsessive thoughts, fears and concerns which had dogged him for months past. He felt an overwhelming sense of friendliness towards the three soldiers who had introduced him to such a dramatic release from his mental turmoil. Chuck and Mike smiled at him, both clearly in a similar state. Dave Cartwright, however, was merely watching with his customary calculating look. This wasn't personal, it was business and he knew that his customer base had just expanded.

Half an hour later, Tom began to feel sleepy. The relaxation of his body, and the calming of his mind, was finally chasing away the insomnia that had bedevilled him. He managed to gather his wits enough to tell them he was going back to his own quarters. Dave reminded him that he wasn't going anywhere before he'd paid for the heroin. Smiling happily Tom pulled a wad of notes from his pocket and stared at the roll of tatty paper. He laughed. Money seemed such a frivolous thing all of a sudden. 'Take what I owe you, mate,' he invited Dave, who duly took a handful. Tom had no idea how much, nor whether it was a fair amount for the drugs Dave had supplied him. It didn't matter.

He surprised himself by finding his way back home without any difficulty. Although he felt largely disconnected from reality, he discovered there was a central part of his brain which remained reasonably clear and could function on a practical level. He made his way to his bed and crawled in fully dressed. For the first time in ages, he slept the sleep of the just for the entire night.

Tom awoke the next morning more refreshed than he could remember in a long time, but in the cold light of day it struck him like a thunderbolt what he had got himself into. He pulled the bag of heroin from his trouser pocket and studied the innocuous-looking brown powder. He knew all the horror stories about addiction – had, indeed, seen it among the ranks of the army. Alcohol had always been his drug of choice – and prior to the last few months he rarely ever drank heavily. His sensible head told him to take the powder and flush it down the toilet immediately. Yet he found himself putting the bag of heroin back in his pocket. The relief from his troubles had been so dramatic that he knew he would be prepared to take any risk with his health for even a temporary respite. Anyway, he reasoned, the guys had assured him that inhaling it didn't lead to addiction in the way that injecting it did. He pulled out the depleted bundle of notes from his other pocket. Either heroin was a more expensive drug than he had realized, or Cartwright had fleeced him. The big Yank, he realized, was a man who would do nobody, other than himself, any favours. He resolved that, before buying anything further from Cartwright, he would agree the price first, and pay up before he took it.

Later, Tom realized that that was the only sensible decision he had made. Although resolving to keep the heroin use to a minimum, to use it only in extremis when he desperately needed sleep or his mind was totally messed, within a couple of weeks his usage was creeping up and he was constantly looking forward to his next smoke.

For about eight weeks he was using heroin every night before he went to bed, and had not a single nightmare over that period. It was such a relief that he didn't care whether he ended up a totally drug-dependent wreck. Anyway, he persuaded himself, it was a temporary difficulty he was going through; once the nightmares faded of their own accord, or at least once they were out of Iraq, he would no longer need to take any drugs. He clung to the notion that he could give up the heroin in an instant when he chose to. Cartwright continually assured him 'chasing the dragon' wasn't addictive, but a small uncompromising voice in his head told him he was using ever increasing amounts, trying to achieve the level of calm he had experienced from the previous smoke.

As his heroin consumption increased, Tom began to notice other physical effects. His normally ferocious appetite was virtually non-existent. Even when he tried to force food down for the sake of his strength and health, he found he could not eat much without it making him retch. In fact, he was nauseous much of the time. He began to feel agitated again and became increasingly irritable and sullen with his patrol, shouting and swearing at the men as the effects of his last smoke wore off. The symptoms worsened as the weeks passed, until he could think about little other than struggling through to finding a bit of privacy for his next smoke.

'You're worse than a fuckin grizzly with a migraine,' complained Bob Brannigan eventually. 'We've just about had enough of it.'

'Aye,' agreed Bunny. 'You've had a real sense of humour failure. Where's the laughs we used to have?'

'Go fuck yourself,' snarled Tom. 'We're in a fuckin war zone, not on a teddy bear's picnic. I don't see much to be sweetness and light about.'

'It's not like you, Tom,' Joey said, for the umpteenth time. 'And look at the state of you, you're stick thin – those fatigues are hanging off you.'

'What d'you expect with the shite we get to eat.'

Joey shook his head. 'You're ill, mate. We can all see that. I'm begging you to go and see the MO. He can give you something to sort you out.'

'Shut the fuck up,' said Tom bitterly, and stalked off.

Even worse than all the things he now recognized as due to heroin addiction, he was dismayed to find that his obsessive worries were returning with a vengeance. It was drummed into all military personnel that the condition of their equipment while on patrol was of the utmost importance. An essential part of each day's routine was checking that their weaponry was in full working order and ready to fire if need be. Tom checked and re-checked his machine-gun, but this obsession soon failed to satisfy him and he ordered the rest of the patrol to do likewise. Much to their annoyance, he stood watching while they went through the routine again and again before he pronounced himself satisfied.

Days before Christmas, Kilo 6 set up a check-point in a small town to the south-west of Baghdad. Tom and Shortarse were up on the back of the LRPV providing cover for Joey, Bins and Bunny while they stopped and searched vehicles heading in to the town centre. They had been on station for less than an hour when the sounds of rapid gunfire and screaming suddenly erupted in the market square round the next corner.

'Let's go!' shouted Joey to Bins and Bunny as he sprinted to the LRPV and leapt into the driver's seat.

'Wait!' ordered Tom from the back.

'Wait? Fuck it, Tom, we need to get in there fast,' yelled Shortarse. 'Like *now*!' It was the first time in his career that he had questioned an order, any order.

'Wait, I said! Are you fuckin deaf or stupid? Check your weapons!'

'What?' asked an incredulous Joey.

'Check them! Check your fuckin weapons! Call in air cover.'

As the sound of gunfire, screaming and mayhem escalated, and terrified civilians fled past them from the Sunni v Shia terror, the men checked their weapons as ordered and waited.

Some minutes after the shooting stopped, Kilo 6 tentatively approached the market. They were met with a horrific scene resembling a blood-drenched human abattoir. The bodies of men, women and children lay everywhere.

'We could have fuckin stopped this' Joey hissed at Tom as they attended a boy lying moaning in the gutter, both his legs shattered by bullets.

'No, we would have made it worse.'

The final bond of loyalty the men had for their sergeant, snapped in the shame they felt. Snapped in the heat of his compulsive indecision. They knew what was happening in the unprotected market. A turkey shoot. They did nothing. They did nothing wrong because they did nothing, but innocents were slain in a violent cleansing that would forever leave them feeling dirty. If it had been cowardice, then maybe that would have been understandable. But it was not cowardice, it was misplaced loyalty and their final let-down. The tragic final straw for the troopers of Kilo 6.

CHAPTER THREE

Lieutenant Colonel Gardiner found it hard to believe what the two senior troopers from Kilo 6 were telling him. Sergeant McCartney had always been one of his most reliable and competent men. No longer, it seemed. He listened closely as Joey Stevens explained how McCartney's personality had changed. 'It's been ever since the incident at the road-block on the Amman Road, sir. He seems to have taken the deaths far harder than the rest of us.'

'Do you know why that would be?' asked the CO.

'No, sir. Tom's the very last person I thought would react like this. Everyone knows he's not exactly the biggest bleeding heart in the regiment. I've tried to get him to talk about it but he won't have it.'

'He won't talk to any of us now, sir, about anything,' added Bob Brannigan. 'Tom and I have been best buddies for years, but he won't even have a tinny with me or the other lads in the patrol any more.'

'Hmm,' said Gardiner. 'That can't be good for the morale of the unit?'

'No, sir.'

'But worse than that, sir, he's now making bad – and often unsafe – decisions,' said Stevens.

'When he makes any decisions at all,' added Brannigan. 'Much of the time we're carrying him, while he goes through the motions. He's lost it. He can't do it anymore, and he's too proud or stubborn to admit it.'

Gardiner looked grave. 'Thank you for bringing this to my attention, men. Rest assured I shall consider what's best here.' With a heavy-handed salute they left the matter with a man who would take action. It wasn't long in coming.

Sergeant McCartney was ordered to report to the medic at Al Asad base the following morning. It proved to be the last day he would spend on active duty with the Australian army.

Nick Waring, the medic, welcomed him in friendly fashion. 'Sit down, Sergeant McCartney. We're just going to give you a good check-up to see how you're doing. Before we start, is there anything about your health which is giving you cause for concern?'

'No.' He was on edge, suspicious. What did they know? What had been said? Paranoia stalked his reason. Was he being set-up?

Waring flicked through the papers on his desk. 'No problems with sleeping, or ability to concentrate, for example?'

'No.' They know, don't they?

'Any symptoms of feeling run-down, tired and so forth?'

'No.'

'I understand you were involved in an unfortunate incident about eight months ago which led to an official investigation. Can you tell me how that affected you?'

Tom glared at the hapless medic. 'Look, can we just get on with this examination? I didn't ask to come, so let's cut the crap.'

Corporal Waring knew a stonewall when he came up against one. He wrote on the file that Sergeant McCartney had no medical complaints to report, and commenced the physical examination. It revealed nothing other than inflammation of old shrapnel wounds on his right leg. The scales indicated that he had lost twelve kilograms since last weighed.

When Lieutenant Colonel Gardiner read the file, he ordered Tom over to the main coalition hospital to see Brigadier Andrew Nimmo, senior Australian army medical officer and consultant psychiatrist.

'Come in, come in Sergeant McCartney,' the Brigadier welcomed him into the consulting room, a beaming smile on his weather-beaten face which, together with his tough wiry frame, marked him as a man who enjoyed outdoor pursuits. 'Will you join me in my morning cup of tea? Or would you prefer coffee?'

'Coffee please, sir,' replied Tom, immediately felt wrong-footed by the Brigadier's unconventional approach. This wasn't the doctor-patient relationship he had been expecting.

'It's a grand name you've got there Sergeant. My dear old Grand-mother Forbes's maiden name was McCartney. Where are you from?'

'Melbourne, sir.'

'Brisbane boy, myself. The family left Glasgow for Brizzie when I was a youngster. It's my Scottish roots, I'm sure, which give me the taste for this tea.'

'My grandfather McCartney was from Glasgow, sir. He came over when he was a boy, but I understand he developed a taste for whisky, rather than tea.'

'And is that a taste you inherited?'

'I seldom drank the stuff, until recently, sir.'

'*Uisge beatha*, they call it back in the old country – the Water of Life. Strange that, don't you think, since it's been responsible for much death and a whole load of misery down the centuries? Never touch it myself.' Nimmo broke off while Paddy, the ward orderly, placed a cup of coffee in front of Tom. 'Beautiful place Melbourne. Your folks live there?'

Tom began to reply but found himself unaccountably emotional. He took a mouthful of coffee, and managed to keep his voice under control. 'They both died when I was young, sir.'

Nimmo nodded in sympathy, his silence encouraging Tom to continue. He found himself explaining how his father, a marine engineer, had drowned when his ship was lost in a typhoon in the South China Sea. 'I was just a year old at the time. Then my mother died from breast cancer when I was four.'

'Tough luck soldier. Who raised you?'

'My mother's folks.'

'And I hear you've had a hard time of it in the last few months. Would you like to talk about what happened on the Amman road?'

Tom's first reaction was to clam up, but Nimmo's words brought the vision of Donna Mulhearty rising like a phantom in his mind's eye. The kindly concern in the old Brigadier's eyes reminded him of his Grandpa Shaw. For the first time since the incident, he opened up, and talked honestly about his feelings. It had been his fault. He hadn't stopped it happening; it was his failure of command. The sleepless nights, the nightmares, the flashbacks, the obsessive behaviour and paranoia, it all came pouring out. All but the fact that he had resorted to illegal drugs to try to make the problems go away.

Nimmo watched Tom closely as he told the tale. He noticed the slight tremor in his hand as he held the coffee cup, the pallor of his skin, quite unexpected in one who'd been brought up in Australia and spent the last year or so under the merciless Iraqi sun. He noted the soldier's agitation, fiddling with his hair as he spoke, and his air of wariness, the way he deliberately avoided his gaze.

Nimmo made notes on the pad in front of him, then looked directly at Tom. 'There's one more thing you need to admit to me before I can help you. You've been taking drugs, haven't you? Heroin, at a guess.'

Tom contemplated denial, but this was his chance to find redemption through confession. He flashed a wary glance at the doctor and nodded, resigned to whatever action his admission might bring. 'I just wanted to get some peace from it all,' he said, his voice unsteady.

'Sergeant, I saw your problem a thousand times over in Vietnam. You have what we call post-traumatic stress disorder. PTSD, in short. Just like you, soldiers there were persuaded, wrongly, that heroin would help. But, as you've found, all it does is add another problem on top of the PTSD. We can help you with that, but first we need to get you off the heroin. Neither of these can be done overnight, so you will be staying here for a while.'

Nimmo watched compassionately as the young sergeant finally broke down. The fears and anxieties of the past months welled up and he quietly wept. 'I'm sorry,' he gasped, trying to stem the flow of his tears.

'Don't be,' said the Brigadier, beginning the process of filling out the paperwork to admit him to the hospital. 'Better out than in, as they say.'

Once Nimmo completed his forms and Tom had regained his composure, the doctor spoke again. 'You will have to be totally open and frank with me, Tom. That's the best way to crack this problem. And, as my part of the bargain, I promise I'll be equally frank with you.'

He went on to explain how bottling up emotions connected with the traumatic event only made things worse. 'If you try to bury it away from your conscious mind, it'll come out in your unconscious. What happens in the flashbacks is not merely a memory of the event, but in effect an actual re-experiencing of it, day in and day out. As for the nightmares, they are part and parcel of your subconscious blaming yourself, whether warranted or not. We'll work through this together and you will, I promise, get your life back in order.'

He paused, and banged the flat of his hand on the desk for emphasis. 'What won't do you any good – in fact, quite the contrary, what is certainly going to do you a great deal of harm – is the continued use of heroin. I'm seeing more and more heroin use here and I fear another Vietnam-scale drug problem. I saw many soldiers' lives destroyed by heroin addiction in Saigon; I know the damage it does. So take that as a not-so-friendly warning. I propose to put you on methadone, a synthetic pain killer which is used to control withdrawal effects from the heroin addiction. It is without doubt the best available treatment I can offer you. It won't be a quick process, and I can't promise you it will be easy. But it will work, as long as you are prepared to work at it too, and take it exactly as prescribed.'

Tears welled again in Tom's eyes. He stared at the floor and nodded his head. Brigadier Nimmo leant over and placed a hand on his shoulder. 'I can see you're shattered. Let's call it a day at that and we'll have another chat tomorrow.'

Dawn brought little hope. Tom declined breakfast and sat alone with his fears in the patients' small day room. He watched Nimmo enter the ward and speak to the charge nurse. Of course they were talking about him.

The Brigadier came into the day room and smiled when Tom rose from his chair and stood to attention. 'Relax. I'm not one for formalities.' He shook Tom's hand and pulled a chair over beside him. 'Sorry to hear you didn't get much sleep, but that will settle over the next few nights with the methadone. Is there anything you'd like to discuss this morning?'

'Yeah, there is, sir. First, can you tell me more about post-traumatic stress? I don't want to sound like I'm boasting, but I can handle violence. Well I could. I don't need to tell you that I've had to deal with a fair bit of it in the past nine years with the SASR. Despite what happened at the check-point, I wouldn't have put myself down as a candidate for getting a psychological disorder through it.'

'Perhaps not, Tom, but nightmares, flash-backs and panic attacks are the classic symptoms of PTSD that even the most battle-hardened soldiers can suffer. Shell-shock they called it in the old days.'

'That certainly fits the bill with me, but probably the worst thing of all is not getting a decent sleep. It leaves you completely shagged out mentally and physically.'

'Yes indeed. Individuals with post-traumatic stress feel anxious about sleeping partly because they lie there anticipating insomnia and partly because they worry about nightmares. If we can help you get off to sleep you'll have fewer nightmares and feel better during the day.'

'That's all I ask,' said Tom

'Tell me, have you suffered any head injuries? Researchers in the States are currently suggesting a physical as well as a psychological element to PTSD. They believe it might be caused by actual structural damage to the brain.'

'I've certainly been bashed about in judo, karate, and hand-to-hand combat training, but that's about it. We were close to exploding Iraqi tanks once and that made my teeth rattle.'

'Tell me more.

'For weeks we were behind Iraqi lines tailing a big column of their tanks and heavy armour. Within hours of the war starting I radioed in the column's coordinates. I was expecting time to get clear away from it, sir, but the American pilots must've screamed across the desert at supersonic. They were there in minutes. I couldn't believe it. Those boys were raring to go and we came very close to being fried by friendly fire. It was quite a fireworks display. The Yankee shells just about vaporized the tanks.'

'If you were close enough to catch shockwaves it may have caused some mild brain trauma, but I'd be more concerned about depleted uranium. The top brass keep insisting that the use of DU in tank-busting shells is safe, but I'm not convinced. Much bigger fish than me in the medical profession have expressed grave concern about the radiation hazards to our troops, if not indeed civilians and the whole atmosphere. As for mild brain injuries, they are not being diagnosed because guys like you believe getting knocked around is part of the job and don't complain. Problem is, repeated episodes of seemingly mild trauma can have accumulative effects.'

'What you're saying is I could actually have some form of brain damage?'

'I don't know. It's possible. Irrespective of whether PTSD is due to psychological or neurological problems or, indeed, both, if left untreated, patients are more likely to engage in anti-social behaviour such as drug and alcohol abuse.'

'Brain damage, drugs, alcohol, anti-social behaviour! Christ I'm there already.' Tom laughed for the first time in weeks. 'Euthanasia might be the best solution all round,' he added, holding his arm out for the injection

Brigadier Nimmo laughed. 'Don't worry. No need for us to resort to that *just* yet. We'll get you better.'

Tom swallowed hard. 'I hear your reassuring words, but I've been thinking about it all night and something inside tells me I'm not going to get through this nightmare.'

'Go on.'

'My father had problems with booze and violence, and I wonder if I've inherited it.'

'Tell me more.'

'My mum lived with her folks – she was teaching in a local school before she met my father, and ended up with me in the oven. They were both in their late thirties when they got hitched. I'm told he was a decent bloke when sober, but liked the grog and was in the boozer all too often. He would deliberately start arguments with Mum and gave her worse than a black eye on occasions. My grandpa Shaw ended up hating him. He told me that when news came in about him being lost at sea, he offered up thanks to whatever gods had ordained it.'

'Does your grandfather Shaw have a problem with alcohol abuse?'

'No, he hates it. On one of my earliest leaves from the army I was back in Melbourne with my old mates getting stonkered every night. He came to my room one day when I had sobered up and had a long talk. He told me about my father's problem with alcohol and that he and Gran were worried I was going the same way.'

'Did it make you cut back?'

'Yeah, it did. It was the first I'd ever heard this and it came as a bit of a shock. He told me that my dad's father, Thomas McCartney, also had a drink problem. He was apparently a big bear of a man with a reputation as a hard man in Melbourne. During the war he was a wharfie down on the Melbourne docks, and enjoyed drinking heavily and brawling in the bars around the port. One night, according to what my grandpa Shaw read in the newspapers, he deliberately provoked American sailors standing chatting on the deck of their warship.'

'Not something I'd recommend.'

'No. A mob of them ran down the gangway and apparently there was one helluva fight. The papers reported that three Americans ended up with broken bones, but my grandfather had finally bitten off more than he could chew. The following morning his battered and bloated body was found floating in the harbour. His guts had been spilled with a Bowie knife and the fish were nibbling them.'

'Pretty traumatic all round,' winced Brigadier Nimmo, who came from several generations of genteel, middle-class people.

'It gets worse – if we go back yet another generation, my great-grandfather McCartney apparently also died young, and was said to be full of booze at the time.' Tom paused and looked across at the doctor whose sympathetic and non-judgemental bedside manner had brought him to talk about things he had never told anyone. 'So, for whatever reason, the last three generations of males on the McCartney side have all died relatively young and seem to have shown addictive and aggressive behaviour. Grandpa Shaw reckons they were all psychopaths.'

'And you're twenty-seven years old with an imagination in overdrive.'

'That's correct, sir. I've been no stranger to booze and violence myself recently.' Tom grimaced as he visualised smashing the bottle on Jim Tranter's head in a drink-fuelled rage. 'It's as though some curse is on the McCartney men and I'm next in line. That day in my room with Grandpa Shaw, I insisted that he tell me everything he knew about the McCartneys. He explained that my great-grandmother McCartney was the first to come out to Melbourne with her two young children. Her husband had been badly wounded in the First World War and died sometime later. A rumour followed her out from Glasgow that she had been having an affair with a rich and dashing officer at the time. It had even been hinted that she was responsible for having her husband murdered. She was, by all accounts, a real looker in her day. Anyway, whether any of that is true or not I don't know. But what I do know is that I come from a completely dysfunctional family and a long line of head bangers on the McCartney side. Grandpa Shaw knew this of course, and he cried that day as he begged me to cut down the booze. It was the first time I'd ever seen him show any real emotion. I promised and I kept that promise for the next eight years.'

'Until the events on the Amman road.'

'Yes sir, until Donna Mulhearty began to haunt me. I've done some really crazy things in my time in the army. Chancer McCartney is not my nickname for nothing, but I got results. More recently, though, I've heard that some of the lads have taken to calling me Psycho Sarge. They wouldn't dare say it to my face, of course, but could they be right? Maybe I *have* inherited some nasty mental condition from the McCartney side? What if this PTSD is punishment for bad things I've done in my life?'

Tom stopped and slumped in his chair, feeling at one and the same time exhausted from the effort of relating past events, and relieved at finally getting them off his chest.

Brigadier Nimmo gave him a few moments to recover. 'There is indeed a genetic vulnerability to certain psychiatric conditions, but it's not a foregone conclusion that you will inherit a disorder simply because several of your first-degree relatives suffer from it. For example, arguments about alcoholism being a disease or an inherited trait have been going on for many years. As for any concerns you might have about being a psychopath, I'd need to delve deeper into your background before I could comment on that.'

'Fire away.'

'Did you feel loved by the grandparents who raised you?'

'Gran was always giving me hugs and kisses.'

'And how did that feel?'

'Good. Yeah, it felt real good, though I can't say my childhood was a happy one. I guess I always felt rootless. If only they'd told me years earlier that my mother died from cancer and hadn't abandoned me, I could have accepted it. It would have saved me all those lonely nights bubbling myself to sleep. They *should* have explained, sir, shouldn't they?'

Nimmo's head rocked. 'Hindsight is a wonderful thing, but yes, perhaps it would have been best. You certainly do appear to have a bruised sense of abandonment. Nowadays we are much more frank with kids, but I'm sure your grandparents believed everything they did back then was in your best interest. Seeing their daughter with black eyes, then dying so young, must have been devastating for them.'

'Yeah, I never thought about their pain. Don't get me wrong, I love my gran, and Grandpa Shaw too. They were always strict with me, but kind.'

'How strict? Corporal punishment?'

'Nah. They hated violence of any sort. They were unhappy when I told them I was joining the army. Most arguments between us were about school. It wasn't my favourite place. Grandpa regularly checked my homework but eventually gave up because it led to so many rows. They made me attend piano lessons for a while despite the fact that I didn't want to go. Christ, I wish now they had been stricter on that one. When I was about nine they were really pissed off with me when I went along and joined the judo club without telling them. They eventually came round when they saw the instructors were good people. Strangely enough, they were pleased when I got my black belt.'

'What was the problem with school?'

'I'm not sure. I was always waggin it. I liked geography and history, but much of the time I'd sit staring out the window. Day-dreaming

I suppose. Dreaming about camping in the bush or joining surfies down the bay. I always enjoyed the outdoors and sport. Most of the teachers just gave up on me. Snozzle Smith, the maths teacher, tried his damnedest to get me interested, but failed. I'm not blaming the school or the teachers, it was a good school.'

'Did you get involved in fights?'

'A few.'

'Go on.'

'In one instance, in my first week at the Academy, I was messed about by a couple of bully boys from the third year. Not just me, they picked on other kids just up from the primary. I gave them a little judo lesson they would never forget.'

'How did that feel?

'It felt good. It felt really good, but not because I hurt them. Good because it humiliated them in front of all the other first years. They never bullied another kid after that.'

'Did *you* pick fights?'

'No, but I never ran away from one.'

'Did fear enter the equation?'

'D'you mean fear of being hurt or fear of hurting someone?'

'Either. Both.'

'Playground punch-ups never bothered me. I was a hundred per cent confident I could handle any fight. It didn't trouble me if I hurt somebody. If I was fighting there was a very good reason for it and they deserved it. I'm usually in control of aggression, but sometimes it's difficult. I might not feel fear, but neither do I enjoy violence if that's what you're going to ask next.'

'If you are involved in violent incidents nowadays, do you experience any remorse afterwards?'

'As you well know, sir, the SASR is not big on remorse or regret. Who dares wins. What has to be done has to be done. I just do it. I didn't dwell on it until this. I don't know why I've been so overwhelmed by the Amman Road stuff.'

'Have you ever been in trouble with the law?'

'No. I was once caught nicking a chocolate bar from Woodrow's sweet counter when I was a kid, and Sergeant Armstrong from the local cop shop came round to the house. He read the riot act to me in front of my grandparents. They were upset. I learned from the mistake.'

'Getting caught?'

'No' Tom laughed, 'stealing and upsetting them.'

'Romantic relationships?'

'A few. Maureen Reilly was the big one though. That romance lasted two years until I joined the army. It broke my heart when I opened that letter at Campbell barracks.'

Brigadier Nimmo scribbled a few notes then sat back. 'Well, Tom, I had your file faxed over from Regimental HQ in Australia. It includes a full report on the psychological assessment carried out prior to your promotion to Sergeant three years ago. Rough, tough and uncompromising, perhaps, but mentally stable.' Nimmo reassured him that neither he nor anyone else thought of him as having psychopathic tendencies.

Relief to the tedium in hospital came in the form of regular visits by Brigadier Nimmo, a long-serving army man and a keen walker and climber. He took on the role of informal mentor to the untutored but quick, perceptive and intelligent younger man. They had regular discussions in the stark common room connected to the ward where Tom was obliged to spend many hours each day. His only other respite was an hour spent working out in the hospital gym, used for the rehabilitation and physiotherapy of patients.

Tom hated taking methadone, and repeatedly told Nimmo how much he disliked the heroin substitute. Several times he had poured the green liquid down the sink when the nurse looked away. Nature proved the point shortly afterwards when he suffered recurrence of severe withdrawals and a rapid deterioration of his condition. On one occasion Nimmo found him lying in bed at midday, and with a cursory glance at his sweaty, agitated state, immediately assessed the situation. 'This is why you must continue to take the methadone. I'm surprised at you; I thought you would have more sense. You'll not crack this addiction unless you stick to the rules.'

Tom smiled ruefully. 'Sorry sir, I know while I'm in here your word is law. And I promise to do better.' He pushed his unruly blond hair from his eyes and fixed the Brigadier with his direct gaze. 'But only if you promise to tell me the whole truth. You see, it seems to me that these symptoms have nothing to do with heroin withdrawal. I think I'm now addicted to methadone, and that it's withdrawal from that I'm experiencing.'

There was a pause. He could see Nimmo was gathering his thoughts. Over the weeks he had come to recognize his thoroughness when put on the spot. The silence was proof he was thinking very carefully before committing himself.

Tom continued: 'My question is, can you absolutely guarantee I'll be able to stop methadone and stay drug-free?'

Nimmo shook his head. 'The short answer is that I can guarantee nothing. Although many addicts succeed in getting off both heroin and the methadone, some are still tempted by cravings. And if they do return to heroin use, they very quickly find themselves back at square one. In such cases the best preventative measure may be to keep them on a long-term maintenance dose of methadone.'

'So this so-called cure may be nothing of the kind,' said Tom, disappointment bordering on disillusionment.

Nimmo shrugged. 'Sorry. That, I'm afraid, is what you condemned yourself to when you first took the heroin.'

'Is there nothing else you can prescribe? No alternative?'

'No, this is the best option available. Which is not to say that there aren't alternatives. Just none that have been cleared by the powers that be as an approved treatment.' He looked sympathetically at his patient, whose agitation and frustration were all too evident. 'For instance, some years ago I read about a new drug called ibogaine. It was heralded as a wonder treatment for all sorts of addictions, but I can only assume it was never approved by the drugs licensing authorities, because it seems to have sunk without trace.'

Tom sat up, his eyes wide open. 'Let me get this clear. You're saying this other medicine might be a genuine cure?'

Nimmo shrugged. 'Who knows? What I am saying is that I can't offer it to you as a treatment. So while you are in my hospital, you will continue to take the methadone.'

Nimmo liaised regularly with Tom's Commanding Officer who made it clear that a return to active duty after recovery from addiction was not something he could countenance. That being said, for Tom's and the regiment's sake, he did not want to go the route of a dishonourable discharge. The fact that he was shortly due to complete a nine-year stint with the army gave Lieutenant Colonel Gardiner a much more discreet route out of his dilemma.

Several weeks later, Tom was summoned to Nimmo's consulting room. When he entered he was surprised to find his Commanding Officer sitting at the senior medical officer's desk.

'Good morning, Tom. Hope you're feeling better.'

'Yes sir, thank you. I'm much improved.'

He waved his hand towards the only other seat in the room. 'Sit down, Tom. You'll be wondering why I'm here, so I'll get straight to the point.'

'Thank you, sir.'

'I don't think we need to go into the reasons – you will understand them, I'm sure – but we think it would be best, for you and for the Regiment, if you did not apply to extend your service when your term finishes shortly.'

Tom nodded. It was news he had been dreading and his first reaction was utter dismay. The regiment had been his life and his love for nine years, and the thought of starting afresh elsewhere was daunting to say the least. But he swallowed his disappointment, stood and saluted his Commanding Officer. 'Yes sir, I understand. Thank you, sir.'

Gardiner saluted him in return, then came round the desk and shook his hand warmly. 'Despite recent events, I can truthfully say you've been a credit to the Regiment, Tom. I'm sure you'll make as much of a success of your future.'

Tom appeared calm when Gardiner left, but Nimmo was sufficiently concerned he might take it badly, that he ordered suicide watch for the next four days. He need not have worried. Once Tom adjusted to the fact that his army career was over, he found he was genuinely looking forward to a new start. A weight had been lifted from his shoulders, and he felt happier and more relaxed than he had for months. There was life beyond in civvy street.

On March 31st 2004, Sergeant McCartney had served his full nine years with the Australian army. He sat with Nimmo in the day room, both drinking the doctor's favourite tea and discussing what the future might hold. 'I have to advise you though,' warned Nimmo, 'that even though you are now officially a civilian you will not be going home until I feel you are well enough to travel. And if you disagree with that, you're going to have to shoot your way out of the hospital.'

Tom laughed. 'Well, it would sure be a novel way to discharge myself! You wouldn't forget me in a hurry.'

'I'm not going to forget you,' said the older man seriously. 'And I do hope we keep in touch once you leave.'

Tom felt a great affection for the doctor who had done so much to help him get his life back on track since the terrible event on the Amman road. 'I'd like nothing better, sir.'

There was a companionable pause as both men looked forward to future meetings. Then Nimmo continued, 'So, will you miss the army? It'll be a big change. A whole new life.'

Tom nodded. 'There's no doubt it'll take some adjustment, but, to be honest, I'm relieved. The thought of signing on again and coping for another three years doesn't appeal to me. The memory of that day will never leave me and I couldn't handle anything like it again. I've seen people die before, friends, comrades and enemy. It's strange that the death of those peaceniks rattled me so much. If I deserve punishment, PTSD sure is one helluva sentence to serve.'

'It certainly is a nasty condition,' agreed Brigadier Nimmo. 'Are you au fait with Edmund Cook?'

'Sorry?'

'Edmund Vance Cook. He was a Canadian poet who wrote about soldiers suffering from PTSD long before it was even recognized as such. "I have seen men march to wars, and then I have watched them homeward tread. And they brought back bodies of living men, but their eyes were cold and dead".'

Tom gulped air and sat in contemplative silence absorbing the powerful words. Nimmo immediately regretted using them and tried to reassure him. 'You are definitely over the worst of it now, Tom. You're on the mend. It's been a rough ride, but you're a tough cookie in many more ways than one. Let me tell you something else Cook wrote. "Did you tackle that problem that came your way, with a resolute heart and cheerful? Or hide your face from the light of day, with a craven soul and fearful? Oh, a trouble's a ton, or a trouble's an ounce, or a trouble is what you make it. And it isn't the fact that you're hurt that counts, but only how did you take it. You are beaten to earth? Well, well, what's that? Come up with a smiling face. It's nothing against you to fall down flat, but to lie there that's a disgrace. The higher you're thrown, why the higher you bounce; be proud of your blackened eye. It isn't the fact that you're licked that counts; it's how did you fight and why?"'

Tom smiled, leant over the MO's desk, and shook his hand warmly.

'Yeah, I've bounced back, sir, and that's thanks to you. I'll never be able to repay you.' He added that he felt he would be ready to leave hospital soon but would not be going straight home to Australia. For months he had felt intimidated by the thought of coming face to face with the wrath of the Mulhearty family, but could not admit to himself, or anyone else, that he was running away.

'I want to see Europe, the UK especially. I need time to decide what to do with my life and I'm going to spend some time abroad before taking the old surfboard out again on Bells Beach. First stop, I'm going to Scotland, to Glasgow, to find my roots. To meet the people and see the places that made my family – and ultimately, me. And lastly, I intend to discover the truth about those stories and the skeletons in the family cupboard. If there is some curse making us McCartney men die young, I might not be able to stop it, but at the very least I want to go knowing what the hell it's all about.'

Nimmo nodded. 'I'm pretty sure we've all got a dark secret or two in our family histories. You'll like Scotland, though. It's a strange country in many ways, a mix of all that's good and bad in any one place. It has some of the most beautiful places you'll ever see – and also some of the roughest. My father was a general practitioner and his brother too, working in the poorest areas of Glasgow.'

'Bit of a family business, then?'

Nimmo laughed. 'Yes, and my cousin Walter is a consultant in the Royal Infirmary in Glasgow. He showed me round one evening when I was staying with him. There's a lot of knife crime in Glasgow and they get dozens of stabbing victims in the Royal every week. I found it quite astonishing – and upsetting – that they need to have police officers on duty every night in the Accident and Emergency department to protect the nurses and doctors from drink and drugs-fuelled violence.'

'So, would I be welcome in Glasgow?'

'Everybody's welcome there, Tom. It might be a horrific picture I'm painting for you, but Glaswegians are definitely among the friendliest people in the world.' He smiled. 'And with your good looks, you'll definitely be a great big hit with the Glasgow girls.'

'That's settled then, Glasgow here I come.'

Tom was eager to go. He knew that he needed to move on quite literally. Make a fresh start, try something new. The anticipation took his mind off his worries and his condition improved apace. Within a few weeks Brigadier Nimmo had given him his blessing to leave and, abusing rank to get things moving quickly, organized permits, references and a flight out with the RAF.

'I suggest you continue on the same dose of methadone for another three to four months, then reduce it very gradually. I'll phone Walter tonight and he'll recommend a good Glasgow GP. It's crucial that you have somebody to turn to if the problem recurs in any way, a GP who knows the score with methadone.'

Tom thanked the Brigadier profusely, adding that he had concerns about arriving in the UK while taking methadone. 'You mustn't stop taking it suddenly,' warned Nimmo. 'It's very important that you remain on this dose until you are settled somewhere and get some order back in your life. Then you can begin a slow reduction as advised by the doctor there. You can take methadone and lead a normal life. No one needs to know apart from your doctor and the dispensing pharmacist.'

Tom returned to Al Asad to collect his few personal belongings. Joey Stevens had been promoted to sergeant and was now in charge of Kilo 6. They'd be in good hands with Joey. He organized a drunken bout of happy reminiscence. Bridges were rebuilt. No one mentioned the tragic incident and all wished him well. Promises were made to keep in touch; addresses checked, mobile phone numbers recorded. The phrase of the moment was simply 'take care, mate'. Hands shaken, backs slapped, honour and face saved in true military style, Tom boarded the flight to RAF Lyneham in England in the certain knowledge he would never be back in Iraq.

CHAPTER FOUR

ARMED ONLY WITH HIS BACK PACK, Tom stepped off a train at Glasgow Central Station on a cold blustery evening in late April 2004. He walked around the city centre and mingled with groups of excited young people arriving for a night out, dressed – many of the girls underdressed, he couldn't help noticing – to impress. The constant squeals of laughter and the number of smiling faces seemed strange, but wonderful, after war-torn Iraq. He wandered into an old-fashioned, unpretentious pub on Hope Street and, although their Glaswegian accents were so thick he could barely understand what they were saying, found both staff and customers extremely friendly. Immediately he ordered a beer, a man nursing a whisky at the bar asked him where in Australia he was from. It took him some time to decipher the almost impenetrable Glaswegian dialect.

'I'm from Melbourne, mate. My ancestors left Glasgow about a hundred years ago, and I'm over to see where they came from. Hopefully even meet up with some long-lost relatives.' He didn't mention Iraq – that was an area of discussion he didn't want to get into ever again.

'Ma aunty an uncle live oot in Australia,' put in the dark-haired barmaid. 'Near Bondi beach in Sydney. Ah'm gaun oot tae visit them at the Glesca fair. Ah cannae wait.'

Soon others in the bar were joining in the conversation. It seemed that everybody in the bar had a relative in Australia. By the time his new friends bought him his fourth beer, he felt as comfortable in this foreign city as he had felt anywhere. 'I know it sounds corny,' he said, 'but it's like I've come home.'

Maudlin after the alcohol, and the Glaswegian welcome, Tom continued his walk round the city centre, recalling old photographs of Glasgow his grandparents had treasured. He imagined his ancestors walking along these very pavements on Sauchiehall Street a century earlier, laughing and joking in the infectious Glaswegian way. He thought of the mother he hadn't seen in twenty-three years. His last memory was of tears running down her cheeks while she cuddled him and stroked his hair and face. Just four at the time, he was thinking that she didn't look so pretty when she was crying. He was screaming when he was pulled from her arms, and driven away in a car. If he had known that he was never to see her again, he would have screamed louder and clung tighter. His gran and grandpa Shaw were kind, but couldn't compensate for the abandonment he felt. It was many years later that he learned his mother had terminal breast cancer and didn't want him to see her waste away and die. When told this at the age of sixteen, he found it hard to forgive his grandparents for keeping the truth from him. That was a difficult time when he had run wild, causing them heartache. They were, by then, well into their sixties and out of their depth with an angry, rebellious teenager. On joining the army, the memory of his mother was placed in a small, seldom-visited, recess of his mind. This evening, walking along Sauchiehall Street, he missed her.

His train of thought was broken by a young couple standing laughing outside a hotel. The name over the door seemed unaccountably familiar and, on an impulse, he walked in and booked himself bed and breakfast for the night. The Sandyford Hotel proved to be inexpensive and clean and the food good and plentiful. Checking through his papers the following morning, he discovered that the GP Nimmo had recommended worked in the nearby Sandyford Health Centre. Trusting to fate – or maybe it was just luck or coincidence – he changed his booking to an open-ended stay. He walked the short distance to the surgery, but was unable to get an appointment for four days.

Tom was relieved to find that Kirsty Crawford lived up to the glowing recommendation Dr Nimmo had received from his cousin Walter. Friendly but brisk, she rose from her desk to shake his hand. In her mid-forties, her severe trouser suit and white shirt were understated but very smart, not a speck of dust or a crease to be seen. Her dark hair was cut in a short, unfussy style, almost masculine, but the subdued make-up and slight trace of perfume she wore softened her just enough to stop her appearing too much of a threat.

'Do sit down, Mr McCartney.' She gestured towards a chair at the end of the desk. 'I know a bit about you,' she said, indicating a letter she had clearly just been reading. 'Dr Andrew Nimmo speaks very warmly of you.'

'And Dr Walter Nimmo speaks just as warmly of you,' returned Tom, smiling.

'Well, we're honours even,' laughed the doctor. 'So, this is your first visit to Glasgow?'

'It sure is, and I love it.'

'And where are you staying?'

'Just around the corner in the Sandyford.'

'Will you be looking for somewhere more permanent?'

'I'm not sure yet. Depends on how things – on how I – get on, I suppose. I'm feeling unsettled.'

'Yes, Dr Nimmo has given me a pretty detailed explanation of what you've ben through. Not something you'll recover from overnight.'

When Tom didn't reply, she continued: 'You wouldn't thank me, I'm sure, for pussy-footing round difficult subjects, and I hope you'll be honest with me. That's the best way I can help you.'

Tom sighed. 'I've been through several kinds of hell out in Iraq over the past year. I've just about managed to hold it together, with the help of the Brigadier, Dr Nimmo. But that was at the level of friendship. I can't say the doctoring from the others out there really helped me. I'm still pretty messed up. No offence meant, but I'm not sure that you, a civilian, can do more than they did.'

'You should know, Tom – may I call you Tom? – that I'm an ex-army medic myself. That's one reason why Walter thought of me. So, although I've not been in Iraq, I've seen my fair share of battle trauma. And I think – I hope – with my understanding of where you're coming from, together with the advantage of your being distanced from the forces and no longer being bound by that culture of – shall we call it "brushing things under the carpet"? – that I can help you to exorcise your demons properly.'

Tom raised his eyebrows in surprise. That at least explained her military bearing and dress.

'So, do you think we can give it a try?' she said. 'I will, of course, continue prescribing the methadone with the ultimate aim of reducing it to nothing. But we do need to address the PTSD; it's pointless getting you off the drugs if you're still suffering the effects of the stress.'

'And how do you propose dealing with that? More drugs? Because that's the last thing I want.'

'We could, of course, go along the drugs route. Some people find anti-depressants very helpful, but they are not without their side-effects. My favoured course of action for you would be to get you to talk about it.'

'I've talked about it out there until I'm blue in the face,' retorted Tom. 'There's nothing more to say.'

'Hmm, I beg to differ. Remember, I know how the army operates. Let me guess, you were debriefed in an interrogation room, which was aimed first and foremost at getting the best PR spin on it?'

'Go on.'

'Then they paid lip service in the hospital to getting you to talk about it. To come to terms with what happened – and to persuade yourself that you couldn't be blamed, and shouldn't blame yourself, for what happened. You're at war and while at war unfortunate incidents happen blah blah blah but a soldier has to pick himself up and get on with the next job blah blah blah. Is that about the flavour of it?'

Tom smiled. 'Okay Doc, very good. But what can you offer that they didn't?'

'I'm guessing they never got you to open up about your feelings – your deep-down emotions, the hurt, the anger, the anxiety. And most of all, the guilt. Not something a soldier is supposed to feel, is it?'

Tom fidgeted in his chair and she looked keenly at him. 'Are you okay with this? Tell me to stop if it's too uncomfortable.'

'I'm shit scared about stirring it all up again,' he admitted. 'I'd hoped that coming here, far away from everything that's happened, would help me to put the past behind me and to bury the bad stuff.'

'I'm sure it will, eventually, but I guess at the moment you're still very raw. You haven't really had time to find a proper way to come to terms with it. On top of all that, you've just become a civvy, in a strange country, living out of a suitcase in some soulless hotel room. No job, no friends. Until you also take measures to find some permanence in your life, to decide what you're going to do – even how long you're going to stay – I predict you won't be able to put the past behind you. How can you, when you haven't got a future to look forward to?'

He nodded ruefully. 'You talk a lot of sense, Doc. I'm in limbo at present, that's for sure.'

'Tell you what. I'll give you your methadone prescription, then why don't you come back next week and we'll talk some more. In the meantime, give some thought to what I've said, and maybe try making some plans. If you had something to occupy your mind, that might go some way towards stopping you obsessing about the past. Because whatever you may say, I don't believe you've buried it at all.'

Tom spent the days getting to know his new surroundings, walking the streets of Scotland's largest city for hours on end. Walking into the city centre he noticed the distinct character of the different areas which he passed through, some no more than a street or two. The poorer quarters leading into the city suddenly changed to a serious 'shop until you drop' zone. One street was lined with big chain stores crammed with merchandise, still a novelty to him after his stay in Iraq where the people were deprived of even the basic necessities of life. He came to George Square, the true geographical heart of the city, surrounded by grand baroque-style Victorian edifices and dotted about with imposing statues of Scotland's great and good on high granite plinths. The square was packed that lunchtime with folk eating sandwiches, chatting, and generally making the most of an all too rare sunny day.

Heading south from the square he found himself in the Merchant City. Not many years ago its huge and impressive buildings, built by the fabulously wealthy Glasgow merchants who made their money from trading goods, both human and physical, had been neglected and were falling into dereliction. But the whole area had been given a new lease of life, enlivened with upmarket designer shops and bars, coffee shops and restaurants every few steps, while chic apartment buildings were going up in any available space between the substantial old granite and sandstone buildings. As he continued on his city safari to Glasgow Green and the River Clyde, he crossed over the river to the south bank and found an area with a hotch potch of tired developments dating from the 1960s and 70s, closed shops and grim-looking pubs. But even here there were signs of the rebirth of Glasgow which was shedding its reputation as a tough, dirty city full of drunks and criminals. The riverside was being lined with new residential developments and even further from the river attempts were being made to improve the facilities and homes in the poorer areas such as the notorious Gorbals, once a watchword for all that was bad about Glasgow.

On another day Tom explored the leafy West End, welcoming the showers and cool fresh breeze from the Clyde after the stifling heat of Iraq. He was impressed with the architecture of the grand Victorian houses and the beautifully decorated high-ceilinged rooms he glimpsed through the windows of gentrified tenement buildings.

The long walks had given him plenty of time for reflection. Dr Crawford's words had struck home. He had to accept that rather than burying the past, parts of it were re-emerging. He found himself remembering more and more about his mother, and angry conversations about her with his grandparents. He began dreaming regularly about her, surrounded by shadowy-faced Shaw and McCartney relatives.

His vague plan to drift around Europe for a year or so, no longer appealed. He had to accept that he wasn't going to recover from his trauma overnight, and needed some sort of settled existence. Glasgow had already become a very attractive option.

On one of his route marches, he stopped to read the adverts in a recruitment agency's window on Renfield Street. Despite his months of drug dependency, a very healthy bank account built up over his army years meant money was not a problem. Financially he didn't need a job, but he was getting depressed with this solitary existence. There was nothing in the window which suited his particular skills – none of them seemed to require knowledge of how to kill an enemy at twenty paces, he reflected sardonically. He went inside and smiled at the pretty young assistant, whose name badge informed him was called Anna.

'Good morning,' she said. 'Can I help you?'

'I think I might be looking for a job, Anna.'

'So you're not sure?' she laughed.

'I suppose it depends what you can offer me.'

'What sort of job might you be looking for, Mr?'

'McCartney. Tom McCartney. That's the problem, Anna, I really don't know.'

He realized the words sounded rather pathetic, and was relieved that Anna continued, in her professionally pleasant way, 'Not at all, Mr McCartney, that's not a problem for us. If you'd like to fill in this form, we can see what the agency computer comes up with.'

Twenty minutes later, Tom handed his reasonably accurate, but not totally honest, CV back to her. She made an appointment for him to return in a couple of days, when hopefully she would have a selection of vacancies for him to consider.

'Thanks, Anna, you're a star. I'll see you on Thursday, then.'

'I'll look forward to it,' she replied, then blushed.

Tom laughed. Now that didn't seem quite so professional.

The following day, he went along to his second consultation with Kirsty Crawford. When she suggested yet again that he needed to discuss his feelings about the incident that had led to the PTSD, he was very reluctant to do so. 'I discussed it at length with the counsellor in the hospital over there. The last thing I want to do is stir it up again. I haven't dreamed about it for some time now. In fact, I'm dreaming more frequently about my family. That's got to be an improvement.'

'Maybe, maybe not,' said the GP. 'Dredging up unresolved issues from the past is a classic symptom of stress.' She glanced at a pile of papers on her desk and pushed them towards him. 'Have you seen these?'

Tom picked them up and riffled through the stack. He was amazed to see they were all UK newspaper and TV reports on the Amman Road shooting, which Dr Crawford had presumably extracted from their online archives and printed off. There were dozens of them, each one giving its own spin on events.

'They make interesting reading,' continued the doctor. 'As much for what they don't say as what they do. I'd be fascinated to know the truth – from the horse's mouth, as it were.'

Tom skimmed through report after report, and was astonished by the amount of information that had actually been disclosed. Much of it, he told the doctor angrily, was pure supposition, some of it complete baloney. 'But that doesn't change the fact that I was responsible for the deaths of four civilians.'

'That's not what the army concluded,' Dr Crawford reminded him. 'Why do you believe you were responsible for the death of – what was her name?'

He was reluctant to discuss it. The doctor showed no signs of wanting to hurry him.

'Donna Mulhearty was her name. A thirty-four year old Australian. She was pretty, with blonde hair and the most vivid blue eyes I've ever seen. Tom Cahill was an older American guy, a Vietnam War veteran turned peace activist. God knows what he looked like; there was nothing left of his face. Guiseppi Del Buon, an Italian peace activist, was in the back of the car. He was cremated when the petrol tank beneath him went up. The Iraqi driver. I didn't actually fire my weapon that day, doctor, but I might as well have. I had the patrol so bloody tightly wound up that a bus-load of kindergarten kids might have got it.'

Dr Crawford persuaded him to further elaborate on his anxiety about the deaths and on his feelings about leaving the army. She prescribed the same dose of methadone and asked him to return in one week. He slept fitfully that night and for the first time in months, the skinned corpse of Donna Mulhearty returned to haunt him.

Cursing the GP for stirring up old nightmares, he was tired when he arrived at the recruitment agency for his appointment with the lovely Anna. The computer had matched a number of possible vacancies, but Anna advised him that many of them were unlikely to suit. 'I can't see you as a bouncer at a nightclub, can you?'

Tom shook his head emphatically. 'No, certainly not. I would have stayed in the army if I wanted that sort of aggro.'

'And I don't think a driver for a security company would be quite your cup of tea either?'

Tom looked pointedly at her. 'You seem to think you know a lot about me, young lady.'

She pushed her glossy dark hair away from her eyes. 'I guess that means I'm right then.'

He laughed. 'So what else have you got for me?'

She placed two job adverts in front of him. The first, as a personal fitness instructor in a health club, was certainly one he would follow up. The second vacancy, however, was altogether more interesting:

Luxury world-class hotel and health spa on 240 acre private estate requires the services of a general security and celebrity protection specialist with occasional chauffeuring duties. The successful applicant will:
Be totally discreet.
Possess impeccable social etiquette.
Have good dress sense.
Be in top physical condition.
Hold a clean driving licence.

Salary by negotiation. Accommodation provided.

Anna proved to be as intrigued as Tom by the vacancy. 'It sounds like a dream job,' she said. 'Just like The Bodyguard. I love that film.'

'Nah, Whitney Houston's not my cup of tea.'

'Well, at least you're younger than Kevin Costner. Not that that's saying a lot.'

Was that a compliment? He read the advert again and looked down with mock disgust at his crumpled shirt. 'Good dress sense? Perhaps not.'

Anna laughed. 'Don't worry, Mr McCartney, I'm sure you scrub up well. A shave and a nice interview suit and shirt and tie from Slater Menswear and you'll be a dead cert for the job!' She told him she'd pass his details on to both the hotel and the health club, and would contact him if he was invited for interviews. Leaving the office, Tom glanced back at Anna and spotted three other girls straining round their computer screens to get a look at him. On an impulse, he went back. 'Listen, you wouldn't fancy coming out for a drink this evening, would you?'

'Sorry, I'd love to, but I don't think my boyfriend would like it. And he's even bigger than you!' she laughed. 'There's a crowd of us meeting up tonight. Why don't you come along?'

Tom met Anna, her boyfriend Jamie, and a group of their friends for a meal at an Indian restaurant in the city centre before moving on to a nearby club. He'd missed this sort of social life and female company during the past few years. Army life was fine, but inevitably it was rare that the conversation strayed very far away from the job. Anna and the other girls were bubbly and light-hearted, while Jamie and his mates had an endless supply of good jokes. Tom laughed more than he could remember for months – maybe years.

The club emptied around 2 a.m. and large groups of people in various stages of inebriation stood laughing and chatting on the pavement outside. Suddenly, off to their right, an argument developed between two females and rapidly progressed into a fight. The girls were punching and scratching each other, and pulling clumps of dyed blonde hair by the roots. Anna attempted to move her group of friends away, but the men stood mesmerized by the spectacle. Several drunks egged them on to greater efforts as they ripped each others' short, tight clothes off. When the heaviest of the pair gained control, and repeatedly banged her opponent's head on the ground, a young lad intervened and attempted to pull her off. He would regret his Good Samaritan act for a long time to come. Three men in casual designer clothes ran over and began kicking him. He put up a spirited defence, but was soon lying curled up on the pavement with vicious kicks raining down on his head as though it were a football. No one moved to *his* aid.

'Enough! Fair's fair.' shouted Tom.

'Leave it. Leave it, Tom. C'mon, let's get out of here.' Jamie grabbed his arm to pull him away. 'Those guys are complete bams. Fuck it man, don't get involved.'

Tom broke Jamie's grip and pulled at the jacket sleeve of one of the thugs. 'Fair's fair, I said. You're gonna cause that boy permanent damage or worse.'

'Fuck off ya wanker or you're gettin it,' shouted the man as he spun round and, much to Tom's surprise, almost landed a punch on his face. Green to amber, then red. He stood still, his breathing controlled, his instincts honed by years of military training. They were the enemy. They had chosen to attack.

Anna and the other girls screamed as two of the thugs drew knives and lunged at their new Aussie friend. Not big knives – not army knives – but weapons nevertheless, and dangerous even in the grip of fools. That's what they were, fools – idiots with knives – thinking they were invincible. They rushed forward with snarls bordering on contempt. They'd sort this meddling fucker. No feint, no quick manoeuvre to dissemble. A slash across his face would mark the moment. Tom dipped his left shoulder, sidestepped right, and took out the first with two fast karate chops to the neck. He fell senseless to the ground. The second, already committed to attack, had no time to break step. For a nano-second his brain told him it 'wisnae happenin' but searing pain proved it had. Tom grabbed the knife wielding arm and smashed it down on his upcoming knee, snapping radius and ulna as if little more than dry kindling for a camp-fire in the outback.

Number three turned to flee so he was facing the wrong way when Tom caught him in an arm lock and propelled him through the air. The crash of body on gutter was outplayed by a sickening crack as his thigh shattered.

'Call an ambulance,' said Tom to no one in particular. He turned the lad who had been kicked unconscious into the recovery position, and carefully wiped blood from his mouth and nostrils with a piece of torn dress. 'Probably best call two' he added, as police sirens gave warning that they should all move on. He stood up and quickly shepherded his friends away from the carnage. No-one quite knew what to say.

Tom heard nothing about his job applications, and found it hard to keep his spirits up. Daytime television and the anonymous hotel room were getting on his nerves, so he was really pinning his hopes on the job which included accommodation. If his application wasn't successful, he would start looking for a place of his own. The days became wearisome and long, the nights no better than before. They were still there – the old ghosts. Much more dangerous than wee boys with knives.

Returning to the surgery at the appointed time, he complained about the renewed nightmares, and flashbacks of Donna Mulhearty's death. 'That's why I try not to talk about that day,' he explained. 'I just want to forget about it.' Surely it was obvious? Why do doctors think they know better?

'I'm sorry to hear that, but burying your memory of the dead woman is not going to prevent her attempting to grab hold of you in a nightmare. You need to express your feelings and talk about her.'

Though he smiled and nodded as if in agreement, he was far from convinced.

Dr Crawford advised him to speak to a clinical psychologist. 'Recovery from post-traumatic stress disorder can be a prolonged process, and living alone in a hotel room in a foreign country is not conducive to recovery. It might also be helpful for you to discuss anger management.' Where did that come from? What had she heard? Anger management?

His affairs took a turn for the better when Anna phoned and asked him to call in at the employment agency. 'Well done, Tom. You've got an interview for the security job. Maybe I should advise them to issue serious health warnings to any potential intruders there.' She lowered her voice. 'You were very brave – and very lucky. Those guys are dangerous. They'd stick a knife into their grandmother without a second thought. You have to be more careful. This is a big city – not the outback.'

He looked back at her with a blank stare that should have said enough, but Anna was born and bred in a country where women only stop once they've finished, 'There's a bit about it in the *Daily Record*. Says the polis are looking for some boy from the army, so you're fine. You're from Australia.'

She smiled and handed over a letter with the time and place of interview. 'It's the Mar Hall Hotel, about half an hour's drive from here over the Erskine Bridge. Very posh – right out of my league! So we've got a few days to get you looking the part.'

They arranged to meet up during her lunch-break later in the week, when she would take him shopping for clothes. He headed straight off to visit second-hand car showrooms.

Forty-eight hours later he drew up outside the agency in a BMW convertible, and honked the horn. Anna came to the door, her eyes wide with surprise. She dashed from the agency in pouring rain. 'Where did you steal this from, cobber?'

'Just a little something I picked up. But God knows if I'll ever have the top down.'

As he drove through town, life felt good. He had a pretty girl by his side and all he needed now was a nice suit and the good fortune to persuade the management at Mar Hall he was the man they were looking for.

The car's soft-top was down when Tom drove west out of Glasgow in glorious sunshine and crossed the Erskine Bridge over the River Clyde. Following the directions he had been given, he soon came to the discreet sign for the Mar Hall Hotel. He turned off the public road beside an old sandstone lodge house and onto a driveway which wound through sun-dappled woodland. About 500 metres along the drive, there was a clearing on the left-hand side and he caught his first glimpse of the hotel. He came to a stop, struck by how impressive it looked. A solid, square Victorian Gothic style building with nests of turrets and chimneys was set against a background of the river Clyde and gentle hills. The stone was a patchwork of colours from a warm, honey blonde all the way through granite grey to black.

Tom continued down the driveway, even more excited at the thought that he might soon be living and working in such a beautiful place. He pulled up in the car park and smiled at two life-size bronze stags standing on their own small lawn. Straightening his tie and brushing creases from his trousers, he walked through the grand arched doorway of the hotel and approached the reception desk. A young women was sitting there speaking on the telephone, head bowed as she wrote something down. When she looked up and smiled, he took an involuntary sharp intake of breath. Her glossy copper-coloured hair graced a slim face with the fair complexion of a classic Scottish lassie. She had fine and delicate features with beautiful hazel eyes.

'Good morning sir, can I help you?' she asked in a gentle Scottish accent which had none of the urban harshness to which he was now accustomed.

'Tom McCartney. For an interview with Mr Osborne.'

'Ah.' She recognized the name, 'Please take a seat. He'll be with you shortly.'

Tom was introduced to the hotel's general manager, Frank Osborne, his assistant, Nadine, and to the operations manager, a smart, somewhat severe, middle-aged woman whose name he didn't catch.

Though he had tried to anticipate what they might ask, he was genuinely surprised by the thoroughness of their questions and acquitted himself as best he could over a rigorous interview. The manager and his assistant were friendly and immediately put him at ease, although the operations manager was less approachable and never relaxed enough to crack a smile. Osborne explained that the main element of the job was hotel security, with bodyguard duties and driving when requested. The salary did not quite match his army pay, but the package included a self-contained apartment and meals. The operations manager was most concerned to ensure that their celebrity guests would never have any reason to complain, and that their head of security should be personable, discreet and reliable, as well as able to provide a high level of unobtrusive protection. She fired so many hypothetical questions at him as to what he would do if his charges were targeted by over-eager fans, paparazzi, angry ex-spouses or even kidnappers, that he felt his head beginning to spin. But dealing with the unexpected had always been his natural territory. He resisted the urge to dismiss the challenge of such lightweight intruders and tell them about his daily diet of snipers, bombers and religious fanatics. He unpicked each question and found suitable solutions to the apparent satisfaction of the panel.

At the end of the interview, Frank Osborne shook his hand. 'Thank you, Mr McCartney. If you'll make your way back to Reception, I've arranged for Julie Anderson to show you around the hotel.'

On the whole, apart from the tricky evasion of a question about his health, he reassured himself that the interview had gone very well.

The short guided tour confirmed Mar Hall as everything the marketing spiel had boasted. From the décor to the demeanour of the staff, the five-star menu to the formal gardens, there was an ambience of quality, an air of restrained good taste.

The hotel felt good to him, it felt right and, quite bizarrely, it felt as if he'd been here before. A comforting sense of familiarity struck him as soon as he walked into the Grand Hall, a stunning room with a high vaulted ceiling from which hung dazzling crystal chandeliers. A few guests were relaxing in the comfortable chairs and sofas, enjoying morning coffee as they chatted or read the newspapers. Why was it so familiar? This sense of déjà vu was disconcerting. He put it down to light-headedness as he followed Julie Anderson around, watching her slim body and smelling her tantalising perfume.

The hotel was a tranquil and welcoming place, the guests at ease and relaxed. The ever-present but discreet staff attended to them in a quiet, friendly way. It seemed so natural, so appropriate. This is what happens here. Comfort and joy. Yeah, it could be Christmas every day in this stunning haven. It was another world.

Julie led him outside to the formal gardens and their centrepiece, a huge Cedar of Lebanon, at least as old as the house itself. They stood side by side, looking back towards the building which stood as a monument to an age of class. A haven from the darkness of industrial Scotland.

'So that's our humble hotel,' said Julie. 'Not bad, is it?'

'Not bad at all,' Tom agreed, looking down at her laughing eyes.

At that moment, she received a message on the pager. 'Mr Osborne's waiting for you in Reception. Hope it's good news.'

'Believe me, so do I.'

Frank Osborne smiled broadly at Tom and shook his hand firmly. 'Congratulations! Welcome to Mar Hall. That is, as long as we haven't put you off the place already?'

'Certainly not, I'm going to love it here.'

Osborne took him to the apartment in the south attic which would shortly be his home. It had a spacious lounge, kitchenette, bedroom and en-suite, and best of all overlooked the gardens with the majestic cedar centre stage.

'Thank you so much, Mr. Osborne. The apartment is... the entire hotel is, well, is quite amazing. I'm going to really enjoy working here and you can be assured of my total commitment and loyalty.'

They agreed that he would start his new job on the first day of June.

Tom climbed into the car, re-crossed the Erskine Bridge and swung in the opposite direction from Glasgow. Twenty minutes later he stood under clear blue skies, cheerfully throwing pebbles into the sparkling waters of Loch Lomond. He hummed the tune over and over, but remembered only one line of the famous old Scottish song about the bonny bonny banks of Loch Lomond. Ten miles further up the lochside, loving the feel of his new car under his hands, he took a fork in the road and soon found himself in the magnificent Glen Croe with mountains rising steeply on both sides. The road climbed towards the highest point of the pass, the quaintly named 'Rest and Be Thankful', then dropped down to the sea at Loch Fyne where he sniffed the ozone and thought of surf-boards.

Tom enjoyed a superb fresh seafood lunch at the oyster bar, and heads turned as the handsome, smartly dressed, Australian paid the bill and walked to his car. On the drive back to Glasgow, he thought of Julie Anderson while singing along to Good Vibrations on a Beach Boys CD. There was something alluring about her that attracted him like a powerful magnet, and it had been difficult to keep his eyes off her on the tour of the hotel. It was a good day to be alive, indeed the very best since Iraq.

Dr Kirsty Crawford had seen numerous patients' spirits rise through gaining meaningful employment, but seldom in such a dramatic fashion. She enjoyed Tom's infectious enthusiasm as he told her about the hotel and his new job there. 'Thank you so much for putting that idea in my head, doctor. It really was good thinking, excellent psychology.' He asked if he could remain her patient after moving from Glasgow, but she explained it wasn't possible. She blushed deeply when he thanked her profusely, put his arm round her, and kissed her cheek.

The BMW crossed the Erskine Bridge several times over the next week as he drove out 'just to have a look'. And, he half-hoped, maybe even catch a glimpse of Julie Anderson. He was moving on.

CHAPTER FIVE

FRANK OSBORNE GREETED TOM on his first day and left him to settle in. 'Come to my office in a couple of hours, and I'll introduce you to the rest of the staff.'

The attic apartment was, of course, nowhere near as luxurious as the guest bedrooms, but it was warm and comfortable despite a cold wind rattling the windows. There was everything he needed, including a music system and personal computer. As his terms of employment included all meals, he couldn't see he'd ever want to use the fitted kitchen to do more than heat up the occasional pizza.

Ever thankful for the precision of his military training, Tom had his few belongings arranged in neat and logical sequence within minutes. He booted the computer and promptly surfed the Mar Hall website. He was impressed to see it had already been updated to boast that a 'robust' martial arts expert and former SAS soldier was in charge of security, and available to ensure the privacy and personal safety of any guest who required the service. Although there were hints that some wealthy and famous clients had stayed there, the watchword of the hotel was discretion, so no names were mentioned. Tom, who was no more immune than anyone from curiosity about the glitterati, felt almost childishly excited at the prospect of working with them.

A grand baronial house, originally the family seat of the Earls of Mar, had stood on the Erskine estate for more than five centuries. In the early nineteenth century, when the wealthy Lord Blantyre purchased the entire estate, his family demolished the original sixteenth century castle and completed the present Mar Hall in 1845.

Tom was surprised to read that the house had not always been the scene of gracious living. In 1916 the then owner, Mr Thomson Aikman, offered free use of the house, gardens and extensive grounds as a military hospital to care for the huge numbers of maimed and limbless part-survivors of the battlefields of the First World War. Named the Princess Louise Hospital, but primarily known as Erskine, it received the first of many thousands of badly wounded soldiers in October 1916. It continued treating the wounded from every conflict of the twentieth century, but in 2002 the hospital moved to new, purpose-built accommodation nearby. The house and estate were sold and given a fresh lease of life by its new owners. A multi-million pound restoration reinstated the former glories of the Regency mansion when it was transformed into the luxury Mar Hall hotel.

Somewhat pensive, Tom made his way to Frank Osborne's office. The fact that he was now, quite accidentally, living and working in a place which had, for many years, such a close identity with the soldier's fate – more specifically, with the seriously wounded and maimed victims of war – struck him as a supreme irony. Possibly this was the best place he could be to continue his recuperation from the damage that war had inflicted on him.

During the course of the morning, Frank introduced Tom to many of the fifty or so staff who worked in the hotel. He was impressed with the manager's relaxed and friendly manner with everyone from Jimmy Newman, the recently appointed Head Chef, to the youngest room maid.

On their return through Reception, Julie Anderson smiled warmly as he shook her hand. 'I was pleased to hear you got the job. Hope you enjoy working here as much as the rest of us.'

'I'm sure I will. I'm really looking forward to getting to know you – and everybody else – much better.'

'Sit down, sit down,' invited the manager, moving a pile of glossy brochures from a chair in his office. 'So now you've met some of the team. As you see, they're a friendly bunch, and I feel sure you'll fit right in.'

Tom could see that Frank was a man who liked to be hands on and approachable to his staff. Not one for standing on ceremony himself, he already felt that it would be good to work for him.

'So Tom,' Frank continued, handing him a chart, 'This is the management structure of the hotel. You'll see that you report either to me or to Jean Marchant, our Operations Manager, whom you met at the interview.'

Tom frowned instinctively as he remembered the severe woman from the interview panel.

Frank laughed. 'Her bark's worse than her bite, I promise you. I'm sure you'll charm her just like you have certain other members of our female staff.'

Tom looked sharply at him. Was his interest in Julie Anderson so obvious? 'Yes,' continued Frank, enjoying himself, 'Nadine my assistant and young Stella on Reception are both very taken with you. Couldn't stop singing your praises – my guts would have been garters if I hadn't appointed you. So, I'm delighted to welcome you to our team – for a far more serious reason than the girls! Since the hotel opened we've been attracting high-profile guests. The press and fans have tumbled to this fact, and on a number of occasions have been causing a nuisance by coming in and approaching our celebrity guests.

'I repeatedly expressed my concerns about lack of security to the hotel owners, but they insisted they couldn't see a problem. That was, until a female celebrity who shall remain nameless – let's call her Britney – was accosted while strolling through the hotel gardens. Photographers from the tabloid press had been snooping around outside and one of them chanced his arm to get an exclusive. The owners were forced to take some action – either that or lose our celebrities altogether – and they came up with the money to create your post. The hotel is open to the public as well as resident guests and since it's difficult to keep undesirables out, a strong security presence is needed.'

Tom listened closely as Frank explained what was expected of him. It was hoped that his mere presence would deter over-eager celebrity-spotters and also reassure guests – both the famous and the unknown – that their protection from disturbance was paramount.

'So we need you to be noticeable but discreet, if you can manage that balancing act. As for dress, all our "on display" staff wear collar and tie, so I'd like you to do the same. When requested by a guest, you'll be assigned as their personal bodyguard. I can't say how often you'll be involved in such work, but it will take priority over your routine security duties. Suites at £1,000 per night for a celebrity guest, plus rooms for their entourage, are a significant earner, and we expect the availability of personal protection will make the hotel more attractive to them. You will also be available to such guests to drive them to and from airports and specific venues, or on sightseeing trips, rounds of golf etcetera. The majority of your time, however, will be spent on routine night security duties around the hotel and the estate. Like an insurance policy, sort of thing, or the Fire Brigade, or Lifeboat – there if needed, but hopefully never required. You're paid for a forty-hour week and I don't expect you to spend your entire life on duty in the hotel because you live in it. It's certain that you'll be kept busy for prolonged periods when guests request your protection services, so chill out at other times. Carry your mobile so Reception or the night porter can contact you. Following earlier incidents, the bar staff are now well trained at recognizing potential problems and defusing them diplomatically. If a guest gets so drunk that he or she becomes a complete nuisance to other guests or staff, it's our own fault for allowing it to develop to that stage. I trust your professionalism, Tom.'

'And you can count on it,' Tom assured him.

'Andy Hutton, our groundsman, uses a Jeep for his work and it'll be available for your use at night and weekends. In the meantime, I'd like you to take an in-depth look at potential security hazards in the buildings and grounds.'

'That all seems clear,' said Tom. 'What I'll need is a plan of the hotel and the grounds to help me identify any problems.'

'Right, I'll get those to you before the day is out.'

By the end of the day, Tom had looked at every room, nook and cranny in the venerable old building and its modern swimming pool and gymnasium annexe. Again, he had that unaccountable feeling of familiarity as though he had been there at some time in his past.

The following morning Tom's time was his own, and he decided to introduce himself to Andy Hutton. He found the groundsman in his garage-cum-workshop to the rear of the hotel. 'I've been told I can make use of your runaround,' he explained, jerking his thumb towards the bright red Suzuki four-wheel drive. 'So I thought I'd come and make myself familiar with the beast.'

'Good tae meet ye,' said Andy, wiping his hand on his overalls before offering it to Tom. 'Ah've heard all about ye.' Andy Hutton's job clearly kept him fit. Despite his advancing years, he was lean and wiry, with the look of a man who had spent his life working out of doors.

Tom laughed. 'There sure ain't no secrets in Mar Hall. I'll bet you already know I had four fried eggs for brekkie.'

'Aye, we do have a very sophisticated bush telegraph, right enough.' Andy looked at his watch. 'How about ah drive ye out tae the furthest reaches of the estate an the local village? It'll help ye get yer bearings an ye can have a wee turn behind the wheel, if ye like.'

'Dinkum.' Nothing could go wrong.

The hotel sat within parkland overlooking the River Clyde to the north, and the Kilpatrick Hills rising beyond. Andy drove the Suzuki down to the river, and eastward along its sandy beach for half a mile. They passed under the carriageway of the Erskine Bridge, which towered several hundred feet above, to one of the estate's original gate lodges. Andy pulled up on an old cobblestone slipway and explained that a ferry had once plied to and fro here on the quarter-mile crossing to Old Kilpatrick. It had been made redundant when the Erskine Bridge was built some forty years earlier. Today, torrential rain swept the placid surface of a river that somehow seemed devoid of purpose. Where were the great ships? The old order changeth, or something like that. Tom mused on a past long gone and once more sensed that déjà vu.

They took the old ferry road, looping back west round the perimeter of the estate and the outskirts of Erskine new town. A mile further on stood Erskine Parish Church and the grey sandstone lodge at the entrance to the avenue for Mar Hall. Another mile to Bishopton, and Andy pulled up outside his local, the Golf Inn. 'Fancy a pint of real Scottish ale? It'll give us time for a chat.'

Not slow to recognize a man on a mission for information, Tom accepted the offer graciously. He guessed that anything he divulged about himself would soon find its way round the hotel. Andy explained that he had been employed as a groundsman by Erskine Hospital for almost forty years, and was delighted to stay on when asked by the new owners. He knew every inch of the estate and it was clear from the way his eyes lit up as he talked that he was passionate about it. He was vastly knowledgeable about the flora and fauna of the Scottish countryside and took great pride in his self-assumed role as a conservator. When Tom talked of his expeditions to the Australian outback, Andy was fascinated to hear about the weird and wonderful plants and animals to be found there. 'Ah would love to visit those places,' he said, with a faraway look in his eyes.

'Well, if you ever do,' said Tom, who had already warmed to the old man, 'I can find you any number of friends who'll be delighted to put you up and show you around.' That boast was once true, wasn't it? Funny that. Did he even have a single friend in Oz now? Christ, he was so keen to get back, he turned west at Baghdad then north to Scotland. There were some not-so-friendly Aussies who would like to see him, though, ask a few questions and get a few answers. Donna Mulhearty, could you just fuck off and leave me alone? His mood lost its casual ease and he found himself withdrawing to darker thoughts.

When they walked from the pub an hour later, the sun made a fleeting appearance and the saturated ground glistened with pools of sparkling rainwater. If you could bottle that you'd make a fortune in Iraq. Fuck! Even in this haven Iraq demanded his attention. Would he ever get it out of his head?

'Ye want tae drive, young man?' Andy asked, breaking the spell, and handing him the keys. On the way back to Mar Hall, Tom pulled over to admire the gabled sandstone lodge house at the entrance to the avenue down to the hotel. It reminded him of a mini Gothic mansion in an old movie. Andy explained how it had been bought some years earlier by his 'guid' friend Roddie Anderson when they worked together as groundsmen on the estate. Roddie had since taken a job as night porter at the hotel. His daughter, Julie, was also working there as a receptionist during university term breaks.

'I met Julie,' said Tom. 'Very welcoming and friendly and ...'

'Aye an very pretty too,' Andy interrupted. 'Just like her mother.'

'I hope I get to meet her.'

'Ah'm afraid not,' said Andy, shaking his head sadly. 'Rachel died about six or seven years ago. She collapsed just along the avenue from here. Poor Julie was on her way home when she found her mum lyin dead in the snow.'

'What a tragedy,' said Tom. 'She must have been devastated.'

'Julie an her father both. Rachel wiz a lovely woman. Such a loss tae everybody.'

Tom put the jeep in gear and drove on along the avenue. Two hundred yards beyond South Lodge, and just past the spot where Rachel Anderson had died, Andy told him to swing off-track and drive through the woodland.

'This is more like it' he yelled, laughing as they bounced along between the ancient trees. 'We used to chase roos like this, back home.'

'This is called The Big Wood,' shouted Andy, 'We don't have any roos, but you'll find plenty of deer straying down fae the hills. Keep headin in the direction of the river.'

On the edge of The Big Wood, at the most westerly point of the estate, they came to an ancient wooden bench taking full advantage of the magnificent panorama which opened up to the west before it.

In the foreground, the manicured greens and fairways of the Erskine golf course sloped down to the Clyde. In the middle distance, the river opened up like a large lake with Dumbarton, Greenock and other towns and villages dotted along its banks. Beyond, to the west, rose majestic mountains which marked the edge of the Scottish Highlands.

'That's what we call the Tail-o-the-Bank.'

'Stunning,' said Tom, looking out over the spectacular view. It was as good as anything he'd seen in Australia. 'Such a bonny country.'

'Glad tae see yer pickin up the lingo. Ye'll be wearing the kilt next.'

'Don't think I haven't considered it!'

'Come an see this,' said Andy, beckoning him through wet grass to a huge beech tree which stood alone in a clearing. Almost the entire trunk and lower branches of the centuries-old tree bore witness to romantic couples who had carved their names deep into its bark. Tom wandered round the trunk of 'lovers' tree' and saw thousands of initials, many dating from the early 1900s. Although the grand old beech had suffered a huge number of lacerations, and several major limbs had clearly succumbed to the damage, it was still producing a magnificent canopy over 100 feet in the air.

Driving on through the woods, they emerged at the formal gardens in front of Mar Hall. Tom thanked Andy and shook his hand warmly. 'What a beautiful, beautiful place this is. It sure beats driving around the fuckin desert. If it's okay with you, I'll take the jeep out on the estate occasionally? I wouldn't want anyone stealing it on my watch.'

'She's aw yours, Sheriff.'

Tom went to his apartment, took his daily dose of methadone, and slept for several hours before showering. He was unaccustomed to wearing a tie, but pleased with the image he presented in the mirror. 'What am I supposed to do now?' he asked himself, and his stomach immediately replied. Downstairs, the hotel kitchen was buzzing.

'Organized chaos!' shouted Chef Newman with a huge grin as Tom looked on in fascination. 'Since it's officially yer first night on duty, Ah'll make whatever takes yer fancy.'

'One of those famous big Aberdeen Angus steaks topped with langoustines would go down a treat.' Thirty minutes later, he sat in the staff room watching television and enjoying the best surf and turf he had ever eaten.

'Okay?' enquired Newman when Tom returned his plate to the kitchen.

'Pretty average, Chef,' he replied, shaking his head. 'A small steak down under is six times the size of that morsel you served up. God knows how I'm gonna survive till breakfast.' He laughed as a freshly peeled orange flew past him. 'Nah, fantastic tucker, mate. Perfect, thank you.'

A scattering of guests with post-prandial drinks sat around chatting when, rather self-consciously, Tom walked through the Grand Hall. It was the gathering place, the hub of the hotel, and he had never seen such classic opulence. Crystal chandeliers suspended from the beautifully curved and ornately carved ceiling created the perfect ambience in this elegant room of almost cathedral-like proportions. The Grand Hall was furnished with period antique furniture including Louis XIV chairs, plush sofas, drapes and tapestries. The scent from flower arrangements created a heady mix with the expensive perfumes and colognes of the guests. By day, sunlight flooded through a south-facing wall of towering windows; this was the first time he'd seen it at night, and the whole room was transformed, sparkling with a thousand lights reflected from crystals dangling from the chandeliers. Not a penny had been spared on the décor of the hotel. No wonder it was a magnet for the rich and famous.

Tom walked through to the bar and discreetly asked the young barmaid if everything was in order. Problems in the lounge and cocktail bar, while exceedingly rare, were not unknown. Frank Osborne had told him how one drunk and unaccommodating guest threw a crystal glass against the wall when gently encouraged to go up to bed at 3 a.m. More seriously, on another occasion a barmaid had left in tears after being sexually harassed by several members of a well-known English rock band. Frank had personally instructed the band to pack and leave, and contacted the police. He would not tolerate his staff being physically or verbally abused by anyone, no matter how rich or famous.

Tom was confident that he could defuse potential trouble with his gift of the gab – aided naturally by his intimidating height and the width of his shoulders. He would certainly not hesitate to deal with any troublesome guest if required. Tonight, in the gentle, friendly ambience of Mar Hall, the notion of violence seemed totally absurd. It was always quiet before the storm, a voice reminded from deep within.

Roddie Anderson, the night porter, sought Tom out when he came on duty. A handsome man somewhere in his fifties, he had a ruddy complexion and a neatly trimmed grey beard. Tom found him every bit as pleasant and friendly as Andy Hutton had said.

'I think I'm about the last to meet our Australian superhero,' he teased. 'Julie tells me the girls have been trying to work out if that's padding you've got on under your shirt, or if it's all you.'

'One hundred per cent pure kangaroo meat,' replied Tom, delighted that Julie had been talking about him to her father, and was it just his shirt?

'Well, big man, I wouldn't be brave enough to call you Skippy to your face. Seriously though, I'm pleased you're here because I sometimes feel a bit vulnerable during the night. We get these bloody paparazzi sneaking about outside in the dead of night when they know a big celebrity's in residence. Some of them are eager to make a name and you need to be careful, these guys can be ruthless.'

'No need to worry now, Roddie. You've got a bodyguard here who's ruthless. It's those fuckers who need to be careful.'

Later, as the last guests wandered off to their rooms, and the dining room staff readied the place for the following morning's breakfast, the hotel gradually settled down for the night. Every hour, Tom stood up to tour the building, but Roddie told him to relax. There were no unwelcome interruptions and the hotel slept in monastic silence apart from Tom and Roddie's quiet chatter in the Grand Hall.

'Andy Hutton took me up past your house today. A really nice place you have there. Maybe I shouldn't mention this, but Andy told me about the terrible thing that happened to your missus.'

Roddie shook his head, smiling sadly in reminiscence. 'Aye, she was my best pal for thirty years. Julie adored her and it broke our hearts when she died. The doctor reckoned she was dead from a massive brain haemorrhage before she even hit the ground. It's maybe a merciful way to go, but not when you're just in your late forties and never had a day's illness. In the months and years afterwards, I didn't think I could ever be happy again, but then I met Susan and we've got very close.'

Tom was amazed how quickly the time passed as the two men drank tea and got to know each other. When the morning staff appeared, he checked the hotel then changed into running kit and jogged down by the river. It was a glorious morning with the sun making an appearance over the Kilpatrick Hills. A pair of grey seals chatted on the beach while three swans flew in close formation downstream, inches above the calm surface of the river. The tranquil scene matched his mood and it was difficult to believe that the Clyde had once been one of the busiest rivers in the entire world. Andy had explained how bow to stern lines of merchant ships once sailed past here every day of the year, heading to and from the Americas and every corner of the mighty British Empire.

He ran along the sandy beach, trying to imagine huge ships like the Queen Elizabeth and Queen Mary passing here on their way from their birthplace just a few miles upstream at Clydebank. He thought Andy had been swearing when he called them 'the mighty Cunard Queens'.

Tom returned to his apartment feeling relaxed after his first night on duty. The job so far seemed to be everything he had hoped for, and more. Best of all, his colleagues were far more welcoming than he had expected. But he had to admit to a little disquiet on that front as he took a bottle from his bathroom cabinet and poured out his daily 80ml dose of methadone. 'What the fuck would they think if they knew I was taking this shit?' he asked himself as he drank the medicine, hating the fact that the doctor insisted he should continue it. For the first time in a year, he was thoroughly enjoying life, not least because the horrific dreams and flashbacks of the post-traumatic stress disorder had all but disappeared. His contact with Andy and Roddie had been a great tonic. He had not enjoyed such companionship since before that desperate day on the Baghdad-Amman road. The nightmare of heroin addiction seemed to be over. Dr Crawford maybe didn't know as much as she thought about the speed at which he would recover.

As he got ready for bed, he decided that he would continue taking the methadone for another few weeks until he had settled into the job. Then, no more living a lie, he would stop it completely. His mind at rest, he went straight to sleep, awaking ten hours later with the sheets and duvet virtually undisturbed.

CHAPTER SIX

'I STILL CAN'T BELIEVE I LANDED A JOB on the other side of the world where they pay me for eating fantastic grub and simply being around the place, and what a place! Honestly Roddie, I love it here. After our chat yesterday, I went down by the river and watched the oyster-catchers and seals on the beach. It's a miracle how a river once so badly polluted can recover.' It was Tom's second night on duty and he and Roddie were back in the Grand Hall.

'It is that,' Roddie agreed. 'If my old man came back from the grave and I told him that salmon were happily swimming up the Clyde past Dumbarton and Erskine, he would declare me insane. In his day, it was like a cesspool.'

Tom listened with interest when Roddie went on to discuss how his late father had moved to the mainland from Islay, a beautiful island off the west coast of Scotland, when appointed manager of a whisky distillery near Dumbarton. Generations of the family had worked in the famous Islay malt whisky distilleries, but Roddie broke with tradition and trained in land management.

'I don't remember my own father,' Tom explained. 'He died when I was a baby. And my mother died just a few years later.'

'That's a tough thing for a kid to handle.'

'Sure was. My mum's parents brought me up, so I guess I was luckier than some orphans.'

'But no substitute for the real thing. Do you know much about your parents?'

'My grandparents only started talking to me about them when I grew up and insisted I wanted to know everything about my background. William, my father, was first engineer on an oil tanker lost in a typhoon in the South China Sea. It's reckoned the massive ship had a fault in her hull and suddenly split in two. They didn't even have time to get a mayday out, so it must have gone down like a stone. My mother was a primary school teacher until I came along when she was in her late thirties. She played piano and, according to Gran, was a beautiful singer. She died when I was four, from breast cancer. My grandparents are a reserved couple and rarely, if ever, spoke to me about her when I was a boy. I think they felt it would upset me too much. They should have, though, because by not telling me they fucked my head up.'

Tom hesitated, unsure whether to discuss the deeply personal stuff he had divulged to the old Brigadier. 'I didn't find out what happened to her or my father until I was a teenager. I never knew him, and I only have some photos and a very vague memory of her.' Tom fell silent. It always took him by surprise how much the thought of his mother still affected him.

Roddie poured tea and gave him time to settle. 'But you'll have Scottish blood in your veins? Being a McCartney an all?'

'Yeah, on both the Shaw and McCartney sides of my family, and that's why I decided to head for Scotland. Since I was a kid I've always wanted to travel the world – it's one of the reasons I joined the forces – and Scotland has always been high on my itinerary. Apparently my dad loved to travel, so I guess I inherited the travel bug from him. I'm told Mum was a real home bird.'

'Ever thought about tracing your family tree?'

'I'd love to, but I haven't a clue where to begin. My grandfather, Thomas McCartney, and his sister Marion, were youngsters when they came out to Melbourne with their mum, and were the last of our line born in Scotland. They emigrated very soon after their father died around the time of the First World War. My Shaw ancestors also came from Scotland, but they emigrated much earlier, in the mid nineteenth century.'

'There's enough to get you started,' said Roddie. 'See, most of the Scottish genealogy records going back to 1550 are accessible through the Scotlandspeople website. I've traced many of my own ancestors back as far as the seventeenth century and constructed a large family tree.'

'That sounds really interesting. I'd love to see it sometime. Maybe do my own.'

'Aye, but be prepared for some surprises. You never know what you'll find; cattle thieves, highway robbers, and that kind of thing. Why don't I speak to Susan and arrange a date that's suitable for you to come over and have dinner with us? I've got a fine collection of whiskies if you fancy a wee tipple, and we can have a look at the website to see what comes up on your family.'

'Love to,' said Tom, wondering whether Julie would be there too.

'Right, let's do that. Phone your grandparents and get every scrap of information they have about your ancestors. We'll need it to get started.'

On a Saturday evening, a couple of weeks later, Tom walked along the avenue with a bottle of expensive wine. He was in a reflective mood. Though he and the night porter were a generation apart and appeared to have little in common, they had many discussions during the wee small hours while on duty together. Despite their differences, Tom was fond of Roddie. It was a strange friendship in many ways, but he instinctively knew that the older man – an avowed pacifist – liked him. Perhaps it was down to Roddie having spent a lot of time over the years talking to military men at the hospital. He guessed that Roddie was also quietly attempting to sow seeds in his mind and saw in their relationship a worthy challenge of sorts to educate him about pacifism. Roddie was opposed to the invasion of Iraq and the war, but had never once tried to ram his views down his throat.

One night, Roddie had suggested to him that harmonious dialogue was much more likely to allow people to move forward together than the age-old adversarial antagonisms of I'm right, you're wrong, and that disagreement and confrontation simply lead to entrenchment of opposing views. If everyone's opinion is considered equally important, it allows people to work out their differences amicably and violence should never be necessary.

He had wanted to argue the point with Roddie but pressed his own pause button. Violence was part of life. Christ, if there was one thing he knew how to handle, it was violence. His life was built on violence, his McCartney roots soaked in violence. He could have given a hundred good examples why violence was sometimes the only answer, but his respect for the older man made him hold fire.

Roddie opened the porch door before Tom could knock, and shook his hand warmly. A quietly attractive woman, her dark hair greying, emerged. 'Tom, this is Susan,' said Roddie, a look of affection and pride in his deep-set eyes.

'Delighted to meet you Tom. I've heard such a lot about you and it's high time I put a face to the stories.'

'It's very kind of you to invite me to your home.'

Roddie and Susan exchanged glances and she laughed. 'Oh, it's not my home, I have my own house in Bishopton.'

Roddie ushered Susan and Tom before him into the hallway. Inside, the grey sandstone lodge was homely and welcoming, and the delicious smell from the kitchen reminded him of Granny Shaw's house in Australia.

'I've offered to move out, so Susan can move in permanently,' said a familiar voice, 'but Dad won't hear of it.'

Tom looked up to see Julie coming down the stairs. It was the first time he had seen her in other than the hotel reception uniform, and she looked stunning in a simple, low-cut, summer dress. Nice one; he'd hoped she'd be part of the dinner party.

'I can't blame him for wanting to keep you close. I'd feel the same way myself,' he said without thinking.

Julie laughed, her eyes sparkling. 'What a compliment, Mr McCartney. I'll have to watch my step with you.'

He followed her into the sitting room, where he was immediately inspected by two glossy black Labradors, wagging their tails in the anticipation of finding a new friend. 'Beautiful dogs,' said Tom, fussing over them.

'That's Corrie with the red collar, and Skye in blue,' said Roddie 'the most demanding members of the family.'

'And I can see that your family is important to you,' said Tom, nodding towards the many photographs that adorned the room. Some older snaps showed Julie as a baby, while others had been taken at every stage of her life as she grew from a lively little girl to a composed young woman.

'That's Rachel when we were in Kenya the year before she died,' said Roddie, indicating a large framed photo on the mantelpiece. 'And this is one of Susan and I taken last year.' He squeezed Susan's arm and turned to smile at her before continuing round the room filling in details and dates.

Tom noticed he deliberately bypassed a group of photographs on the wall by the door. 'What about these?'

Roddie explained that some were of Rachel taken many years ago on a Campaign for Nuclear Disarmament protest outside the Trident submarine base on the Clyde. 'And these are Julie and me on the big anti-Iraq war demonstration in Glasgow with about a hundred thousand other protestors.'

'I can see who Julie takes after,' said Tom, taking a closer look at the young Rachel, and studiously ignoring the implication of the other photos.

'Aye, she does that,' replied Roddie, immediately adding, 'Look Tom, I know you believe the war and occupation of Iraq are justifiable and necessary. We'll just have to agree to disagree on that.'

'Of course I would never fall out with you over that. Each of us does what he thinks is right and believes in. I believe we're doing a good job out there overthrowing an evil dictatorship and helping the Iraqi people to democracy.'

'Some democracy for the tens of thousands of innocent men, women and children slaughtered by the Coalition,' Julie hissed. 'Not to mention the legacy of depleted uranium weapons slowly poisoning the rest of the population.'

There was a moment of awkward silence. What was that about depleted uranium? Why did others know about it, while he and the squaddies were kept in ignorance?

'Sorry, Dad. Didn't mean to embarrass you, but it's not something I can ignore.' She kissed her father and Susan. 'I'm meeting Davie for a curry and a few drinks. Don't wait up.' She barely glanced at Tom. He felt like he'd taken a sucker punch. Julie had another date! And Christ, she didn't half speak her mind.

Roddie took Tom through to his study in a large extension at the back of the lodge. Its patio doors openened onto the bright and colourful cottage garden. Shelves of books, and a big open cabinet heaving with bottles of Scotch whiskies, covered the walls. A computer, music system and racks of CDs were neatly arranged in a corner. Two comfortable chairs sat facing out to the garden, one with a set of headphones resting on its arm.

'Try this for starters,' said Roddie, pouring a small measure from a 1974 Ardbeg. With Brigadier Nimmo's words about the dangers of *uisge beatha* ringing in his ears, Tom nosed and tasted the amber fluid like a professional, while his host looked on expectantly.

'Magnificent, Roddie. Absolutely magnificent.' He drained the glass, savouring every last drop.

Roddie nodded. 'My favourite. And perhaps it should be at £330 a bottle.'

Tom looked at his empty glass. 'Fuck sake! I'd have taken it more slowly if I'd known.'

Roddie laughed, took the glass from Tom's reluctant grasp and poured a much bigger measure. 'It's okay. I didn't say the son of one of Islay's best-known whisky men paid that for it, now did I?'

Tom sipped it appreciatively, 'I'll take this one more slowly...' He paused and looked at Roddie anxiously. 'I'm sorry for upsetting Julie.'

'Ach, you hit a raw nerve there. Easy done. She's got her mother's passion, right enough. I blame it on the red hair and that fiery belief in justice and hatred of warfare in all its forms. That's what made her decide to study history.'

Tom raised his eyebrows. 'Yeah.' He paused without realizing it. 'But why is she working in the hotel?'

'She insists it's to save me forking out money for her studies, but I'm not sure she isn't just using that as an excuse to keep an eye on her old man here. She works there in the summer holidays, and most other breaks from the university.' Roddie looked at his watch. 'Anyway, we've an hour until dinner. Let's find out if you've got any skeletons in the family cupboard.'

They pulled chairs over to Roddie's computer and sat down with generous measures of whisky. He typed in www.scotlandspeople.co.uk and Scotland's national genealogy website appeared. 'Which side would you like to look at first?'

'The McCartneys.'

'Okay, but to get started we need some information from two generations back. Do you know which district of Glasgow they came from?'

'Sorry, mate. Glasgow is all I know. Grandpa Shaw tells me I was named after my grandfather, Thomas McCartney. Thomas's mother, my great-granny McCartney, was called Mary. She brought Thomas and his sister Marion over to Australia sometime during the First World War when they were kids. Grandpa Shaw says a rumour went round Melbourne's Scottish community that my great-grandfather, Angus McCartney, had died back home in Scotland in mysterious circumstances. Within weeks of his death, Mary shot off to Australia with their two children. I don't know why, who or what she was running away from. It seems to be some kind of dark family secret. She got married to an Italian immigrant a year or two later, but apparently he was a nutter and used to beat little Thomas up. Everything went pear-shaped for her and the kids.'

'Hhmm. We might discover more about that from his death registration, but first of all let's see if we can trace Thomas McCartney born in Glasgow in the years around the Great War.' Roddie typed the name into the statutory register index of births and christenings and, within seconds, a list of twelve Thomas McCartneys born in the city between 1900 and 1916 appeared. Tom pointed to a Thomas Louden McCartney born in 1911. 'The middle name Louden rings a bell.'

Roddie hit another key and further details of the birth appeared: Thomas Louden McCartney, born March 15, 1911, Royal Maternity Hospital, Rottenrow, Glasgow. Father: Angus McCartney. Mother: Mary McCartney, maiden surname Louden. Residence: 34 Colinton Street, Port Dundas, Glasgow.

'Brill Roddie, fantastic mate.'

'Whoaaa there, hang on a minute. It probably is him, but let's check it out to be absolutely sure. It wouldn't be the first time I've gone off on the wrong track. If you don't get everything absolutely spot on at the beginning, genealogy can be a disaster. '

Roddie methodically went through the other eleven Thomas McCartney births. None had parents named Angus or Mary. 'Okay, I'm prepared to accept that it's your grandfather. Next we go to the marriage register and search for an Angus McCartney who took a wife called Mary Louden.'

Roddie entered the details and within seconds had the wedding registration of Tom's great-grandparents: Angus McCartney, aged sixteen, had married Mary Louden, aged sixteen, in the vestry of the Church of Scotland, Cowcaddens, Glasgow, on December 15, 1910.

'Thomas was born in March 1911,' exclaimed Tom. 'So a shotgun wedding at the age of sixteen. Fuck sake, Roddie, that's eleven years younger than I am.'

Tom's great-grandfather, Angus, was described on the marriage register as a locomotive engineer's helper, living at 34 Colinton Street, Port Dundas, Glasgow. Mary was a domestic servant from 107 Milton Street, Cowcaddens, Glasgow.

'Look over here at this column,' said Roddie. 'It gives us the names of *their* parents: Angus's dad, your great-great-grandfather, was one

William McCartney, a locomotive engineer. Your great-great-granny was Elizabeth McCartney, maiden name Elizabeth Winning.'

Tom was bouncing with excitement at how quickly they had obtained the information. 'Amazing, truly amazing. We're back four generations already.' He asked if they could find out what his great-grandfather, Angus McCartney, had died from. Roddie brought up the register of deaths in Glasgow, and searched through lists of every man named McCartney who had died there around the time of the First World War. There were no Angus McCartneys among them. It seemed the mystery surrounding his death wasn't going to be cleared up so easily.

At the dinner table, a respectful toast was raised to Angus and Mary, the sixteen-year-old newlyweds in 1910, and their son, Thomas, born three months later. An excellent meal was crowned by a considerable number of different whiskies from Roddie's collection. A great night, though the disappointment and embarrassment of Julie's outburst still rankled.

The following Tuesday night, Roddie took a desperate call for help from Tom and went to his attic apartment. His young Australian friend was sitting on the edge of his bed trembling, sweating profusely and unrecognizable from the giant of a man charged with hotel security. 'My God, what a state,' said Roddie, feeling Tom's brow for fever. He adamantly refused the suggestion to call a doctor, but took the two paracetamol Roddie found for him a few minutes later.

'Christ Tom, I hope it's not my whisky did this to you. I've had a few heavy sessions in my time, but a hangover lasting three days is a new one on me.'

'Roddie,' he whispered painfully, unable to look the older man in the eye. 'I'll be honest with you. This is no hangover. It's very difficult for me to explain, and I don't want to get you involved in my problems, but in the short time I've known you I've come to trust and respect you.'

'I'm a good listener,' said Roddie reassuringly, 'and very discreet.' For almost an hour he sat quietly, fascinated and shocked in equal measure, while Tom gave an account of the past year and more of his life. How he came to be prescribed methadone and why he had stopped taking it just forty-eight hours earlier.

Along with virtually every other person in the western world, Roddie had followed newspaper reports and news bulletins about the road-block killings of the peace activists. He had, like many, been far from convinced by the official accounts. Looking Tom directly in the eye, he asked him if he was telling the absolute truth about the deaths.

'There would be no point in me lying to you, Roddie. From the minute it happened I told the truth and I've never wavered from that at any time. Kilo 6 was a man down, but we gelled and I actually preferred five man patrols. Presley shouldn't have been there. It was my fault for agreeing to take him. He was a nice enough kid, and oh so desperate to please me. I think he looked on me as some kind of tough-guy action man. Maybe I was acting out that role for my grand little audience of one that day and exaggerated the danger we faced. He was frightened, and his nervy index finger was wrapped around that trigger way too tight. It was my fault. I'm not blaming him. No. But had it been just the five of us that day, things would have been okay.'

Tom took Roddie's arm firmly and looked him in the eye. This was no apology. 'Don't think it wasn't dangerous for us out there. It was very, very dangerous. Some American boys from our base had just been killed at a road-block and none of the rest of us was particularly keen to go home in a body bag. Agree with the war or disagree with it, it can be a fuckin nightmare out there for the troops. My own theory is that Donna Mulhearty recognized the uniform and my regimental Excalibur badge. When she jumped out to greet us, an older guy – an ex-US marine who was sitting in the back – realised that her sudden movement was dangerous in such a situation, and tried to stop her. Maybe that's what spooked young Presley who was round that side of the car. He thought she was reaching into her bag for a weapon. Of course the brass put their usual spin on it to deflect criticism, but the final, official accounts were not entirely lies. I've re-lived it a million times – blamed myself every time for allowing it to develop to what it did – and here I am, a fuckin junkie on methadone, cursed by my fate. Maybe Donna Mulhearty is determined to get even with me from beyond the grave.'

Roddie went to Tom's bathroom cupboard and returned with the bottle of methadone. 'You can't stop taking medicine just like that,' he said irritably, and poured 80ml into the small plastic measuring cup. 'Do those army doctors know bugger all?'

Rather than explain that it was his own stupidity, Tom merely shrugged his shoulders and swallowed the methadone. He'd said enough for the moment.

'Try and get some rest,' said Roddie, as he headed out the door. 'I'll see you later.'

Tom lay on his bed wondering just how much later 'later' would be, or indeed, if Roddie would ever speak to him again. The methadone coursed through his body and he fell asleep.

Six hours on, Roddie answered Tom's unspoken question by taking him up a breakfast tray of toast, scrambled eggs and coffee. 'Been thinking about this all night,' he said, putting a reassuring hand on Tom's shoulder. 'I know who's responsible for the deaths and it certainly isn't you or the young rookie.' He offered no further explanation and Tom sought none. There was a kind of presumed absolution in the words that were used. He wasn't responsible? Yeah, he'd love to believe that.

Roddie went off duty and home to bed. An hour later, restless and wide awake, he switched on his computer and typed 'methadone withdrawals' into the search engine. Immediately, the first page of over two thousand results appeared. He read articles explaining how some individuals, who had been prescribed methadone as a substitute for heroin, became just as physically dependent on it as they had the heroin. Withdrawal symptoms from methadone were every bit as severe, if not more so, than withdrawals from heroin. Coming off the drug was a slow process. It had to be gradually reduced by small amounts over a long period of time.

Roddie's attention was drawn to an article claiming that iboga, a substance extracted from an African shrub, might with just a few doses, cure addiction to methadone and much else. He printed copies of relevant articles and took them to the attic apartment when back on duty that night. Tom was feeling very much better and it was clear that the sudden cessation of methadone had indeed been responsible for the 'bad hangover'.

'I've been reading up on this and, at the risk of teaching grandmothers to suck eggs, I was correct in saying that any reduction in dose will have to be done slowly, and under the advice of a specialist.'

'Yes, I know that, Roddie, but I felt really well, and I thought I could handle stopping it myself. I hate being dependent on this shit. I feel as though I can't move on while it's dictating my life.'

'Better that than making yourself ill, my friend.' Roddie smiled ruefully. 'Although I don't suppose anybody's been able to stop you acting headstrong before.'

Tom thanked him profusely for his understanding and kindness. 'What can I do to repay you?'

'You can do the same for me some night, and you can agree to go and see Dr McKenzie in Bishopton. He's a good man – a good doctor.'

'Okay. But I'd think him a whole lot better if he could find me some miracle cure for this addiction.'

'Well, just read this.' Roddie handed him an article on iboga. 'Not sure if it's a crock of horse manure, but it might be worth following up?'

Tom scanned it and immediately recalled Brigadier Nimmo mentioning this. 'The CMO out in Iraq talked about this stuff. Said there was no way he could prescribe it, but I know the old guy well enough to realize he said nothing without a purpose. He was telling me to go away and find out more. In the upheaval of moving countries, finding a job and all that, it went completely out of my head. He called it ibogaine, but it appears to exactly the same stuff.'

'Ah well,' said Roddie, seriously, 'seems like there's some fate lead you to me, and me to this. I'm a strong believer in destiny.'

Tom switched his computer on and turned back to Roddie. 'I'll find out more about it on the net. There is of course a very serious issue we should discuss. You'll have realised that hotel management know absolutely nothing about this. They would never have offered me the job if I'd been upfront.'

Roddie acknowledged that with a single nod of his head.

'The last thing I want to do is make you complicit in this sleight of hand, that kind of thing. I'll understand if you feel you need to inform management.'

'Ach, don't be so daft. I'm not a man to let down a fella who needs support.' He looked Tom up and down mock-appraisingly. 'And don't forget, I've got my own reasons for keeping you here, big man, so let's just say I'll keep your guilty secret, and hold it over you just to make sure you keep your eye out for me. A little friendly blackmail can work wonders, I've always found.'

Tom laughed with relief. 'Yeah, right, I hear ye. That sounds like the sort of blackmail I can live with. Thanks, Roddie. You're a real mate.'

'That's all I ask,' said the older man simply.

Left alone, Tom turned to the web for information on iboga, and was astonished to get one hundred and forty thousand hits. Numerous reports stated that it had the ability to remove the symptoms of drug withdrawal and cravings. It was claimed to have considerable potential in the treatment of addiction to heroin, cocaine, methadone and alcohol, and was also useful in treating tobacco dependence. It had often proved successful as a 'one-shot' medication for pain-free withdrawal, but multiple doses given over a period were sometimes required. Because the drug altered consciousness and could cause severe nausea and vomiting, the risk of choking to death on one's own vomit made it essential that individuals, if self-treating at home, had a 'sitter' with them when under its influence. Jesus. Why don't people know about this? You'd think it would be in everyone's interest to use it to end dependency. He read on.

Later, through the night in the Grand Hall, Tom outlined his findings. 'This is quite a story that you came across, Roddie. The drug comes from an extract of the root bark of a West African shrub called Tabernanthe iboga. In 1962 an American heroin addict, Howard Lotsoff, acquired some and took it hoping it would give him a hit. It didn't, but the very next day he found his heroin craving had completely disappeared. When he gave it to other heroin addicts to try, their cravings disappeared too. After years of heavy-duty heroin addiction Lotsoff was drug free, and so convinced the iboga had cured him that he tried to develop it under the name ibogaine as a proper treatment for all addicts. When he began to make some headway, the U.S. authorities arrested him on trumped-up drug conspiracy charges. He spoke in court about iboga's huge potential for treating a wide range of addictions, but the judge ordered his testimony stricken from the record and threw him in jail. Nowadays it's possible to get the treatment under supervision in a clinic, but you have to go abroad for it and it is very expensive.'

Tom outlined how the iboga extract had been used for centuries by certain African tribes, such as the Bwiti and Dogon in West Africa, during their rite-of-passage initiation ceremonies. He flicked through some articles he had printed from the web. 'Here's what one scientist wrote about it:

The iboga root extract causes the initiate to be emotionally and spiritually 'reborn' and take his place within the group as a true adult. The

Bwiti believe that the dreamlike descent into the unconscious caused by the drug leads to a reconnection to the tribal lands, and visions of the ancestors. If the initiation proceeds well they believe that the initiate travels back in time to actually meet the ancestors.

'Visions of the ancestors!' Roddie snorted, and shook his head derisevly. 'Meet the ancestors! Is that not a movie?'

'I'm serious. This is for real. The African tribes believe iboga allows them to see hidden spirits and discover who they truly are. They say it enables them to travel through different dimensions, and planes of existence, to the other world of the dead and make contact with the ancestral spirits.'

Roddie laughed. 'Travelling might be in your blood, Tom, but travelling back through time to meet your ancestors? Come on, give us a break!'

'Scoff all you like, mate, but listen to what this French chemist who studied the Bwiti has to say about it:

Iboga brings about the visual, tactile and auditory certainty of the irrefutable existence of the beyond. It causes dream-like visions to appear: some describe it like a film being shown on the inside of the eyelids; others talk of characters acting out roles as though a play was taking place inside the head. West African cultists believe that, in the almost comatose state induced by the drug, the soul leaves the body and wanders around in the land of dead ancestors.

'If true, it would certainly be a unique way of studying your family history,' said Roddie, laughing. 'Who needs the genealogy website if you can take this stuff and travel back through time to meet them?' It was a thought that hadn't occurred to Tom.

Medical centres in various parts of the world offered a full treatment package with ibogaine. A government-licensed clinic in the West Indies charged £5,000, while another in Panama charged £9,000. Alternatively, individuals were able to purchase the medication from suppliers and self-treat at home.

'Ideally you should have blood and liver tests, and a cardiograph and psychological assessment,' Tom explained, 'but I've had all that recently. I hate taking methadone, Roddie. Fuck it, I'm definitely gonna try this.'

Tom traced an internet source of the drug in Slovenia. The price was £80 for a capsule of 98% pure ibogaine hydrochloride. He ordered six capsules, paid with his credit card, and waited impatiently for them to arrive. The flashbacks and nightmares had now gone, but he was determined to get off methadone and back to full mental and physical fitness as soon as possible. The only thing he had omitted to tell Roddie was that people had died taking ibogaine. Great phrase, that 'need to know' basis. God bless the old military, they have phrases for every deception.

CHAPTER SEVEN

WHEN THE IBOGA ARRIVED the accompanying leaflet warned in red letters:

The combined effects of altered consciousness and vomiting may lead to danger of death by choking. The patient must ensure that another person remains in attendance until the dreamlike state, which may last for a period of up to 24 hours, is over.

Roddie remained sceptical and reluctant to get involved. 'I know you're a risk-taker, but Christ, Tom, you've no idea what might happen to you. Have you read the list of side-effects? What happens if you develop an adverse reaction?'

Tom shrugged. 'Well, I don't suppose they call me Chancer McCartney for nothing. If I wasn't a risk-taker I would never have messed about with heroin. Anyway, when you've been in battle zones and faced death from suicide bombers, rockets, guns and road-side bombs, the risk from this little capsule is nothing to worry about.'

'No, I suppose not if you put it that way,' said Roddie.

'The only other option,' Tom continued 'is to go abroad for supervised treatment. Firstly, that means a delay. How many months might it take to set that up? And secondly, it could mean losing my job. They're not going to be happy about me swanning off to Panama or the West Indies or wherever, for some unspecified reason – or even for a holiday – now, are they? I love this job, and this place and you people.' He grasped Roddie's shoulder. 'I'd rather take my chances with this than risk losing what I have here.'

Roddie smiled. 'I wouldn't like to lose you, either. You've a way of getting under the skin, big man.'

Tom picked up the innocuous looking padded envelope which had arrived through the post from Slovenia. 'I've read everything I can find on it, and I'm convinced this is my best chance to break free from methadone. And listen to this.' He rifled through his papers. 'I printed this off this morning:

In addition to its usefulness in helping overcome addiction, some experts believe the iboga extract has considerable potential in psychotherapy, particularly in the fields of trauma and conditioning. It can facilitate closure of unresolved emotional conflicts through its ability to enhance retrieval of repressed memories. Ibogaine allows patients to view their past experiences in an objective manner, which enables them to confront personal issues that were previously unapproachable. One expert's work with ibogaine was sparked by his earlier interest in the use of drugs in the treatment of war-related trauma in the wake of World War Two.

'I read this to mean that it can help me avoid a recurrence of the post-traumatic stress – the very thing that led me into drugs in the first place.'

'But what if it leaves you with worse problems? It sounds like one powerful substance, and even the best regulated pharmaceuticals have inherent dangers. If it's safe, why haven't they licensed it in Britain? It's not something you should go into lightly. Why don't you discuss it on the q.t. with Dr McKenzie? He's very discreet.'

'Come off it, Roddie. He said I should keep the methadone going, but you know I can't ask him to be party to my taking a substance considered illegal in this country. What about his Hippocratic oath?'

Roddie finally nodded his head in resignation. 'I'll help you out on one condition. Susan and I keep absolutely no secrets from each other. I'd need to tell her if I was to get involved here, Tom.'

'Sure, mate, I can understand that. Yeah, of course you have to tell her. It's cool. I'm confident that she'll understand. And what about Julie?'

'What about her?'

'Telling her?'

'Only if you agreed to it.'

'I'm not questioning your daughter's integrity, Roddie, but would she actually be able to keep it to herself? You know what some women are like.'

'She is totally dependable. Without question.'

'Fair enough. It would be bloody difficult for you to get involved if they knew nothing, so you should be open about it with them.' He was about to add that he'd already blown his chances of a relationship with Julie, but didn't.

'Okay,' said Roddie. 'Given that I know you're headstrong enough to take it without anybody around to keep an eye on you, I insist that you don't take it unless I'm present.'

'Thanks, Roddie. I can't think of anyone I would trust more to sit with me.'

After comparing their upcoming shifts, they agreed that the following Saturday morning would be the best time to take the iboga.

Roddie was at the flat at 6 a.m. just as Tom was rousing – they'd agreed on 7 a.m. but Roddie wasn't going to allow him to give in to the temptation of taking the capsule before he arrived. 'I didn't sleep well last night,' he explained when Tom opened the door, rubbing the sleep from his eyes. 'Too apprehensive, I suppose.'

'Let's get on with it, then,' said Tom, waving him in.

'Now, you're sure you don't want to change your mind?' said Roddie 'It's no problem if you do – this has got to be something you're completely happy with.'

'Not at all. I'm really fired up about it – curious to know what's gonna happen. Fuck sake, Roddie, it's gonna be an experience if nothing else!' He picked up the instruction leaflet for a last read through. 'The commonest problem is vomiting, but I've chundered plenty through drink in my time to cope with that.'

Roddie frowned. 'Well, here's hoping that's all we have to contend with.' He busied himself fetching a bowl, a glass of water and a towel, and setting them ready beside Tom's bed.

'Okay, Nurse Anderson' said Tom. 'Everything ready?'

'As ready as it'll ever be.'

Tom swallowed the capsule and lay down on his bed. Five, ten minutes passed in stiff silence, Roddie anxious and guilt-ridden, Tom prone and keen to experience this miracle cure. Nothing. Silent eyes sought reassurance, but there was no noticeable change. 'Look at us,' said Tom, 'wound as tight as a couple of old women waiting for the last number on the bingo card.'

'Aye lad, the tension's killing me. How are you feeling?'

'Perfectly normal. Seems nothing's gonna happen immediately. We should do something to pass the time.'

'What, like I spy?'

'Well, as I'm about to drift off to sleep – of a sort – maybe you should tell me a soothing bedtime story.'

'Hmm, never was much good at the 'once upon a time', even when Julie was a child. Rachel, though, she was a grand storyteller. She'd just make up these wonderful stories straight out of her head. Julie could never get enough of them.'

'Tell me more about Ju…, about Rachel. How did you meet?'

'It's the family history you're after, is it?' said Roddie with a grin. 'Or just a certain part of it. You know, I find it amazing that a hard man like you is so soft underneath.'

'We've all got our vulnerable spots, Roddie.'

'Aye, right enough,' said Roddie, lapsing into reminiscence. 'I thought I was tough until that day I met Rachel. There I was, in my late teens, the Dumbarton lad in London for the first time. It seemed like the centre of the world – and like half the world was there. It was a huge Campaign for Nuclear Disarmament march and the first protest I'd ever been on.'

'Ironic really, that at the same age I was being trained how to kill people in a dozen different ways.' Tom coughed and gulped in air.

'You okay?' asked Roddie, studying his face. 'You're looking a bit green about the gills.'

'Just a touch of nausea. Think it's starting to take effect. Go on with your tale.'

'So anyway,' continued Roddie, his face softening as he thought back, 'There I was, in the midst of this mass of humanity moving towards Trafalgar Square and all I really had eyes for was this girl just in front of me. Couldn't even see her face. It was her beautiful long, glossy, auburn hair that mesmerized me. It was hanging down the back of her corduroy jacket, just a few inches in front of my nose. I was so close I could smell the shampoo, and it was all I could do to stop myself from reaching out and running my fingers through it.'

Tom laughed, realizing as he did so that both Roddie's voice and his own laughter seemed located away in the distance somewhere.

'I was so tied up in the fantasy of burying my face in that glorious hair – at the same time feeling guilty that it was far more important to me at that moment than stopping the world blowing itself to kingdom come with atom bombs that I stumbled, instinctively putting my hands out to stop myself. I wonder now whether it was my own subconscious that caused it, because there I was, touching that wonderful hair, just as I'd been imagining.'

'Subconscious my arse.' Tom swallowed involuntarily. He felt distinctly nauseous, and a cold sweat was forming on his brow.

'Do you want some water, pal?' Roddie asked, picking up the glass from the bedside table.

'No, I'll be okay. Go on with the story. Did she slap your face?'

'I thought she would, but she turned round and I could barely believe it when she asked in a Glasgow accent if I was okay. When I apologized and she heard my own Scottish accent, her eyes lit up and she gave me a huge smile. Her smile was even brighter than her hair. I tell you Tom, my bloody heart melted. I was absolutely smitten.'

Roddie stopped when he saw that Tom had finally drifted off. 'Good luck, pal,' he murmured. 'Hope you don't need it.'

Tom found himself in a twilight world. In the half-light he could sense, rather than see clearly, crowds of indistinct figures jostling to push themselves to the fore, as though trying to impress themselves on his notice. Once his eyes had gradually adjusted, he realized that many of them were familiar figures from his past. Several were old school friends, still as young as when he'd last seen them; a kindly neighbour from the Melbourne street where he'd lived with his grandparents – she'd always had sweets in her pocket for him; his first judo teacher; and, outnumbering them, numerous army colleagues, men he'd served alongside in many different countries. Then he realized, with a shock that made him physically recoil, what they all had in common: they were dead, every one of them. The soldiers had been killed on active service or in tragic training accidents. One man, whose name he couldn't grasp, had died on a climbing trip in the Himalayas. He remembered reading about it.

He felt deeply moved as he recalled those brave soldiers and the other souls. These were the lands of the dead, he was certain. The African legends were true. His heart quickened. This had to be one of the greatest adventures of his life.

Without warning, the gloom lifted and he was in a hot, searingly bright landscape. The manner in which the characters moved, and the scenes changed from one to the other in front of his eyes, was surreal; he felt fully absorbed in them and yet distanced, divorced from them. It was like watching a film on a huge wraparound screen, in full technicolour with surround sound, but made so much more real by the addition of smell and the taste in his mouth. He could taste the air. How odd. The only thing he couldn't do was to physically touch anything.

His eyes adjusted to the light, and he felt a wave of fear and dismay wash over him when he saw where he was. Donna Mulhearty walked towards him with a smile. There was an ear-shattering burst of gunfire and he experienced, once again, the devastating sight of her death.

'No!' Tom yelled, and sat bolt upright in bed, gasping for breath and only vaguely aware of Roddie's concerned face as he jumped from his chair to assist him.

'Tom, what's wrong?' Roddie saw real fear in his eyes, the pallor of his face and sweat on his brow.

Tom could barely hear, much less respond. When a wave of nausea overwhelmed him he struggled to get to his feet but found himself disorientated, with poor coordination and muscle control. Roddie held the sick-bowl at the ready, but nothing came up when Tom's body went into spasms with the force of repeated retching. The attack passed and Roddie splashed his deathly grey sweating face with water.

'Dear God, Tom, why are you putting yourself through this?'

The eyes that looked at him were unfocused. Tom slumped back on the bed and re-entered the dream-world in a completely different place. Tears sprang to his eyes; this was his earliest memory made real. He looked at himself as a child clinging to his mother, her gaunt, jaundiced face wet with tears. They were in what he now recognized as a hospice but he recalled painfully how, when he was that four-year-old boy, he thought it was a new home she had moved to without him. They were both crying as she stroked his hair and face, kissing him fiercely, murmuring over and over through her sobs: 'Be a good boy for Granny, Tom. Promise Mummy you'll always be a good boy.' The adult Tom felt anew the unbearable pain of his childhood, of thinking his mother didn't want him to be with her any more. He saw Granny Shaw walk forward into the picture, and take hold of the young Tom, her strong arms kind but firm as she pulled him away. 'I don't want to go, Mummy! I don't want to go,' he screamed at the top of his voice. Heartbroken, his mother buried her face in the pillow, not looking at him once as his grandmother took him from the room.

The picture changed instantly, like a cut between scenes in a film, and Tom's distress gave way to calmness and tranquility when he saw himself as a baby being nursed at his mother's breast. She looked healthy and beautiful and was happily humming the lovely Brahms lullaby. The sound of footsteps interrupted the ecstasy – loud, heavy footsteps on stairs followed by the crashing open of a door. A tall man with an unruly shock of blond hair came staggering in, clearly the worse for drink. The smell of alcohol on his breath and clothing filled the room.

'Look at you there idling your time away! Where's my dinner?

'Stop shouting, you've made him cry now.'

'I'll make him fuckin cry!' When the man drunkenly lurched forward, the adult Tom instinctively balled his fists, but was left helpless and frustrated when he found he couldn't intervene. Of course, when he later considered it dispassionately, he realized it was inevitable that, even though he might in some mysterious way be able to observe these scenes from his life – observe his father for the first time, intervention was simply not an option.

William McCartney staggered and crashed against a dressing-table, and his wife took the opportunity to gather up the baby in a blanket and run from the room. Crying and gasping for breath, she held him tight and ran downstairs into the black night, her footsteps clattering on the street.

Tom's eyes flickered. He caught the briefest glimpse of Roddie before the effects of the drug washed over him once again. He heard a piercing scream, and yet another distressing scene came in to focus. A young boy, aged about three or four, crashed head first from the roof of a small shed, on to a pile of ashes and stinking rubbish on the ground in front of him. Rats scrambled from beneath the boy and darted in all directions. Fresh blood from a head wound ran through the boy's blond hair, down his face, and into his mouth. Tom's immediate impulse to go to the unconscious child's aid proved futile and, yet again, he could only watch helplessly. He looked around, trying to make sense of it all. Towering walls of blackened sandstone rose all around him like a prison yard with small windows. Ancient gas lamps created an eerie yellow glow in thick, freezing fog and the smoke that belched from a hundred or so tenement chimneys above.

Two older children climbed down from the pitched roof of the small building, on to a wall, then jumped down beside the boy.

'He's no deid izzy, Wullie? Tell me he's no deid,' cried the younger boy, a ragged child of about six.

'Ur ye aw right, Thomas?' Wullie whispered in his ear. 'Ur ye aw right?' He shook the child with one filthy hand and wiped blood away from his mouth and nostrils with the other. 'Ees mammy's gaunny murder us fur takin him up oan the roof.' When Wullie began yelling 'Mrs McCartney, Mrs McCartney', Tom's suspicions that this scene had a connection with his grandfather, Thomas McCartney, were confirmed. The thud of numerous old wooden sash and case windows opening above drew his eyes away from the distressing scene. Anxious faces were immediately thrust out from the tenement windows, their collective instinct recognizing that something was seriously wrong – and whatever it was, it was everyone's problem.

Several women ran from adjacent closes. 'Whit happened, Wullie, whit happened?' shrieked one of them.

'Get him inside.'

'Maisie, put the kettle on.'

'Diz he need the infirmary?'

'Whit happened, Wullie? Ye need tae tell us whit happened.'

'He fell heid furst aff the wash hoose roof,' blurted Wullie, and burst into tears. 'Ah'm sorry Mrs McCartney ah'm awfa sorry. S'no ma fault. Ah thought he'd be awright.'

Tom watched Mrs McCartney pick the boy up and run with the other women through a close crammed with an assortment of old junk. He followed them up a narrow, turret-like, winding stone stair case with flaking green walls. They passed a small wooden door on a half landing, and the stench of urine and shit almost made him vomit.

Three flights up, on the top landing, Mrs McCartney and her neighbours rushed into the house on the right. Tom followed them into a short dark hallway and through a door. He immediately scanned the room as he would on an SASR mission. His initial reaction was one of pleasant surprise. It was bright, clean and cosy. Beside the white distempered wall to his immediate right was what looked like a home-made chest-of-drawers-come-sideboard. On the wall opposite the door was an open, recessed window that overlooked the back court and the scene of the accident. Below the window, a single deep tub with a swan neck tap reminded him of an old trough he had once seen on a farm. Attached to the sink was a large, well-scrubbed, wooden draining board. Over on the wall to the left, a large black iron cooking range had a coal fire blazing away in the grate. On the range, a heavy-looking iron kettle and a black pot were boiling in anticipation.

An elderly, grey-haired woman sat in a soft easy-chair to the left of the fire rocking a baby's crib with her foot. Above her, suspended from the high ceiling, a wood and rope pulley sagged under the weight of drying clothes. To Tom's immediate left sat a big wooden table covered with an oilskin, and four chairs. On the wall behind, a curtain hung over a large recess with a bed just visible.

'Splash ees face wae cauld water, Mary,' advised one woman.

'Slap ees back,' suggested another, 'ee's maybe swallied ees tongue.'

Mary did both and everyone gasped when young Thomas opened his eyes, as if waking from a cat-nap, clearly wondering what all the fuss was about. 'Whit's wrang Mammy? Why are aw the mammies here? Whit's happened? Is ma faither no hame fur ees tea yet? Ah'm starvin. Can ah get a piece till the tea's ready?'

Tom barely understood a word, but joined in the laughter. Communal relief was registered with knowing nods and sighs of satisfaction. They would not have passed muster as paramedics, but as emergency teams go, this was one of the most formidable he had ever seen.

The neighbours made their way out. Mary removed Thomas's blood-stained coat and sat him up on the draining board. Tom took stock. It was true. The iboga was working. Roddie's cynicism and scorn were unfounded. It induced visions of the past just as the African tribes-people said it did. He was watching his grandfather, Thomas McCartney, as a little boy some ninety years in the past. He could see his ancestors – in vivid three dimensional colours. They could not see him. Communication was a one-way process. He could hear them, but he had no voice for their ears.

Mary, he reasoned, was his great-grandmother. A short, slim young woman with glossy auburn hair, she had an exceedingly pretty, freckled face. He puzzled over the plump old lady wearing a long, wrap-around pinny and heavy cardigan. She had a round, kindly face with her grey hair in a bun. The pupils of both eyes were so opaque that it was readily apparent she was blind. As she rocked the baby in the crib at her feet, Tom saw that her ankles were enormously swollen and literally hanging over her tattered house slippers.

'Keep yer legs oot the road, son,' Mary told Thomas as she lifted the kettle of boiling water with both hands and carried it over to the sink.

Pouring half of it in, she added cold from the tap and stirred it with her hand until the required temperature. 'How's ma big wounded sodjer?' she asked, stripping off the rest of his tattered clothes and giving him a kiss on his bloodied head. 'In ye go, son. A nice bath then Mammy'll tear up an auld sheet an bandage yer poor heid. It's payday so mibby yer faither or yer granfaither'll gie ye money tae buy sweeties when they get hame fae work.'

'Mibby they'll baith gie me money if ye make the bandage really big, mammy.'

'Aye ah'll dae that son, an efter yer tea ah'll take ye doon tae Jeannie Spittall's.'

'If ah get money tae buy sweeties ah'll gie some tae ma Granny Cartney.' When the old lady thanked him, and Thomas smiled across the room at her with warmth that put the fire to shame, the penny dropped for Tom. Here was his grandfather's granny McCartney, and therefore his own great-great granny McCartney.

Tom watched tears run down Mary's cheeks as she washed Thomas, and the reality dawned that her beloved son might have been killed in the fall. Life was such a fragile gift. Turn round and it could so easily be gone.

'It's aw right mammy. Don't cry,' said Thomas. 'Ah'll gie you some sweeties tae.' Mary wiped her tears and chuckled. She dried him with a warm towel, bandaged his head, and dressed him in a man-size cotton shirt. He snuggled into his Granny Cartney's arms by the fire and dozed off. Mary washed his bloodstained clothes in the same warm water and hung them on the pulley.

'His clothes are done, Lizzie. Ah don't know how am gaunny afford another coat.'

'How did he manage tae get up oan the roof?' asked Lizzie, looking down on her grandson with unseeing eyes.

'Bella Ramsey's boys lifted him up. He must've slipped on the wet slates an went right oe'r the side heid first.'

'Ah might've guessed it wiz them. Did ye gie them a shirikin?'

'Naw, ah'll hae a word wae Bella the morra. They're no bad boys; just a bit stupit sometimes. Since John enlisted, she's no been keepin them under control.'

Lizze nodded. 'Aye, Bella jist seems tae let them dae whatever they want. You'd be better keepin Thomas away fae them.'

'Easier said than done. He's a laddie wae an adventurous mind. Ah pray tae God he'll be aw right, Lizzie.' Mary knelt down beside her mother-in-law and gently stroked her sleeping son's face.

Tom felt a keen sympathy for Mary as he pondered the pain she would feel if she knew that her angelic little blue-eyed boy was destined to die one warm night in Melbourne harbour with a knife in his guts.

'Tripe an onions fur the night's tea, hen,' said the old woman, sniffing the big pot boiling on the stove beside her. 'Their favourite. They'll be hame any minute an run up the stairs when they smell it.'

'Aye, we're lucky, Lizzie; there's a lot a wimmin cook a decent dinner, but their men jist head straight tae the pub on pay day. Half their pay ends up in the publican's till then they come hame drunk an gie their wife a beatin cause the dinner's burnt.'

'That's somethin nae wummin should have tae suffer. Ah can honestly say William's never done that tae me in aw the years we've been married.'

'Christ, Lizzie, there's no a man in the whole a Glesca wid dare dae that tae you.'

'Aye, yer right there,' said Lizzie, with a laugh. 'An your Angus knows it's far safer fur him tae follow ees faither's example or he'd be needin a big bandage on *his* heid.'

Both women laughed heartily, confident that their men would be home just as soon as they got off the tram from work.

'Ohhhpen Ohhhpen,' came a friendly call from halfway up the tenement stairs when William McCartney and his son, Angus, trudged up ten minutes later than their usual, regular as clockwork, homecoming time. A draught of cold air blew through the small house as they walked in.

'Jesus Joahnny! Whit in the name a God happened?' blurted Angus, the instant he saw his bandaged boy. Tom was taken aback by the extraordinary resemblance between himself and his great-grandfather. Other than being about three inches shorter, and marginally slimmer, the striking young man with the dirty, oil-smeared face could be him.

Before Mary could explain, Thomas opened his eyes and smiled adoringly at his father. 'Ah fell aff the wash hoose roof, Daddy. Mammy says you'll maybe gie me a penny tae buy sweeties at Jeannie Spittal's.'

'Sorry son, that bandage isnae big enough tae justify ye gettin a penny,' said Angus seriously, while turning to wink at Mary.

'No even a ha'penny?' Crestfallen, Thomas's face creased, lower lip pouting.

'You stop teasin the wean,' said Mary, slapping the back of Angus's head playfully. 'Look at that petted lip.'

Angus lifted Thomas from his granny's lap and hugged him. 'Ah'm only kiddin pal. A bandage that size is worth at least two pennies. Gie yer Granda Cartney a big hug an ye'll get a penny fae him as well.'

Thomas's granda gave him a hug and sat down at the fire beside Lizzie, gently rubbing the side of her arm with a huge, oily hand. Having worked out the relationships, Tom marvelled at the fact that here before him sat his great-great-grandparents whose names he and Roddie had traced on the computer at South Lodge: William McCartney, locomotive engineer, and Elizabeth McCartney, maiden name Winning. William, with a full head of thick, tousled blond hair, looked to be in his mid to late fifties. Lizzie appeared older.

'Sound the gong for dinner,' said Mary in a posh voice, ladling huge helpings of tripe and onions onto plates. At that moment, Tom would have given his right arm to be able to sit down and join them. These people – his forebears were poor, but they were decent, kind and good people. Watching them, and listening to their conversation, he felt a warm connection to each and every one of them.

'Smashin, hen,' said William, before licking his plate and patting his daughter-in-law's shoulder. 'Fit fur a king that wiz.'

Tom looked on when they pulled their chairs round the coal fire in the big range and sat chatting happily, drinking cup after cup from the massive iron teapot. Mary nursed baby Marion at the breast for twenty minutes before handing her over to Angus. 'Ah'm takin Thomas doon tae the shop,' she said, wrapping an old shawl round his shoulders. 'We'll need tae get him a new coat. The auld yin's done.'

'We cannae afford a new coat,' said Angus benignly, but William and Lizzie immediately insisted they would somehow find the money for one.

Twenty minutes later, Tom felt another cold blast of air hit the room as mother and son returned from Jeannie Spittal's with brown paper bags full of sweets.

'Ah've got plenty for us aw, Granny, but Mammy says you've no tae eat too many or you'll die a beeties.'

The adults in the room burst out laughing at the little boy's misunderstanding. 'Aye, that's right son,' said Granny Cartney, holding out an open hand. 'But we've aw goat tae die a somethin – an beeties'll dae me jist fine.'

Mary hugged Thomas and kissed his bandaged head. 'Diabetes, right enough. If that's true, Jeannie Spittal's got enough sweeties doon there tae kill the whole street. It's a right wee Aladdin's cave that shop, an she's got the patience ae a saint the time she takes servin the weans.'

'Jeannie asked me if ah'd been tae France,' said Thomas, emptying the bags of hard-boiling sweets on the table and separating them into different coloured piles.

'France?' repeated his puzzled grandmother. 'Whit wiz she askin ye that fur?'

'France is where aw the sodjers go tae fight the Germans, Granny. Jeannie said ah looked like a wounded sodjer jist back fae France.'

'Aye, Jeannie's right enough, son.'

There was a pause in the conversation when Thomas went round handing each of them a sweet.

'Ah'm goin tae France!' blurted Angus. There was a moment's silence. Not even the fire cracked. Eyes flashed questions yet unasked. The room was suddenly uncomfortably warm.

'Yer goin tae no bloody France,' Lizzie retorted with a certainty that brooked no objection.

'We've been tellin ye since the war started that yer no goin,' added Mary, her voice with a pleading edge.

'A'hm goin tae France an there'll be no more arguin aboot it.'

'Yer goin tae France!' shouted Mary. 'Yer goin tae France! Before this bloody war we agreed tae go tae Australia tae start a new life, no fur you tae go tae France tae get killed. Whit's brought this on again all of a sudden? Ye agreed tae finish yer time at the works an get yer journeyman's ticket. Dear God, Angus, we cannae afford a coat for the wean's back an yer wantin tae bugger off tae France.'

'It's no that ah'm wantin tae *bugger* off tae France – it's ma *duty* tae go tae France. Ma duty tae fight fur ma country. Plenty at the work are enlistin. They're sayin the war'll be o'er by Christmas. Ah'll be left lookin like a coward if ah don't join them.'

'Whit's happened, William? Somethin's happened fur him tae be talkin like this,' said Lizzie perceptively. 'Only last week we aw agreed that John Maclean wiz right when he said the war had bugger aw tae dae wae fightin fur freedom, an everythin tae dae wae greedy, rich buggers makin piles a money. They make the money, the workin class provides the cannon fodder. That's whit wars are always aboot. Yer no goin Angus, an that's the end ae it.' Dishes clattered angrily. Lizzie had spoken and would have no more discussion.

William broke a short period of silence. 'Did ye notice we were a wee bit late gettin hame the night? When aw the workers piled off the trams at Dobbies Loan, there wiz a bit of a stushie. Some wimmin were waitin there haranguin the men an handin them white feathers.'

'White feathers! Ah'll white bloody feathers them,' shouted Mary, startling the baby. 'Suggestin yer a coward! They'll no be there the morra night handin oot white feathers tae the men, rest assured aboot that. There'll be white feathers stickin oot their arses if ah get a haud ae them.'

Tom could feel the terrible tension in the room, but young Thomas unwittingly broke it. 'Mammy! Quick mammy! Ah need a number two. Can ah dae it in the pottie? The smell doon in the cludgie makes me sick.' There was laughter all round when he added that his 'number two' would smell okay because he'd eaten so many sweeties. Mary pulled open a curtain revealing the bed in the recess, and took an old porcelain potty from below it. Thomas quickly pulled the tail of his shirt up and sat on the potty. The adults looked away, pinching their noses and laughing. 'More sweeties, more sweeties! Quick! Gie him more sweeties,' shouted his grandfather. 'Ah'll run doon tae Jeannie Spittal's an get another two bags before the smell gets us.'

Thomas sat laughing and holding his nose. 'Aye, quick, Granda. More sweeties, more sweeties.'

Angus picked up the potty when Thomas declared himself finished, and Tom followed him out the door and downstairs to the half-landing. The muggy smell of ice-cold fog swirling up through the stairwell was instantly overpowered when Angus opened the door of the tiny cubicle. It comprised the communal toilet for four different families. The floor was sopping. There was no wash-hand basin. The toilet paper comprised a wad of ripped-up newspaper pieces dangling on a piece of string nailed to the wall. Tom retched at the stench of urine and shit. Angus tipped Thomas's number two into the other brown stuff in the bowl, urinated into it himself, then pulled the chain that hung from a high cistern. 'Fuckin thing,' he grumbled, as the toilet bowl filled to the brim and waste spilled on to the floor. Christ, thought Tom, that's a thousand times worse than having to crap out in the desert.

'Right mister! Time fur bed,' Angus announced an hour later. Without a grumble, Thomas took his father's hand and led him through the cold hall to the even colder bedroom. From the light of a gas mantle, Tom watched with some sadness, and much longing, as Thomas lay down in a small wooden cot bed and his daddy tucked him in under a pile of old coats. 'Night, night, son. Ah love ye.'

'An ah love you Daddy. Will ye tell me a story?'

'The morra night, son, yer faither's awfa tired the night.'

Thomas lay still for a few seconds, the big white bandage all that was visible. He popped his head up and began to sing:

Tell me a story,
Tell me a story,
Tell me a story before ah go tae bed
Ye promised me, ye said ye would,
Tell me a story if ah wiz good,
Tell me a story before ah go tae bed.

Never having known his own father, Tom felt his heart might burst as he watched and listened to his great-grandfather, Angus McCartney, sit down and relate a magical fairytale to his adoring son.

Ten minutes later, Angus slipped quietly away from the child's bed and turned off the gas mantle. 'Night, night, ma wee wounded sodjer,' he whispered almost inaudibly.

'Night, night, Daddy,' came a drowsy reply. 'Can ah go tae France wae you tae keep ye safe?'

CHAPTER EIGHT

TOM WAS ELATED. Whatever his expectations had been, it surpassed belief. 'Thanks for being here with me, Roddie. Give me some time to think this all through and I'll tell you about it. It was amazing. Mind-boggling. Literally out of this world.'

'Hmm,' said Roddie, clearly not convinced. 'I expect an account, but right now I have a family and dogs which need my attention.' He looked at his watch. 'Six o'clock. They'll be thinking I've set up home with you!'

Tom walked down to the Clyde and strolled along the deserted beach, occasionally stopping to skim flat stones over the water. The calm, still evening matched his mood. The tantalizing glimpse of his ancestral home in Glasgow had left him with a deep warm feeling of connection with his past that had never been there before. He had always known a certain rootlessness, an emotional void which he had filled by joining the adrenaline-charged SASR, but this privileged view of his ancestors did something profound to his whole psyche. He belonged. A broken chain had been reforged and he could see, almost touch, the links to his past. He was taken by surprise by a sudden acute awareness that he, Tom McCartney, was the last link in that chain. Until this moment he had never seen himself as a father – maybe because in his own past, childhood had been a time of anxiety and loneliness. He wouldn't wish that on anyone else. But the connection to his roots made him, for the first time ever, think about having children of his own.

In a reflective mood, Tom walked under the piers of the bridge to the cobblestone slipway of the old ferry and gazed across the river. He recalled Andy Hutton telling him how he had stood at this very spot as a boy in the fifties and waved his aunty Fiona off to Australia. Fiona, and several thousand other Scottish emigrants, had lined the prom-enade deck of the Captain Cook that day as tugs guided her down-stream from Glasgow at the start of the month-long voyage to Sydney. Andy and his entire extended family had searched fruitlessly for Fiona among the sea of faces up on the ship, yet waved frantically. They might not see her, but she would see them. There was not a dry eye when a piper stood on the slip playing a farewell lament *Will ye no come back again?* and the captain gave the great white liner's horn a blast to say thank you and farewell.

Did Mary and her two children stand crying on the deck of some big liner when it took them away forever past this very spot? He had seen with his own eyes that she and Angus were a loving couple, and could only guess how broken-hearted she must have been at leaving Scotland without him. Having witnessed them together, he now considered the suggestion that Mary could have been in any way responsible for Angus's death, preposterous. His early euphoria ebbed in a rising tide of emotional attachment. These were his family, for Christ sake.

Back at the apartment, Tom logged on to the Scotlandspeople website and searched the Glasgow records for his McCartney family. The 1901 census returns showed they were living at 34 Colinton Street, Port Dundas with seven other families in the same close. His great-great-grandfather, William McCartney, was then aged fifty, and his wife Elizabeth fifty-one. Tom was surprised that Lizzie was only a year older than her husband. The ravages of time always seem unkinder to women, or was it due to her diabetes? In 1901, William and Elizabeth had six children living with them at Colinton Street: William Jnr aged 27; Bunty, 22; John, 19; Alexander, 16; Mathew, 15 and Angus aged 6. So, Angus was the baby of the family, a late child, and Lizzie had been forty-five years old when she had him.

Tom turned to the Glasgow births section on the website and typed in Elizabeth Winning. After several false leads he found his great-great-grandmother's birth registration. It shook him. She had been born in the City Poorhouse. The child of washerwoman, Agnes Winning, of 45 College Street, Glasgow, her date of birth was February 10, 1850. No father's name appeared on the registration. Elizabeth was described as 'Illegitimate.'

'Thank you, Elizabeth Winning,' said Tom to himself. It was strange to reflect that if it hadn't been for that little bastard born in a Poor House having a baby at the age of forty-five, he wouldn't be sitting there right now. Hey, how many times had he been called a bastard and worse besides – and here was proof that, give or take four generations, it was true? Nice one, cobber.

Tom moved on ten years to search the 1911 census returns for Colinton Street, but they were not available. A vivid recollection of the stench from the blocked drain in the dunny on the half landing made him feel sick. Strange how he could see, hear and smell the vision, but not speak in it. By November 1914 – the time of his vision – all the children had left the parental home, apart from Angus who was now aged nineteen. He had married Mary several years earlier and both of them, plus three-year-old Thomas and baby Marion, were living with William and Lizzie.

Angus had four older brothers and a sister. Surely there had to be offspring from that lot living somewhere in Glasgow today. His genealogical research, and the vision, made him curious about the possibility of discovering Scottish relatives. He would pay a visit to Colinton Street, but before that he would go to South Lodge to tell Roddie his incredible story.

The following morning Tom walked along to South Lodge. He was warmly greeted by the Labradors before Roddie made mugs of tea and lead him through to the study. He was keen to speak about the amazing iboga experience, but Roddie asked if he'd wait until Susan and Julie returned from the shops. Roddie reassured him that, while both women were shocked when told about his recent past in Iraq, they were understanding and supportive.

Tom and Roddie sat chatting while classical music played quietly in the background. Roddie was in a philosophical mood. 'You'll realize from our discussions that I've got very radical views on life.' He gestured to the books lining the walls of his study. 'The more I read about what's going on in the world, the more radical I become.'

Tom was astonished at how well-read and informed Roddie actually was. His own meagre breadth of knowledge left him feeling quite inadequate. 'I have to admit that I very seldom read. At school I was always too busy messing about with the gang or playing sport to pay attention to lessons.'

'I was much the same,' said Roddie. 'But I get great pleasure from reading now. As I've said before, you've an open invitation to browse and borrow any book that takes your fancy.'

'I'm gonna take you up on that. It's about time I began my real education.'

'Good man, but think on this. No matter how early or how late in life we begin our education, it will never be completed.' Roddie stood up and changed the CD, choosing Brahms' Symphony No 2 from his large collection of classical music. He was extending Tom's musical appreciation as well as stretching his understanding in other areas. Kylie Minogue it was not, but Tom had to admit that the calm state induced by the music was something he would have found useful in the past.

'I can see your musical taste needs working on,' said Tom, as he looked through Roddie's collection. 'It's somewhat restricted.' He took a CD from the shelf. 'Rumours, Fleetwood Mac! That's a small step in the right direction.'

'Never heard it. Must be one of Susan's or Julie's.'

'I can't believe it! Now this really is a classic. Tell you what, you choose some books for me and I promise to read them provided you listen to this and give me your honest opinion.'

'It's a deal' said Roddie, clunking his mug of tea against Tom's. He ran his fingers along the bookshelves and picked out *The Collected Poems of Hamish Henderson,* and *Everyman's Poetry. Rupert Brooke & Wilfred Owen.* 'Take these for starters.'

Julie and Susan joined them for lunch. They were of course late, but that appeared to be a relatively common attribute of the species. Tom told his story. He stayed calm and underplayed events, rather than have it appear that he was embellishing.

Roddie was sceptical and frankly dismissive. 'You've certainly got a lively imagination, Tom. It seems pretty obvious that you've had vivid dreams with iboga. Not horrific dreams like those you had about skinned corpses, but vivid dreams none the less.'

'I can assure you it was much more than just vivid dreams,' said Tom, rather more sharply than he intended. He felt disapointed and unhappy with Roddie's response and, for the first time since they'd met, irked by him.

'Maybe it induces hallucinations rather than vivid dreams,' Julie ventured in an equally skeptical manner before excusing herself. She would have to 'rush off' for a back shift on reception.

Susan smiled and turned to wink at Roddie when Tom immediately offered to walk back to the hotel with her.

'I'm sorry if we appeared indifferent,' said Julie, as they walked slowly along the driveway to Mar Hall. Despite the rain, and her claim that she'd be late for work, she seemed to be in no hurry. 'Whatever caused it, it was certainly interesting. It seems to have made a big impression on you.'

'Vivid dreams? Hallucinations? Who knows? Maybe you're right, but it was very, very real to me, and you've no idea how much it affected me. It's changed my attitude to so many things – the importance of family, for starters. Knowing where we're coming from, who we are and why we're the way we are.' He struggled to find words which effectively described what he had experienced. 'It was astonishing, quite amazing.'

Julie looked at him thoughtfully, her footsteps slowing even more. 'And what about your attitude to war?' The question hit him unexpectedly, but he realized that she had every right to ask.

'Yes, that too, I suppose. Seeing how shocked they were when Angus said he was going to war, brought it home to me. The working class provides the cannon fodder.' He stopped, perplexed. Those words, those very words. Someone else had voiced them. Recently.

Julie's face lit up. 'Yes! That's the thing – it's the poor and the innocents who suffer, and the effects of that war are still being felt today. What I mean is that it affects our whole understanding of war and why it's so important to know the real reasons behind it, and not to be taken in by the beguiling words of politicians. They blatantly lied in 1914, and they blatantly lie today to send yet more young men and women to war. As you were.' Her voice trailed off into the sodden woods. Cold raindrops were running down her cheeks, but her face was flushed with passion.

'Well, maybe so,' Tom agreed reluctantly. 'But there's always more than one side to a story – more than one reason for going to war.'

'But how can that ever justify lying to the very people they are sending to their deaths?'

'In certain circumstances I would say that maybe, just maybe, it's worth it for the greater good. Maybe the end can justify the means. And there's no way to be entirely sure until we've had the benefit of hindsight.'

Julie came to an abrupt halt and turned to face him, agitated and pushing her wet hair from her eyes. 'So you're saying that it's okay to invade Iraq because we can't know what the verdict of history is going to be?'

Tom flinched. Her words felt like a direct attack on him. 'You're just being simplistic. You can't make a direct comparison between two wars ninety years apart just like that. There are very different issues involved.'

'Of course we can make comparisons – how else is anything ever going to change?' Anger crackled through her words. 'The warmongers deliberately create villains and enemies then use propaganda and jingoism to tee us up for a war against them. It happened in 1914 and it continues to happen. And even worse, how can soldiers, people like you, be prepared to go and shoot innocent civilians?'

Fuck sake. What exactly had Roddie said to her about him? 'Where do you get fuckin crap like that from?' he asked quietly, his jaw tense.

'I get fuckin crap like that from keeping my eyes, ears and mind open to what's really happening in the world,' she said through gritted teeth. 'And I get it from men like Jimmy Massey who are brave enough to tell the truth.'

'And who is Jimmy fuckin Massey when he's at home?'

'Oh, just a staff sergeant in the US Marines who admitted publicly that his platoon killed at least thirty unarmed civilians in Iraq last year, including women and children at road-blocks.'

'Sounds to me like your Sergeant Massey talks through his arse.'

'Well, so too must all the other soldiers who came forward to confirm his allegations.'

Tom immediately felt wrong-footed, and said nothing. He was used to getting his point across in a totally different manner.

'Massey left the army in disgust and now obeys his conscience rather than orders. According to him, the invading forces in Iraq are behaving like "a bunch of pitbulls loose in a cage full of rabbits". Soldiers are feted as heroes, but the real heroes are guys like Massey with the guts to stand up and tell the truth.'

'Never at any time in all my years in the army did I consider myself a hero,' said Tom quietly. He was seething inside and struggling to keep a tight rein on it. 'Nor did any of the thousands of other soldiers I know. We were just ordinary people who behaved like ordinary people. We could be bad or good, or brave or frightened, on any given day.'

'I wasn't implying that you personally considered yourself a hero. The point I'm making is that treating soldiers as heroes is a cynical ploy to get young men to enlist and keep them fighting.'

'A lot of good, decent men and women are risking their lives over there,' said Tom, tersely.

'I'm not suggesting that there aren't any brave soldiers in Iraq, but most of them don't understand why they are there, or what it's really about.'

'Yeah, we're all just thickos dodging bullets and suicide bombers.'

'That's not what I'm saying.'

'If only we'd had the vast experience of life you've had, and sat on our arses scribbling notes at a clever university, we too might have turned out like smart-arse know-alls.'

'Oh go fuck yourself,' hissed Julie.

They walked the rest of the way to the hotel in stony silence before she stormed off to reception without even a cursory 'goodbye'.

Her words cut deep. He was disappointed and angry. She was so fuckin convinced her view was right in black and white, with no room for the shades of grey he had been aware of during his entire career as a soldier. Anyway, soldiers aren't taught to think about politics. He was versed in reaction, survival, procedure, loyalty and duty. His beliefs may have been compromised at times, but he'd always relied on his own moral compass and brought his patrol back alive. She was too harsh in her outspoken opinions. He sighed ruefully, recognizing that he liked to be as unerringly right as she did. They were similar in that respect, if no other.

A hot shower washed away some of the anger. He felt no need to take methadone and poured himself a very generous measure of malt whisky instead. Maybe not clever, but let's see how it goes. He sat down by his window overlooking the rain-sodden gardens with Roddie's book of Hamish Henderson poems. What was it his training manual said? Find out how the enemy thinks. This might be a start.

CHAPTER NINE

ON A DULL, OVERCAST MORNING, Tom finished his night shift and headed off to Glasgow to find Colinton Street. The city was grey and disinterested. It had that Monday morning feeling and you could almost touch the listlessness. Leaving the M8 in central Glasgow he drove along Dobbies Loan and, quicker than he imagined, found Port Dundas. It sat on a hill just one mile north of the very heart of Glasgow. He pulled in beside a graffiti-daubed snack trailer, whose lack of tyres suggested it had a quasi-permanent pitch, and automatically asked for a coffee and a burger.

'Cheese-burger, veggie-burger, burger-burger, bacon-burger?'

It could have been a votive prayer. The prices were cheap and the offerings nasty. The pungent smell of recycled fat hung around the trailer, fuelled by the preferred cooking style. Everything fried. This was cholesterol central and Tom quickly revised his order to a coffee and a question.

'Colinton Street? Never heard ae it, Jimmy. Ur ye sure ye've gote the right name? There's nothin here except the industrial estate.' The perfectly rotund wee man behind the counter stood there proudly surveying the surrounding factory units, proof positive that too many burgers spoil the broth.

'Yes, definitely Colinton Street, but for some reason it's not shown on this.' Tom brandished the street map with growing frustration.

'Does the name Colinton Street mean anythin tae you, Isa?' Burgerman shouted above the din of the hissing steam coffee maker. 'The wife wiz brought up here,' he explained before Isa could answer. When she did, she spoke at a furious rate of knots, apparently without breathing.

'Yer aboot forty years too late tae see Colinton Street, pal, it wiz razed tae the grun when they built the motorway through here. Ah wiz born an bred in Maitland Street ye know an we used tae take oor bogies up tae the wee bridge o'er the canal at the top a Colinton Street an we'd start there an race aw the way doon tae Port Dundas Road. Ah remember wee Bandy Williamson built a bogie wae giant pram wheels an the furst time he went oan it, it went doon Colinton Street that fast he couldnae stoap an went straight intae a caur on Dobbies Loan an broke baith eez legs. Made him walk funny. That's why eez called Bandy. If ye go tae the right there up Townsend Street then turn left at the tope ye'll come tae a wee bridge o'er the canal. Where dae ye come fae yersel anyway, is that a South African accent?'

Disappointed, Tom paid for the coffee. He explained that he was Australian with a fair amount of Glaswegian, and especially Colinton Street, blood in his veins. He had caught only snippets of her rapid-fire Glasgow vernacular, but headed in the direction she had pointed, looking for a bridge over a canal.

Minutes later he came to a ten-foot-wide, hump-back, wooden bridge on the canal and sat on its side rails. Isa's coffee tasted sour and was exceptionally weak. Its singular merit was that it was boiling hot. Even its dubious aroma was overpowered by the heavy odour from a whisky distillery on the opposite bank. A middle-aged man wearing a life-preserver stood on the bank watching children in expensive-looking, brightly coloured, fibre-glass dinghies learning to sail on the canal. Another man sat in a rubber inflatable with the outboard on low throttle, bobbing in and out among the half dozen small boats, shouting instructions. Twenty yards away up on a grassy bank, the rusting hull of a sixty-foot long canal boat, a partly buried reminder of industrial decay, lay forlorn. What tales could it tell?

'That's a scheduled ancient monument yer sittin on, mister!' shouted the man wearing the life preserver with the logo British Waterways sewn on. Tom jumped down from the rails of the bridge, chastised like a naughty schoolboy.

The weather-beaten man laughed and walked over. 'It's okay, Jimmy. Ah'm sure it'll last another two hundred years if you're prepared to sit there and guard it.'

'This is two hundred years old?'

'Aye an mer. From 1790 tae be precise. It's called a Bascule Bridge. A man would stand here and when he turned this big cog wheel, half of the bridge came up. Same again with another man on the opposite bank and, Bob's yer uncle, the boats could sail through.'

'I hope they had fewer holes in them than the hulk there.'

'Aye, it's a bit of an eyesore right enough, but I'm hopin we can get it restored an displayed. The barges carried millions of tons of goods on the canal in their heyday. That's one of very few remainin. It's part of our heritage – it deserves a better fate.'

'The canal must have been busy back then.'

'Aye, very busy – Glasgow was the second city of the Empire, no less.'

'Not Melbourne then?'

The waterways man laughed. 'I'm guessin from yer accent that's where yer from?'

'True blue, but the woman in the snack shack thought I was South African.'

The man threw his head back laughing and almost tipped backwards into the canal. 'I'm surprised wee Isa stopped talkin long enough tae actually hear yer accent.'

In companionable silence, the two men watched the children sailing, some quite expertly, as the man in the inflatable shouted encouragement.

'It's a bit different from the auld days,'said the man. 'There's an old framed photo of the Dundas basins in our head office an it shows every single berth taken by barges an ships.'

'Ships! Ships came along here?'

'They sure did. The canal was built to take sea-goin vessels. Not the big riggers, of course – but smaller sailin ships from the Irish and North Seas weighing up to about a hundred tons'

'They'd be pulled along by horses on the towpaths, I suppose.'

'Aye, in the early days, that's right, but when the steam ships came along, the horses just about disappeared. Then canal's day was o'er when the railways opened up, and it gradually fell into disrepair.'

The man invited Tom to join him and they walked along the towpath on the canal's south bank. 'So what brings you to Glasgow?'

Tom simply explained his mission to find Colinton Street.

'Well, your satellite navigation system's working fine, my friend. In the old days three Bascule bridges used to cross the canal here in Port Dundas. One of them was the Colinton Street Bridge. The bridge at the basin there is the only survivor.'

Looking about to ensure he had the correct place, the man led Tom further along the bank.

'Right here. The Colinton Street Bridge crossed the canal at this exact spot. Colinton Street ran down the hill from here in a long sweepin right-hand curve tae Port Dundas Road an Dobbies Loan. The auld tenements, an the big cooperage, in Colinton Street were bulldozed about forty years ago.'

'What's a cooperage?'

'A place where they make wooden barrels for the whisky industry. It was an ugly big buildin that ran down the right hand side of the street from here. The motorway was built across the bottom of the street, separatin it from Dobbies Loan. As ye can see, the industrial units here are all recent. Few people who knew Colinton Street back then would even recognize the place today. What's the name of the family yer lookin for?'

'McCartney. My grandfather was a boy in Colinton Street during the First World War. He lived with his mum, dad, and grandparents in their house up a close at number 34.' Tom went on to describe the room and kitchen in detail.

'My God, the place was demolished forty years ago but ye describe it like ye lived there yourself. Somebody in your family obviously kept a good diary.'

Tom laughed. 'Yip, an excellent diary.'

'I don't know of any McCartneys living about here, but that's not surprising because, as you can see, nobody lives around here now. There's no doubtin, though, that your ancestors would have walked across the bridge here many, many times. I'll guarantee ye that when your grandad was a wee boy he would have played right at this very spot catchin baggie minnies in the canal.'

Tom encouraged the man to tell him more about the bridge and the waterways, and he explained that construction of the canal had been completed in 1790. 'It links the River Forth on the east coast of Scotland to the River Clyde at Bowling on the west.'

'Bowling! Is that not just across the river from Erskine?'

'Aye, that's right. I used tae cross on the Erskine Ferry many years ago with ma mother when she visited her uncle in the military hospital there.'

'That's where I'm working, sorry, not the hospital, the hotel.'

'Aye, ah heard the hospital moved away an the old buildin was turned in tae some swanky hotel. What are you doin there?'

'Ah nothing permanent.' Tom avoided the question. 'It's just a temporary job to get some cash while I'm over here researching my family history.'

'Now, this might amuse you,' said the man, keen to get back on to his favourite topic of conversation. 'Talking about Bowling, there's a series of locks along the canal that allows it tae climb from sea-level at Bowling to 150 feet above sea level at Port Dundas here. When the canal first opened, Glasgow folk would look up from the city centre and see ships on the hill sailing past the tops of the houses.'

Tom laughed. 'I'll bet a few of them thought they were hallucinating – or maybe had too much to drink!'

'Are ye partial tae a wee dram yourself?'

'Yes, especially if it's Ardbeg at £330 a bottle.' Tom explained Roddie's source.

'Aye, we've all got our wee sources,' said the waterways man, looking at his watch. 'Ach well, nae rest for the wicked, better be gettin back to work.'

'Thanks, mate, that was really interesting.'

'Not at all, it's a real pleasure tae talk to someone wae a genuine interest. It's been ma passion as well as ma job for forty odd years. I'm only sorry I couldn't help ye with a lead on the McCartneys. If ye try the Old Port Tavern further along by Speirs Wharf, some of the old codgers in there might be able to help you. Good luck, big man.'

Tom strolled round the canal basins of Port Dundas for half an hour before walking along to Speirs Wharf and the pub. Not quite the last chance saloon, but he had a sense that strangers should beware. A couple of obvious regulars glanced up from their newspapers as he walked into their smoke-filled local.

The world may have radically changed, revolutions come and gone, but the Old Port Tavern had survived such niceties by confounding time. It had aye been, and the regulars cherished their monument to an earlier age. They sat where they always sat, safe in a space where they knew they belonged. The nicotine walls and dark-stained ceiling gave the bar its own five o'clock shadow but, like everything else, behind the gruff exterior that is quintessentially Glasgow, the bartender was outwardly welcoming.

'McCartney,' he shouted to the room at large. 'Diz anybody know the McCartneys that used tae stay in Colinton Street? This big fella here's tryin tae find them.' The atmosphere in the pub changed instantly.

One customer got up and left, his pint, three-quarters full, abandoned in haste.

'Who wants tae know?'

'You the polis?'

'Yer a fuckin debt collector, aren't ye?' snapped a small wiry fellow aggressively.

'Hey lads, let the man speak,' said the barman. No-one else had moved, but protocol as practised in the Old Port demanded that a stranger identify himself. There were too many official predators in society as it was, all wanting information – police, social workers, lawyers, court officers. No-one you could trust.

Tom was finally allowed to explain his mission and soon found himself seated among a group of Glaswegians, all the more welcoming when he bought a round of drinks. The man who had made his escape peered cautiously round the door, breathing heavily. 'It's okay, Jimmy, ye can come back in,' said a jovial-looking bald man. 'He's no CID. He's an Aussie.'

'Aye, and ye can bring that hot mobile phone wae ye,' said his neighbour.

'Ah've jist thrown it in the fuckin canaul,' said Jimmy mournfully. He lifted his pint from the table and downed it in one. Barely five feet tall in his thick-soled shoes, he looked Tom up and down. 'Whit the fuck dae they feed you on oot there in Australia, big man? Hauf a coo aff the barbecue every night?' For the next hour, Tom enjoyed a spontaneous comedy show as the men vied with each other to see who could make him laugh loudest.

Wee Jimmy remembered Colinton Street and its terrible slums. Tom left with a very positive lead on a McCartney family connection. Apparently there was a small engineering works, further north of the city centre, which had been owned by the McCartney family for three generations. He went back to his car, drove straight there, and asked the young woman at reception if the boss was in.

A rotund middle-aged man immediately appeared from his office holding his hand out. 'Now there's a fine upstandin McCartney if ever ah saw one.' Tom guessed he'd already been forewarned by somebody in the Old Port Tavern.

'Ah'm Mathew McCartney, pleased tae meet ye. Now, let's take a look at ye,' said Tom's new-found relative, taking him into the light from the plate-glass window before giving his verdict. 'Jesus wept, yer ma Uncle John's double.'

Mathew – or Mattie, as he was known to everybody – was the third generation Mathew McCartney to have run the light-engineering works. Mattie explained that his grandfather, who had started the business in 1920, was an older brother of Tom's great-grandfather. Mattie was an amiable man and showed great interest in Tom's research as they chatted about family connections for the remainder of the afternoon. They could not quite work out their actual relationship to each other, but it mattered not. Family was family, in Mattie's book, however distant.

'An now, young man, you'll be comin hame wae me tae share a bite tae eat,' said Mattie, checking his watch.

Tom protested, 'Oh no, please don't put yourself out.'

'We don't take no for an answer. Sadie would never let me forget it if I didnae bring ye home tae meet her.'

Half an hour later, Tom was sitting in a luxurious villa in the northern outskirts of Glasgow at Lenzie, nursing a glass of beer. Mattie's wife was a buxom woman, determined that Tom should be impressed by her considerable skills as a cook. The meal she effortlessly served was as good as anything he'd eaten at Mar Hall.

Thereafter, Mattie summoned a dozen or so relatives. Among them was his brother James, who brought along a copy of their family tree that he had painstakingly compiled. Tom was amazed to find that it went back beyond 1700.

'I never realized I had so many relatives,' he said, looking round the room, and noting family resemblances wherever his eyes fell. 'It's amazing to suddenly discover all these other McCartneys and so many of you still living near each other.'

'We're a close-knit bunch,' said Mattie.

'Aye, find one McCartney an ye can be sure there'll be another close behind,' put in his brother James.

'Ah hope you'll visit us aw regularly now we've found each other,' said an elderly aunt, holding out her glass for a refill. She had said little during the evening, but had consumed, Tom noted, vast quantities of whisky on the quiet. Her technique was Olympian in practised perfection. One by one she summoned a nephew, niece, brother or grandchild to talk privately with her and, unerringly, at the end of this private audience they would get her a 'wee drink'.

Tom smiled at her. 'I'd love to, but now I must love you and leave you.' He went round the room shaking everyone's hand. 'It's been great meeting you all.'

'It's been a pleasure,' agreed Mattie 'and we'll see each other again soon.'

CHAPTER TEN

DAILY SWIMS AND LONG RUNS helped Tom settle down after the spat with Julie. Physically, he felt as fit and healthy as he had done in a long time. Mentally, his head was clear, the nightmares gone. He was able to look forward, not back to the events that he feared would define his life for all time. Crazy how you know immediately when you're ill, but getting better could be a state of mind. Did the air smell purer, or did he just want it to? Had a single dose of iboga cured him? Irrespective of whether it had or not, he would be taking more. He knew that the moment he surfaced from the astonishing vision. Just a little lie should convince Roddie that a full course was required. If Roddie wasn't prepared to sit with him again, tough. He would go it alone.

Despite Roddie's protests and reluctance, he arrived early at the apartment with sandwiches, reading material, a Sony Walkman and a number of his classical CDs.

'Here for the long haul then, mate?' Tom asked. 'Fingers crossed this dose helps. I'd hate to puke my guts up for nothing.' He took a capsule and lay very still on the bed with his eyes closed. Roddie sat in silence, anxiously watching over him. After some twenty minutes, when he considered all was well, Roddie quietly clicked a CD into his walkman.

Tom felt a rush of exhilaration when, once again, he experienced the strange sensation of being both in, and yet separate from, a cinema film. The whirling, indistinct images, phantasms of his past, cleared away and the picture became clearer, although still vague as though covered by a veil of white fog.

He was standing on the Bascule bridge over the canal at the top of Colinton Street. It was snowing heavily with about six inches blanketing the barges and masted boats moored in the canal basin. They were all stuck fast, prisoners of the gripping ice, shrouded in virginal white as in a Bruegel painting.

Two young lads were running and sliding on the frozen canal, jubilant at their success in finding a new playground. 'C'mon, Thomas,' one of them shouted. 'It's great fun. Let's see how far ye can slide.'

'Ah'm no allowed tae play on there.'

'Yer jist a wee mammy's boy, McCartney' said the older of the pair, whom Tom now recognized as Bella Ramsey's son, Wullie. Thomas pulled a face and trudged across to join a group of other children preparing to sledge down Colinton Street. He was about a year older than in Tom's first vision, making him about five years old in the mid-winter snows of 1915.

Most of the children were wearing cast-off adult jackets or coats. Clearly too big for them, they were held with string tied round the waist, the sleeves roughly cut to size. Tom could see that they were basically old rags, but the children were having fun and looked warm in them. Like their coats, footwear was a hotchpotch of old, worn, adults' shoes or boots, with string wound round the uppers and soles to hold them on to the feet. Tom was shocked to see one boy running around barefoot in the snow like someone from a Dickens novel.

An older girl shouted to Thomas to sit with her on a battered tin tray. She pushed off down the Colinton Street slope and he shrieked with joy as the tray gathered speed and they shot past his close at 34. Who would have imagined such fun would one day be an Olympic sport?

On Tom's right, running away from the canal down virtually the entire length of Colinton Street, was a grim-looking building five or six stories high. It resembled an old warehouse he had seen in the Melbourne docks area, its tiny windows covered with vertical iron bars making it look like a prison. It was clearly the cooperage the British waterways man had described. On the left was the four-storey sandstone tenement he had visited in the earlier vision. Hundreds of chimneys along the roofs above belched dark grey smoke, and like every other building, it was blackened by years of constant pollution.

Tom walked off the bridge to follow Thomas down Colinton Street, and heard an angry voice shout: 'Ah'll kick yir fuckin arses, ya wee bastarts!' He turned to see Wullie, and his brother George, on the deck of a small steam ship, lobbing snowballs into its smoking funnel. Tom chuckled when a man jumped down from the boat to chase after them and slipped on the icy towpath, landing painfully on his dignity. The laughter of Bella's boys and the other children sent him into a hissing fit of temper. He got to his feet and lashed out at Wullie with a vicious kick. The blow landed on the boy's back, above the waist, and sent him crashing to the ground, badly winded. The red mist having descended, the boatman then made for Wullie's younger brother. Instinctively Tom tried to grab him, but he was restrained by an invisible force and found himself unable to intervene. He looked on helplessly as the raging boatman picked George up with one massive hand and drew the other back in a fist.

'Ah'm sorry mister, ah'm sorry! We wur only playin,' screamed George, a look of terror on his face. Tom yelled loudly at the man, but no sound came. The boatman was about to smash the little boy's face when he pulled his punch, unballed his fist, and dropped him on the snow. He went over to Wullie and yelled: 'Don't let me catch you two near the Gypsy Queen again. We're aw sick comin in tae the port an you two causin bother. Dae ye hear me?'

Ashen faced, Wullie got up, rubbed his back, and took his wee brother's hand. 'Aye, we hear ye.'

Daylight faded, but the children played on. Tom watched a man trudge up through the snow holding a long, slender tube with a flickering flame at its end, and a short wooden ladder on his shoulder. He stopped at each lamp post, climbed the ladder to open a valve below the glass lantern, and lit the mantle with the flame. The glow from the gas lamps miraculously transformed the dreary Colinton Street into a Christmas card.

The serenity of the scene was suddenly shattered when a cacophony of sirens, whistles and horns blasted Tom's ears. He tried to recall if Glasgow had suffered air-raids during the First World War. Did the Zeppelins fly this far north? The children sledged on unconcerned, and the penny dropped. Thousands of men poured from the distillery, and the many other factories and warehouses around Port Dundas. The mass of skip-bonneted humanity moved quickly across the bridge, down Colinton Street towards Port Dundas Road, and was gone. Within minutes the children were flashing ever faster past Tom on the impacted snow.

A sash and case window rattled open above and Mary shouted down from the top floor: 'Thomas! C'mon up son, yer tea's ready.' Without a grumble, he left his friends and walked over to the close at number 34. Tom followed him in through the close and a smell of cat's urine changed to the human variety when they passed the toilet cubicle on the half-landing. It hit him hard every time. How could people live like this?

'Ohhhpen. Ohhhpen.' Thomas mimicked the friendly call Tom had heard Angus and William make the previous year when they climbed the stairs.

The kitchen was exactly as Tom remembered it, with a welcoming coal fire blazing in the range. Baby Marion, now around eighteen months old, toddled about on the floor at her granny's still badly swollen ankles.

'Strip aff the wet clathes, son. Ye'r like a wee frozen snotter,' said Mary, holding up a clean shirt and trousers to warm at the fire. 'Ye'll get a big bowl a broth shortly when yer grandfaither gets in.'

Thomas pulled off his sodden clothes and placed an icy cold hand on his granny's cheek. 'Ye should come sledgin wae me, Granny. It's rer fun.'

'Ah wid love tae, pal, but can ye jist imagine yer fat aul granny sledgin doon tae Dobbies Loan like an express train an knockin a tram caur o'er oan its side?'

'Maybe ye would keep goin till ye gote tae Buchanan Street station wae aw the other trains.'

Granny chuckled at the thought. 'Ah hope yir daein whit yer mammy telt ye an jumpin aff the sledge well before ye reach the tram lines.'

'Aye, Granny. A wiz goin doon wi Nancy oan her sledge, but we were stopin before we reached the bottom.'

'An ah hope ye've no been standin oan the ice oan the canaul. There's many a wee boy fell through the ice an got drooned. Their mammies never, ever saw them again.'

'Aye, Granny, ah mean naw, Granny. Diz that mean the wee boys are still doon there? Wullie an George were slidin oan the canaul, but ah kept aff it. A man gave Wullie an awfa kick.'

'Whit?' said Mary, turning her full attention on Thomas, her face darkening ominously.

'A man kicked Wullie an he went flyin an couldnae breathe. He wiz gonnae punch George.'

'Are you tellin me fibs?'

'Naw, Mammy. Granny knows ah don't tell fibs, don't ye Granny?'

'Aye, ah know that fine, pal. Wee boys that tell fibs go tae the bad fire. Whit wiz Wullie up tae that the man kicked him?'

'Ah didnae see whit happened, but Morag Nisbet said she heard the man shoutin at Wullie an George an they jumped doon aff the Gypsy

Queen. The man jumped doon efter them, an fell oan his bahooky. They wur aw laughin an he got up an kicked Wullie.'

'Ah'll take the soup doon an speak tae Bella,' said Mary. 'You play wae yir sister till ah come back.'

Mary lifted a black pot of bubbling broth and poured half of it into another. Tom followed her down two flights of stairs, where she opened a door without knocking and walked in with the soup. The kitchen had exactly the same layout as the McCartney's, with a big black range, but it lacked the homely feel that Mary had created. Bella was sitting on her own by a smouldering fire looking desolate.

'Have ye no shouted them in yet, Bella?'

'Ah'm surprised ye havenae heard me shoutin oan them. Ah'm surprised the whole a Glesca hasnae heard me. They just dae whit they want noo. Ah've nae control o'er them.'

'Thomas's jist telt me a boatman gave Wullie a hard kick an wiz gonnae punch George. Maybe they've been up tae somethin an they're scared tae come in.'

Bella gave a wry laugh. 'Maybe a good kick's jist whit he's needin. Whit their baith needin.'

'A good kick, Bella, is the very last thing the weans need.'

Tom watched Mary add coal to Bella's fire then fill a kettle with water and place it, and the broth, above the heat. He followed her as she went out through the close and walked up the now deserted street to the bridge. In the darkness he could just make out Wullie and George sliding on the frozen canal. He shivered, recollecting another time, another world, when little boys their age would sail right there in their expensive dinghies.

'Wullie, George, time tae come in boys,' shouted Mary. 'There's a nice pot a broth for ye's in the hoose.'

Mary walked back down the street between Wullie and George, a friendly arm round their shoulders.

'Thomas says a man gie'd ye an awfa hard kick the day, Wullie, is that right?'

'Naw, Mrs McCartney, he's tellin fibs.'

Mary took the boys back to their house and told them to strip off their sodden clothes. They did so without embarassment and Tom was shocked to see how thin and filthy they were. Wullie had an angry, red weal from the boatman's boot on his back.

'Right, put these shawls roon ye an eat up yer soup. Ah'll come back doon when Thomas's granfaither's been fed.'

Mary stormed back up to the canal and battered on the hull of the Gypsy Queen. 'Did you kick wan ae the weans?' she demanded when the boatman stuck his head out the door of the small cabin.

'Whit the fuck's it got tae dae wae you?'

'It's got everythin tae dae we me. Wullie's faither's no here tae sort ye oot, nor ma man, but there's still a few in Colinton Street that's no away in France. You listen tae me mister, if ye even look at any the weans the wrang way again, yer tub'll be at the bottom ae the canaul an you'll be inside it. Dae ye understaun whit am sayin?'

'Ye'd better make sure they've gote plenty back up.'

'Somehow ah don't think they'd need it ya wee niaff, but ah'll make sure.'

Twenty minutes later Mary pulled a zinc bath from under the bed in the recess in Bella's kitchen. She sat it near the now roaring fire, emptied the boiling kettle in, then added sufficient cold water to make it safe.

'Who's first?'

Mary laughed and joked with the boys as she scrubbed each of them clean. She told them to dry themselves with the towels she had placed near the fire. Bella sat in her chair smiling a sad smile, but took no part. Tom could see that the shirts they put on were men's shirts, but they were warm and dry.

'There ye go. How does that feel, ma wee Geordie?' Mary asked as she bone-combed nits from his hair.

'It feels good, Mrs McCartney.'

'Aye wee man, ah'll bet it feels good. Noo, a want ye baith tae gie yer mammy a big cuddle, an when she tells ye tae go tae bed, ye go. Will ye's dae that fur me?'

'Aye, Mrs McCartney.'

Mary was about to leave when Bella stood up and hugged her. 'Thanks, Mary.'

'Nae need for thanks. Ah' know Bella Ramsey would be the first tae step in if ah wiz needin a wee hand. Jist one thing, Bella.'

'Whit's that?'

'It's the weans that are needin hugs, no me.'

Upstairs, after Marion and Thomas were asleep, Mary, Lizzie and William sat round the fire drinking tea.

'They're gaunny end up in a home,' said Lizzie. 'The way things are wae Bella it might be best aw round.'

'No way, Lizzie. They're good boys that's just no gettin any attention since their faither got blown tae bits in France. The poor weans were as black as the Earl a Hell's waistcoat, an ye should see the mark that bastart left oan Wullie's back. It's no their fault. Aw the wimmin are tryin tae gie Bella as much support as we can. She'll pick up. It's only two months since she gote the telegram.'

'Whit's happenin wae her rent arrears?' asked William.

'She told me she's just gettin deeper an deeper intae debt since the landlord increased the rents. Quite a few wimmin livin in the the Port are strugglin badly, an they're aw feart they're gonnae be evicted like poor Magret Burns last week. There's Bella, an wee Bridie Docherty, fae Colinton Street, an another three or four on Dobbies Loan. They're expectin the Sheriff Officers any time. They could be oot on their ears by the end ae the week. Bella cannae feed the weans, let alone pay the extra rent they landlord bastarts are demandin.'

'Aye. Nae wonder she's ill,' said Lizzie. 'It's a bloody disgrace.'

'It's mer than a disgrace, Lizzie. They were telt their men were heroes. Killed o'er there fightin fur king an country, an noo the landlords are tryin tae squeeze every last penny they've got oot them. Pennies they've simply no got. Ah'm gonnae dae somethin aboot it. They are not gonnae evict Bella or any more women fae Port Dundas. The wimmin leadin the rent strikes across the river in Govan huv got it doon tae a fine art. When their men are oot at work in the shipyards, they keep a close watch oot fur the Sheriff Officers in their bowler hats. As soon as they're spotted comin in tae a street, the wimmin ring bells, blaw trumpets, an batter auld pots an trays tae summon help. Aw the wimmin run oot their hooses fae every street nearby an cram in tae the closes and stairwell's so the officers cannae evict the poor soul that's behind wae their rent. They pelt them wae flour an rotten eggs an the buggers run fur their lives.'

'The men in the work were talkin aboot Mary Barbour an Helen Crawfurd jist this efternoon,' added William. 'As well as leadin the rent strikes, they're stirrin up a lot a workin folk tae come oot against the war. Ah hear the government's gettin worried that the unrest they're causin in Glesca could spread tae the rest ae the country.'

'Aye, well if the Govan women can stope the evictions, so can we,' said Mary. 'Ah'm gonnae go oe'r on the ferry the morra an have a word wae Mrs Barbour an Mrs Crawfurd. It's high time us Port Dundas women got oor act thegither.'

'Good on ye,' said Lizzie. 'Ah jist wish ah wiz well enough tae join ye. Lizzie McCartney here in her day would've scared the livin bloody daylights oot the Sheriff Officers. Is that no right, William?'

'That's right enough, hen. Ah wiz jist thinkin that we could beat the Germans within days if the government sent you an a couple a battalions a women fae Port Dundas an Govan o'er tae France.'

Mary laughed, and sat staring quietly into the flickering fire, her heart, her thoughts, her fears elsewhere. 'Thank God ah've got you two tae look efter me if somethin bad happened tae Angus,' she said, breaking the silence.

'Oor Angus'll come hame tae us in one piece,' William responded immediately. 'Don't you fret aboot that, hen.'

Mary stood up and walked to the window. Tom saw tears glisten in her eyes when she stared out at the heavy snow falling into the back court middens below.

'Ah wonder where ma big sodjer is the night. Whit if it's snawin like this in France an he's lyin oot in the open?' No-one answered, each lost in their own version of a silent prayer.

Tom wanted to take her in his arms as tears ran down her face and her shoulders began to shudder.

CHAPTER ELEVEN

TOM FOUND HIS LEISURE time over the next few months taken up with social visits to the Glasgow McCartneys. Tracing your family roots is an exciting project, but if you don't stop to think of the consequences it may come at a cost. They all wanted to take the Australian scion of the family under their wing, and if he wanted to put off a call on a distant maiden aunt, Mattie was not going to allow it. According to him, Aunty Betty, or whoever else it might be, would feel her nose had been put out of joint if he didn't pay a visit as soon as possible. One relative in particular, Mandy, was clearly smitten by him. At first he had thought of the pretty blonde as a caring cousin, and that was fine, but she clearly wanted a deeper relationship. He had always been particularly interested in blondes, but despite all that had happened between him and a fiery red-head, he could not get her out of his mind.

Tom maintained his friendship with Roddie and they still enjoyed long discussions when their night shifts coincided. He had been invited for meals at the lodge with Roddie and Susan several times, and made time to read the books he borrowed from Roddie's study. International politics was becoming more and more interesting to him, and he surfed many web articles relating to the origins of the Iraq War. After an intensive six-day spell on protection duty with an A-list celebrity temporarily resident at Mar Hall, he drove up to South Lodge. He found his friend pottering in the garden, and was immediately invited in for a cup of tea.

'I've not got time at the moment, Roddie – got stuff to catch up on after being tied up for the past week.'

'Ah yes, your beautiful Australian charge. Julie's been telling us all about her.'

'Oh she has, has he?' said Tom, grinning as he made a mental note to rib her about her avowed disinterest in the activities of the rich and famous. 'I've called in for two reasons. Firstly to return this batch of books – some of the stuff in them is mind-boggling, and I'd like to discuss it further with you when we get some time. I've checked the duty rosters and we're on again together in a couple of nights.'

'Fine,' said Roddie. 'I enjoy our night-time chats and it keeps my wits sharpened to have somebody questioning what I've long taken for granted.'

'The second thing is, I'd like to cook you and Susan a meal to thank you for your hospitality since I've been here.'

'Funnily enough, Susan was saying only yesterday that we should invite you over for a meal.'

'Well, how about a compromise? My problem is that the apartment just isn't big enough to entertain you properly. Would Susan agree to me cooking dinner here for you?'

'I'm sure she'd be delighted.'

'I'll make the curry a family in Afghanistan once cooked for me.' He turned to go, then paused. 'I'd love Julie to sample it too. Do you think she'd come?'

Roddie shrugged, his face unreadable. 'I think you should ask her that yourself, Tom.'

He headed back to the hotel where Julie was booking in a newly arrived couple. He waited while she dealt with them then approached the reception desk himself.

'So you've got rid of your pop star girlfriend, I see,' were her opening words.

'I'm surprised you even noticed she was gone,' said Tom, coolly.

'Only because things can get back to normal here. The entire hotel's been in a state of hysteria.'

'But you haven't, of course.'

'Certainly not. She's only a woman like the rest of us.'

'So that'll be why you've been passing on a full account of her activities back home?'

Julie flushed. 'That's for Susan's benefit – she never missed her years ago when she was in *Neighbours*.'

Tom laughed. 'If you say so.'

She glared at him. 'Yes I do.'

'Anyway, I'm here to invite you to a meal cooked by my own fair hand. Your dad has kindly agreed to let me prepare dinner for the three of you at South Lodge.'

'Yes, I'll come,' she replied, rather ungraciously.

'Right then. I'll fix a date with your dad. Better let him know when you're available.'

Julie looked down at the register. Tom walked away with a smile on his face.

Several weeks later – on a Saturday afternoon, Tom carefully wrapped a gift of crystal decanter and tumblers, and packed it into his backpack along with about a dozen different ingredients for his Afghan curry. The air was cooler than it had been as he walked through the woods to South Lodge. He took his time, relishing the fresh smell of damp leaves and stopping to examine the huge variety of fungi which had appeared in the wet undergrowth.

Despite a light rain, Roddie was in his garden as usual, Corrie and Skye close by doing their own form of pottering. They bounded up to Tom when he appeared, greeting him like an old friend.

'They treat you as one of the family now,' said Roddie approvingly, wiping his hands on a rag before shaking Tom's hand.

'The weather reminds me of what my grandparents said about it always raining in Scotland. Clearly they were telling the truth.'

Roddie laughed. 'Aye, so much for global warming. You might've brought some Australian sunshine over with you.'

'The mushies are coming up everywhere in the woods,' Tom remarked. 'I recognized some, but plenty I've never seen before.'

'Ah, the first signs of autumn. It's a season that has far more character about it than the summer months. And just wait till the leaves start turning – you've never seen anything so beautiful. Some days those woods look like they're on fire.'

'Mushies aren't the only things out today. The bloody bitties were trying to eat me alive in the woods.'

Roddie laughed. 'The terror of Scotland. Weather like this sends them into a feeding frenzy.'

Tom scratched his head and arms. 'They're as bad as the bloody mozzies in the tropics.'

'The midges have Scotland under permanent siege from May to September. Come up with an answer to the little buggers and the Scottish Tourist Board will hand you a few million quid. They're probably the main reason your ancestors, and just about everyone elses, emigrated to Australia.'

'I thought they were all convicts sent out there in shackles,' said Julie, as she came down the stairs.

Tom smiled, but said nothing. Was that an attempt to be funny or a snide insult about his family?

Following Roddie into the kitchen, he unloaded the contents of his backpack onto the large wooden table and handed him the gift. 'A little something for babysitting me when I take the iboga.'

'Ach, you shouldn't have,' said Roddie almost gruffly, although Tom guessed from the slight reddening of his face that he was pleased, nonetheless. 'That's what friends are for.'

Roddie placed the parcel carefully on the table but made no attempt to open it. 'Right, chef,' he said, making great show of tying on a flowered apron which was hanging on the back of the door. 'You've to treat me as your assistant today. It'll earn me Brownie points if I can learn how to cook the girls something other than bacon and eggs!'

Julie lifted the parcel up. 'What is it?'

'It's a little thank you present,' said Tom.

'Oh, he won't like that,' she teased. 'He just hates getting presents, don't you, Dad? You realize he won't open this until you've gone. Saves him the embarrassment of having to show how pleased he is.'

'How about opening it for him then? I'd like it to be used this evening.'

'You bet. Now I love opening presents – even if they're not mine!' Carefully unwrapping the parcel, without tearing the paper, Julie held the dark blue box out to her father. 'Do you want first look inside?'

'No, Julie, wouldn't want to spoil your fun.'

She slowly lifted the lid. 'Oh, how gorgeous. Look Dad, you'll just love them.'

Roddie's eyes sparkled almost as much as the crystal as he held first the decanter, then one of the whisky tumblers up to the light. Tom looked at him discreetly and noticed the faintest glistening of tears in his eyes.

Much to Tom's surprise, Julie walked over and kissed him on the cheek. 'Thank you for being so kind to him. Even if he might not be able to say so himself, I know he'll treasure them. Okay,' she added as she went to the sink to wash her hands. 'Assistant chef number two reporting for duty. Tell me what to do. I'm all yours.'

I wish, thought Tom, still aware of the touch of her lips on his face.

Roddie and Julie both proved able helpers. Onions, tomatoes, garlic, ginger and green chillis were prepared, and Tom fried them in ghee. He added various spices and a delicious, exotic aroma soon filled the kitchen.

'Wow! That smells amazing,' said Julie. 'Davie'll be jealous he's missing out on this. He even has curry for breakfast.'

Tom cubed lamb and soon had it simmering in the large pan on the hob. Roddie disappeared and came back with a bottle of one of his favourite whiskies. 'Might be a bit early, but we need to christen these glasses so I can thank you properly for such a handsome gift. But only on the understanding,' he went on, with a stern glance at Tom, 'that if you do need to take another iboga you call on me and don't embarrass me with expensive gifts.'

'Okay,' said Tom, toasting his friend. 'I'll consider you in credit – at least for a little while.' The silence as the three savoured the whisky was broken by the sound of a car door closing outside.

Susan walked into the kitchen sniffing the air and enthusing about the smell. 'How wonderful to see you, Tom.' She kissed him, and then Roddie. 'I hear you're getting on almost as well with your relatives as you are with your famous Australian girlfriend.'

Tom laughed. 'Yeah, she's one hot sheila,' he joked. 'Even offered me a job.'

'I'm sure that's not all she offered you,' said Julie.

'You bet.'

Roddie shepherded them through to the living room for a comfortable seat. He crushed up pages of an old newspaper and placed them in the grate, piled chopped kindlers and several small logs on top, and set it alight. Within minutes a blazing fire cheered the room.

Tom described his trip to Port Dundas. 'No rich forebears or famous celebrities, I'm sorry to say, but I discovered Glasgow is full of McCartney relatives and every one of them falling over themselves to welcome me to the fold.' There was much hilarity when he recounted jokes told by the Old Port Tavern men.

'It's hard to beat the Glesca banter,' said Susan. 'And I believe you've been treated to some fine home-cooking these past months. Perhaps it's in your genes.'

'Maybe,' Tom laughed. 'It sure would be nice to know that I inherited something worthwhile. Someone sitting not a million miles from here would say that cooking would've been a better use of my time these past years. Mattie's wife, Sadie, is the excellent cook, so unfortunately it isn't coming down through McCartney genes.'

'Roddie tells me that you're finding them all very pleasant.'

'Yeah. They're friendly folk, and go out of their way to make me welcome, but the novelty of meeting new relatives seems to have worn off. I don't particularly enjoy going over there so much now.'

'Oh, sorry to hear that, has something happened?'

'No, everything's fine, Susan, but I much prefer coming here. This is a comfortable home where you can kick off your shoes and sit back with your feet up at the fire and relax.'

'Aye, and remember you're always welcome to do just that,' said Roddie.

'Thanks mate. They live in a big house with all the trapping of wealth. You take off your shoes there too, but it's to protect expensive carpets rather than to relax. They've got everything, but don't seem to have a clue about what's happening in the world. My McCartney rellies at Colinton Street were completely different. They lived in poverty, but took an interest in what was going on. They shared what little they had with neighbours, and everyone seemed to help each other through the bad times.'

'My mum told me it was like that when she was a wee girl living up the gangway in Whiteinch, 'said Susan. 'The neighbours always rallied round to help if a family was struggling. If a man was layed off, or killed in an accident in the shipyards, a collection went round and they gave everything they could without a fuss.'

'Yeah, Granny Shaw said it was like that in Melbourne when she was little. People seemed to care a lot more for each other back then. At Colinton Street they sat round the fire sat for hours without television or computer games and they actually discussed serious things, and took an interest in what was going on.'

'Community spirit,' said Roddie. 'They had nothing yet they shared. Today we have the lot, but never seem satisfied and always want more. People know the cost of everything, but the value of nothing.'

Tom nodded. 'Consciously, or otherwise, Roddie, you've helped me understand these things. For the first time I'm starting to question why the things that happen in this world happen – question where the truth lies. I'm not flattering you, mate, when I say I've learned more from you and your books in the last few months than in my entire life.'

'Well that's quite a compliment. Thank you. But community spirit is not the only thing that's gone, Tom. The language, culture and creativity of the nation were passed down through the generations by way of story-telling, poetry and song. That too has been lost in a couple of generations. Mind you, they also had the capacity to fall out terminally over religion or politics, and life for the working class was a bitter struggle for survival.'

'I can understand that, and I'm beginning to see that as a soldier, thinking for myself is exactly what I was taught not to do. You just mentioned the importance of oral traditions, but I've never read poetry let alone recited it until you gave me your books. The language of Wilfred Owen and Hamish Henderson, and the power of their words, is astonishing. They blew me away. I can see why people in authority didn't like them.'

'Absolutely. They've given you some new things to think about. As for your present day McCartney relatives, they're no better or worse than the rest of us addicted to the material things in life. After years of the lowest common denominator and superficial celebrity culture, the vast majority of the population now hasn't a clue about what's really going on. But that, my friend, is exactly what the powers-that-be want.'

'Spot on, Dad. They encourage us to think about little other than trivia. Aldous Huxley was spot-on when he predicted we would become a trivial culture through our almost infinite appetite for distractions. Those in power dictate what we see and hear on the television and what we read in the newspapers. Almost the entire population of the Western world sits goggling at a television screen for hours every night while the most potent communications force ever known short-circuits our critical faculties and cons us into apathy. We see and hear what Rupert Murdoch and his cronies want us to see and hear. They give it their spin and, hey presto, it's a fact!'

'Yes, Julie, I hear what you're saying,' said Tom. 'The war I went to fight in Iraq was about removing a dictator and allowing the ordinary men and women of Iraq to achieve democracy. Saddam had weapons of mass destruction and was threatening peace across the entire region if not the world. That's what.'

The colour drained from Julie's cheeks. She rose to her feet, frustration written all over her face.

'Let me finish what I was saying before you spit the dummy, again,' said Tom. 'I was going on to say that that's what I went to Iraq believing. That's what most of the troops sent to Iraq went there believing.' He gave Julie the briefest of smiles and she sat down.

'Just like Angus in 1914, I was spoon-fed propaganda and lies, if not actually brainwashed. I've got your dad to thank for helping me, for guiding me, to an understanding that's very different from what I previously thought about Iraq. Your own Prime Minister insisted that Saddam had weapons of mass destruction and the capability of unleashing them within forty-five minutes. My mates and I went out there thinking we were saving the world from imminent disaster. It was all fuckin crap, sorry about the language, Susan, but how could we soldiers know that? You obey, you serve. You're in the army.'

Julie looked across at Tom, fixing her gaze on him as she spoke. 'I'm sorry for interrupting you. You're right. We all need to open our eyes and our minds. All I ask is that my future children, the world's future children, are allowed to grow up in a peaceful caring world. But these madmen sure as hell aren't going to allow that.'

'Fair enough, but you can't deny that Saddam Hussein was a madman and bad news for many of the Iraqi people.'

'Believe me,' Roddie responded immediately, 'I had no time for Saddam or his henchmen. Some of us were protesting about him while Britain and the US were pandering to him and actually supplying him with chemical weapons of mass destruction. Donald Rumsfeld, Bush's Defence Secretary, was out in Baghdad not that many years ago glad-handing Saddam and presenting him with solid gold riding spurs.'

Julie excused herself, went to her room, and returned seconds later with a little book of poetry. 'You like poetry, well listen to a few lines by Paddy Hogg, a good friend of mine. He wrote it before the Iraq War had even started. It's an address to Tony Blair and a very sharp parody of Robert Burns. Believe me, Burns would've approved.'

When peace protestors take the street
And Westerners Iraqis meet
We think upon the very poor
Whose blood Saddam has bled before
The refugees who fled his reign
His terror, torture and its pain
So distant, far across the world
Their plight has many banners furled.

O' Tony! Were they half say wise
As taen thine ain good folks advice
We warned thee weel 'Not in our name'
Thou are nae Churchill fash'd on fame
Resolutions frae October
Demand action, fair and sober
Gie inspectors time and silver
Evidence convicts a killer
We prophesised that late or soon
Saddam's regime would tumble doon
Though we now hae facts that damn him
British weapons once did arm him
The arsenal now that he has got
Is from the U.S. and our lot!
You know his weapons and deceits
You have copies of the receipts!

U. N. embargos kill the poor
Go count the bodies on a tour
This we do to curb his power
But come the day and come the hour
The roar of shells and guns and tanks
Increase the profits in the banks
Of arms companies and their greed
Who rub their hands while others bleed.
The innocent will die in droves
Or starve in want of fish and loaves.
This is no cynical left-wing view
It's what the rich and callous do.

Julie handed the book to Tom, but her passion was now on fire and she
gave him no time to respond. 'Paddy, as far as I'm concerned, is spot on.
Britain and the United States armed the bastard for years then, when
the Frankenstein monster we had created abused the devil's friendship, we bombed the shit out of Iraq's infrastructure. The Iraqis are
now living in a country where the electricity, water and sewage infrastructure has been destroyed. With their oil, these poor folk should be
among the richest people on the planet, but they're living in conditions

far worse even than at Colinton Street in 1914. Oil should have brought them material wealth, but it – or, should I say, western greed for it – has brought them nothing but death, destruction and misery. The Americans are merely continuing the rape of Iraq that we, the British, began ninety years ago. That's where the truth lies.'

'Believe me, I'm trying to discover where the truth lies,' said Tom, a despairing look on his face. He had made a reasonable comment about Saddam being a madman, but felt he was once again under personal attack fom Julie. 'As your dad knows better than anyone, I've had a hard time trying to make sense of my life over the recent past. My descent into drugs and madness after we killed those innocent peace activists; the visions where I saw my ancestors living in poverty; your dad's gentle education; and not least, your refusal to let me ignore the implications of my choice of life – not to put too fine a point on it, as you don't – as a paid killer. I hardly know who I am any more, let alone where the truth lies.'

After a moment of embarrassing silence, Roddie leaned over and put a hand on Tom's shoulder. 'I'm sorry if you feel Julie's having a pop at you, Tom. She's not.'

Susan made to stand up as the timer on the cooker pinged, but Julie stopped her and went through to the kitchen with Tom. 'I'm very sorry,' she said, grasping his hand tight. 'You'll realise by now that I get a bit excitable at times. Never at any time did I intend to imply you were a paid killer, so please forgive me if that's the impression I gave. I assure you that is not what I think.'

Tom called Roddie and Susan through to the kitchen and Roddie sniffed appreciatively as Tom carried bowls of food to the table. Julie didn't wait until she'd sat down before she tried it. 'Yum, tastes as good as it smells,' she smiled warmly at him. 'You have hidden talents.'

The curry was greeted with effusive compliments for the chef. The embarrassing moments were put aside and there was some light-hearted banter over dinner before they went back through to the living room for coffee.

'You are one superb cook, my friend,' said Roddie. 'Thank you for a most wonderful meal.'

'Hear, hear,' agreed Julie, with a genuinely friendly smile that warmed Tom's heart.

CHAPTER TWELVE

DRESSED IN HER PINNY AND tattered slippers, Lizzie was sitting in her chair by the blazing coal fire in the range. Marion was sitting at the table, playing with a home-made dolls' house and two small, roughly carved, wooden dolls.

'Ah'll never remember aw this, Lizzie,' mumbled Mary, as she anxiously paced the kitchen with a sheet of notes. 'Ah don't know why ah said ah'd dae it.'

'Ye don't need tae remember it, hen, jist read it straight off the paper.'

'Ah suppose so, but if ah dae that it'll look like ah hav'nae bothered aboot it. Ah want tae show that ah care. Show that ah'm interested an committed.'

'Mrs Crawfurd knows fine well by noo that yir committed,' Lizzie reassured her. 'Stoap worryin.'

Mary glanced out the kitchen window. 'The rain's still peltin doon. Maybe naebody'll turn up.'

'It's a bloody disgrace that that wee shite McTaggart wouldnae let ye have the hall in the Boatmen's Institute fur yer meetin. Ah'll be geein him a shirikin the first time ah see him. Maybe the wee niaff fae the Gypsy Queen had a hand in it efter you threatenin him.'

Tom knew where he was in an instant and watched breathlessly, trying to grasp what they were talking about.

'When ah first asked McTaggart he said aye, but then when ah explained it was fur a meetin aboot the rent strikes, he said naw. Ah suppose he wiz scared he would get intae bother if the committee heard aboot it.'

'Scared is an understatement,' said Lizzie. 'Ma wee boy's oot in France bravely facin the German army an their shells an bullets, while he sits doon there terrified ae a stupit boatmen's committee. Ah jist hope he's never faced wae eviction himself an needs some help.'

'They're gatherin,' said Mary, looking down at the middens below. 'Ah'd better get doon before Mrs Crawfurd arrives.'

'Mind'n invite her up fur a cup a tea.'

'Ah'll dae that. Wish me luck, Lizzie. Ma mooth feels that dry ah can hardly swallie never mind talk.'

'Ye'll be fine. How many times dae ah need tae tell ye tae stoap worryin?'

'Aye, ah'll be fine,' said Mary, pulling on an old raincoat and taking deep breaths to relax the knot of anxiety in her stomach.

Tom followed her downstairs past the stinking toilet to the back middens, and was astonished to see that a crowd of about two hundred women had gathered in the pouring rain. Minutes later a hush fell over them when Mary went over to greet two other women who came through the close at number 34. 'Thanks for comin, Mrs Crawfurd. Ah wisnae sure if ye'd be here in this weather.'

'Nice to see you again Mary,' replied the tall, robust woman who was dressed in an ankle-length black raincoat and wide-brimmed black hat. 'Miserable day right enough, but the good fight must go on. Looks like you've managed to get a decent turnout. Well done.'

'Aye, well done,' echoed the other woman, holding out her hand to shake Mary's. 'Ah'm Agnes Dollan. Sorry ah missed ye when ye've been oe'r at Govan.'

Mary led them over to a makeshift platform she had set up earlier beside the wash house, and took her notes from her pocket. Self-consciously, she began to read in a faltering voice, attempting to drop her broad Glasgow accent and speak 'properly'. 'Mrs Crawfurd resided in, sorry, Mrs Crawfurd was born in the Gorbals in Glasgow. Her father was a baker, a master baker and ...'

'We cannae hear ye Mary,' interrupted a women halfway back in the midst of the crowd. 'Ye'll need tae speak up.'

'Aye ye'll need tae speak up, hen,' shouted one of the many women leaning out listening from their tenement windows.

'Jist imagine yir geein oor Angus a shirikin an we'll aw hear ye,' shouted Lizzie from her top floor window.

'They'll hear her across the watter in Govan' shouted another, as the crowd laughed and relaxed.

Mary joined in the laughter, but looked very anxious. Mrs Crawfurd leaned in to whisper words of advice and encouragement. 'You're doing fine, Mary. Take some deep breaths and start again. Look up at the women at the back and speak out loudly to them. Just be yourself. Just speak naturally. These are your ain folk. You're among friends.'

'Go'n yersel Mary, hen,' shouted a woman in the crowd.

She took deep breaths and briefly looked at her sodden notes before crumpling them and throwing them in the midden.

'Sorry aboot that. Ye can aw see that ah'm nervous, but ah'll dae ma best. Ah would like tae thank youse aw for turning oot tae hear Mrs Crawfurd an Mrs Dollan on such a rotten day. Thousands of women have been attendin their talks in different parts a Glesca an ah wiz confident you wouldnae let me doon when ah asked them tae come and speak in Port Dundas.'

The women gave a roar of approval. In a loud clear voice, Mary thanked them once again for attending. 'We've aw heard aboot Helen Crawfurd an her activities o'er the years wae the suffragettes. Ah for one support her in that, an hopefully sometime in the comin years she'll succeed in gettin the vote for us. Ah also support her anti-war stance, an ah support…'

'Aye, an so dae ah,' shouted a number of women.

'Good,' Mary replied, 'that's good. Ah'm gaunny hand ye oe'r tae Mrs Crawfurd noo. Naw ah'm no!' she immediately shouted and laughed at herself. She was beginning to relax and grow in confidence as she spoke in public for this, the first ever time. 'Ah'm gaunny tell ye a wee bit aboot her first. Mrs Crawfurd wiz born in the Gorbals. Her faither wiz a master baker, an when she wiz a wee lassie he took the family doon tae England tae try an get a better life fur them. They did get a better life, but they came back tae live in Glesca when Helen wiz a teenager. She wiz totally shocked when she saw the poverty an terrible conditions for the workin class folk in the city here. She married Mr Crawfurd, a minister in the Church of Scotland, but sadly he died. Helen has devoted her life tae the betterment ae conditions for women an workin class folk in general. She's been in prison mer than once fur protesting wae the suffragettes. Ah'm sure many of ye read aboot the time she was tryin tae protect Mrs Pankhurst fae police brutality when the polis broke up the big suffragette meetin in the St Andrews Halls here in Glesca. She got sentenced tae a month in Duke Street Prison an went on hunger strike. She's the secretary of the Glesca Women's Housin Association an she's been organisin the rent strikes wae Mrs Barbour and Mrs Dollan here. Ah'm gonnae shut up noo so she can tell us aw aboot it.'

Mary felt a great surge of pride as the women of Port Dundas clapped and cheered her little introductory speech. She glanced up at her top floor window and smiled at Lizzie who was leading the applause.

Mrs Crawfurd stepped forward and spoke without notes. 'Thank you so much for inviting us here today, Mary, and thank you for that nice introduction. A big thank you also goes to you, the good ladies of Port Dundas, who have turned out on such a dreich morning. Mary assured us you would take up the challenge and it's due to her single-handed efforts chapping on so many doors, and putting posters up around the streets here, that you heard about this meeting. Mary's been over to Govan several times in the past week to meet Mary Barbour and myself. She's distressed and angry that some of her good friends and neighbours in Port Dundas are facing eviction. One poor soul on Dobbies Loan, whose husband is a prisoner of war somewhere in Germany, was thrown out on the street with her children just a few weeks ago. She was the first to be evicted in Port Dundas and we need to ensure she is the last.

'It's a miserable morning and I won't keep you standing out here for long, but before explaining the rent strikes I would like to say a little about the war. As Mary rightly said, I am against this war. I know many of you have men fighting over in France and that some of you will have lost a husband, a brother, or a son there. I am aware that those husbands, brothers and sons went to France believing they were defending their country. I would never decry their bravery in doing what they did, for they believed the war was a just and noble cause. I know you will take comfort from that, and I'm sorry if I upset you, but I believe that this war was, and is, totally unnecessary. I believe that the fine young men from Port Dundas, and all the other districts, towns and cities, are away fighting and dying not for some just and noble cause, but for the benefit of millionaire capitalists who started this war in the first place.'

'Aye,' one of the women interrupted, 'and then the widows an weans are thrown oot their hooses cause they cannae afford the rent increases.'

Mrs Crawfurd nodded in agreement. 'And that's exactly why we are here today: to try and find ways to prevent these evictions. No matter what side they are on, the young working-class men firing shells and bullets at each other will gain nothing from this disastrous war. As I say, I genuinely believe that and it would be hypocrisy for me not to speak to the truth as I see it. I have to be truthful – we all have to be truthful if hundreds of thousands more young men that comprise the cream of our country's youth are not to die needlessly in this hideous slaughter. I know these are not popular words but.'

'Naw but they're true. She's right.'

'Aye, yer right, Mrs Crawfurd,' shouted others in the crowd. Tom moved among them and could see some women shed tears. Many were distressed. None left. The women listened intently as Mrs Crawfurd continued: 'I'm going to move on now to explain a little about the background to the rent strikes. The central areas of Glasgow have always been densely packed, but since the war started, the flood of people coming into the city to work in the big armaments and war-related industries have made the situation even worse. There is a great demand for housing which the government has failed to meet. Every available house, and I'm including those that are in a very bad state of repair with little or no sanitation and infested with rats, has been filled. Housing for incoming workers becomes steadily scarcer month by month as the need grows and grows. And you, of course, know what the outcome is. With the terrible overcrowding and high demand for housing in the city, some landlords look on it as a golden opportunity to make pots of money through introducing big rent rises. In some districts, Govan and Partick for example, the rents have been increased by as much as twenty per cent in the past year. It is a blatant example of war-time profiteering. With these rent increases, and the steep rise in the cost of living this past year, everyone is struggling desperately to keep up, especially women with big families who have a man at the front or have lost him to the war.'

'Aye – yir right again, hen.'

'The current housing laws allow landlords to evict tenants who are in arrears with their rent, and to confiscate all their possessions to cover those arrears. So not only are the poor people made homeless, their possessions are taken. First, the landlords send in debt collectors to try and intimidate folk in arrears into paying. If that doesn't work they call in Sheriff Officers to serve writs and carry out the evictions.'

'It's a bloody disgrace' shouted a woman to a chorus of support. 'Scandalous so it is.'

'Aye, a bloody shameful disgrace,' shouted another. 'As you say, Mrs Crawfurd, they tell the widows their men died heroes. Tell them lies aboot the true causes of this war and the reasons their men were killed. Then, they allow the widows and the weans tae be thrown on the street cause they've nae money tae pay the rent. Ah'm with ye Mrs Crawfurd.'

'Aye, an whit wid the men at the Front dae if they knew it wiz happenin?'

Another chorus of approval greeted this comment and the women began talking to each other with great indignation about the injustice of it all. Mrs Crawfurd gently regained control and continued. 'Thank you for that support, but I have to suggest to you that if you condemn the evictions, and those who order them, there is no point simply talking about it because nobody, but nobody, in authority is listening. You have to take direct action. That's what the ordinary women of Govan and the ordinary women of Partick have been doing for months now through their local tenants' defence committees, and their campaign of non-payment of rent increases. They have succeeded in stopping the evictions there, and if we can mobilise and generate working-class action right across the city we can stop them everywhere. And not just in Glasgow. Women in other cities will take heart and follow our example. Irrespective of your different religious and political views, and indeed the views of your men, hostile or otherwise to you being here this morning, this is about us women coming together and demonstrating solidarity. I am well aware that some women have attended rent-strike meetings despite their men having forbidden them, but we are getting support from men in the factories. I can let you in on a little secret: right at this very minute Mary Barbour is meeting with the local workers committee at Parkhead Forge. The men in the munitions factories are so furious at these evictions that they are threatening to stop armaments production. Mary could have the twelve thousand workers at Parkhead out by this afternoon.'

'An no before time.'

'The Munitions Act might make strikes illegal, and the stopping of output a criminal offence, but the government can't jail twelve thousand people and it knows that fine well. We are also getting support from the Govan shipyard workers and political support from the Independent Labour Party and other political groups.'

Cheers filled the packed back court and middens.

'You can do this, ladies. You can stop evictions in Port Dundas if you have the will to do it and, by your attendance here this morning, I'm very, very confident that you have that will.

'I think I'll stop there and hand over to my friend Agnes Dollan, who is going to tell you how the women in Govan and Partick have directed their will into action. I should emphasise that Agnes and I are not here to tell you what to do. This is not about any one person or any one group dictating to others. This is your home patch and you must decide on the best and most suitable course of action for Port Dundas. You are the women who might suffer if you join the rent strike and refuse to pay the rent increases, so you are the ones who must decide. Probably the best advice I can offer you is to have constant meetings and keep one step ahead of the Sheriff Officers at all times. I wish you, and any loved ones you have in faraway places, all the very best of luck.'

When the raucous applause for Mrs Crawfurd died down, Mary introduced Agnes Dollan. She spent twenty minutes detailing how the Govan and Partick women had brought the evictions in those districts to an end.

Fired with enthusiasm, Mary then confidently stepped forward and asked if, having heard Mrs Crawfurd and Mrs Dollan, any of the women of Port Dundas would join her in organising a rent-strike committee. A sea of hands went up.

'Are we gaunny let the landlords increase oor rents?' shouted Mary.

Back came the roar 'Naw!'

'Are we gaunny let the Sheriff's men evict another Port Dundas family?'

'Naw!'

'Are the Port women gaunny show solidarity?'

'Aye! We'll aw stand thegither.'

The sodden mass of single-minded women cheered and clapped. This would be their fight too, and this was their chosen battlefield.

Mary invited Helen and Agnes up for a cup of tea and a heat by the fire, but they declined because they were running late and had to get a tram out to Maryhill for yet another meeting. The women of Glasgow were on the march.

Tom stirred briefly in his bed at Mar Hall and took a sip of water from Roddie before succumbing again to the iboga. He found himself back in the kitchen at 34 Colinton Street. It was frosty outside, and some days after Mary's meeting in the back court. Lizzie was sitting snoring in her chair by the fire when Mary burst in with Thomas and Marion. 'They're comin, Lizzie' she shouted breathlessly. 'They've been spotted on Cowcaddens Road an they're comin tae evict Bridie. Watch the weans for me. Ah'll need tae get doon there quick.'

Mary rushed to open the window and began clattering a big iron pan and ladle together. 'Eviction at 10 Colinton Street, eviction at 10 Colinton Street,' she shouted at the top of her voice, and continued the racket as she hurried down the stairs. Women ran from their closes towards number 10, banging metal trays and blowing whistles. A bugle blasted from a nearby tenement window. Women rushed up past Jeannie Spitall's from Townsend Street, Port Dundas Road and Dobbies Loan. Some fifty of them crammed into Bridie Docherty's tiny room and kitchen. Double that number jammed the close and stairs outside her door.

Bridie sat shaking and crying by her stove, overcome both by the injustice and this massive show of community spirit. Imagine. Just for her.

A woman from Dobbies Loan tried to comfort her. 'Don't worry Bridie, the bastarts'll no get anywhere near here tae evict ye. Are they gaunny get anywhere near Bridie, girls?' she shouted and a roar of 'Naw' went up inside and outside the house.

Seven men strode purposefully up past the Boatmen's Institute into Colinton Street. The Sheriff Officer and his two officials were identifiable by their smart suits and bowler hats. Four burly minders accompanied them. A group of close-ranked women and children carrying banners proclaiming THERE WILL BE NO EVICTIONS IN PORT DUNDAS moved forward at the close mouth and began shouting at them. The Sheriff Officer stopped and imperiously pointed a finger at the women. 'In the name of the Sheriff of Lanarkshire and the City of Glasgow, I order you to move aside. Failure to comply with my instruction will result in your prosecution and possible imprisonment.'

He may have thought that sufficient, but this was not Caesar's Rome. Glasgow women did not take such instruction from the agents of Satan. The women stood their ground, but said nothing.

'I order you to move aside now. You are obstructing an officer of the Crown.'

'Yer arse in parsley,' shouted one of the women. 'Away an bile yer heid. We're no movin anywhere.'

The Sheriff Officer nodded to the burly minders and one of them walked forward to within inches of the woman at the front. 'Move!'

'Naw! You move. Move yir fat arse oe'r tae France an show the Germans how big'n tough ye are. Ah'm no feart fae ye an ah don't think the German sodjers would be either.'

'Aye,' shouted another woman, 'get yersel a uniform an a boat tae France an show them how brave ye are. Ma wee brother's only half yer size an he's away fightin fur ees country.'

The other heavies stepped forward to join their colleague and one of them shouted directly into the faces of the women. 'The Sheriff Officer is no gonnae tell youse again, Move!' He put his hand on a woman's arm to pull her away from the close, and she spat in his face. 'Ya dirty wee bitch' he shouted and instructed his colleagues to help him remove her from the crowd. She started yelling and struggling when the men grabbed her, but the rest of the women around the close stood frozen to the spot. No-one knew what to do next. Bravado and loose threats were one thing – but these were the Bailiff's men.

A women leaning out of a window above, screamed abuse at the men and threw a paper bag full of soot down over them. The black charcoal dust burst like a water balloon and broke the spell. On cue, the women sprang into action and began smacking the men with whatever they had in hand. Blows rained down in their fury.

Dignity lost, self preservation takes over. The burly minders released the woman and retreated with the three officials. One of their own had been knocked to the ground, however, and within seconds a baying pack of angry women formed a tight circle round the dazed man, and goaded him. He picked himself up from the street, cowed by the snarling she-wolves of Port Dundas, and held both hands up in the surrender sign. The circle of wolves opened and allowed him to escape.

'Now bugger off the lot ae ye,' shouted Mary, 'an don't ever come near Port Dundas again wae yer eviction notices or yer threats.'

CHAPTER THIRTEEN

Sitting by the apartment window, Roddie looked up from his book when he heard Tom give a quiet cough. Tom had initially planned to tell him everything but, given his attitude to the first visions, decided otherwise. 'Thank you so much for being here with me again, mate.' He sat up and nodded more to himself than his friend.

'That's no problem. Happy to oblige just as long as it helps, and doesn't hinder your recovery.' Still that undercurrent of scepticism. Couldn't really blame him – these visions had to be experienced.

Tom showered, made himself cheese toasties, and sat eating them by the window. He relived every moment of his presence at Colinton Street. Christ, Mary was one spirited young woman with strong views about injustice and war. Her stand against the eviction of Bridie and other poverty-stricken widows made him feel proud that he came from such committed stock. He pondered the poverty poor Bridie must have endured. Her husband, the father of her six children, was lost forever somewhere in France. The massive rise in the standard of living between those poor people and the present day was mind-boggling. Fuck-sake, what would Mary, Lizzie and William, struggling to get by on a pittance while Angus was away fighting Germans in France, make of a McCartney boy driving in to Port Dundas in his German car costing £30,000? What would Thomas, Wullie and George think if they went up to the canal and saw boys their own age dressed in designer gear, learning to sail in expensive dinghies? How could they make sense of it if they walked down Colinton Street and watched thousands of cars flash past every minute on an eight-lane motorway just yards away? What would Lizzie McCartney, the wee bastard born in a poorhouse, make of him sitting in a hotel where it cost £1,000 for a suite for the night? We don't know we're living, as Roddie would say. He finished his snack and his musing and went down to the hotel foyer.

'Got time for a break?' he asked Julie. 'I'm feeling in need of a bit of company.' It was more of a plea than a question.

She checked her watch. 'Looks like coffee time to me.' They walked together to the small staff-room beside the kitchen in a silence that felt awkwardly solemn. 'What's up?'

'Your dad sat with me again this morning when I took an iboga. I had another vision – sorry, hallucination, about Colinton Street.'

'It certainly appears to have hit you hard' Julie said, instinctively reaching out to him.

Tom's mood instantly lightened and he squeezed her hand. Realizing what she'd done, she flushed and gently took it away.

'I'm surprised at just how much it's affected me,' he admitted, looking down at her.

Julie gave him a little smile. 'Yeah, I'm beginning to think that you're just a big softie underneath the rough tough exterior.'

With a day off the following Sunday, and Scotland dressed in early autumnal colours, Tom decided to head out for the day. Hotel guests spoke enthusiastically about their visit to the beautiful Trossachs, Scotland's first national park, and he had resolved to check it out for himself, if and when the sun next appeared.

He drove past South Lodge, and on an impulse reversed and stopped outside. Roddie appeared from behind the house, and gestured towards the sky. 'Beautiful morning.'

'Sure is. I'm off to make the most of it – and I'd like you to come with me as my guide round the Trossachs. How about it, mate?'

'Sorry. I've got plenty to keep me busy here.'

'You sure? I'd enjoy the company. Be a good day out.'

Roddie shook his head. 'Susan'll be over later, and I'm going to …' He plunged his hands in his pockets and fiddled distractedly with his change. 'Well, that can wait.'

'What can wait? What have you got up your sleeve?'

Roddie grinned and tapped his nose knowingly. 'Tell you what, why don't I see if Julie fancies a day out? She's wasting a beautiful morning lying in her kip.'

'Okay, if you like.' said Tom, transparently nonchalant.

'That'll be a yes then,' Roddie's grin widened. 'To tell the truth, I could do with her out of the house for a few hours. Got some serious business in hand.'

'She says give her thirty minutes to get ready, but between you and me, safer to make that forty.'

'Great! No offence, Roddie, but she'll make a far more attractive companion than you. And now, I've got half an hour to find out what all the mystery's about.'

'You can try all you like, mister, but my lips are sealed.'

It took Julie less than twenty minutes to shower, throw on the sundress he'd admired previously, and declare herself 'ready'.

Roddie looked pointedly at his watch. 'It's a record-breaker!'

Julie simply smiled and patted him on the cheek. 'Bye, Dad, see you later.' She moved Tom's road map from the passenger seat and climbed into the car. 'No need for this. I've been visiting the Trossachs since I was a child.'

'Okay,' said Tom. 'I'm completely in your hands. Take me to your favourite places.'

They crossed the Erskine Bridge and Julie directed him onto a country road through rich farming land.

'Beautiful countryside,' said Julie.

'It is beautiful,' Tom agreed. 'Takes the breath away. It's a beautiful morning, beautiful country, and beautiful company.'

'Yes, I could easily get used to this,' Julie responded with a warm smile.

'And what might your boyfriend have to say about that?'

'Boyfriend? What are you on about?'

'Davie.'

Julie threw her head back against the head-rest, laughing. 'Davie! Davie Kirkwood! He's a very dear friend, but not my boyfriend. We've been buddies since first year at university and I'm sure we'll be good buddies for a long time to come.'

'Sorry, my mistake.' Strewth, why didn't I ask earlier? You little ripper.

Tom pulled into the car park in the village of Aberfoyle, which proudly proclaimed itself 'The Gateway to the Trossachs', and found a coffee shop. Julie looked him directly in the eye. 'I'm sorry for saying those horrible things to you that day on the avenue. I hope you can forgive me.'

'Yeah, of course. And I'm sorry for the nasty comments that I made. Maybe we should both say sorry and start from scratch?'

'Yeah, let's do that,' said Julie with a smile. She drank her cappuccino and regaled him with childhood memories of family days out to the area.

'I can tell how much you still miss your mother.'

Julie sighed. 'There are so many things I wish I could share with her. She always loved me to tell her about the things I'd been doing.' She looked at Tom and smiled a little shyly. 'I have to admit that even now, there are certain special things that I talk to her about – in the privacy of my own head, of course.'

On an impulse Tom took her hand. 'Maybe today might be one of those "special things".'

'Slow down, cobber,' she said, mimicking his accent, flushing at the intense look in his eyes. 'Let's make a move? There's so much to see.'

They took the steep and winding Duke's Pass through the Queen Elizabeth Forest Park towards Loch Katrine. Tom negotiated the many tricky bends on the road and Julie read to him from the tourist guide he'd picked up in Aberfoyle.

'The Duke's Pass was built in 1855 by the Duke of Montrose. Prior to that only a pack horse track led over these hills.'

'Thank heavens for the Duke,' said Tom, patting the steering wheel. 'I don't think this pack horse would be so happy on a dirt track.'

'The Trossachs and Loch Katrine in Scotland have been known for their scenic attractions ever since Sir Walter Scott wrote "Rob Roy" and "The Lady of the Lake" in the early nineteenth century.'

'I can see why he was inspired by the place,' said Tom, as they rounded a bend to yet another glorious vista, the sunshine highlighting the reds and russets where the first leaves were turning to their autumn colours.

At Loch Katrine pier they mingled with visitors from every corner of the globe, and boarded the quaint little coal-burning steam ship, *Sir Walter Scott*. Every day in summer the ship sailed the waters of Loch Katrine, surrounded by imposing mountains which on that still September day were reflected crystal-clear in the mirror-smooth waters.

The tourist guide droned on, feeding the busy boat with fact and myth in equal measure. Tom was interested in statistics that showed some fifty million gallons a day were drawn from the loch, via a twenty-six mile long aqueduct, to provide Glasgow with fresh drinking water. At the time of construction in the 1850s it had been one of the most ambitious and complex engineering projects in Europe, and ended the epidemics of typhoid and cholera in the burgeoning industrial city.

'Now there's a sobering thought,' said Tom. 'If it weren't for this loch, my ancestors might never have survived those epidemics – and I might never have been born.'

'And then who would I have got to drive me out here today?' Julie laughed up at him, her copper hair gleaming in the sunshine.

'I'm sure they'd be queuing up for the chance.'

'I'm glad it's you.' She hugged his arm and drew in his powerful warmth.

Several elderly musicians with accordions struck up a set of dance tunes under a large colourful canopy amidships. Almost immediately, a couple of elderly Glaswegian women stood up and slowly waltzed to the music.

'Let's dance,' said Julie.

'Well, I suppose I could try – but I have to warn you I've got two left feet. I reckon the antipodean sun must have burned away the dancing gene from my branch of the McCartney family.'

During a lull in the music Tom walked over and asked the band leader if he played requests.

'Sure, what's it to be, *Waltzing Matilda*? Now there's a thing, boys,' he said to the others in his quartet, 'I don't believe we've ever played that on the old tub before.'

Tom laughed. 'Yeah, ta, mate. Waltzing Matilda would be great, but I had been thinking of something a bit more romantic.'

The band leader nodded, 'What's her name?'

'Julie.'

'And where does the beautiful Julie hail fae'?'

'Erskine but Dumbarton originally. Home town of this fine ship.'

The band members muttered some words to each other and nodded. 'Leave it with us.'

Tom returned to Julie's side and they joined the rest of the passengers in heartily singing the old Australian song.

'That was for me,' said Tom as the song finished. 'And this one's for you.'

The band leader had a fine voice. He smiled at Julie and sang a beautiful old Scottish love song, *Dumbarton's Drums*. It could have been written for her.

Tom put his arm round her shoulder and she responded by turning her face up to his and kissing him. Remembering Roddie's description of his first touch of her mother Rachel's glorious auburn hair, he ran his hand through Julie's, caressing and smelling it. She snuggled in close. Few words were spoken between them for the rest of the cruise. All that had to be said could wait. Time seemed to stretch endlessly before them – time which, at that very moment, they both knew they would spend together.

The open-top with its happy, hungry occupants passed through the village, Brig o' Turk, and along the winding north shore of Loch Venachar. They stopped in Callendar and walked hand-in-hand into the Roman Camp Hotel for lunch. Two hours later, they finally took their eyes off each other long enough to see that the restaurant had emptied.

Julie reached for her purse, but Tom put his hand on hers. 'Oh no, you don't.'

'Well, let me go halfers then.'

'Certainly not. That's something else, apart from dancing, we don't allow in the lucky country.'

'Okay, you win this time, but in future we share everything.'

When they returned to South Lodge, Roddie and Susan enjoyed Julie's radiant happiness as she related the story of their day in the Trossachs. When she eventually paused for breath, Susan took Tom through to the kitchen on the pretext of helping her prepare supper. A loud shriek came from the lounge and Julie rushed into the kitchen.

'Susan, oh Susan!' She dissolved in tears and hugged the older woman tightly. 'It's fantastic, marvellous, oh God, I'm so happy for you, for Dad.' She turned to Tom and flung her arms round him. 'They're getting married! Dad and Susan are getting married.' She rushed from the kitchen, wiping her eyes and they could hear her footsteps pounding as she ran upstairs. Tom followed Susan through to the living room where Roddie was standing by the window, looking pleased, if a little embarrassed. 'Congratulations, cobber,' said Tom, shaking his hand. 'So that's what you were being so coy about this morning. When's the buck's night?'

Roddie put an arm round Susan. 'I thought it was time I made an honest woman of her, but I'm not sure that Julie and you haven't stolen our thunder. She's always had a knack of upstaging me.'

'We couldn't be more delighted that you're officially "going out",' said Susan. 'We've been hoping for some time that Julie would fall for you.'

'And what made you believe I would be interested?'

'The boy thinks we're daft,' said Roddie. 'Everyone could see you were a gonner when you first set eyes on her.'

'Am I so transparent?'

'Aye, when it comes to women we all are.'

Tom looked towards the ceiling. 'Are you sure she's okay?'

'Too much emotion for one day, that's all that's up with her,' said Susan. 'Give her a few minutes. She'll be down shortly, I'm sure.'

'Okay. When she reappears, tell her I'll be back in ten minutes.' He jumped into the car and drove to the hotel. On his return, with two bottles of expensive champagne, Julie was waiting at the lodge door for him, her tears dried, holding a framed photograph of her long-deceased mother. 'I had to confirm Mum was okay about it – and she is; she's delighted that Dad's found happiness again.'

Later, as they got ready for bed, Roddie remarked to Susan that he hadn't seen Julie so animated and bubbly since her mother died.

'Well, we both know who that's due to, don't we?'

'Aye, it's the first time I've seen her really loved up.'

Roddie turned the light out, and Susan voiced an afterthought. 'I just hope he doesn't suddenly decide to return home to Australia.'

If they had seen Julie staring forlornly after Tom's car an hour later, and walking sadly upstairs to bed, they would have wondered whether he hadn't already done just that.

It was Julie who had suggested they go for a walk. 'I think we're being spied on,' she laughed, looking up from the garden at the bedroom curtain twitching. 'The house is too small to be really alone – and that's what I'd like.' She slipped her hand into his and they wandered along the driveway, the harvest moon shining through the trees, dappling the ground in silver. Julie chattered on about the wedding; Tom was silent, enjoying just having her by his side. They made their way along a path and Julie led him to the old wooden bench Lord Blantyre had been accustomed to sit on so many years ago. The Clyde was laid out before them, its water shining in the moonlight, wisps of mist drifting over the surface and settling in the folds of the hills beyond.

Julie seemed over-excited with all the emotion of the day – and the champagne perhaps. She was still talking, almost to herself, planning the things they might do. Tom touched her lips with his fingers and pulled her in close, 'Shhh. Just calm down and listen to the silence.'

Their tentative kissing and caressing grew urgent and frantic, and he could feel her excitement and desire grow. He unbuttoned her blouse, fondled her breasts and nipples, and all too rapidly approached a point of hyper sexual arousal. Julie was the first female he had been in a relationship with for several years. This was all gonna happen too quick. Slow down. Oh for fuck sake, slow down!

Julie made a strange little whimpering noise, ran a hand down over his belly, and unzipped him. He gently pushed her hand away.

'What's the matter?' she moaned.

Sucking in lungfuls of air, he stood up and zipped his trousers.

'What's wrong?' she asked, tugging at his hand as they walked back to South Lodge. 'I don't understand. Tell me, Tom, please.'

'I'm sorry, I can't. Not now. You'll have to trust me.'

'I do, but it seems you don't trust me.'

He shook his head distractedly, searching for the car keys in his pockets. 'I've got something to do first.' Afraid to hold her again, afraid that the response of his body would weaken his resolve, he got into the car after a final brief kiss and drove away towards the hotel.

CHAPTER FOURTEEN

TOM WAS IN AN ALMOST unbearable state of emotional frustration by the time he got back to his flat. He switched on the computer but couldn't concentrate on the screen, stood up and paced round the room, kicking the furniture and cursing himself for upsetting Julie. He desperately hoped he hadn't spoiled their relationship before it had begun. What must she be thinking? 'Fuckin dipstick,' he berated himself. 'Putting it off because you're afraid to face up to bad news.' He wondered whether he had been wise, refusing to tell her – he'd upset her enough anyway, would it really have been worse to tell the truth? But it hadn't seemed the time or place to confront her with the brutal realities of his life. He resolved he would do in the morning what he should have done months ago. And whatever the outcome, Julie had to be told.

Unable to sleep, pumped up by the adrenaline of fear, he was standing outside the health centre before Dr McKenzie's receptionist opened up. 'Can you fit me in to see the doctor today please?' he pleaded when she asked if he had an appointment. 'I'll sit and wait until he's free – it's very important.'

Julie meanwhile had gone into work early. She immediately climbed the back stairs to Tom's flat and knocked on his door. There was no answer, and she went down to reception and tried to settle to her work. Just before noon, Susan rang. 'Are you all right, dear? You were away so early this morning.'

'Yes, I'm fine,' she lied. 'Couldn't sleep.'

Susan laughed, 'I'm not surprised. Anyway, I've rung to say your dad and I have decided we want the wedding to take place as soon as possible – no point hanging about at our time of life. I wondered if you could think of somewhere nice we might be able to book a wedding reception at short notice – say a month or two off.'

'I'll give it some thought,' promised Julie, looking up to see a delivery boy behind a huge bunch of red roses. The envelope was addressed to her and the card inside simply read: We need to talk. Big cedar, 4 pm at the end of your shift. Love you. Tom.

Four hours later, Julie handed over at reception to Stella. Tom was waiting, pacing restlessly back and forth. When he spotted her, his face broke into a relieved smile and he opened his arms wide. Julie ran straight into them and they kissed hungrily as though they had been apart for months. They took the path into the Big Wood and Julie turned to look intently at him. 'Shoot,' she commanded. 'Tell me. What is it we have to talk about?'

He took both her hands and inhaled deeply. 'This isn't going to be an easy thing for either of us. I went to the GP this morning, and he's arranging an appointment for me with the department of nuclear medicine at the Western Infirmary.'

'But what's the problem? I didn't realize you were ill. Why didn't you tell me?'

'I hope I'm not, but if I am, it's something which will affect our whole relationship.'

Tom tried to find the words to explain. Julie squeezed his hands and waited.

'You know enough about the Iraq conflict to understand the implications of what I'm going to say. Depleted uranium!'

Julie's hands flew to her mouth. She felt as though she had been physically struck. She knew exactly what the implications were.

'I'm sorry, Julie. I discussed it with your dad months ago, but I didn't get checked out. I know I should have, but I put it off. Fear, I guess. Fear of the terrible impact a positive result would have.'

'I just can't imagine why I never thought of it,' said Julie. 'I've read so much about it.'

They discussed the depleted uranium problem as they slowly walked through the woods. DU was used on a large scale during Operation Desert Storm in the first Gulf War in 1991. Incorporated into the tips of shells and missiles, it vastly increased their ability to penetrate tank armour. When fired, DU shells ignite upon impact, burn at an extremely high temperature, and vaporize uranium into tiny particles of radioactive dust. If inhaled, the particles lodge in the body and emit radiation indefinitely.

Tom explained that contaminated soldiers fathered children born with severe defects. A recent report from the London School of Hygiene and Tropical Medicine that he'd read, stated that babies whose fathers fought in the first Gulf War had a greater than fifty per cent chance of having physical abnormalities such as large heads, finger deformities and missing arms or legs. It was hideous.

'What's more, soldiers just like me returning from Iraq have been found to have depleted uranium in their semen, and contaminated their partners. I could never take that risk with you, Julie.' He pulled her in close. 'That's why I ran off last night. I desperately wanted to make love, but it was something I – we – might forever regret. I'm deeply sorry I upset you.'

As they walked towards Blantyre's seat, tears of anger and compassion glinted in Julie's eyes. 'God, Tom, I couldn't bear it if that was your fate.'

'In spite of all that's happened with DU, they're using it again over there,' said Tom bitterly. 'Everything I now know I got from your dad's books and the internet. The fuckers certainly never explained any of it to us soldiers.'

'Nor to civilians,' said Julie. 'The US military and the British Ministry of Defence have consistently lied about it. It's reckoned that hundreds of thousands of innocent civilians are suffering horrendously from it in the Middle East, but the bastards insist its use in battlefield weapons poses little or no threat to health. Even that bloody useless American puppet, the United Nations, classified them as illegal weapons of mass destruct...' She stopped mid-word and screamed as the blast of a shotgun shattered the air close by in the Big Wood.

'What the fuck?' said Tom, instantly dropping to the ground for cover, pulling Julie off her feet and tight beside him. 'Down. Stay down,' he whispered.

'Poachers!' Julie gasped. 'It'll be poachers, you daft sod.'

'Poachers?'

'Aye, after rabbits. They're the bane of Andy's life. He's forever ordering them off the estate but they just tell him to "fuck off, old man". It'll be one of the Stewart boys, maybe both.'

'They do, do they? The Stewart boys? I'll "fuck off" them,' raged Tom and, in a flash, was up and away through the undergrowth. These people needed to know who was in charge of security on this estate. The script had changed, and they clearly hadn't read it.

'No, Tom!' Julie picked herself up and ran after him.

Boab Stewart, who prided himself in his poaching craft, was completely unaware of the former SAS man's advance. Assumption breeds complacency, and complacency disarms the senses. The Erskine estate was an easy picking, always had been. A couple of rabbits, some pheasants in season, and away. At best he would be home in twenty minutes with his plump catch. At worst he would trade insults with the groundsman who knew better than to involve the police. Even if he had been primed for trouble this afternoon, Boab would have been unable to do much about it. The first he knew of Tom was a heavy boot thumping his backside.

'What the?' Both question and expletive were lost as he sprawled forward into the undergrowth, shocked and unable to comprehend what was happening to him. Tom ejected a cartridge from the shotgun and smashed it irreparably against a tree.

'Right, fucker. On your feet! You're next!' He effortlessly pulled the poacher up with his left hand, and balled his right for a punch.

'Tom! No Tom. No! Leave him alone!' screamed Julie, running to intervene. 'No violence, Tom. No violence.'

He kept a tight grip on Boab's army camouflage jacket and took several deep breaths. 'The lady says "no violence", mister. What about you?'

'Ah'm no looking for any trouble, pal. Jist a rabbit or two for the pot. You're the one that seems tae be keen on violence.'

'Take it!' ordered Tom, releasing him and pointing to the dead animal. 'It's the last you poach from this estate, and it's the last time you tell my mate Andy Hutton to fuck off. Do you read me?'

'Ah read ye,' said the chastened man as he trudged off with the crippled shotgun, leaving his prize behind. 'Ma brither'll no be happy about what ye did tae his gun.' Boab tried to exit with dignity, hoping the remark would sound something like a threat.

'You and your brother both. I find you here again with a gun, and you'll each wear a barrel where the sun don't shine.'

Brushing leaves and dirt from her clothes, Julie was far from amused. 'Why do men always have to look for solutions with their fists? You didn't need to do that – you could have given him a warning,' she said sharply.

'Firstly, he wouldn't understand any other way. Secondly, that was a warning. Catch him or his brother again and they'll not be able to poach an egg.'

They continued on through the woods in silence. Tom concentrated on his breathing to bring his heart rate down. 'What if your tests are positive?' Julie eventually asked. 'What do we do then?'

He kissed her passionately, trying to block out the dread he had felt in the pit of his stomach since the beginning of the long sleepless night. 'I can't think about it yet,' he lied. 'We'll wait for the results.' He couldn't upset her further by telling her he had already made his decision. If contaminated, he would be booking a one-way ticket home to Australia. Alone.

'What in the name of God is happening to the rest of the world with this poison?' Tom asked as they walked along the path to South Lodge

'It's blowing all over the planet now,' said Julie. 'Getting into the food chain, into the oceans, and potentially affecting all living things.' She bent to pick a golden leaf from the ground. 'Possibly even this. It's a tragedy for the world – a despicable and evil crime against humanity being perpetrated by Britain and the United States, and what's worse, in our name.'

The easiest, least embarrassing, samples to give at the clinic were blood and urine. The consultant tried to reassure him, saying there was a good chance he had escaped contamination. 'The way things are just now you've more chance of catching MRSA by coming to the hospital here.' Well, that was reassuring, surely?

Tom knew that he had to prepare himself for the worst. No use convincing yourself everything would be fine – only to be given the devastating news you dreaded. During the painful period of waiting, he spent more and more time at South Lodge with Julie, not knowing what or how to feel. Wanting answers now, but only the right answers. He couldn't bear to be alone for long; demons gathered in his mind whispering doubts, mocking moments of optimism. Life was cruel: he had found the woman he wanted to spend the rest of his life with, but was facing the prospect of having to turn his back on her for her own sake. As the black thoughts grew he began to feel the insidious poison permeating his body. Began to picture the horrendous health problems he was likely to face in later life. Christ, when he joined the army he only wanted to do his duty and save the world. No mention was made of post-traumatic stress, addiction, uranium poisoning, mental breakdowns and a legacy of decay. And what of the boys who lost legs

and arms, or were left for blind or seriously impaired in a dozen different ways? Was anyone spared? If they brought the whole regiment back
together in twenty years time, how many of their lives would have been
truly fucked by that war?

Julie was determinedly cheerful and upbeat about the whole business. 'We'll have four of the most beautiful and intelligent children
you've ever seen,' she said.

'A boy then a girl then a boy then a girl.' He played along despite
his deep-felt belief that it would never happen. 'We'll buy little boogie
boards and I'll have them surfing before they can walk.' He pulled her
onto his lap and they kissed and cuddled – Julie continually reassuring
him that everything would be fine. Both offered up silent prayers that
he had escaped contamination. They did their best to distract themselves, but the tension in South Lodge mounted as the days crawled
by.

'You should go for a walk in the hills together,' suggested Roddie.
'The two of you sitting here getting more and more stressed isn't helping any of us.' He took out a map and offered a few suggestions. Tom
quickly settled on Ben Ledi in the Trossachs. His first day spent with
Julie had been there and it ensured that beautiful area a permanent
place in his heart.

'Ben Ledi it is,' agreed Julie, mirroring his thoughts that, if it was
good news from the hospital, they would return to the Trossachs
together many times in the future.

'Let's try to forget about it today,' said Tom, as he drove north. Magnificent autumnal colours greeted them as they drove into the Queen
Elizabeth Forest Park with Ben Ledi rising beyond, for almost 3,000
feet. He parked on the shore of Loch Lubnaig and they walked along
a forest track up on to the slopes. As they climbed steadily towards
the summit, some of the most beautiful scenery in Central Scotland
opened up before them. Julie pointed across the Forth Valley to the
castle town of Stirling some thirty miles to the east and, beyond Ben
Lomond to the west, a range of mountains locally known as the 'Arro-
char Alps'.

'Ben le Dia,' said Julie when they reached the summit. 'Gaelic for the
hill of God. It's one of several interpretations of the name's origin. In
centuries past, on the first day of May, folk from the surrounding villages and farms climbed right to this exact spot on the top here. It was

the Celtic New Year and they celebrated with an old Druidic rite: the lighting of the Beltane fires. To symbolize the dying of the old year, the home fires were extinguished before midnight and hundreds of people came up here after dark to light a ceremonial bonfire'

'That would have been quite a spectacle.'

'It must have been. Ritual dictated that each of them should leap through the fire before sharing the food they had brought with them. After feasting, they lit flaming torches from the bonfire and carried them back down to re-light the hearth fires. The purifying flame from the hill-top fire symbolized the Celtic sun god, Bel, and kept their homes warm and safe over the following year.'

Tom smiled at her. 'My, you've certainly been doing your home-work.'

She laughed. 'I love all those old legends and rituals, don't you? I think it's my Celtic blood – pure undiluted romance running through my veins.'

'I suppose those sorts of things kept the community close in those days,' said Tom thoughtfully. 'Pulling together must have been impor-tant for their survival – it would have been a hard enough life anyway. Not much time for romance, I imagine.'

'Well, I can always make time for romance,' said Julie, kissing him. 'And next May Day, you and I are going to climb back up here and repeat that ancient rite with our very own Beltane fire.' He pulled her close and silently prayed to the Celtic sun god that she was right.

After a gentle walk down to the car, and lunch at the Lade Inn, Tom drove back to Erskine and dropped Julie off at South Lodge.

'Tom, a Professor Lever's secretary phoned trying to get hold of you,' said Stella at reception when he walked in to Mar Hall. 'She tried your mobile a few times this morning with no response. Asked if you would contact her as soon as possible. '

'We were hill-walking in the Trossachs. Reception must be bad there.' He tried to sound nonchalant. Unsure of his own reaction, and unwilling to display emotion that might make him look weak, he went outside and phoned the hospital on his mobile. The wait seemed end-less as he was passed from the hospital switchboard to the department, then to the professor's secretary. 'Oh, Mr McCartney, Professor Lever told me he wanted to discuss the results with you himself. Hang on while I put you through.' Tom knew it was bad – the worst – it had to be when the professor insisted on speaking to him personally? Finally he answered the phone. 'I wanted you to know straight away,' he said cheerily, 'you're clear, young man. Not the slightest trace of radiation. Urine, blood, semen; each and every test was perfectly normal. Well done.'

Tom heard 'clear' and 'well done', and struggled at first with the meaning. 'Thank you so much, sir,' he said, a wave of relief sweeping through him. 'You've just made my day – my life in fact!'

He raced to South Lodge with the news, and Julie hung on to his neck as he danced her round the garden. 'No doubt?' she asked eventually.

'No doubt. The professor says there's not a trace of radiation. Every test was clear. Time to celebrate?'

She pressed her groin tight against him, kissing him long and hard. 'Yes, Sergeant McCartney, time to celebrate. Where?'

'The apartment?'

Julie looked up at her own bedroom window. 'Hmmm.'

At the hotel, they headed up the back stairs, but Julie pulled her hand from his. 'Wait here,' she ordered, 'there's something I need to do in reception. Two minutes.'

She returned on time and, offering no explanation, hurried him along a back passage towards the guest rooms. Stopping outside the Junior Suite, Julie produced a key from her pocket. 'It's vacant tonight,' she whispered, opening the door and pulling him in. 'You wanted a celebration.'

Sunlight flooded into the suite the following morning as Tom lay gazing at Julie, asleep beside him. Never in his life had he felt as happy and content as he did now, watching her slow, rhythmical, breathing and feeling her breath on his cheek. 'Love you deep, Julie Anderson.'

Her hazel eyes opened and a lazy smile broke across her face. 'And I love you, Tom McCartney,' she whispered, and rolled on top of him.

'Fancy some breakfast?' asked Tom some time later. 'I'm famished.'

'Me too. Must be all that exercise.'

'Certainly beats the Mar Hall gym.'

Tom picked up the antique phone and adopted a posh English accent to speak to room service. 'Yes. Yes indeed, my dear, the Junior Suite. Arrived late last night. Full cooked breakfast for both of us please yes, and bucks fizz with your best Dom Perignon. Yes, twenty minutes will be fine, thank you. You are most kind.'

The puzzled expression on the waitress's face turned to a huge smile when she knocked on the door of the suite and wheeled the breakfast trolley in. 'Just wait till I tell them we have famous guests!' she said, setting the table as carefully as she would for genuine millionaires.

They walked through the Big Wood to South Lodge, kicking up fallen leaves and enjoying the freshness of the autumnal air. Roddie and Susan warmly congratulated Tom on being given all clear, and the foursome sat round the fire discussing the horrendous expense involved in organizing a wedding.

'Guess we'll just have to make do with beer and crisps in the Golf Inn, dear,' Susan joked.

'I'm sure you can manage something a wee bit nicer than a pub' said Julie. 'I made some enquiries and this is what I suggest: a marriage ceremony and reception at the conference centre in the old stables block along the drive.'

'Now that sounds interesting. I've heard great things about the catering there,' said Susan.

Roddie nodded approvingly. 'It's a beautiful old building since they renovated it. So as long as it's affordable.'

'It's very reasonable, Dad, and Tom and I are going to contribute to the costs, as our wedding present to you, aren't we, Tom?'

'Of course,' he agreed, not betraying the fact that it was the first he'd heard of it.

Julie laughed. 'They've given me a list of dates it's available. We can book it as soon as you settle on one.'

'There's something else you should know,' said Susan. 'We've decided to move from here, and live in my house in Bishopton.'

Julie was visibly shocked at the thought of the house of her childhood, and a million happy memories of her mum, being sold. 'Oh right,' she said bravely. 'But I'm surprised you want to leave here, Dad.'

Roddie looked sad. 'Well, you know how it is. Things change in life, and now that the mortgage is cleared.' He smiled and crossed the room to kiss her on the cheek. 'I'm only kidding you. Of course I could never sell it, sweetheart. I want, we both want you to stay on here.'

'Tom, come and help me prepare lunch,' commanded Susan, rising from her chair. 'Roddie and his beautiful daughter have things to discuss – and if I'm not mistaken, it involves you.'

Tom was already aware that Susan had a lucrative hairdressing business and a nice house in nearby Bishopton. Since both her children were married and away, she and Roddie would have it to themselves.

After some ten minutes together, father and daughter came into the kitchen smiling and demanded to know what was for lunch.

'Is there anyone you would like to invite, Julie?' asked Susan.

'No-one, apart from Davie.'

'And you, Tom?'

'I'd love to have Gran and Grandpa Shaw over from Melbourne to meet you all, but they're both in their late eighties and very frail now.'

'Perhaps they could make it for the next big wedding,' said Susan, looking at no-one in particular.

CHAPTER FIFTEEN

TOM HAD NOW BEEN OFF methadone for months and remained mentally and physically well. There was no need for him to take iboga again, but he lied and convinced Roddie otherwise.

'Are you okay?' asked Roddie, when Tom became restless some twenty minutes after taking the capsule. He sat up, unsteadily, his face pale and wet with perspiration.

'I think I'm gonna be sick. Best get the bowl on standby.'

'It's right here. Do you want some water?'

He didn't answer. Feeling nauseous, clammy and fidgety, he slumped back. Roddie was anxiously watching his every move. He rolled over out of his bed, staggered to the bathroom, and vomited repeatedly into the wash basin. Strangely disembodied and befuddled, he could feel Roddie standing behind, supporting him. Tom turned the cold tap on, splashed his face with water, and glanced bleary-eyed into his shaving mirror. The face that looked back was an ashen grey colour, and he was perplexed to see that several deep, ugly scars had appeared on his cheeks and forehead.

No, he was wrong; very wrong. The sick man bore a striking resemblance to him, but the blond hair and scarred face definitely belonged to his great-grandfather, Angus McCartney. A nurse, who was dressed in an old-fashioned ankle-length uniform, helped him remove his shirt then sponged his face and deeply scarred upper torso. A wave of horror broke over Tom when he saw that Angus was tragically maimed. His left arm and both legs were missing, he was a part-man, part-survivor, alive but grossly mutilated. The nurse helped him dress in a clean shirt of coarse grey material, then re-settled him into a battered wooden wheelchair.

'Bad turn there, Angus. Hope it's not what we're feeding you,' she joked as she wheeled him along a gloomy corridor.

'It's what those German boys fed me, Mabel, that's ma belief. Maimed me inside an out.'

'Ach come on, where's your normal cheery self today? Let's see that sparkle in your eyes before you make your grand entrance and rejoin your pal.'

Angus sighed. 'Ah suppose ah've got more tae be thankful for than some of the poor buggers in there.'

'That's the way. Somebody's got to keep the men's morale up, and you're the lad to do it.' She paused outside a door and smiled affectionately at him. 'It's men like you, the ones who make the effort, that make our job a little easier. We do appreciate it, you know.'

Angus forced a smile. Indicating the door, he gave the thumbs-up sign with his remaining hand. 'Okay, Mabel, over the top, charge!'

The nurse winked at him, rubbed his shoulder, and turned her back to the door. Pushing it with her behind, she manoeuvred the clumsy wheelchair backwards through the entrance.

Tom struggled to take in the shocking sight that followed. The huge room smelled foul with cigarette smoke, urine, and stale body odour. It was damp and dingy with a range of old, cheap, furniture and nicotine-stained drapes and curtains. But there was no mistaking the beautiful French windows and tall vaulted ceiling of the Grand Hall at Mar Hall Hotel – or, as he was now seeing it, Erskine Hospital. Just as in Mar Hall today, the Grand Hall was the hub of activities in the hospital. Sunlight flooding in through the towering windows revealed not the well-heeled clientele of the luxury hotel, but a crowd of broken young men in their twenties and thirties. They were uniformly dressed in coarse grey shirts, blue trousers and jackets. None had his full complement of limbs. Men with their feet or entire legs missing sat in wooden wheelchairs while others, who had been spared a lower limb, limped around supported by an artificial leg or crutches. Wicker bath chairs on wheels, a sort of mobile bed, were used by the most badly wounded young men who were mutilated beyond belief.

Two nurses, in their long blue serge dresses, white aprons and starched white hats, walked in from the gardens through the French windows. In the far corner, a concert party of well-intentioned ladies attempted to brighten the atmosphere by singing familiar songs. Several men were enthusiastically joining in with their rendition of 'Pack up your troubles in your old kit bag', while others paid no attention and sat talking amongst themselves. Perhaps they understood the irony.

When the nurse pushed Angus's wheelchair alongside one of the mobile beds, Tom gasped involuntarily and felt his heart thumping in his chest. The young man's face was covered in a mass of ugly scars. He had lost not only both arms and both legs, but both eyes. Fuck sake. What God allowed this? What wrong had this young man done to deserve it? There was no future for him, no hope, no getting better. You don't grow eyes or arms or legs. How could his heart continue to beat?

The young man turned to Angus with a concerned smile, as though he could still see.

'Back from spewing your guts up then. Feeling better?'

'Right as rain, Johnny-boy, right as rain,' said Angus, with an obviously forced cheeriness. 'Ye cannae keep a good man down.'

'Aye, especially not with that Mabel mopping your brow,' joked Johnny, with a mock leer. 'Mind you, ah'd be happier if the good man kept his food down.'

Angus laughed good naturedly at the thought of Mabel mopping his brow. 'An how in the name a hell would you know she disnae look like the back end a one ae they new tanks?'

'Ah can tell by the sweet sound of her voice – and by the way you flirt with her whenever she comes near.'

'Up to your old tricks, are you, boys?' asked a small, dark man who had quietly approached them during this exchange. 'I'll be getting more complaints from the nurses – they tell me you give them a dog's life.'

Angus looked up and smiled. 'They wouldnae be happy withoot us tae complain aboot, Sam. Ye know they love us really.'

'Hello, Dad,' said Johnny, as the older man sat down beside him and grasped his shoulder in greeting. 'Five minutes late today, ah see.'

His father checked his watch and shook his head. 'Right again. Beats me how you do that, Johnny. Have you got a clock inside that head of yours?'

'Well, ah'm not much use for anything else – Angus'll tell you that. He does everything for me, including feeding me and wiping my arse.'

'That's right,' said Angus, 'and he's no best pleased when ah try to do both at the same time!'

The older man joined in the laughter, but Tom could see a bitter sadness in his eyes as he gazed on what was left of his son.

'I know I've said it many times before, Angus, but I'm so grateful to you for looking after my boy. And I know Johnny's dear mother, God rest her soul, would say the same if she was still around.' He probably couldn't voice the truth. Thank God she was dead. Thank God she never saw him reduced to this.

'Okay Dad, that's enough of the maudlin stuff,' said Johnny briskly. 'What treats have you got in your bag for us?'

'I've got you both some fags, as usual, and your Aunty Maggie's made you this fruit cake.'

'Bless her,' said Johnny. 'She's the best cook in the whole of Scotland.'

'Whit's that ah see,' called out one of the men sitting close by. 'McVeigh's got cake, lads.'

'Hey Johnny, pass it over here,' added a plump man sitting across the room from him. 'You wouldn't want to see your old mate starve, would you?'

'Little chance of you starving, Henderson,' Johnny called back good-naturedly. 'You could live off your fat for three months.'

Their corner of the room was filled with good-natured laughter and cheeky comments, paralleled as insults to maintain that aura of manly banter.

'Put it away,' said Sam.

'Aye, it's too good for these reprobates,' added Angus. 'It'll no last two seconds if they get their hands on it.'

'Hey, pipe doon you lot,' called out a voice from the far corner. 'Yer drownin oot the singin.'

'Sorry, very rude ae us,' said Angus graciously. 'Tell ye what; ask the ladies tae come further o'er this way so the McVeigh duo can join in the singin. If Aunty Maggie's the best cook in Scotland – well, Sam and Johnny here are the best tenors.'

'That sounds an excellent idea,' said a severe-looking lady who was obviously in charge. 'Come along girls,' she instructed, imperiously beckoning the others to follow her. They moved to the centre of the room, carefully guiding their expensive dresses between wheelchairs and basket beds, feather hats waving all before them. These women would not normally have given this sort the time of day, but this was their contribution to the war 'effort'.

'Christ, that face would turn milk soor,' Angus whispered to Johnny. Then, turning a beaming smile on the leader, 'Ah compliment you, Miss…'

'Mrs Townsend,' said sour face.

'Ah do beg yer pardon, Mrs Townsend. Can ah just say how delightful it is tae see youse aw so finely turned out. A bevy a beauties tae brighten oor day – an such divine singin. Ye obviously have a rare musical talent, Mrs Townsend, tae produce such a refined choir.'

She positively preened herself under Angus's charm offensive, oblivious to his mocking sarcasm, her face even relaxing into the semblance of a smile. 'We have a duty to use the talents the dear Lord gave us, young man.'

'Tell us what they're like, Angus,' said Johnny in a low voice. 'Any lookers?'

'Aye, that there are, specially the red-head in the front row. What a sweet face an figure she has. She reminds me of Mary.'

'Can you get me an introduction? Surely she'd go for a fine figure of a man like me.'

'How could she resist? But if she's anythin like ma Mary, she'd eat ye alive.'

'Get her over here right now.'

'Shh,' said Sam, 'they're about to start.'

First, the ladies sang a sweet version of 'If you were the only boy in the world, and I was the only girl', then the men joined in a rousing rendition of 'It's a long way to Tipperary'. The full rich voices of the McVeighs, father and son, commanding centre-stage, even among the crowd of practised singers. When the song ended, one of the concert party – the red-head that Angus had singled out – suggested a little timidly that maybe Johnny and Sam would entertain them all with their favourite song.

'Yer in there, Johnny-boy,' whispered Angus.

'Ah knew she had the hots for me,' laughed his friend.

'What will we sing, son?' asked Sam.

'You know the one.'

Sam frowned. 'Are you sure?'

'The lady asked for my favourite. The lads love it too.'

Sam shrugged uncertainly as Johnny began to sing:

While on the road to sweet Athy, hurroo, hurroo
While on the road to sweet Athy, hurroo, hurroo
While on the road to sweet Athy
A stick in the hand and a drop in me eye

A doleful damsel I heard cry
Johnny I hardly knew ye.

As Johnny began the chorus, Angus sang along, waving his hand to encourage the other men to join in.

With your guns and drums and drums and guns, huroo, huroo
With your guns and drums and drums and guns, huroo, huroo
With your guns and drums and drums and guns
The enemy nearly slew ye
Oh my darling dear, ye look so queer
Johnny I hardly knew ye.

On the second verse, Sam joined in, closing his eyes against the tears that welled there. Mrs Townsend's face formed back into its stern lines as she took in the meaning of the words.

Where are the eyes that looked so mild, huroo, huroo
Where are the eyes that looked so mild, huroo, huroo
Where are the eyes that looked so mild
When my poor heart you first beguiled
Why did ye skedaddle from me and the child
Oh Johnny, I hardly knew ye.

The men joined in with the chorus, and some of the younger ladies in the concert party began to pick up the words. They faltered and fell silent, however, as Mrs Townsend, lips pursed, shook her head disapprovingly and fixed them with a steel-eyed stare.

Where are the legs with which ye run, huroo, huroo
Where are the legs with which ye run, huroo, huroo
Where are the legs with which ye run
When first you went to carry a gun
Indeed your dancin days are done
Oh Johnny, I hardly knew ye.

On the next chorus the young red-head bravely began to sing, despite the obvious disapproval of Mrs Townsend. Emboldened, her friends joined in, their feet tapping to the infectious tune.

With your guns and drums and drums and guns, huroo, huroo
With your guns and drums and drums and guns, huroo, huroo
With your guns and drums and drums and guns
The enemy nearly slew ye
Oh my darling dear, ye look so queer
Johnny I hardly knew ye.

Quietly, Johnny sang the next verse alone.

Ye haven't an arm, ye haven't a leg, huroo, huroo
Ye haven't an arm, ye haven't a leg, huroo, huroo
Ye haven't an arm, ye haven't a leg
Ye're an eyeless, boneless, chickenless egg
Ye'll have to be put with a bowl to beg
Oh Johnny I hardly knew ye.

Every man in the room then sang the chorus and final verse with gusto, those who could, stamping and clapping as the song reached its climax.

They're rolling out the guns again, huroo, huroo
They're rolling out the guns again, huroo, huroo
They're rolling out the guns again
But they never will take our sons again
No they never will take our sons again
Johnny I'm swearing to ye.

Appreciating the ghoulish sentiments of the anti-war song, Tom felt a bond of brotherhood with these soldiers – a different war, a different era, but they used the self-same black humour as he and his comrades to cope with the terrible horrors they had experienced.

Mrs Townsend cleared her throat, her shock at the brutal harshness of the song evident on her face. 'Perhaps you know something more appropriate?'

'This one's my favourite, ma'am,' said Sam respectfully.

The room fell silent as Sam and Johnny prepared to sing. This was a treat which the men had heard before, and they didn't want to miss a moment.

Their heart-rending version of 'Roses of Picardy' drew a spontaneous burst of applause, and surreptitious wiping of eyes here and there.

The concert ended with the national anthem, after which the ladies walked among the men, doing their duty, handing out cigarettes and small bags of sweets. The young red-haired woman approached the McVeighs shyly. 'I just wanted to say how beautiful your songs were.'

'My friend told me how beautiful you were, so we sang it just for you,' replied Johnny gallantly.

'You've made her blush, Johnny,' said Angus.

'Just like a rose of Picardy,' said Johnny, bowing in her direction from his bed.

She glanced round at the sour-faced choir leader, and seeing that she was occupied talking to the matron, leaned forward and gave Johnny a quick peck on the cheek. 'You're a lovely man,' she said.

'Look who's blushing now,' said Angus.

'Emily!' The commanding voice of Mrs Townsend filled the room. 'Come here this minute!'

'Yes, Mother,' said the red-head, scurrying away from Johnny's side.

'God, ye had a lucky escape there,' said Angus. 'Be thankful ye cannae see whit she's gaunny grow intae.'

Tom had noticed a tall, distinguished-looking man of about thirty-five enter the room during the singing. Moving with a stiff gait, he limped across the Grand Hall and stood at Angus's side, joining in the singing with a pleasant baritone voice.

Angus was clearly delighted to see him and introduced the new arrival. 'Sam, ah'd like ye tae meet a good friend of mine an Johnny's – Captain Michael Farquhar.'

'It's an honour to meet you at long last, Captain. I've heard so much about you,' said Sam, holding out his hand. 'We've somehow managed to miss each other at visiting times. Any friend of Angus's is a friend of the McVeighs.'

'The feeling is mutual,' said Farquhar in an upper-class English voice, with just a hint of Scottishness to it. 'May I take this seat? Only I can't stand for long – the old tin leg gives me seven sorts of gyp.' He sat down and stretched out his right leg, manoeuvring it to a comfortable position with his hands. They sat and chatted while the ladies continued their rounds of the room, Farquhar absent-mindedly massaging his left knee.

'Seems to me you've trouble with both your legs, sir,' said Sam.

'Yes, 'fraid so. Although the surgeons did a jolly excellent job saving the left one, at times I wish they had taken them both off and had done with it. The old bullet wounds repeatedly break down with infections. Give me a dreadful time. I was discussing with my surgeon just last month whether it might yet be better amputated.'

Sam shook his head and tutted.

'How long did they keep ye in this time?' Angus asked.

'Almost three weeks. I can't fathom how you, Johnny and the other lads cope with being in hospital permanently. Just that short time drove me to distraction. Saving grace was the nurses are wonderful.'

'Which hospital were you in?' Sam asked.

'Craiglockhart Hospital in Edinburgh. Just like Erskine, a truly wonderful place.'

'Except for officers only' said Johnny.

'Well yes, it is for officers.'

There was a pause.

'I can't say I've seen any of the other ordinary soldiers in the hospital being visited by their officers,' said Sam, breaking what could have been awkward silence.

'No, it's not seen as quite the "done thing",' admitted Michael. He explained that he and Angus were badly wounded at the Somme and stretchered away after lying helpless in a trench. Though Sam had heard the story many times from both Johnny and Angus, he listened intently as Captain Farquhar went on to describe how the remains of his right leg had been amputated at a field hospital, the left being saved only by the speed, dexterity and skill of the elderly English army surgeon.

'After that, Angus was shipped out here to Erskine, while I was sent to Craiglockhart. I was only there for six weeks initially, but I've been in and out since.'

Michael stood up and walked awkwardly up and down. 'Gives me gyp if I sit down too long, and just as bad if I'm on my feet too long,' he explained. 'Can't win!'

'So how did you two meet up again?' Sam asked.

Michael sat down and readjusted his artificial leg. 'When I decided to trace the young soldier I carried from the field that bloody day, my father and friends attempted to persuade me that it wasn't a wise move on my part. It wasn't the "done thing", always that – not the done thing. Well, I don't always do the "done thing". We were thrown into that madness together. I had to know if Angus…' The sentence was left unfinished, but everyone understood the sentiment.

Sam grumbled. 'People would get on so much better in this life if they did the "right thing" more often than the "done thing". When you're as old as me you'll see that even more clearly.'

'The authorities weren't interested in helping me trace Angus. Truth be told, they were positively obstructive. It took me weeks to track him down, to even find out that he had been sent here to Erskine. Thereafter it took weeks longer to persuade the Commandant here to grant his permission for me visit him. I believe they were concerned that my presence might cause dissension in the ranks.'

'Aye, even though yir man here had been awarded the military cross fur his bravery that day,' put in Angus.

Michael continued, 'Money always talks. A generous donation was enough to persuade them that no harm could be caused by allowing me to visit Angus here. Six months ago I finally visited him – and as I got to know him, to become, I hope Angus will agree, more than an acquaintance, a firm friend. As you know, he and Johnny are inseparable, so I couldn't help but get to know him too.'

'They're like Siamese twins,' said Sam.

'Aye, with only one limb left out the eight between the pair of us,' said Angus. 'If ye want the truth, it's Johnny's friendship, spirit an sense of humour that gies me the will tae keep goin.'

'Aye, and vice versa,' said Johnny.

'And as for Michael here,' Angus continued, 'he's the one who stops me goin crazy – as ah would do if ah wiz stuck inside here twenty-four hours a day, every day. Ye know, Sam, this man comes tae visit me even on days when he's clearly in a lot of pain. Without the slightest grumble he pushes me in the wheelchair away up through the woods tae Lord Blantyre's seat or o'er on the ferry tae The Grapes fur a pint.'

'It's about the only exercise I take, Angus, so no bad thing.'

The singers waved goodbye and departed in their large limousines.

A young fellow who had enjoyed the concert commented: 'Not bad talent there, boys. But you'd better watch out for that wee red-head's mother, Johnny.'

'Ach, the young ones are nae better,' said another man disparagingly. 'They're just a bunch of upper-class, patronizin arseholes.'

'Steady on, man, there's no call for that sort of language,' said Michael sternly. 'They come here as an act of charity, whatever their social standing.'

The man spat contemptuously. 'If it wisnae for the upper classes spoilin for a fight ah reckon we'd never have had tae go tae war in the first place.'

'Aye, and if it wisnae for privileged upper-class bloody officers sendin us o'er the top,' growled another, looking pointedly at Michael, 'a few more of us might have come back in one piece.'

'Hey, hey hey!' interjected Angus. 'A bit more respect there – the Captain saved ma life.'

An argument quickly broke out in the hall with men shouting and cursing at one another. The sliver of gallant resignation that was presumed on these men, sat over a cauldron of uncompromising bitterness. Cut through the top-soil and a thousand justified resentments escaped like molten lava hissing and swirling in a path of self-destruction.

'Here we go again,' said Johnny. 'You're a load of arseholes yourselves,' he shouted, adding his voice to the din. 'I for one am proud of what we did out there.'

'We'd have been better handin over tae the Jerries,' said a darkhaired man with no legs. 'They'd run this country better any day!'

This was greeted by howls of outrage from various quarters of the Grand Hall.

'Get me oot a here fur fuck sake, Michael,' said Angus, shaking his head. 'We'll leave the McVeighs tae sort oot the warrin factions an hope they don't kill too many of them.'

Farquhar wheeled Angus through the French windows leading out to the garden, and over to the shade of the huge Cedar of Lebanon which dominated the lawn. He sat down on a bench, adjusting his legs to be as comfortable as possible. 'Well, I can understand some of those sentiments,' he said. 'Some officers are a little – high-handed, shall we say, when dealing with the ordinary soldier.'

Angus looked sideways at his friend. 'Aye, and ah seem tae recall a certain Captain Farquhar wiz yir average toffee-nosed git when he first took up post as oor officer.'

'You're right, Angus. But you have to remember that I didn't know any other way to behave. It's a terrible thing to say, but all my experience at home, boarding school and officer training, taught me that power and control always came from those above with the money, and obedience came from those below.' He sighed and massaged his knee. 'I don't blame you for disliking me back then.'

'Aye, well you proved tae be a better man than many of ma so-called mates there. They were too busy tryin tae save their ain hides that day tae think about savin me. No that ah blame them fur that – ah don't know how ah'd have reacted if you'd been the one lyin bleedin tae death in no man's land and ah'd been in the trench.'

'Water under the bridge, Angus. Water under the bridge. You know, in a strange way the war showed me that privilege counts for nothing. It taught me more about people than any amount of expensive education and privilege. What is important at the day of reckoning is how we treat our fellow human beings, whatever their class.'

'Ah couldnae agree more. Talkin about privilege, it's the twelfth of August – thought you'd be out shooting with the old Purdies to bag the first of the season,' said Angus with a reasonable attempt at an upper-crust accent.

Michael laughed. 'As you well know, old chap, I'd probably miss him at ten feet. Better chance of dropping the blighter with the blunt end.' Both nodded. Their meaningless pleasantries filled the time but avoided real reflection.

'It's been a long thirteen months for us,' Angus added, becoming serious. 'Thirteen months since baith oor lives were fucked that first day at the Somme.'

Michael could only agree and the two men lapsed into silence. A convoy of four battered ambulances drove into the avenue and nurses and porters began to assemble on the hospital steps. What tragedies lay inside? How many would survive the first month? How many more pleas would cry in the night to end the misery? Boys who might make a recovery, but never kick a ball again. They had abandoned their legs and their youth in the mud of France, and now they came here, to recover or to die. Ah to be so lucky.

Tom's vision became less distinct, and gradually the image of Angus and Michael turned to black, like a fade-out on a cinema screen. Simultaneously he felt himself floating towards consciousness, and his eyes opening involuntarily. He saw Roddie's concerned face peering over him as he moved restlessly on the bed, but before he could speak, his eyes closed again. The quiet of the hospital garden on that reflective summer's day, was transformed by a shaking jolt that hurled him back to a very different place.

The noise of explosions battered his ears, the smell of cordite and mud were acrid in his nose and mouth. His senses were so overwhelmed by the physical brutality of the scene playing out all around that it took him several minutes to re-acclimatize. Nausea and anxiety washed over him again as he realized with a shock that he was at the front line in the midst of a First World War battlefield. A feeling of dread left him shuddering involuntarily. He guessed he was about to discover exactly what happened to his great-grandfather at the Somme.

Although he had fought in the thick of battle himself, watching the scene as an unarmed observer was so much more shocking. He regained control of his feelings and tried to engage his military mind, to assess and make sense of what was going on around him.

The sun was shining over a churned-up field. In the distance the spires and towers of small villages broke the horizon. Both before and behind him he could see endless lines of trenches, snaking away for miles to the left and right. What, no doubt, was once fertile land was pocked with shell holes more deadly than disease. Heavy artillery bombarded the trenches directly before him in a devastating barrage, throwing huge, billowing mounds of earth into the blue sky. Periodic massive underground explosions caused the ground to convulse as though at the epicentre of an earthquake. Thousands upon thousands of shells screamed directly over his head like demented banshees attempting to escape from hell. Nothing was as it should be. Nature was in chaos.

Without warning, the barrage stopped and in the almost disorientating silence which followed, tin whistles blew. A line of tens of thousands of soldiers climbed from their trenches and began walking slowly and deliberately towards the opposite trenches. Advancing with fixed bayonets before them, the British troops were weighed down by heavy woollen uniforms and a multitude of weapons and equipment which seemed to hang from every part of their bodies. They picked their way delicately across no-man's-land. There was a look of determination on their faces that Tom instantly recognized, the grim faces of a body of men who were there to do exactly what they had been told to do. Their duty.

The silence lasted for no more than a few seconds. The British artillery began a barrage over their own men's heads, their shells always exploding just in front of the advancing line. There was no reply from the Germans. It seemed that British heavy artillery had succeeded in pounding their trenches with sufficient accuracy to prevent return fire.

The soldiers began looking at each other with surprise and relief. Their steps became more confident, they strode out a little faster. It was working, just as the officers had said it would.

Suddenly, a single burst of machine gun fire erupted from the German lines. It was followed by another and another. Horrified, Tom watched helplessly as the British soldiers were mercilessly mowed down by the German machine gunners. Despite this, those still on their feet continued to advance, firing back as best they could.

The German artillery now dropped their sights onto no man's land, raining a hail of shells down on British troops. Although Tom knew the explosions could not touch him, he flinched and ducked as shells burst around him. He crouched for cover in a trench, surrounded by Scottish soldiers wearing khaki kilts that seemed so inappropriate on a field of death.

He looked around, searching for a face which he felt sure would be there. It was but two feet away. Such a familiar face, instantly recognizable, so similar to his own. Angus. Private Angus McCartney, his great-grandfather, looking just as he had seen him at Colinton Street. A feeling of dread and utter helplessness washed over Tom for he knew he was about to witness something terrible. He wanted to grab Angus, to yell at him to run, to hide, to do anything but advance across that field of slaughter.

In the trench, an officer shouted instructions to the men to prepare for this, the second wave. Turning round, Tom recognized Captain Farquhar. Several soldiers crouched in fear. Their resolve snapped, incapable of movement, they were crudely advised by Farquhar that they could either take their chance now or face a certain firing squad in the morning.

At that moment a chorus of sharp whistles blew all along the trenches, heralding the legions of hell to visit their worst on the unblooded volunteers. Friends among the ranks shook hands and wished each other well. Some were trembling, some were crying, others vomited or their bladders and bowels involuntarily opened. Many seemed strangely calm, prepared now to walk with their God.

Tom watched helplessly as Angus went over the top. His mouth formed a silent scream: 'No!', but the vision took its inexorable course. He knew from his own limited appreciation of military history that the first day of the Battle of the Somme had been described as 'the blackest day of slaughter in the history of the British Army,' with over 57,000 casualties in the first few hours alone.

Within yards, a withering hail of German machine gun fire tore many of the men to pieces. Several took no more than one step. Their bullet-riddled bodies fell back into the trench with blood spurting over friends waiting in turn to go over.

Tom watched in terror mixed with admiration, as his brave ancestor moved unhesitatingly across the killing field, stepping over more and more of his dead and wounded comrades as he headed towards his fate. Huge clumps of earth flew into the air and Tom felt his guts churn when the kilted remains of a lower torso with one leg landed just in front of Angus.

And then it happened. The scene which Tom knew he was helpless to prevent played itself out pitilessly. He started thrashing wildly as a German shell exploded immediately in front of his great-grandfather. Angus's body spun high in the air and landed virtually in a sitting position on the rim of the smouldering crater. Quite astonishingly, Angus was still conscious. Looking down, he saw torn, bleeding flesh and gleaming white, splintered bone ends protruding from what had been his thighs. The enormity of what the explosion had done to him hardly registered, seemed more a matter of interest than anything else. Instinctively putting his hands down to stem blood loss, he realised that no left hand or arm was there. That was when it hit him. He screamed loud and long for his mammy and daddy, but no one could hear. Even God ignored his desperate pleas to take him quickly, and he began to claw at the mud with his remaining hand in a futile attempt to drag himself back to his trench.

In that trench, thirty yards away, Farquhar watched in horror through a box periscope. He could see Angus screaming and shouting, but was unable hear his words. Tom thrashed around on the bed in agonies of distress as he vainly tried to run to Angus's aid.

Forming the shape of a pistol with his remaining hand, Angus pointed at his right temple. 'Shoot me!' he screamed repeatedly at Farquhar. 'Shoot me. Do it! Do it you stupit bastard! Do it *now*!'

Trembling with fear and the horror of it all, Captain Farquhar grabbed an Enfield rifle and climbed up to the edge of the trench. He aimed at Angus's head and was about to pull the trigger when he shouted something quite incomprehensible, threw down the rifle, and rushed towards him. Grabbing Angus's remaining limb, he swung him up onto his shoulder and darted back. Two steps from safety, machine gun bullets ripped into the back of Farquhar's legs, pitching both men into the trench. As they landed face to face within inches of each other amidst the blood, vomit and shit of the dying and the dead, blood-curdling screams rose from the very depths of their souls.

CHAPTER SIXTEEN

Tom opened his eyes to see Roddie standing anxiously over him. 'Bloody hell, Tom! You had me worried there. I thought you were having a seizure or some sort of convulsion the way you were thrashing about on the bed. I was damn near close to calling an ambulance.'

Tom was stunned to find himself still lying on his bed in Mar Hall, soaked in perspiration, the sun streaming through the window. His entire body was trembling from the explosions, noise and sheer emotional trauma, and he now knew the literal meaning of the term 'shell shock'. It took a supreme effort to comprehend that what for him had taken place in the here and now, was actually ninety years and many miles removed in time and space.

He lifted his arm and peered through watery eyes at his watch. 'Fuck sake' he exclaimed involuntarily when he saw it was 4.30. 'Is that right – I've been lying here a full nine hours?'

'Aye, right enough,' said Roddie. 'Except for the pleasant interlude when you staggered to the bathroom to puke. Not that you really woke then – seemed you just lost consciousness again while you were standing.'

Tom tried to make some sort of sense of it all. 'I know you're not gonna believe this, Roddie, but I've been at the fuckin Somme.' He swallowed hard. 'Saw my great-grandfather blown to bits.'

Roddie looked shocked and agitated. 'You don't know how glad I am you're out of that. It's dangerous! Doing you much more harm than good. No more, Tom. I'm having nothing more to do with this and neither must you.' There was no anger in his voice, just finality.

Roddie left and Tom stood at the apartment window, gazing down at the massive cedar dominating the lawn below. He could see in his mind's eye the figures of Angus in his wheelchair and Farquhar sitting on the bench massaging his knee. He felt drained, deeply sorry and desperately inadequate as he thought back over the events. It had happened. He had been there. There was nothing he could say or do to explain it. Nothing he could change. Angus was brought from the Somme battlefield and had been right here in the Grand Hall at Erskine with such terrible wounds. Was that why the place felt so familiar when he first arrived? Surely not.

He cobbled together a quick pasta dish and went straight to his computer. Googling Battle of the Somme, he was surprised to find how many photographs there were, taken during the battle itself. Weary, anxious faces staring into camera lenses from the head-high trenches; men with wounded comrades on their shoulders, wading through mud; more men, mounted on heavy artillery, almost lost in clouds of smoke; so many images of the bodies of young men, sinking in mud. That was the real tragedy. Young men. The lost generation. Why oh why did no-one call a halt to such slaughter? He looked at picture after picture, finding it difficult to reconcile the vision, the sense of actually being there, with images on a computer screen.

Tom shook his head, struck anew by the strangeness of his experience. The images he had in his head were so much more real than these grainy old pictures. What he had seen hadn't been like photographs or even watching old films. He had felt and smelled and heard the violence, the fear, and the despair of those poor, brave soldiers. Of his great-grandfather.

The first day of the battle, 1st July 1916, was described over and over again on website after website. Millions of words traced the events leading inexorably to the loss of 57,000 British and Commonwealth troops – one third killed, the rest terribly wounded – on the first day, a figure which remains a one-day record for any battle. But despite the disaster of that first morning, the battle continued with very little chance of success until 18th November, before it was finally called off.

The German army had swept through Belgium on 4th August 1914 and quickly occupied large swathes of French territory on the Franco-Belgian border. By the end of the first battle of Ypres in November that year, the Western Front was taking shape with lines of opposing trenches running for hundreds of miles from the English Channel to the Swiss border. Facing the Germans in the north was the British Expeditionary Force. The French army massed further south.

The German army had been dug in to its trenches for many months when the original battle-plan for a French and British summer offensive was proposed in early 1916. The French and British armies would carry out the attack against German lines in the closest co-operation, acting as one united army in an area near the river Somme where the British and French lines converged.

In February 1916, however, a mighty German offensive at Verdun to the south resulted in massive numbers of French casualties and the abandonment of the original plan. The Somme would now be a large-scale diversionary attack, mainly by the British Fourth Army. The British Third Army to the north would exploit the gap expected to be created in German lines, and make a breakthrough with cavalry. The French Sixth Army would attack from the south. My, how straightforward are the plans of battle, drawn by experts across pristine maps as crisp as the uniforms that believe in them.

The Germans had two well-prepared lines of parallel trenches at the Somme front, and a third under construction. They took in many sleepy French villages, including Beaumont Hamel, Thiepval and Fricourt, all of which would be obliterated by the months of battle.

The opposing armies had been entrenched for a considerable time and the German command had made best use of that time by ordering the construction of lines of defence, and facilities that were far superior to those of the British. They had built a massive network of tunnels and chambers, with interconnecting passageways, deep into the workable chalk. The underground facilities were protected both by their depth and by massive steel girders and wooden beams. Terrified as they were, the German soldiers sat out a week-long British heavy artillery barrage in relative safety in shelters and dormitories twenty feet below ground level. They had multiple exits, drainage sumps and pumps, complete cooking facilities and anti-gas curtains. Some of the underground German facilities even had their own electric lighting powered by generators.

From 24th June, and for an entire week before the actual battle began, British artillery bombarded the German lines with one and a half million shells – more than had been fired during the entire first year of the war. The grand plan was to destroy the German defences with the bombardment. British soldiers would then attack the enemy after walking across no-man's-land, behind a 'creeping barrage' of British artillery, fired from the rear.

The week-long heavy bombardment, however had failed to destroy the German tunnels or concrete machine gun posts, and simply turned most of their barbed wire defences into an even more impenetrable mass. Immediately the bombardment ceased and the British infantry attack began, German soldiers poured out from their underground shelters through interconnecting passageways to man their machine gun posts.

Of the brave souls who made it up to the German line, most were riddled with bullets as they attempted to climb through the tangled mess of wire, many with their kilts caught in the barbs. One survivor described the German wire as being so tight and densely packed that it was almost impossible to see daylight through it. The First Newfoundlanders regiment left the trenches with 752 men, and 684 of them were dead or badly wounded within half an hour.

British soldiers being brought up to the front as reinforcements could see clearly through binoculars that the German machine gun posts and wire defences were intact. The men were incredulous that the generals had given the offensive the green light. That very day, those men would be ordered over the top themselves. Day after day, month after month, Field Marshall Haig ordered hundreds of thousands of men out to face the German machine guns.

Tom struggled to understand how he had been able to witness exactly this – watch it actually unfold before him and see his great-grandfather mutilated in the carnage without any prior knowledge of the details of the battle. How could it be? If he'd read the facts from a history book or from the internet before he had the vision – then fine, it could be explained, but he hadn't.

He looked at his watch and found he'd been browsing the net for almost three hours, growing evermore disillusioned and angry as he read deeper into the background of the disastrous British tactics. As he figured it, the men at the top were totally to blame for the fiasco. In their Headquarters well behind the front line, they had blithely sent twenty thousand young men to their deaths that morning – deaths which could have been prevented if they had listened to the voices in the trenches. And then, to compound their failings, they had continued the offensive for four long months. All for what? Little or nothing, it seemed, other than the wholesale slaughter of hundreds of thousands of soldiers. They played by the rules of war. Was that it? Did the High Command think of war as a global game of grand moves and set rules? But this wasn't cricket. It was an unforgiveable risk. They were gambling. That's it. They were engaged in a worldwide game of roulette with the odds firmly stacked against the common man. Jesus Christ. Was Roddie right?

Looking out at the big cedar, his head still full of heartbreaking images of the battlefield, he felt as though his feet were still stuck fast in mud. How he had wanted to save Angus. The more he struggled to get free and drag his great-grandfather from the battlefield before the inevitable explosion tossed him in the air and broke him, the deeper he sank into the quagmire. The feeling of powerlessness and hopelessness he had felt in the vision stayed with him, making him restless and uncomfortable. He showered, went downstairs to the Grand Hall, and walked across the original polished floorboards to the exact spot where Angus had sat next to Johnny McVeigh. He saw again in his mind's eye the broken men, some bitter, some resigned, who had given all; heard the songs of Johnny and the ladies' concert party; smiled as he remembered the pretty young Emily whose compassion for Johnny had been so evident. It had happened here, right here.

He wandered out to the big tree and pondered on Michael and Angus's discussion on how their experiences during and after the war had changed their lifes. Like Michael, he now seriously questioned his own acceptance of the wars he had been involved in – the conviction that he was doing his duty to defend the civilized world against whoever had supposedly been identified as aggressors. Had he been as much a victim of the 'men at the top' as Angus and Johnny and all their compatriots – in fact, all the soldiers on both sides in that terrible war? The 'war to end war' as it had been called. Tom, fresh from war in Iraq, was struck by the irony of that phrase. A phrase that had been trotted out naively, trustingly, by the press but which, he now realised, had been fed to them by disingenuous men of power and influence with who knows what vested interests in warmongering.

He walked pensively through the Big Wood, distracted, without any purpose other than to keep moving. Every detail of the vision was clear in his head. His anger and sadness were tinged with a sense of wonder at the strangeness of an episode he felt almost privileged to have experienced. He compared his great-grandfather with the image an earlier vision had given him of his own drunken father terrifying his mother. Angus had been, and remained, a good, kind and caring man despite the horrors he endured and the terrible wounds he suffered.

Tom sat for a while on Lord Blantyre's seat which was renowned as the old estate-owner's favourite thinking place. He looked out over the Firth of Clyde and imagined the great ships sailing down the river, taking many thousands to what they hoped was a better life in Canada, Australia or New Zealand, among them his own great-grandmother, Mary. How awful it all must have been for her. Not only had Angus been ripped apart that day in 1916, but her whole life and all she knew and loved. They should have enjoyed a happy life together. War had ruined it.

Tom couldn't help but compare it with his own situation. Years spent either on exercise or fighting in wars and conflicts in various parts of the world, had affected his chances of settling down with a woman in much the same way. He sighed, stood up, and made his way to Julie at the lodge.

CHAPTER SEVENTEEN

TOM WAS DEPRESSED AFTER the vision. He couldn't shake it off despite spending as much time as possible with Julie, the best thing he knew for brightening his mood. As the week wore on his despair deepened. He was sleeping badly and, in addition to constantly reliving the sight of Angus being mutilated on the battlefield, flashbacks to the shooting of Donna Mulhearty had recurred.

He did his best to hide the extent of his troubles from Julie, but she had quickly learned to read him more accurately than he liked. 'We need to do something to get you out of this black hole,' she said one afternoon when she got back from university to find him still in bed in his apartment.

'Don't you think I've been trying? Seems there's nothing else I can do except wait for it to go away again. So I might as well stay just where I am.' He turned his back on her and pulled the covers over his head.

'Oh no you don't! You ain't getting rid of me that easily,' she said, sitting on the bed, and pulling the covers off him. 'This is obviously a recurrence of the PTSD – and you told me often enough that talking to Brigadier Nimmo helped you through the blackest times, so shoot.'

He turned back towards her and gripped her hand. 'Listen Julie, I'm no good for you. I'm a mess, and I don't think I'll ever get over this properly. I've been thinking seriously about it and I can't ruin your life with my misery. As soon as I've worked out my notice I'm going back to Melbourne. You'll be well rid of me.'

Tears sprang to Julie's eyes, but she blinked them back and jumped to her feet purposefully. 'I've never heard such crap in my life! Do you really think I'm going to sit back while you wallow in self-pity?' Suddenly all energy, she started tidying his flat, picking up his clothes where he had thrown them to the floor and taking dirty plates through to the kitchen. 'Go back to Australia, my arse. There's a wedding to help me organize, don't forget – and I seem to recall talk of teaching you to dance, travelling the length and breadth of Scotland and, last but not least, having four babies! So don't think you're going to shirk your responsibilities by slinking back down-under!'

For the first time in days, Tom laughed. 'God, your father was right when he told me I didn't know what I was doing taking on a red-haired woman.'

Julie lay on the bed and they held each other tight. 'Promise you won't leave me,' she whispered.

'I promise.'

They talked long into the evening, and his mood began to lift. He agreed that he should try distraction therapy. Over the next few days he was kept busy riding shotgun for an exceptionally rich international banking executive whose singular disappointment was that no one tried to kidnap him. Tom helped with Roddie and Susan's wedding plans, swam many lengths of the hotel pool, and jogged round the grounds. He and Julie had long chats, but there was one topic he avoided discussing with her: desperate to know what happened to Angus, he was going to take more iboga. Roddie wouldn't be there to sit with him, and he risked the danger of choking to death if he vomited, but he would go it alone.

Tom locked the apartment door and set out a towel, basin and glass of water by his bed. He switched off his mobile phone, swallowed an iboga capsule, and lay down. Thankfully he had no nausea, but nothing much else was happening either. Had the drug lost its potency? He was considering taking another, when a bad smell filled his nostrils and the blurred image of a familiar passageway came into focus. He knew it was just below where he lay, the very corridor Julie had taken him along when he got the all-clear from Professor Lever. The hotel's luxurious and fragrant Junior Suite, however, was a stark place and stank of urine, antiseptic and, worst of all, putrifying flesh. Men lay in old wooden hospital beds, arranged in rows of five down each side of the room. They took the place of the huge four-poster bed he and Julie had made love in for the first time.

Johnny McVeigh's bed was on the far right hand side beside one of the room's two large windows. Tom was shocked to see how pale, gaunt and ill he looked. Angus sat in his wheelchair beside the bed, holding a cup and pleading with Johnny to sip some water. Sam and Michael stood on the other side at the window, looking out at a huge warship bristling with guns being guided downriver by three tugs.

'Leave him, son,' said Sam, gently as he turned to Angus. 'Let him sleep now.'

Angus nodded, put the cup down, and began to sob.

Michael turned from the window and spoke quietly to Sam. 'I'll take him out for a break. He's never left his side for days.' Michael walked round, put a consoling arm round Angus's shoulder, and manoeuvered his wheelchair away from the bed. 'Come on, I'll treat you to a pint in the Grapes.'

Angus had regained his composure by the time Michael pushed his wheelchair past the new hospital bowling green being constructed alongside the path to the ferry. 'He's dyin, isn't he, Michael?'

'Yes, another infection and gangrene.'

'Aye, he always knew a fuckin wound infection would take him sooner or later. How long?'

'Difficult to say. The surgeon was most apologetic when he told Sam there was no more he could do. We just have to come to terms with what Johnny has already accepted – it's for the best.'

'Never goin tae war in the first place would have been fur the best,' Angus replied bitterly.

Black reek belched from the funnel of the little open-deck ferry as it waited patiently while several merchantmen lying low in the water sailed upstream to Glasgow. The Clyde wasn't so much a river as an artery pumping life into a nation desperate for supplies. The ferryman closed the gate and the ferry, laden with lorries, horses and carts, hauled itself across the river to Old Kilpatrick on two massive iron chains.

Michael limped and struggled up the steep slip, but two young lads saw his plight and hurried over to help push the wheelchair up to Dumbarton Road and along to The Grapes.

A little cheer went up from the regulars when Michael wheeled Angus in. 'Good to see you again, gentlemen. Two of the best is it?' asked the barman, already pulling their pints. Old acquaintances gathered round to listen when Angus explained that Johnny was dying. The atmosphere in the pub turned sombre until Michael scolded the men, saying he had brought Angus over for a pint to try and cheer him up. They began telling jokes and stories, tales that get told in earnest but embellished in drink. Angus's mood lightened somewhat, and another two pints and ten refusals later, they set off back to the ferry.

Tom stirred in bed and sat up just long enough to take a sip of water. When he drifted away again, he recognized the old Erskine Parish Church just along the road from South Lodge.

'We are gathered today to say farewell to our dear friend Johnny McVeigh, who was taken from us at the tender age of twenty-two. We are, sadly, all too accustomed to the passing on of the young men who now make their home in the hospital, tended for so caringly by the selfless staff. Johnny, terribly wounded in the defence of our country, epitomised the spirit in adversity of every man in the place. He brought us all much joy with his beautiful singing voice and tremendous sense of humour. He was also one of the bravest men I had the honour to meet. Never a man to complain, although in many ways he would have been most justified in doing so, Dr Borland tells me he was in constant pain, especially in his last few weeks. But he always had a smile and a joke to brighten everyone's day, right to the end. When I spoke to him just a few days before he died, he was more concerned about his father Sam, and his dear friend Angus, than about himself. "Tell them I love them, and not to be sad. I'm ready to go," he told me. "Tell my family and friends I'm waiting for them. One day we will all meet again."' The hospital padre seemed genuinely moved when he ended his address and led the mourners in singing The Lord is my Shepherd.

Sam McVeigh, dry-eyed but much moved, gripped Angus's shoulder tight when a bugler played the Last Post and his beloved son was lowered into the grave under the sheltering branches of an ancient syca-more tree.

Wiping tears, and working hard to compose himself, Angus took a sheet of paper from his pocket and addressed the mourners. 'This poem was written by Wilfred Owen, a friend of Captain Farquhar's. It's called "Anthem for Doomed Youth", an ah believe it captures our fate so well.' He began to read, his voice shaky at first, gradually getting stronger and clearer as he proceeded. Heads bowed in recognition of the bitter reality that the anthem caught perfectly. Angus had to hold his voice steady when he reached the lines:

No mockeries now for them; no prayers nor bells;
Nor any voice of mourning save the choirs, –
The shrill, demented choirs of wailing shells;
And bugles calling for them from sad shires.

Well, the bugle had now called Johnny to a better place and the ugly fact that Angus knew was, he would not be the last. Sam McVeigh hugged Angus then, standing tall by the side of his son's grave, recited a poem from memory:

He was the most beautiful son on earth
Braver than a hero of antiquity
Gentler than an angel of God
Tall and dark, his hair like a forest
Or like that intoxicating canopy
Which spreads over the Po valley
And you, without pity for me, killed him.

He was my new son
He was the triumph of my betrayed boyhood
And you changed him
In front of my praying hands
Into a heap of worms and ashes
Mutilated, hurt, blinded
Only I know the tragic weight I am carrying
I am the living cross of my dead son
And that tremendous and precious weight
Of such great suffering, of such unbearable glory
Becomes daily harder and more heavy
It breaks my skin
It fractures every joint
It tears my soul
And yet I shall have to carry it
As my sole good
As long as I have one beat of love in my old veins for him
I shall carry him
Sinking on to my knees if I have to
Until the day of my own burial
Only then will we be down there together
A perfect and obscure cross.

'To finish this sad ceremony,' Sam continued, 'I'd like to thank everyone for their presence here today, and for being such a support to both myself and my son over this difficult year since he was brought back from France to Erskine Hospital. Although I have lost my only son, I have gained many new friends while visiting him and,' he looked down at Angus and grasped his shoulder, 'feel I have also been blessed with a second son. As Johnny was blessed by the best friend any man could have, my earnest hope and prayer is that the war which destroyed his life will indeed, as they promise us, prove to be the war that ends all war. And now I would be honoured if you would all join me for a purvey which the hospital kitchen staff has kindly prepared.'

As the mourners began to make a move, a group of Johnny's friends from the hospital had a hurried conversation. A fair-haired lad in a wheelchair spoke up. 'Before we go, Mr McVeigh, we think Johnny would be pleased if we sang his favourite song.'

Sam glanced down at his son's coffin in the open grave, uncertain. Angus gripped his hand. 'Aye, why not. He sang it so bloody often we aw know the words backwards. He'll look down on us right now an join in.'

The young disabled soldier began to sing, his voice clear and tuneful, the others joining in at the chorus, gradually increasing, the volume rose to a rousing finale.

With your guns and drums and drums and guns, huroo, huroo
With your guns and drums and drums and guns, huroo, huroo
With your guns and drums and drums and guns
The enemy nearly slew ye
Oh my darling dear, ye look so queer
Johnny I hardly knew ye.

The funeral party sat in the hospital canteen round tables groaning with beer and whisky provided by Sam. 'Please fill your glasses – and keep them filled,' said Sam. 'Johnny would want you all to enjoy yourselves – something he knew how to do better than most!'

'Ah'll drink tae that,' said Angus, raising his glass and downing it in one.

Plates of steak pie, potatoes and gravy were brought to them, and Sam recharged Angus's glass. He reached across to fill Michael's. 'Liquid refreshment is what you need, lads.'

'Thank you, Sam,' said Michael. 'It's a difficult time for you.'

'I'm most touched that you came to pay your respects to my boy. And please thank Mr Owen for his poem.'

'I will indeed. Like everyone else who knew him, I warmed to Johnny immediately I met him. Such a brave man.'

'The bravest,' said Angus. 'Even o'er these last few days when he was wastin away in front of ma eyes. Ah tried tae get him tae drink, an even eat a wee bit, anythin tae keep his strength up.'

'There was nothing anyone could do for him, Angus,' said Michael. 'Not even you.'

'God rest his soul,' said Sam. He stood up, thanked everyone for attending to pay their last respects to his beloved son, and wished them all well for the future.

When the mourners dispersed, Sam, Angus and Michael moved outside to sit under the Cedar of Lebanon, Angus's favourite spot in the garden. The shadows were lengthening as the afternoon drew on. Angus was still clutching a bottle of whisky, forlornly drinking from it from time to time.

Michael sat next to Sam. 'He's taken it so hard,' he said quietly, gesturing towards Angus sitting in his wheelchair off to one side.

'Yes,' Sam agreed. 'Harder than me, I guess. My overwhelming feeling is that I'm happy for Johnny – that at last he's free of pain. I'm sure he's glad to have finally gone. Although he always put a brave face on it, I know how hard it was for him, deep down.'

Michael looked across at Angus. 'There's another one whose brave face rarely slips.' There was silence as they pondered on that.

'You know, I think I did my real mourning for Johnny a year ago,' said Sam, thoughtfully. 'When he came back from France in that terrible state.'

'Such a dreadful thing, war,' said Michael, striking his artificial leg forcefully. 'All these lives wrecked. The soldiers and their families both. They say that more than four million British soldiers have gone to France, half a million already dead.'

Angus gulped more whisky from the bottle. 'Aye, an don't forget the ones like me and Johnny who came back broken in body or spirit. Ah left for the front fae the Maryhill Barracks wae hundreds of local men. Not many survived an here's me, stuck in hospital ever since. Is that somethin the great British public should be proud of or should they be bayin fur the blood of the fuckers responsible? The rich bastards who sent us there while they stayed warm an comfortable well behind the lines, or at home in their big hooses in London?'

'Hey, steady on Angus,' said Michael, gently removing the whisky bottle from his hand. 'Let's show some respect for Mr McVeigh on this day of all days.'

'It's okay, Michael,' said Sam, smiling affectionately at Angus. 'He's upset about Johnny. I know his feelings on the war. We're all entitled to our views – and Angus has more reason than most to feel bitter.'

'Like father, like son,' suggested Michael. 'It's only a short time I knew Johnny, but it seems to me he was similarly forgiving.'

'A saint and a hero,' said Angus. 'No two ways aboot it.'

Sam nodded, quietly pleased at the compliments to his son. 'Talking of heroes, Michael, there can't be many officers who'd put themselves out to rescue an ordinary soldier – especially not at the risk of their own lives.'

Farquhar fiddled bashfully with his artificial leg. 'One does what one can.'

'Well, what one can do now,' said Angus, 'is pass that bottle back if aw yir gonnae dae is sit there cuddlin it.'

Michael laughed and took a small drink from the bottle, then offered it to Sam. He took it from him but declined to drink and passed it straight back to Angus. 'Here you are, son. You need it more than me.'

Angus raised the bottle, first to Michael, then to Sam. 'Tae ma three fine friends, two present here the day, the third sadly gone before. As Johnny rightly told the padre, one day soon we'll aw meet again. Here's tae that day.' He drained the bottle and dropped it on the grass beside him.

The three men sat in silence, sombre and saddened, contemplating the immediate past and their uncertain futures, letting the sun set over them and Johnny in the churchyard nearby.

Michael took a small blue box from his jacket pocket. 'Today, Angus, on this very sad day for all of us, I'm going to explain the main reason I decided to seek you out. When I compare myself now with the man I was – the man who stood in that trench full of the certainty and arrogance of privilege – I realize that all the men I personally ordered over the top that day are far more deserving of bravery awards than I ever was.'

Michael opened the little box, lifted the military cross from its blue satin-lined bed and firmly pressed it into Angus's hand. 'This is for you, and for Johnny, and for all your other friends from the Maryhill barracks that didn't make it home.'

Angus examined the medal. Handing it back, he opened his mouth to speak, but Michael held up his hand. 'No, don't say it, Angus. I'm not taking it back.'

Angus smiled. 'Well, ah know better than tae argue wae an officer.' Placing the medal in his lap, he raised his arm in a salute to which Michael responded in kind. 'I accept this military cross on behalf of Private Johnny McVeigh, 21571, Argyll and Sutherland Highlanders, and aw the other lads who cannae be here the day,' he said formally. 'Thank you, Captain.'

'No, Private, thank you.'

Choking with emotion, Sam rose from the bench and walked off into the Big Wood. Angus and Michael lapsed back into thoughtful silence, watching the nurses as they pushed other wheelchair-bound patients from the terrace into the hospital.

'Ah don't mean tae sound ungrateful, Michael, but ye didnae do me any favours that day, ye know. Ye denied ma name its immortal place on a war memorial.'

'Truth is, Angus,' said Michael with a smile for his friend, 'I was shaking so much that had I used the Enfield that morning, I'd most likely have shot your remaining arm off.'

'That's the standard of officer trainin fur ye,' Angus joked. 'Fuckin useless.'

'I know how hard Johnny's death is hitting you, and Sam told me how concerned he is about you.'

Angus shrugged. 'There disnae seem much left for me tae live fur noo that ah've no even got ma wee pal tae look efter. Ah feel totally useless. And alone.'

'You're never alone. You've still got friends and family who love you.'

Angus shook his head, struggling to keep his voice steady. 'So why did Mary no come tae the funeral? She knew how hard it would be fur me.'

'I noticed she wasn't there. I assumed you had agreed on that.'

'Aye, well, maybe one of the weans is sick. Or maybe she was short a money fur the fares. That'll be it, short a money.'

'You should have said if there was a money problem – I would have brought her across myself.'

'But the point is, Michael, that ah never knew she wiznae comin. An its been happenin mer an mer, recently. Ye know, she hasnae brought

Thomas or Marion tae see me in the past month. What kind of a way is that tae treat a husband an father? Even a useless wreck like me!'

Michael put a sympathetic hand on his shoulder. 'Our families take it hardest of all,' he commented. 'Why would they not?'

In a low, faltering voice which Tom had to strain to hear, Angus talked to Michael about his wife and family. He thought Mary the nicest and prettiest girl in his school, and had been bowled over with his luck when he realized she felt as strongly about him. They had been inseparable and neither of them had the slightest hesitation about getting married when she fell pregnant.

By that time, Angus explained, he was working as an apprentice with his father building railway locomotives in the huge engineering sheds in Springburn, Glasgow. They were being shipped to every corner of the globe and there was work aplenty. Once he qualified as a locomotive engineer his weekly wage would be adequate to support himself and his new family.

'Ma mother an faither put us up in Port Dundas. Mary adores them and they her. We were so happy, Michael. An when wee Thomas wiz born ah felt as though ma heart would burst wae the pride an pleasure of it aw.'

Michael sighed. 'I wish I had children. Always thought I had plenty of time. Don't suppose anyone will have a cripple like me now.'

'Don't worry ma friend, yer money'll attract them,' Angus joked. 'Three years after Thomas wiz born, wee Marion arrived. We were still only nineteen – just weans oorsels really. We had two weans tae look efter, but Mary wiz wonderful wae them, a born mother.' He paused, lost in thought, a smile on his face.

'The day ah went tae enlist ah came hame feelin like a hero, aw set tae protect ma family fae the evil Germans. Ma mammy an Mary were ragin. They wept for weeks an ah felt as though ah'd personally wounded them. Ma faither took me tae one side an said he was proud of me. Said he would have gone himsel had he been younger. It was him that encouraged me tae enlist, but he was sensible enough never tae say it in front of ma mammy or Mary. They would have murdered him.'

'Not your fault, Angus, not your father's fault. Nobody's fault except for those who dragged us all into this dreadful war in the first place.'

'Ah'm a burden on them now, Michael. Mary's life's in limbo. You didnae do her any favours that day either – it would have been better for her an the kids if ye had put me oot ma misery. Ah think she wants tae move on. That's why she hardly visits noo. Ah'm jist a reminder of how things might've been.'

'I'm sure she still loves you Angus, but it must be so hard for her.'

'Aye, hard it is when ah look at her an see the regret in her eyes. An now, wae Johnny's death, the last wee bit joy's gone fae ma life. Ah've never once complained tae the nurses aboot the phantom limb pains ah get, cause a knew Johnny suffered it worse than me an he never complained. But it's drivin me fuckin mad, Michael. Every night an every day it feels like some bastart's scaldin ma feet wae boilin water. Feet that are lyin in the mud somewhere on the fuckin Somme. Half the men in there get the same problem. Wae that an shell-shock, it's nae wonder we're aw crabbit bastarts. Ah cannae take any mair.'

'Perhaps you should speak to Mr McEwan about it, but I know from personal experience that there's nothing the surgeons can do. Regarding Mary, might it help if I went and spoke to her? If I told her how much you're missing her visits?'

'It's too late fur that, it's too late fur anything.' His voice shrivelled to the brink of despair.

'Do you want to go back in?' asked Michael as Angus began shivering.

He shook his head and looked his friend in the eye. 'Ah'll tell ye what ah really want.'

Michael's colour drained when Angus formed the shape of a pistol with his hand and pointed it at his right temple.

'Do it, you stupid bastard,' Michael whispered in response, repeating Angus's stark plea to him at the Somme when he lay badly wounded and seemingly close to death.

Angus nodded. 'There's nothin left fur me now, dear friend. Ye've got tae help me bring this misery tae an end.'

CHAPTER EIGHTEEN

AFTER THE VISION, Tom wandered aimlessly along the shore, alone with his dark thoughts and no fit person for company. He phoned Julie to say he wouldn't be coming round as planned and went back to his apartment.

He rose at first light, walked along past South Lodge to the old parish church, and entered the silent graveyard. Nothing stirred, neither bird nor beast. He went straight to an ancient tree dominating a corner of the cemetery, and found the absolute proof that the vision had been so much more than a dream. Below the tree stood three small military-style gravestones. The stone on the right carried the regimental crest of the Argyll and Sutherland Highlanders with the inscription Johnny McVeigh, October 21st, 1917. The stone next to it boasted the proud crest of the Cameron Highlanders and the name Angus McCartney. It was dated December 15th, 1917. Here they lay; if not forgotten, certainly unvisited. Bothering no-one in their final resting place. The sacrificial lambs beneath the canopy of the giant sycamore, its branches extending like the wings of a guardian angel.

Ominously, the gravestones revealed that Angus would die within weeks of his chilling plea to Michael for help to end it all. A welling of emotion gripped Tom's throat as he looked around and saw Erskine Hospital war graves spread everywhere in the centuries-old graveyard. War he was used to, he had played his part in a modern context, but the tragedy of the death of so many fine young men was piercingly raw. Angus and Johnny were only boys in their early twenties, for Christ sake. Somehow, the fact that they had fought and died all those years ago struck home far more than the death and misery he had seen around him in his career – maybe because the men he had fought beside were professional soldiers who had chosen to enlist. Although he knew that many hundreds of thousands of young men had been eager to volunteer when the call went out in 1914, had they volunteered to walk helplessly into the carnage such as he had witnessed at the Somme? It seemed to him nothing less than legalized genocide.

He paid his respects to Angus and the other brave soldiers whose lives had been taken so young and so tragically, and headed back along the avenue to Mar Hall. Deep in thought, he was taken by surprise when a voice called out: 'Hey, big man, ignore your friends, why don't you?' He looked up to see Roddie walking the dogs at the edge of the Big Wood.

'Hey Roddie, didn't see you there. Thought I'd be the only one up at this time.'

'Fancy a brew?'

'Yeah, put the billy on.'

Roddie moved around the kitchen quietly to avoid waking Julie. Tom sat at the big table.

'Here, this'll warm you up. She was at her wits end worrying about you last night. We all were.'

'Sorry, mate. I just couldn't face coming round. I definitely wouldn't have been good company.'

'Want to talk about it?'

'I don't want to burden you, but yes, I would like to or I think I'll go mad.'

Tom outlined his vision of the Somme offensive and the horrors of seeing Angus blown to bits. Going on to describe the vision of Johnny's death and funeral, he inadvertently let slip the fact that he had taken another iboga. Roddie almost went ballistic. 'You took more of that stuff when you were on your own! Christ, I don't believe it. You could've choked to death when you were lying there unconscious. The reason I pleaded with you not to was because of the bad effects it was having, but you just went straight ahead and took it again. Just how irresponsible are you?'

Julie heard the commotion and rushed downstairs. 'Calm down, Dad, calm down. What's happened?'

Contrite and composed, Tom explained. He told Julie to head off for her morning lecture, but she refused.

'You could keep an entire team of psychoanalysts busy for a year,' said Roddie with a smile, attempting to lighten the tense mood. 'War, destruction, death, funerals – God knows what it all means. Everything appears to be connected to events in your life. Perhaps it's you confronting perceived guilt about what happened in Iraq. The very thing that caused the terrible upset to your psyche in the first place.'

'Thank you, Dr Anderson.'

Roddie smiled. 'I'll have you know that your man here has a degree in amateur psychology from the University of Life.'

'Okay, I bow to your superior knowledge. Continue with your diagnosis.'

'Well, the symbolism of death figures prominently – the end of a cycle perhaps – something finally over? Hopefully it indicates a closure; that you've stopped blaming yourself for the death of Donna Mulhearty and the others. We all know that dreams are intimately interconnected with events in the dreamer's life. For example, the poem that you say was recited at Johnny's graveside is actually in the book of Hamish Henderson poems that you borrowed from me some time ago. The thing is, Henderson wrote Lament for the Son during the Second World War. It's impossible for it to have been recited twenty-five years before it was written. It clearly indicates all this stuff is coming to you by way of dreams.'

'Two things I can see wrong with your diagnosis. One: I know for sure that Johnny's death is not the end of the cycle. Two: the iboga is not, as you insist, simply causing dreams. I hear what you say about the poem and, yeah, dreaming is clearly part of it, but can you explain how I've just been able to walk directly to Johnny's grave in an old cemetery I've never set foot in before? And what about the pub? Does The Grapes exist?'

'Yes. I mean no. There was a pub in Old Kilpatrick called The Grapes, but it was demolished years ago.'

Tom closed his eyes and recounted everything he could remember about The Grapes: 'It was in an old sandstone building on the canal side of Dumbarton Road, immediately under where the Erskine Bridge now crosses. You entered it through two sets of double swing doors. Each of the four doors had an opaque glass pane with a bunch of grapes engraved on it. The bar was horseshoe-shaped with a large gantry of bottles at the far end and beer fonts on both sides. At the rear, on the right side of the horseshoe, a big picture window looked out on to a lock gate on the canal. On the left was a huge stone fireplace with a large mirror above and an adjacent wall cavity for storing logs. There was fancy plasterwork and original wooden beams on the ceiling.'

Roddie appeared dumbstruck and, for the first time since Tom had known him, either unwilling or unable to offer an opinion. They sat in silence for some time before he responded. 'You've never been in Old

Kilpatrick before and The Grapes was demolished years before you were born, but you've just described it exactly as it was. It's quite incredible, astonishing, contrary to all reason. I don't know what to say.'

'I agree, it's crazy, Roddie, completely crazy, but I'm telling you; I was at the funeral of my great-grandfather's best friend, Johnny McVeigh, who died sixty years before I was born. The iboga seems to put me into a state of conciousness that exists beyond time and space.'

'I haven't a clue what it does, Tom, but whatever it is I can see it's hitting you hard. At first I was concerned about what might happen to you physically, but I suppose your body can take that. What worries me much more is that you'll develop severe clinical depression through this, if you're not already halfway there.'

Julie grasped his hand. 'That's what worries me too, handsome.'

'Dreams, hallucinations, visions,' said Roddie, 'or whatever it is, there has to be some rational explanation, and for the sake of your sanity it really is time to stop. You are doing yourself no favours. The last thing any of us want is for you to go back to those dark and disturbed places your mind visited when you were in Iraq. Call a halt, son. Please.'

What is a Scottish colloquialism, a manner of speech that signifies nothing, hit Tom like a bullet. No-one had ever called him son. No-one he respected, that is. Yeah, Roddie was a father figure who cared for him. That truth had never struck him before.

'I agree with Dad on this, Tom. It's making you ill.'

'Yes. You're right.' Tom stood up to leave. 'I'm sorry for bringing all my troubles to your door. You've both had quite enough heartache to cope with in the past without me adding to it.'

Roddie shook his head and stood up. 'Listen to me, Tom McCartney. You've been nothing but a big bonus in my life since you came into it. I've had more enjoyment in the last six months through our friendship and discussions than I've had in the last six years. Had you been the son Rachel and I always wanted, we would both have been mighty pleased and mighty proud.'

Roddie put his arms round Tom and gave him a tight hug. No man had ever physically embraced him; no man had ever dared. Tears welled in Julie's eyes, and she got up and squeezed them both.

'Now, if you'll excuse me, I'm going to have to love you and leave you. I'm bushed,' said Tom. This tight huddle of friendship and love was what he so absolutely needed. It said: you belong here, but he could not simply admit that this was what he needed. He couldn't because he didn't consciously realize it. 'Thank you for being so kind to me, both of you. I appreciate it.'

'I'm really worried about him, Dad,' said Julie in a low voice when Tom went to fetch his coat. 'He'll just go back to the hotel now and curl up in bed all day.'

'Aye, he's really down. Why don't you take him out somewhere for a few hours?'

'Right, you heard that,' she said when he returned at that moment. 'We've been ordered out for some fresh air. I'm not letting you sneak back into your pit.'

Roddie looked at Tom. 'She's right. You know she is. You need something to take your mind off it. Be back here for teatime the pair of you and Susan and I will have a nice dinner ready for you.'

Tom held his hands up in submission. 'Okay, okay, if you're gonna gang up on me.'

'Yes we are. Borrow Dad's scarf and gloves and let's go.'

'Give me a clue,' Tom demanded as they crawled along in heavy traffic over the Kingston Bridge in Glasgow, Julie at the wheel. 'I guess we're not going to the Trossachs.'

'Correct! We're going on a magical mystery tour,' she replied, and broke into song:

Roll up, roll up for the mystery tour,
Roll up, roll up for the mystery tour,
Roll up, that's an invitation, roll up for the mystery tour.
The magical mystery tour is waiting, I do hope you enjoy the day.

'I enjoy every day I'm with you,' said Tom, smiling for the first time in days as she finished belting out the old Beatles song.

Thirty miles north of Glasgow, they sped past the motorway sign for the slip road to Stirling. 'I guess Stirling Castle and the Wallace monument aren't on our mystery tour. Pity that. I've always wanted to see them after watching *Braveheart*.'

'Another day, handsome, we'll definitely visit them another day.'

'You're not giving anything away, are you?'

'Nope – where would the mystery be?'

The low winter sun broke through as Julie drove along the western by-pass skirting the fair city of Perth and continued north on the killer A9. Twenty minutes later she turned right off the main road and along a winding single track up into the foothills above the snowline.

Passing an occasional farmhouse, she drove a further few miles on along the hillside road then turned right onto a snow-covered farm track which led to an old ruin. 'Easter Auchnaguie Farm,' she said proudly with a wave of her arm, when they stepped from the car. 'Dad discovered that my mum's Macgregor ancestors lived here and farmed this land 200 years ago. I came with her on her first ever visit and she sat on that big rock by the stream there and cried her eyes out. Right at the very spot our forebears would have drawn their drinking water centuries ago. She was overcome with emotion.'

'It's friggin beautiful,' said Tom with genuine enthusiasm. He sniffed the pure air and looked out over the magnificent vista of Strath Tay with the great mountains of Schiehallion and Ben Lawers rising in the west, their peaks sparkling white against clear blue sky.

Julie led him round the outside of the ruin. Over generations of neglect the roof had fallen in, and the outer wall had succumbed to the effects of the wind and rain. They went in through what they guessed had been the front door. Inside it was easier to see that it had once been a home. Julie put her arms round him and hugged him tight. 'Make love to me,' she whispered.

'Here? In the snow?'

'Yes. Here in the snow.'

Round the fire at South Lodge that evening, Roddie and Susan were delighted to find Tom more relaxed and settled after his day out. Roddie produced a large brown envelope. 'I've got something for you, but I'm afraid it's only on loan.'

They looked on in amusement when he turned the envelope over and over in his hands and looked quizzically at Julie. 'You know what this is?' He tapped it, held it up to the light, shook it close to his ear and put it back on the table. 'Well, I wonder what it is. I'll open it later.' When he'd teased her long enough, he opened the flap and pulled out a sheaf of old photographs. His interest was all the more eager when he realized they were old pictures of the war-disabled at Erskine Hospital. There were seven photographs, dated on the back.

'I got them this afternoon. Jean Marchant has them locked away in the safe,' explained Roddie. 'There are lots more recent photos, but these are the only ones from the early years between 1916 and 1925.'

Tom studied them carefully. Several had been taken of the Grand Hall itself, and one of the workshops with men making the artificial legs on which so many of them relied. Another depicted a ward with just a handful of men sitting on their beds during the day, reading and chatting. It must have been stage-managed, for in a sense the horror show looked almost charming. One was of Field Marshall Earl Haig visiting the hospital in 1919. Men with artificial limbs stood to atten- tion while others sat in wheelchairs and saluted as he reviewed the ranks. In another photograph, a group of wounded men and nurses stood outside the French windows leading from the Grand Hall, an old-fashioned gramophone set up to one side, clearly for some day of celebration. My, what fun you might imagine they had if you'd never been there. Yet another was a view of Mar Hall taken from the formal gardens, with the big cedar in the foreground and a number of patients relaxing on the grass beneath it.

Tom thumbed through the sheaf once, then went back to the begin- ning, peering closely at a picture of patients in the Grand Hall, some playing billiards, some reading newspapers, others posing stiffly for the camera. He stood up and moved over to the table lamp, holding the picture closer to his eyes. 'Hey Roddie, have you got a magnifying glass?'

'Right here,' he said, opening a drawer in the sideboard.

Tom studied the photo through the lens for a long moment. 'That's him,' he said finally, in a low voice. 'I'm sure it is.'

Roddie, Susan and Julie stood behind and peered over his shoulders when he pointed through the lens at a man in a wheelchair, half in shadow towards the back of the room. 'Private Angus McCartney. My great-grandfather. It's amazing really, and hard to believe the coinci- dences that brought me here. I never was one to believe in destiny – but now.' He turned the photograph over. 'It's dated November 1917, so it must have been taken just weeks before he died.' Tom carefully replaced the photographs in the envelope, and thanked Roddie profusely.

'I'm glad you like them,' he said, putting a friendly hand on Tom's shoulder. 'And I apologise for my wee tantrum this morning.'

'Forget it, mate.' He gave Roddie a hug. It felt good.

CHAPTER NINETEEN

Tom was in better spirits after Julie's mystery tour. Following his visions of Colinton Street, and seeing Angus at the Somme, the First World War now intrigued him in a way he didn't anticipate. He could look on it as an insider with family interests and what he saw, what the visions showed, was a misery no history book could convey. Did they do this to every war? Write it up in glorious technicolour like any number of Hollywood movies and ignore the cost in human suffering such as he had witnessed? He knew he would be going back. They would object, call him a fool, point out the dangers, but he was going. He had to know exactly what happened to Angus. What they didn't know wouldn't hurt them.

Once again, he locked his apartment door, switched his mobile off, and took an iboga. He lay down on his bed and attempted to will himself back to the hospital. To his consternation, the vision placed him outside a small, brick-built railway station at the edge of a forest. It was a cold, miserable day with heavy rain and darkness falling. He scanned a cluster of wooden houses around the station for signs of life. It was strangely deserted like some hick town in the outback – without the sun, of course.

Outside a rickety wooden shack by the station entrance, the *Daily Mail* billboard announced: HAIG THROUGH THE HINDENBURG LINE. The old man sitting behind the counter of the tiny shop carried on reading his book when Tom walked in and scanned the newspapers. 'Gains being made in fierce fighting at Cambrai' shouted the front page of the *Daily Express* dated 23rd November 1917. Shelves behind the shopkeeper were sparsely lined with packs of cigarettes and boxes of matches, a few cans of corned beef and assorted brown paper bags of God knows what.

Tom left the shop and, ignoring the sign 'Georgetown NFF Strictly Private', walked in through the open doorway of the deserted railway station. He looked along the single-track line and was amazed to see that the station platform stretched for about 200 metres to his right before curving out of view. Half-way along the platform, a covered walkway ran directly away from it into the forest.

The strain of iron on track caught Tom's attention. Great plumes of black smoke announced the arrival of two massive steam locomotives long before he saw them. Joined together, they hauled a long train of goods wagons tentatively round the curve. He watched awestruck as the immensely powerful engines came snorting through the station like living, breathing beasts, and the platform beneath him trembled. The driver of the second engine looked down from his big open cab, but failed to acknowledge Tom when he waved up at him like a small schoolboy. As fifty-odd wagons clattered past through a cloud cover of smoke and steam, he read the words DANGER HIGH EXPLOSIVES, NFF 4, painted on the side of each.

Five minutes after the explosives, a long passenger train drew into the station and stopped alongside him. It was followed in quick succession by three similar trains which now filled the entire length of the platform. He smiled when a cacophany of sirens and horns blasted in the forested area to his right. The last time he heard such sounds he had scanned the skies above Colinton Street for Zeppelins.

Within minutes, thousands upon thousands of women in working clothes poured from the walkway, hair bound by faded headscarves, thin coats a sop to the biting weather. Several looked ill, their skin a jaundiced yellow. Many lit cigarettes and walked straight on to the carriages, slamming the doors behind them. Others hurried to the little store. There were no 'ladies' in such company.

Tom jumped when the driver of the first train sounded the shrill whistle and a great commotion of smoke and steam blasted out around him. He looked up to see the fireman shovelling coal into the warm orange glow of the firebox, and recalled his Grandpa Shaw speaking with great affection about the steam trains of his childhood. Apart from old film clips on television, he himself had never experienced such sights and sounds. Fuck sake, maybe William and Angus built this beaut. Sparks flew when the engine's big drive wheels spun and struggled for traction on the rails. There was something magical, awe-inspiring, about the great machine, defying physics to pull the laden carriages forward. The red glow from an old paraffin lamp swinging on the back of the end carriage was the sole warning to train drivers travelling behind to keep a safe distance. As the packed passenger train gained pace with a slow metrical rhythm, the red blob gradually receded and rocked away into the night.

Tom walked along to the next train in line, puzzling over the relevance of it all, when the mystery was solved. A group of women hurried back along the platform from the shop, and Mary was among them. They held their collars up against the biting wind to light cigarettes, then stepped into compartments. Tom squeezed in behind Mary, just before the whistle blasted and the train pulled out. The carriages had no corridor and, in each section, sixteen women were crammed onto two hard bench seats. In this compartment, Mary and five others had to stand. Tom felt sick with the stench of Woodbine smoke, dirty wet clothes and stale body odour.

'Another day, another dollar,' sighed Mary, grabbing the overhead luggage rack when the train shuddered over points. 'Ah'm shattered, Sadie. It's bad enough workin five days a week in there, but Erchie Simpson wiz roon oor department the day again askin fur volunteers tae work extra weekend shifts.'

'Aye, oors tae. The lassies gied'm dugs' abuse. "It's awright fur you men" Ah telt him. "You've no got tae go hame efter a hard day's shift in here and make the dinner." He kin get stuffed.'

'The wimmin in D22 telt him tae get lost tae, but ah'm gonnae have tae seriously consider it.'

'Ye've got tae be kiddin, Mary.'

'Believe me, Sadie ah wish a wiz. Ah'm skint efter payin the doactor's fees.'

'Right enough, ah never thoat aboot that, but Thomas's better noo so that's the main thing.'

'Aye, thank God. When ah went tae get'm hame fae Oakbank, the doactor said he wiz a lucky boy tae have survived. He telt me three other weans had died fae diptheria in the same ward that very week. Ah jist pray that Marion disnae get it.'

'Christ, don't even think aboot it, Mary. Ah heard aboot a wummin on another shift losin her wee lassie wae diptheria three weeks ago. Poor soul's back at work an she stauns there every day makin bombs an breking her heart. Ah couldnae cope wae losin a wean. Ah'm glad ah've no gote any. Mind you, that daft bugger wrote tae me last month sayin we wur gonnae start wan the minute he steps aff the boat. It wiz always the first thing oan ees mind.'

'Huvin weans?'

'Naw, huvin sex.'

'They're aw the same. If he's anythin like ma Angus he'll no even gie ye time tae get yer knickers aff before he tries tae get in. Mind you, that wiz then.'

'How izzy, Mary?'

'Christ, don't ask. Like a bag a nails! Nothin pleases him. Last month when Thomas wiz in hospital, ah went oot tae Erskine on ma own an he gied me a shirikin fur no takin Thomas wae me.'

'Did ye no tell him?'

'Naw, ah didnae want tae gie him any extra worries. Ah jist said sorry then kept ma mooth shut an waited till he'd calmed doon. It's no jist that. The train an ferry fares oot tae Erskine cost a fortune. Ah cannae afford tae take the weans wae me every time ah go.'

'It must terrible fur him though.'

'Terrible's no the word fur it. He doted on that boy fae the day he wiz born an it's destroyin him that he's no there tae see him grow up, an teach him tae play fitbaw. He loved the fitbaw did ma Angus. Ah know it sounds daft, but he sometimes thinks he's still got ee's feet. Ah've seen him wae tears in his eyes because ae the pain he feels in the toes. Says it's like they're bein dipped in bilin water.'

'Aye, ah mind readin aboot that in the *Sunday Post*. Phantom pains they caw it, an there seems tae be bugger aw the doactors can dae tae stope it.'

'Nothin. They jist have tae grin an bear it.'

'Has ees faither been oot tae see him yet?'

'Naw. Ah cannae figure oot why cause they used tae be that close. Went everywhere thegither. He'll no even leave the hoose noo. He's no the man he used tae be before Lizzie died.'

'It's a right shame aboot ees pal dyin last month.'

'Wee Johnny. Aye, he'll be missin him bad. Ah didnae get o'er tae see him efter it. That'll be another row.'

Mercifully the train had a straight run through and twenty-five minutes after boarding, Tom followed Mary and Sadie off in Glasgow Central. The hands on the station's big clock were approaching quarter past six when they walked through the heaving crowds and out onto

Gordon Street. Long snaking lines of green and orange tramcars filled the streets, but they walked despite the lashing rain.

Halfway up Renfield Street, Tom recognised a big haberdashery shop as the future employment agency which would lead him to Mar Hall. He had stopped at this exact spot in his BMW waiting for the bubbly Anna.

'See ye in the mornin, Mary,' said Sadie with no enthusiasm when she trudged wearily off along Parliamentary Road. Mary walked across Cowcaddens Road, seemingly oblivious to tramcars approaching fast on each side. Minutes later she passed the Boatmen's Institute on Dobbies Loan and briefly stopped outside Jeannie Spitall's shop. Clearly, she had second thoughts and carried on up Colinton Street and in through the close at 34. 'Ohhhpen. Ohhhpen,' she shouted halfway up. However bad the smell on the stairs still was, it was relatively fresh compared to the packed compartment on the train.

Mary took her sodden coat off and threw it over a chair. Seven-year-old Thomas looked up from a book and gave her a warm smile. Marion, now a pretty little three-year-old with wavy blond hair, greeted her mum and held out her arms to get lifted. 'How's ma wee darlin?' said Mary, swinging her round and round.

'Hungry, mammy. Ah'm hungry.'

Mary glanced at William, her father-in-law, and her smile turned to an expression of disgust when he turned the palms of his hands up and shrugged his shoulders. When she opened the door to the big sideboard, Tom could see that it was empty. 'Jist as well ah didnae buy them sweeties,' she muttered. She took the purse from her sodden coat pocket and carefully counted the coppers. 'Mammy'll get ye a nice big bag a chips fae Orlandi's, hen. Ah'll be back in ten minutes.'

Tom was frustrated that he couldn't tell her to sit down and warm herself by the fire and he would go for the chips. No, not for chips. He would go to the very best restaurant in the city and come back with huge sirloin steaks and fudge cake with fresh cream, and a big box overflowing with fruit and chocolates and cheeses. He saw Mary's eyes glisten with tears when she put her sodden coat back on.

William sat in his wife's favourite old chair by the fire. Tom was shocked to see how markedly his great-great grandfather had aged in the two years since his last iboga visit to Colinton Street. The eyes were dull and the face, which had once favourably belied his age, told a very different story. He was but the ghost of the man he had once been, empty, done, a spent spirit, crushed by the consequences of his own stupidity. Every time he looked at Mary he saw what this war was doing. Should he catch her eye, he saw the bitterness, the unforgiving stare that said 'ya stupid, stupid bastart. Ah telt ye, but no, no. You're a man. You men always know better.' And she was right. He wouldn't cry, but inside he bled the tears of hidden guilt.

Mary came back and the children sat at the table eating chips from their wrappings in old newspapers, together with bread spread thinly with margarine. Mary ate hers on the move while making a pot of tea and pouring four cups. Adding the little sugar that was left to one, she handed it to William who was eating his chips by the fire. 'Ah hope it bloody chokes ye,' she said, without malice. It was a straightforward statement of fact. He simply responded with a brief smile.

Later, when she had tucked the children up in bed under piles of old coats, Mary walked through from the bedroom and slumped in a chair. 'First seat ah've had in the last fourteen hours.'

'Wiz it busy the day again, hen?'

'Busy! Ah think there must be three bloody world wars goin on wae the amount a stuff we're producin. We've got 12,000 wimmin workin in there in shifts roon the clocke seven days a week. The gaffer came roon oor section the day an asked fur volunteers tae work extra week-end shifts, an the lassies nearly lynched him.'

'Aye, ah think there's a big push on tae get it aw o'er by Christmas.'

'Aw o'er by Christmas. Aw o'er by Christmas! Now where in the name a hell have ah heard that before? You listen tae me, we'll be lucky if this war's o'er by the Christmas efter next. The mer shells the workin class boys lob at each other o'er there, the mer money goes intae the pockets ae the warmongers an the merchants of death. Every ounce a cordite we produce is money in their poakets.'

'You've been listenin too much tae that John Maclean.'

Tom saw a flash in Mary's eyes which instantly reminded him of Julie at her angriest. 'John Maclean knows far mer aboot this war than you dae. Just don't get me bloody well started the night again. Ah'm goin tae ma bed. Some ae us have tae get up fur work in the mornin.'

'That's no fair an you know it. Ah'd be first oot that door in the mornin if ah wiz able.'

Mary poured herself another cup of tea, placed the pot back on the range, then lifted it again and refilled William's. 'Aye ah'm sorry. Ah'm tired.'

'Are you goin oot tae Erskine tae visit him at the weekend?' asked William.

'Aye ah'll need tae. Ah've no been since Johnny died, an it's oor anniversary soon.'

'He understands, hen. He knows yer tired workin aw they oors.'

'Now how in the name a hell does he know that cause ah certainly havnae telt him ah'm workin? An since you never visit him, how come you know so bloody much aboot whit he understands an whit he disnae understand? Yer aw very clever, you McCartneys.'

'Angus is clever,' William replied forcefully. 'He was always a clever boy. An you know ah've no been well enough tae visit him since Lizzie died.'

'He wisnae very clever when he decided tae go tae France an get blawn tae bits.' Mary waited in vain for a response. 'Well? Wizzi? An you – no stoppin him. He might have listened tae you.'

William gazed at the fire for some time before responding quietly. 'It wiz ma fault he went.'

'Whit?'

'It wiz ma fault. The night we got aff the tram on Dobbies Loan an the wummin handed him a white feather, ah told him that ah'd have been away tae fight for ma country long before then if ah'd been young enough like him.'

Tom felt the tension in the air rising as Mary sat silent for a moment before exploding with frustrated rage.

'It wiz you! It wiznae they wimmin wae their white feathers that made him change his mind. It wiz you, ya auld erse!' She moved to strike him but stopped and began sobbing violently.

William tried to say sorry and placed his hand on her shoulder, but she slapped it away. 'Bugger off. Don't you ever speak tae me or ma weans again. Ever! Ye'r responsible fur their daddy bein blawn tae bits. Him an me will never sit on a sunny beach in Australia because you couldnae keep yer big, stupit mooth shut.' Mary got up and walked to the window. She stood watching sleet lash down into the middens and wept. She had had enough. She had tholed enough.

'That's it!' She finally turned to face William, wiping tears and snotters from her face. 'Bella telt me last week ah could move in wae her an she'd watch the weans when ah'm at work. You, mister, are nothin but a big, stupit, lazy useless auld…'

William agreed and began to cry himself. 'Ah wiz taken in wae aw the jingoism an propaganda. Ah'm responsible for oor Angus lyin there like that in hospital for the rest ae his days. That's why ah cannae go an face him. Ah'm responsible as well for ma Lizzie dyin. She jist couldnae go on livin efter whit happened tae her wee boy. Ah'm sorry, hen,' he sobbed. 'Ah'm so sorry!'

Mary said nothing. She put on her soaking wet coat and slammed the door on the way out.

Tom could see it all, how the war had ripped the heart from not only Angus, but his entire family. He looked out of the window at the stinking middens below and wept along with his great-great-grandfather. William wasn't to know, was he? It was all to be so easy. Everyone had been fooled by the headline hopes. Everyone now suffered except for those who were making a fortune. Is that how wars always work? Misery for most, fortunes for the few? Who called the shots? Who needed wars? Industrialists, arms dealers, oil magnates? No, surely not. That's just conspiracy theory, isn't it?

Half an hour later, Mary came back, drenched, shivering and red-eyed. She put boiling water and tea leaves into the teapot, stirred it, and made two cups. 'Right!' she said, handing a cup to William. 'Ah'm fed up tae the back teeth wae you just sittin there week in week oot feelin sorry for yersel while ah'm knockin ma pan in aw day in that bomb factory. A want ye tae…'

'Ah hear ye, hen,' William interrupted, 'ah'm sorry. Ah know yer doin yer patriotic duty, ah understand.'

'*Patriotic duty?*' exclaimed Mary, incredulously. 'Christ, ah don't believe it. Patriotic duty my arse. Ye swallied their lies aboot the need fur war, an noo ye've swallied their propaganda aboot us wimmin doin our "patriotic duty" an "supportin the war effort" an "workin for victory". Well let me tell ye this, mister, the thousands a wimmin ah work wae are there fur one reason, and one reason only; tae keep some money comin in tae save their weans fae starvin. We work aw day makin bombs in there for the lowest wage the government can get away wae. They say the men are the heroes, but tell me this, dae the men understand whit it's like take knock their pan in in a factory fur ten hoors then come hame an huv tae start cookin meals an clean a hoose – if there's anythin tae cook that is? Dae they understand whit it's like tae dae that and try tae haud a family thegither on their own when there's a bloody war goin on? Dae they understand whit it's like fur mothers an wives tae sit starin intae the fire every night, wonderin if a telegram's gonnae be delivered in the mornin? Ah don't bloody think so.'

William sat with his head bowed as Mary continued to tear shreds from him. 'Don't gie me any mer shite aboot me leavin ma weans an goin oot there in the freezing cauld every mornin because it's ma patriotic duty. If you're just gaunny carry on as before, then we're leavin. If ye want us to stay, there's gaunny have tae be changes. You'll get aff yer erse an help me. If ah'm oot at work fae seven in the mornin till seven at night tae bring some money in, you've got tae look efter the weans. Ah do not mean ye just sit on yer erse an look at them. Ah mean ye read books tae them. Ah mean ye take them oot tae the park an play wae them. Ah mean ye wash them in the sink when they come in, and ah mean get their dinner ready aye, an mine tae fur me comin hame. Ye tell them a wee bedtime story the nights their mammy's too tired. Now dae ye really understand whit ah'm sayin tae ye?'

'Aye, hen. Ah dae. Ah understand.'

CHAPTER TWENTY

Tom and Julie wandered hand in hand through the huge St Enoch shopping mall in Central Glasgow. 'After the desert then four months in hospital in Iraq, I loved this place when I came to Scotland. I was like an excited kid at Chrissie time.'

'Yeah, Mum and I used to do our Christmas shopping here. On one of our days out together, she told me that this place had once been the old St Enoch railway station. She recalled being a wee girl standing on a platform right here with her mum and dad when they were going to Saltcoats at the Glasgow Fair. She started crying and came over all emotional on me.' Tears welled in Julie's eyes. 'I miss her so much.'

Tom pulled her in close when she began sobbing. 'Come on,' he said leading her to a coffee shop. 'Let's have a latte and a cake. Nothing like a sticky bun to cheer you up.'

Julie worked her way through a slice of chocolate cake, still watery-eyed, but under control, and Tom encouraged her to talk about her mother.

'It was such a shock when she died. There I was, just sixteen, and I found her lying on the avenue beside the big wood.'

'It must have been devastating for you.'

'Yes. I have to admit I took it hard. I went wild for a time. Started mixing with a rough crowd at school and got into a bit of bother. I left school, no, I should tell you the truth. I got expelled! Mum must have been turning in her grave.'

'Fuck sake! What did Roddie have to say about that?'

'He barely seemed to notice. He was so completely stunned by Mum's death himself that he hardly spoke and hardly ate. It was a full year before he began functioning again, and it was like I'd lost both parents. I felt it was my fault and that Dad wouldn't talk to me because he was blaming me.'

Tom reached across the table and took her hand. 'How on earth could you blame yourself for that?'

'I believed that if I hadn't been laughing and messing about with my friends after school, I might have been there in time to get help.' Tears filled her eyes again. 'The doctor said that she'd only been lying there a few minutes before I came along.'

'Ah, the what ifs,' said Tom, remembering the times he had insisted to Brigadier Nimmo that it was his fault Donna Mulhearty was dead. The Brigadier had told him he was being self-indulgent. 'Beating yourself up about something that was no fault of your own – or even if it was your fault – is a pointless exercise. You have to put it behind you and move on.' Tom heard himself repeat the words, but did he really mean them?

'Your mum died instantly Julie, even the best surgeons in the world couldn't have helped if they'd been there on the spot.'

She looked at him questioningly. 'How do you know that?'

'Your dad told me about it one night in Mar Hall.'

Julie sighed. 'Yeah, Dr McKenzie told me that too, but it's a hard thing to accept. It was only thanks to Carole and Andy Hutton that I got back on track again. They were so kind and patient with me and Dad. I eventually got a job as a ward orderly in the hospital, but two years of cleaning shitty bums and bed pans was more than enough.'

'Strewth, two weeks would have been more than enough for me.'

'Yeah, it wasn't particularly pleasant for me or the men. Carole persuaded me to pack it in and go to college full time to get my Highers. If it hadn't been for her I'd never have gone to university. Andy would sit for hours on end with Dad, the pair of them barely speaking a word, but he was there for him. It helped knowing that people cared.'

Her words struck Tom forcibly. 'Your dad never mentioned that, but it explains why he's been such a help to me in my own dark periods. He's been there himself.'

'Yes, and we both owe Andy and Carole so much.'

'How do you feel about him remarrying?'

'Between you and me, I'm surprised how difficult I'm finding it. Susan's a lovely woman, and I know she's good for Dad. But even so, deep down I can't help feeling that he shouldn't replace Mum. I feel guilty, disloyal to Dad and to Susan for thinking that – but at the same time it feels like the ultimate disloyalty to Mum.'

'I guess that's only natural.'

'I do my best to hide it – you don't think they realise, do you?'

'I'm sure your dad understands you far better than you think he does. And Susan, I'm sure, doesn't believe she'll ever be a replacement for your mum. She probably finds it as difficult as you do to work out her role in relation to you.'

'I hadn't really looked at it that way.'

'You know, I'm sure she'd like it if you talked about your mum to her. That might help both of you, and you can then move on without having the ghost of your mother affecting your relationship.'

Julie nodded. 'That's a good idea. Maybe I'll take her out for dinner tonight since you and Dad are both working.' She lifted Tom's hand to her lips and kissed it. 'You know, you're not as stupid as you look, McCartney. No wonder I love you.'

'And you're a cheeky young sheila,' said Tom, leaning across the table to kiss her. 'Now, let's go and get my kilt fitted?'

At 3 a.m. the following morning, Roddie walked into the Grand Hall with a pot of tea and a plate piled high with sandwiches. 'Tea's up,' he said quietly into his mobile phone, and laughed when Tom appeared, almost instantly, bounding up the steps through reception with his phone at his ear.

'All quiet out there?'

'As a mouse,' replied Tom, rubbing his hands. 'Winter's here with a vengeance. Must be about minus three. It's a beautiful crisp starry night, though, so I took a quick run round the estate in the jeep. Up around Lord Blantyre's seat is extra special tonight. I can understand why it was his favourite place on the estate.'

'What's your's?'

'South Lodge,' replied Tom, before stuffing an entire sandwich into his mouth.

'Look at the table manners of the man,' said Roddie, shaking his head in mock disgust.

'Sorry, old habits and all that. Out in the wilds, with no one watching us eat, we just bogged in with no thought for etiquette. It was fuel, Roddie, nothing else. Fill the tank up as quickly as possible. I guess I'm bad, but the table manners of some of the guys in my patrol, Shortarse especially, made pigs look refined. I promise I'll be beyond reproach at the wedding and not embarrass any of you.'

'I'll be on my best behaviour too, and far too nervous to be worrying about what you're up to. Julie tells me you ordered your kilt.'

'Yeah, and I have to say it was a strange experience. Never dreamed

I'd ever be wearing Highland dress. It was only to please Julie that I agreed. God knows what the lads in my patrol would have to say about it. There'd be much piss-taking. But Julie insists it looks great on me, and it's surprisingly comfortable.'

'A convert, eh? Glad to hear it.'

'Tell me the score regarding what to wear under it? Julie insists that nothing is worn. She is teasing me, isn't she?' Tom took another sandwich from the plate and, much to Roddie's amusement, nibbled it daintily with his little finger extended.

'It's supposed to be tradition that a true Scotsman wears nothing under his kilt,' said Roddie, 'but it's one tradition that Roddie Anderson won't be following on his wedding day.'

A winter sun struggled to break through as the guests arrived. A piper in full Highland dress slowly paced back and forth playing a medley of tunes at the front of the old stables building. The beaming Australian usher escorted guests from the car park to the wedding room. 'No, not a stitch,' he replied when the hairdressers from Susan's salon giggled at his massive hairy legs and asked if he was swinging free under the kilt. By a few minutes before three, the bride's scheduled arrival time, he had everyone seated.

When the 1934 Austin 16/6, with its gleaming burgundy coachwork, carried Susan through the archway into the quadrangle, the tower clock clearly showed three-fifteen. Being late was her God-given right; every woman's God-given right. The guests clapped, cheered and stamped their feet when Susan's son escorted her in to stand beside Roddie. Tom realised that this would be quite unlike any other wedding he had been to.

A pretty, middle-aged lady stepped towards Susan and Roddie and waited till the noise settled before speaking.

'Thank you, friends. Please be seated. Good afternoon everyone and welcome. My name is Anne Baxter and I am a celebrant of the Humanist Society of Scotland.'

The service was short and simple, but very moving. When Susan and Roddie exchanged the vows of commitment they had personally composed, the deep affection they felt for each other was palpable. Tom felt a lump in his throat.

Anne Baxter continued: 'In the peace and tranquillity of this beautiful place, let us all think for a moment of the step that Susan and Roddie are now taking together. I'm sure that you will all want to join me in wishing for their union to grow in strength and their love to deepen throughout the coming weeks and months and years. They already understand the great joy that comes from giving and sharing; may that understanding continue to grow, and may all of their hopes and dreams be realised – as individuals and as a couple.'

Tom slid his arm round Julie's shoulders. She smiled up at him, her eyes moist with tears, and he was struck once again by the certainty that the deep love he felt for this beautiful woman was mutual.

Cheering and clapping erupted as the ceremony ended. The piper struck up outside and Anne led the newlyweds over to a table to sign the marriage schedule. She kissed Susan and Roddie, wished them all the best, then turned to the gathering. 'And now folks, it's time to party! I have no doubt you will enjoy the rest of the day's festivities as you go on to celebrate here in this beautiful place, and I hope that you will enter fully into the spirit of the occasion by eating, drinking and generally being merry. I have a feeling that you won't let me down on that one!'

'I'll never remember all their names,' Tom whispered to Julie after she had proudly introduced him to yet another group of her relatives.

'Jist kid oan yer fae Glesca an caw aw the men Jimmy an aw the wimmin "hen",' she said, with a broad Glasgow accent. Just then, the genuine article appeared. 'Jules, ma wee darlin, ye've broken ma heart. Here was me aw set tae go down on ma knees and propose tae ye, but ye'r here with this big handsome fella.'

'Can I have a look at the ring before I decide, Davie? If it's a massive diamond sparkler, I might accept.' Julie kissed the good-looking man, and threw her arms round him. 'Let me introduce you to Tom McCartney. And this, Tom, is Davie Kirkwood. You know – the Davie Kirkwood.'

'Pleased to meet you at last, Davie, I've heard all about you. Julie's told me you were the star pupil at the uni.'

Davie gave a big booming laugh, 'I'm no sure the lecturers would agree with that.'

'Tom's an old soldier, Davie, so he has a special interest in the history of warmongering. I was telling him that you know more about it than any man he's likely to meet.'

'And this old soldier sure would be interested in discussing it with you,' said Tom, 'but the womenfolk have warned us that there's to be no talk about politics or anything serious today.'

'Well, I think it's high time two of my favourite men got to know each other.' Julie looked at her watch. 'I'll need to go and mingle, so you're both excused for an hour before we sit down for the meal.'

Tom took an immediate liking to Davie. His Glasgow accent, cropped sandy hair, and huge, coarse hands gave the initial impression that he was as hard as nails – a rough diamond, but he was the type Tom had warmed to when he first arrived in Scotland – the genuinely friendly Glaswegian; full of fun and banter, no ego on display, no pretension.

'Is there nae beer in this place?' asked Davie. 'Champagne's no the right tipple for a Gorbals man.'

'Follow me,' said Tom, heading for the bar.

Julie and Tom waved the last of the guests off, and settled some relatives into Mar Hall. They were tipsily making their way along to the lodge in pitch darkness.

'What a day, what a night!' said Tom. 'Best time I've had in years. Well, not quite.'

'Yes,' Julie agreed. 'The singer and the band were fantastic. I think we could call it a successful Scottish wedding. Didn't you think Dad and Susan looked so happy when they were driven away?'

'Well they would do – they've left us all the clearing up to do tomorrow!'

Julie went up on tiptoe to kiss him. 'You do know Dad thinks the world of you, don't you?'

'Yes, I do, and it's mutual. He, and you, have transformed my life.'

'And you mine.'

Tom was up early. He demolished an enormous breakfast of sausage, black pudding, bacon and eggs, then gave Julie poached egg on toast in bed. 'Well, Miss Anderson, time you got up and set to work. We've a busy day ahead, and remember we've a guest for dinner.'

'I knew you'd like him.'

'Yeah, he seems a decent bloke.'

'Davie is a decent man, one of the best. It's been a long hard struggle for him, but he's getting there. He left school and served his time as a gardener with the Glasgow Parks department before packing it in to go to uni.'

'That explains why he's a bit older than you.'

'He was one of the mature students in our first year and we just seemed to click. I took a gap year and pissed about, but Davie kept his head down and got on with it. He was one of only two in my original year to get first-class honours.'

'Clever as well as decent.'

'Very clever. He was miles ahead of everyone, especially on the First World War. He's doing a PhD now.'

'What's that?'

'Doctor of Philosophy.'

'Wow! You would never imagine it, speaking to him.'

'No, he's completely down to earth with no airs or graces. Says he's a working-class boy and proud of it.'

'How do you become a doctor of philosophy?'

'You need to get a good honours degree then stay on at uni to do original research on your chosen subject – in his case the First World War – then write it all up in a thesis. It takes three years, and at the end you're awarded the Doctor of Philosophy degree.'

'Good on him. I'm impressed. He never mentioned any of that, but he was talking a lot about his ex.'

'Yeah, he was married for about seven years, but unfortunately they split up. It's a real shame because he was upset and I know it still hurts him. Sandra has custody of their six-year-old boy. Davie joined Dad and I when we went down to London for a big Iraq demonstration. They share a love of gardening. Dad thinks he's a gem.'

'Davie, it's you!' Julie beamed as she opened the door and threw her arms round him.

'What a welcome from a beautiful woman.'

'Still on the tools, I see,' said Julie when they sat down at dinner.

Davie turned his big, rough calloused hands over by way of confirmation. 'Sure am, Jules.'

'Sorry, you've got me confused here,' said Tom. 'You're working as a gardener? I thought you were at uni doing a PhD.'

'Aye, but ah still do gardens in the evenins an weekends. The research grant is peanuts, and an estranged wife and a wean to provide for doesnae come cheap. So needs must.'

'It's a crying shame!' Julie protested. 'It took you two years to get the qualifications needed to get into university, four years for a degree, and now three for the doctorate and you still have to dig gardens for a living! It's not a shame, it's a fucking disgrace.'

'Whoa right there, Jules. There are a lot worse things ah could be doin. Somebody suggested teachin!'

'Aye, me too,' she said with a melodramatic shudder.

'Ah hope this big romance isnae keepin you away from your studies.'

'No,' said Tom, immediately. 'She's been studying and working her little socks off since the term started. I make sure of that. I can see another first-class honours on the horizon.'

'More wine or coffee, anyone?' asked Julie, keen to change the subject away from Tom's preposterous suggestion.

'Nae disrespect tae your excellent choice of red,' Davie replied with a cheeky grin, 'but wine's no really ma cup a tea – if you see what ah mean. Ah wonder if the Golf Inn still serves real ale? It's a while since ah was last in there.'

The less than subtle hint was taken and they were soon carrying pints of Harviestoun's Bitter and Twisted through to the snug with its blazing coal fire.

'Nectar,' Davie enthused. 'Pure nectar.'

'Do you still see your boy?' Tom asked.

'Callum, sure, and Sandra too. At least she's talkin tae me again, so who knows?'

'Good to hear that,' said Julie. 'Try and make more time for her, and take her flowers. You can acquire them from yon big gardens you landscape in Newton Mearns.'

'Aye, you're right. To be honest, lack of time thegither was the reason it aw went pear-shaped. With me at university and studyin, then havin tae work weekends for money, we were like ships that passed in the night. It basically took o'er my life and ah shut her and the wean out. That first-class honours came at the cost of a marriage. It was a big mistake. It would have been better all round if ah'd just contented maself workin for the Parks department back then. Ah still love her, you see,' added Davie, surprised at his own frankness – and somewhat embarrassed by it.

Julie rubbed his hand. 'Well, I'm sure Sandra still loves you too. More of your time, some gentle coaxing and who knows?'

Davie laughed his infectious laugh. 'Flowers, time an coaxin. Christ, ye're a right wee marriage guidance counsellor, Anderson.'

'What made you decide to study history?' asked Tom, eager to change the topic to what really interested him.

Davie picked up the empty glasses. 'Let me get a round in before ah answer that. Ah'll no have any more maself since I'm drivin.'

'Stay the night at the lodge, why don't you?' Julie invited. 'Have a few drinks.'

It was a no-brainer. 'Thanks, Jules. That sounds good to me.'

Davie returned from the bar with three pints of foaming beer. 'Why study history? Well, it goes back tae ma school days. Ah wasn't really interested until we got a new history teacher called Mr Hunt. He was the first teacher ah actually sat an listened to and he opened ma eyes and mind tae a lot of things. Ah suppose he's the main reason for ma interest in the subject.'

'Good onya, Mr Hunt.'

'Yeah, he was a good man. He asked me tae do a project on the First World War where ah had tae list the names an addresses of aw the men from our district that perished in the trenches. Then ah had tae get an old Gorbals street map an mark wee red crosses where they lived. It shocked me, absolutely shocked me, when it was complete. Every street in the Gorbals was covered in red crosses. One poor mother in Cumberland Street lost three sons. Christ Almighty, can ye imagine the pain an heartache in that house?'

'Horrendous,' agreed Tom. 'I can understand why that made a big impact, but why did it take you so long to go to uni?'

'Ah left the school at sixteen, got a job, got a wife, got a wean. That's what most of us did. Mr Hunt sparked the interest, but readin books on the First World War remained a pastime. Ah cannae explain why, but when ah was about twenty-five ah developed a real hankerin tae go tae university. Believe me, it was a dream come true when ah got that degree.'

Julie nodded. 'And you're well on the road now to the PhD. Dr David Kirkwood, Doctor of Philosophy. Sounds good.'

'Sounds more than good to me,' said Tom. 'Sounds bloody impressive.'

'Yeah, it is impressive,' Julie agreed. 'It means a few more years struggling without a decent wage coming in, Davie, but it'll be worth all the effort.'

'Ah hope so. Ah love the research an the writing but, at the end of the day, the professors could read ma thesis an chuck it in the bin. It might be too radical, too controversial for them. Only time will tell. What do you see on your horizons, Tom? It cannae be easy for a sodjer tae adjust to civvy street?'

'No, it's been a long bumpy ride.' Tom went on to give Davie a potted history of his life since the day on the Amman road. Julie was surprised at how frankly he spoke about his mental health problems and heroin addiction. When he outlined the iboga visions, Davie fired off what seemed like a thousand questions.

'Well,' said Tom when the pub bell rang for closing time, 'what do you make of all that?'

'You've blown me away with this stuff, Tom,' said Davie, seriously. 'When's your next trip? Have you got plenty of these capsules, because ah'm comin with you?'

'Mind an tell Roddie ah wiz askin fur him,' said the barman as he coaxed his last three customers out through the Golf Inn door and closed it against the biting wind and lashing rain.

Julie hooked out an elbow to each man. 'Grab a wing, chick.' They left the village lights behind and walked into inky blackness on the old ferry road.

'Gie's a song, Jules,' said Davie. 'But for Christ's sake, no a Barry Manilow number.'

Julie felt like singing. The wind was whipping against her face, the icy rain running down her neck, but she felt safe and had a warm, contented glow inside. She began to sing 'It's a long way to Tipperary', and the men immediately joined in.

The following morning they sat in the kitchen drinking strong coffee and nursing hangovers. 'Ah cannae dig gardens when the ground's so wet,' was Davie's excuse for taking the day off. He asked if they could go along to the old churchyard to see the graves of Johnny and Angus.

'Incredible as it sounds, I was actually at Johnny's funeral,' said Tom, looking solemnly at the small, simple headstone. 'I saw him being buried here almost ninety years ago. His dad, Sam, stood ashen-faced on the exact spot you're standing right now. Have you any ideas, Davie? Can you come up with any explanation for it? Roddie insists it's down to the iboga inducing vivid dreams. Julie reckons I'm hallucinating with it.'

'That would certainly seem tae be the logical conclusion,' agreed Davie, 'but last night ye mentioned something about a pub in Old Kilpatrick contradictin that explanation.'

'Yes, just before Johnny died, Angus and Michael went across on the ferry to The Grapes. In the vision, I was in there with them. When I discussed it with Roddie he turned sheet white like he'd seen a ghost himself.'

'You must've been there at some time in the past an forgotten about it,' Davie suggested. 'Half-pissed like we were last night.'

'No, no, Davie, you've missed the point. The Grapes was in an old tenement block demolished a long time ago. One of the piers of the Erskine Bridge stands on that very spot. The bridge was built years before I was even born, so it's totally impossible for me to have been in that pub or know what it was like. Yet, according to Roddie, I described it in fine detail.'

Tom and Julie stood quietly, awaiting Davie's response.

He shook his head. 'There's got to be some rational explanation for it. Look Tom, ah'm no really in tae ghosts or supernatural stuff.'

'No. And neither am I. I haven't a bloody clue what the answer to all this is. I took the iboga to help get me off that methadone shit I was hooked on, not to go swimming around in some supernatural soup that took me beyond time and space.'

Julie tugged Tom's arm. 'I'm getting cold shivers running up and down my spine, standing here talking about ghosts. Let's discuss it at home over nice bacon butties.'

'To be honest, ah've got no explanation tae offer you about the visions,' said Davie. 'Ah'd like to hear more about the African tribes using it to visit the lands of their dead ancestors. Ah was raised a Roman Catholic – altar boy, the lot – but jettisoned it as mumbo-jumbo when ah was about sixteen. Ah like tae have hard factual evidence for somethin before ah'll accept it. Meetin a ghost doesnae quite fit in there.'

'I'm surprised you're so dismissive, Davie,' said Julie. 'You're the one who told me about Samhuinn?'

'Sa what'? asked Tom.

'Samhuinn. It's an ancient Celtic festival. On Ben Ledi we talked about the Beltane festival being held on the first of May to celebrate the arrival of summer. Samhuinn is exactly six months later to mark the summer's end and the arrival of the long dark winter nights.'

'Sorry sweetheart, I'm not following the logic here.'

'It was the most magical night of the year. They believed the veil that separates our world from the underworld was at its thinnest on the thirty-first of October, and they could communicate with the spirits of their dead ancestors. They honoured and respected them by laying out extra food and places round the table. It was like an invitation to them to return for a meal with their loved ones. "The Feast of the Dead", they called it. The custom was simply disguised and adapted by Christians as Halloween, with all its spooky ghost stories.'

'"Feast of the Dead"? Sounds pretty morbid,' said Tom.

'It was far from morbid. They believed death is a happy occasion and not to be feared. I have to admit, though, that I find the happy bit hard to understand after experiencing the terrible pain when Mum died.'

'Yeah, me too,' Tom agreed. 'I would have poo-pooh-ed all this a year ago, but not now.'

Davie nodded. 'The Buddhist equivalent of Samhuinn comes on the fifteenth night of the seventh lunar month – the month of joy. It's astonishin how similar it is tae the ancient Celtic custom.'

'Yeah, I think that was the ceremony I saw once when I was in Malaysia with the SASR. The locals said the ghosts and spirits of ancestors would visit them that day, and they laid on big feasts and gifts. It's an extension of their strong belief in filial piety where individuals respect and love their parents and look after them in old age.'

'Good God!' exclaimed Julie. 'Filial piety! I'm impressed.'

Tom looked chuffed 'Yeah, but being orphaned at an early age meant it was something I never personally experienced. One of the things that struck me about you was the love and respect you have for your dad and for your mum.'

'And for you,' said Julie, leaning over to kiss him. 'I'm sorry I've been so dismissive of your experience with the iboga. Don't ask me how to explain it, but it's fascinating.'

Davie agreed: 'Like you, Julie, ah don't have a rational explanation. It goes against everythin that's now ingrained in me tae say this, but maybe it just has tae be accepted that there isn't one.'

Tom smiled. 'You're both absolutely spot on. God only knows why or how it all happens, but I assure you it does. Like you, Davie, I was never a big believer in ghosts or Santa Claus or the tooth fairy, but this is for real and I just accept it for what it is. It's mind-blowing.'

'It is that, and if it's possible for us tae somehow go back in time tae visit the world of our dead ancestors, why shouldn't it be possible for them tae come forward through time tae visit us at Samhuinn?'

'Many other ancient cultures clearly believe it is,' said Julie. 'They show great reverence and respect for the wisdom of the ancestors, and believe that they actually watch over us, protect us, and guide us through life. I'm absolutely certain my mum watches over me.'

'Before all this I'd have said "bollocks" to that, sweetheart, but the strange thing is, after the visions I now have this wacky feeling that I'm being protected and guided by some invisible force. It's like I'm now on a path that I was destined to walk: the horrors in Iraq; the deaths of the anti-war activists; my subsequent mental illness leading me to the beauty of Mar Hall; the joy of finding you.'

'I'm glad you took that path.'

'I disliked peaceniks, hated them if the truth be told, and actually came here to get away from a family of peaceniks. Then, fuck me, do I not end up in Scotland and find myself in love with one, and embraced into the bosom of a family of peaceniks. Is this all meant to be, or is it utterly random?'

'That's a profound question man has been askin for thousands of years,' said Davie

'My father was lost at sea in a typhoon in the South China Sea. When I was a youngster someone told me that a butterfly flapping its wings in the Amazon jungle could be responsible for a typhoon on the other side of the world, and for much of my childhood I wondered if he would've been okay if only some bird had eaten that butterfly.'

Tom fell silent and searched Davie's eyes for any hint of scepticism or alarm. He found none. 'Between you and me, after my problems in Iraq, then these visions, I pretty well convinced myself I was suffering from some kind of psychosis. Answer me honestly here, mate, do you think I'm some sort of basket case?'

'Ah'm no a psychiatrist, Tom, but ye seem like one of the most grounded blokes ah've ever met.'

'Well, thank you for that vote of confidence.'

'Nae bother, pal. Your experiences wae that stuff are totally fascinatin. Julie's told me a lot about the old hospital, but listenin tae your visions brings it aw tae life for me. Ah'd love tae see the place sometime.'

'Sure, no problem. I'll give you a guided tour this afternoon.'

'Hmm, maybe not a good idea,' said Julie. 'Jean Marchant's duty manager this week and you know what she's like.'

'Yeah, you're right. Sorry, Davie, can we make it another day?'

'Of course.'

'It might be best late on when most of the staff are away home,' said Julie. 'You and Dad can give him a proper tour then. Davie's a night hawk anyway.'

'Good idea. Come over any night that suits you, but phone first to check we're on duty.'

CHAPTER TWENTY-ONE

TOM SAT AT HIS COMPUTER by the apartment window, constructing his family tree. He typed in the date of Angus and Mary's marriage, and it registered with him for the first time that Angus had died on their wedding anniversary. The date on his gravestone, 15th December 1917, was exactly seven years to the day they had wed in Cowcaddens parish church. There had been speculation in the McCartney clan for ninety years and, for good or ill, it was time to discover the truth about his death. The rumour mill had turned long enough. He emailed Slovenia and ordered another six iboga capsules.

Ten days before Christmas 2004, the eighty-seventh anniversary of Angus's death, Tom locked the apartment door and took one of the new batch of capsules. Concentrating hard, and willing himself back to the hospital, he called up the memory of the men being entertained by the concert party with the pretty Emily and her battleaxe mother. Slight nausea passed. He sank deeper and deeper under the influence of the iboga, and the Grand Hall appeared. It was cold, miserable and depressingly dark and colourless in the low light of winter struggling through the tall windows. Outside, snow lay in the garden and on the vast canopy of the cedar. Raised voices echoed round the huge room from a group of disabled men shouting obscenities and arguing over Rangers and Celtic. Angus was sitting in his wheelchair by the French windows, talking to Michael Farquhar.

'She's no comin, Michael. She cannae make it any plainer than that, can she?'

Michael looked at the floor with a pained expression. 'I'm sure there's a reason why she can't be here.'

'Ach, we both know the reason. Just look at me.'

The two men sat staring out at the gardens before Angus made a decision. 'Right! Come on, we're no sittin here aw day. Take me fur a pint an ah'll celebrate ma anniversary withoot her.'

Heavily wrapped against a chill wind, the pair set off on the path along the river. When they reached the slip, a flurry of snow momentarily obscured the ferry waiting on the other side for a line of cargo ships to pass. When it finally reached them, Michael gripped the wheelchair firmly and limped down the wet and dangerous slip to board. Twenty minutes later they entered the welcome warmth of The Grapes.

'Hey lads,' called out a man. 'There's space here, Michael.' He wheeled Angus over and they settled themselves amongst a group of older men sitting drinking round the roaring coal fire.

'It's good tae see you again, boys,' said Robert the barman when he came over with pints and warmly shook their hands. 'I'm very sorry to hear about your friend Johnny dyin.'

'Aye, he's sorely missed aboot the place.'

'Are ye keepin okay yourself? You're looking thinner since ye were last in?'

'Ah've been a wee bit under the weather. No eatin much, you know how it is.'

'Well, that doesnae stop ye drinkin,' added one of the group, 'a whisky tae warm you up, lads?'

Michael thanked him. 'It's very kind of you, thanks, Jimmy, but for once you must let us pay and buy a round for you.'

'Uh uh,' replied Jimmy shaking his head and pulling a handful of coins from his pocket. 'Ye know the rules ae The Grapes. Not one of our Erskine war heroes is tae pay for his drink.'

'Aye,' agreed a third man, emptying his glass. 'Or we'll have tae get Robert tae bar ye – isn't that right?'

'That's right, boys. You've tae allow us tae show our appreciation – no argument,' said Robert.

Good intentions were translated into rounds of drinks. The Grapes regulars had them both 'well oiled' with three pints of best Alloa ale and three double whiskies, before they were allowed to don their heavy coats and leave. The mood was light and convivial, but behind the sugar-coated bonhomie there was a darker purpose. Angus leaned over and spoke to Michael meaningfully in a low voice.

Michael looked anxiously at him as if needing confirmation, 'Are you sure that is wise?'

'Please,' he looked gravely at Michael. 'Today's no like any other.'

Michael grasped Angus's hand and squeezed it in a private show of empathy, then went to the bar and spoke to Robert. The barman winked when he came over and slipped a gratis bottle of Johnnie

Walker inside Angus's coat. 'Take care on the way back, lads. It's fairly iced over out there now.'

The return journey presented even greater danger, for the alcohol made Michael unsteady on the slippery ground. Wheeling Angus's chair down to board the boat, he lost control and they slithered down, inches from the edge of the slip and the black, ice cold, river below. Tom instinctively tried to lend a hand but was unable to intervene. Fate, however, decreed that Angus McCartney's blighted young life should not end in the Clyde. Several other passengers waiting to board, rushed to hang on to Michael and succeeded in pulling the wheelchair back from the brink. They were thanked for their help with a swig from the bottle as the skipper conveyed them to the Erskine bank.

The two were deep in thought as the ferry made its way across. Angus seemed solemn but calm; Michael grew increasingly agitated. He made to speak, but looked at Angus, lost in his own thoughts, and kept silent.

'Would you take me up the ferry road, Michael? Ah'd like tae visit the cemetery.'

Michael pushed him along past the Ferry Inn and Boden Boo cottage on the country road to Bishopton. A long, slow mile, and several swigs of whisky later, they came to the old Erskine Parish Church and graveyard. Lying on Johnny's grave was a bunch of winter-flowering heather. Michael gently picked up the posy to shake off the snow which had settled on the tiny cerise flowers.

'Ees faither's been back,' Angus approved.

Still Michael did not speak.

'At his right side there,' said Angus, pointing to the virgin ground beside Johnny's grave. 'Ah belong at his side.' He looked at Michael, but his friend refused to meet his eye. Angus continued to talk, the whisky making him garrulous. 'Aye, it was a movin ceremony. Ah can see Sam standin here readin his eulogy ...' He paused. 'Michael, ah've somethin tae ask ye. Since ma faither never comes near me, ah'd like you tae say a word or two instead.'

Michael's words broke out forcefully. 'Why now, Angus?'

Angus pondered how best to answer. 'One of the poems your friend Mr Owen wrote explains it so much better than ah ever could. That's why ah'd like you to read it at ma funeral.' Angus wet his throat with more whisky, and began to recite:

He sat in a wheeled chair, waiting for dark,
And shivered in his ghastly suit of grey,
Legless, sewn short at elbow. Through the park
Voices of boys rang saddening like a hymn,
Voices of play and pleasure after day,
Till gathering sleep had mothered them from him.

Some cheered him home, but not as crowds cheer Goal.
Only a solemn man who brought him fruits
Thanked him; and then inquired about his soul.
Now, he will spend a few sick years in Institutes,
And do what things the rules consider wise,
And take whatever pity they may dole.
Tonight he noticed how the women's eyes
Passed from him to the strong men that were whole.
How cold and late it is! Why don't they come
And put him into bed? Why don't they come?

By the end of the poem Michael was reciting with him, tears running down his face.

'Ye'd think he'd written it for me, wouldn't ye?' said Angus quietly. 'Mibbee he did.'

Michael slowly wheeled him from the cemetery and continued on along the road to South Lodge and the avenue to the hospital.

'Mary wheeled me along tae the end of the drive here, an we stopped an daydreamed about livin in a hoose like this. We talked about watchin oor weans grow up in the clean country air, an playin in the big wood there. What would the world have been like if we had avoided this fuckin war, Michael? Ah've often tried tae imagine it, dreamt what it might have been.'

Michael reached down and squeezed Angus's shoulder. 'We all have those dreams.'

The two men fell quiet, adding to the heavy silence of the winter day. After a time Angus spoke again. 'Ah've never asked ye before fur money, Michael, even though ah knew ye would have given me yer last penny. Ah'm countin on ye now tae do me one huge favour. Mary an I dreamed of emigratin tae Australia when ah finished ma apprenticeship. The big sunny country of golden opportunities beckoned, an some of oor pals had already gone oot tae Melbourne. That wiz before the madmen decided tae gie us stupit buggers rifles tae kill other stupit buggers. We dreamt of leavin the Glesca slums an gettin oorselves a nice hoose just like this oot there. Nothin but dreams, dreams, dreams, Michael, cause everythin's fucked now. Ah'm askin if ye'll see Mary an the weans okay wae enough money tae get them oot tae Australia an allow them tae settle intae a new life there.'

Without pause for consideration, Michael said he would be honoured to help. Two hundred metres beyond South Lodge, he pushed the wheelchair onto the path through the Big Wood to Lord Blantyre's seat. The panorama from the bench was spectacular. Snow-covered mountains formed the backdrop as lights twinkled in the gloaming, in the towns and villages scattered along the banks of the Clyde.

Angus swigged from the almost empty whisky bottle. 'She loved me, Michael. Ah'm no gonnae blame her for no appearin the day. She loved me. She deeply an honestly loved me. Neither of us knew what it was like tae even kiss another person, let alone sleep wae them. We chased each other when we were kids in the primary school an we knew even then that we would love each other forever. Fuckin idiotic stupit bastarts fucked it aw up for us wae their glorious fuckin war. They fed us aw that propaganda crap an ah wiz stupit enough tae faw fur it. Did ah ever tell ye aboot the night ah wiz comin hame fae work with ma faither an we got aff the tram at Dobbies Loan? Ah wiz still nineteen at the time. A wummin came up an handed me a white feather. A white fuckin feather! Can ye believe that, Michael? There ah wiz, covered in grease an dirt efter a hard days graft, when this wummin in an expensive coat an a big hat labelled me a coward. That wummin, wae a fuckin plum in her mooth, fae one ae the big hooses in Kelvinside, nae doubt, made me feel so bad that ah went an signed on. Me an just aboot every other bampot on that shift. Mary an ma mother were ragin when ma faither told them aboot the white feathers, but ah went anyway. An ah broke their hearts.'

Angus spoke so quietly that Michael, his emotions churning, had to strain to hear his words.

'Ma mammy never once got tae see me efter ah left the Maryhill barracks that day. She died wae a broken heart, Michael. Ah'm tellin ye, she died because her poor heart broke when she got word that her youngest wean, her wee boy, had been blown tae bits an it would take a miracle fur him tae survive. But noo it's time fur Lizzie McCartney tae see her wee boy again. Tell me that poem yer friend Siegfried wrote about the mother gettin word that her son had been killed.'

'"The Hero",' said Michael, his voice unsteady.

'Aye, that's the one.'

Coughing to clear the thickness from his throat, Michael began to recite Sassoon's poem. The lights across the Clyde appeared to grow stronger as the twilight deepened. The wind had dropped now, and his voice sounded clear in the chill air.

'Jack fell as he'd have wished,' the Mother said,
And folded up the letter that she'd read.
'The Colonel writes so nicely.' Something broke
In the tired voice that quavered to a choke.
She half looked up. 'We mothers are so proud
Of our dead soldiers.' Then her face was bowed.

The two men sat in silence for some time at Lord Blantyre's seat.

'Getting dark, we'd better head back now,' said Michael.

'Okay, it's time tae go, dear friend. Let's head doon the path tae the big cedar.'

Michael pushed the wheelchair through the darkening woods to one of their favourite spots. Angus drained the last drop from the bottle and began to sing. His singing was slightly slurred through drink, but his emotions were held in check. This was his chosen requiem.

Kiss the children for me, Mary
Don't let them pine or grieve
Tell them I'll be thinking of them
Though it breaks my heart to leave.

'Ah love ye like a brother, Michael. Ah hereby absolve ye of all sin an command ye tae have a happy, fruitful life fae this day forth. Now gie me a final hug, ma dearest freen.'

As Angus leaned forward in the wheelchair, Michael bent over to hug him. In one rapid movement he slipped the cushion from behind Angus's back and placed it between his chest and Angus's face. Michael forcefully hugged his friend to his chest for a considerable time, all the while singing 'Kiss the Children for Me, Mary', through sobs and tears.

The scene went mercifully blank. Tom opened his eyes to the sight of his bedroom ceiling, blurred by tears, before fading back into the vision.

A coffin was being lowered into the ground beside Johnny McVeigh's grave. A lone piper was playing the mournful lament, 'Flowers of the Forest'. Among the large group of mourners, Tom recognized many of the faces he had seen at Johnny's funeral. Michael carried out Angus's request with a moving reading of Wilfred Owen's poem, 'Disabled'. The hospital padre said a short prayer, then the fine voice of Sam McVeigh lead in singing a hymn.

Fading away like the stars in the morning
Losing their light in the glorious sun
Thus would we pass from this earth and its toiling
Only remembered for what we have done

Who'll sing the anthem and who'll tell the story
Will the line hold will it scatter and run
Shall we at last be united in glory
Only remembered for what we have done.

Standing beside Michael, dry-eyed but pale, Mary was dressed in a long black coat and headscarf. They turned to each other as the mourners were leaving the graveyard and clasped hands. 'He loved you, Mary. Right to the very minute he died he was singing a song about how much he loved you and the children.'

Her composure finally disintegrated and Michael hugged her as she wept on his shoulder. 'Ah'm sorry, Michael. Ah'm so sorry ah didnae come tae visit him on our anniversary. He died believin ah didnae love him and that is ...'

Her voice broke off in a sob, and Michael reassured her that he understood, and that Angus had understood too.

'Was it a peaceful end?'

Michael nodded, his face grim. 'Yes, very peaceful. He went the way he would have wanted. It's far more upsetting for those of us left to mourn him. Doctor Borland believes that his heart suddenly failed and he died almost instantly.'

'But Angus never had any problems wae ees heart.'

'No, but the doctor says it is something that often happens with multiple amputees. Their heart simply can't take the strain any longer and just gives up. He never suffered any pain, Mary. I can assure you of that.'

'You've been such a good friend tae him – and Johnny too,' she said, placing her hand on the granite headstone over Johnny's grave. 'A better friend than ah've been since.' She shook her head. 'Ah feel so bad that ah could never come tae terms wae what happened tae him.' Her face distorted and shudders ran through her body as she sobbed. 'Ah couldnae bear tae see him in such pain an misery. Ah tried, oh ah tried but it ripped ma heart oot an made somethin close off inside me until, finally, ah couldnae reach oot tae him anymore.'

Michael took her arm and gently led her away from the graveside. 'He's at peace, Mary. No more pain. No more misery. We must both learn to be at peace now ourselves.'

'Ah cannae go back there,' she said, gesturing in the direction of the hospital. 'Too many painful memories. Too many ghosts. Will ye make ma apologies tae Sam an aw the others.'

'I'll do that. Let me take you first to the ferry.'

As his chauffeur drove them along Ferry Road to the slip, Michael took Mary's hand. 'Angus told me you had planned to go to Australia.'

Mary laughed bitterly. 'More impossible dreams.'

The chauffeur drew up by the slip, stopped the engine, and walked away from the car. Michael turned to Mary and paused, as though scripting his words before he spoke. 'Not long before he died, he asked me to help you and the children to go to Australia and start a new life once he was gone. It was as though he knew the end was near.' His words hung in the air for Mary to consider.

'So there is no problem about money. I will pay your fares and ensure that are you settled into decent accommodation with a proper bathroom, and a nice garden for the chidren to play in. I'm led to believe that Melbourne is a very beautiful place with lovely safe beaches for the children.'

'It's too much tae ask. Ah couldnae.'

'No Mary, nothing is too much to ask for Angus, or for you. I told him I would be honoured to help in any way I could, and I say exactly the same to you.'

'Such a big move,' said Mary, but for the first time that day there was life behind her tired eyes, a slight glint of hope.

'That's what Angus wanted, but your plans for the future are, of course, entirely for you to decide.'

'Ah'll need tae give it some thought; ask the weans what they think.'

'Shall I call in on you in a few days to discuss it further?' Michael offered.

'Yes please.' She leaned across the car and kissed his cheek. 'Thank you, Michael. Yir a good man.' She climbed from the car, dabbing her eyes. Michael watched her board the ferry on the first leg of her lonely journey home to Glasgow. He waited until it reached the opposite bank. She never looked back.

CHAPTER TWENTY-TWO

Tom's breath condensed in the freezing night air as he walked back and forth across the Mar Hall car park waiting to greet Davie Kirkwood. 'For fuck sake,' he muttered to himself, when the racket from the damaged exhaust pipe on Davie's van announced his arrival from halfway along the avenue. Tom walked over as Davie parked the dirty, battered Ford Transit alongside gleaming limos and outrageously large 4×4s.

'Christ, Davie, I'm glad you didn't come in that when the war wounded were here. The blokes with shell-shock would've thought it was a machine-gun barking, and been diving for cover.'

'Sorry, but ah hit a pot-hole on the way here. Nah, the truth is ah cannae afford tae fit a new exhaust this month.' Davie eyed up the magnificent building. 'First time ah've ever been in a five-star. They'll probably ask the local scrap man tae come an tow this heap outta here.'

'Don't worry, mate, I'll say you're a reclusive millionaire travelling incognito and I'm on protection duty while you're here. On the other hand, I'm sure the guests trying to sleep would appreciate it being towed away.'

Davie's hearty laugh boomed across the car park 'This place has never been far from ma mind since ye told me about the visions. Are ye sure it's okay for me tae have a nosey?'

'Of course, mate, come on in, Roddie's waiting inside. The guests are away to their rooms, but I doubt if they'll have slept through that din.'

'This was used as the recreation room for the wounded men,' explained Roddie, as Davie cast an admiring eye around the magnificent Grand Hall. 'They called it the Gallery back then. Some of the biggest names in Scottish show business came here to entertain the men.'

Tom felt a lump in his throat when he told them about the beautiful young girl from the concert party kissing Johnny McVeigh, just a few feet away from where they now stood.

After chatting in the Grand Hall for some time, Roddie led them through to the dining room. 'Just look at that ceiling,' Davie enthused, 'it's magnificent.'

'It is that,' Roddie nodded. 'My favourite room in the entire place.'

He lit several candles on the tables, and gold-painted cornices on the intricately carved, vaulted ceiling gleamed in their light.

'What would this have been way back in the early days of the hospital?'

'I'm not sure. When I first came to work here about thirty years ago it was used as the physiotherapy department.'

'Ah reckon that with Tom's visions, he's the man tae tell us what it was back then.'

'Yes, just like every other room in the building during the First World War, it was a hospital ward chock-full of wounded men. They had about thirty beds in here.'

'Mind-bogglin,' said Davie. 'It's difficult tae imagine that now.'

'They had over two hundred beds crammed into the big house, and by 1917 so many wounded men were coming in that they put another two hundred beds into emergency huts outside.'

They moved quietly upstairs to show Davie the bedrooms and luxurious suites. 'Bloody hell,' he whispered when he saw the four-poster bed in the vacant junior suite. 'How many guests have been listed missing in action in there?'

Tom laughed. 'It's massive, eh? The ideal size for rampant sex apparently.' He became serious. 'Believe it or believe it not, mate, there used to be ten beds in this room. Wee Johnny McVeigh died in one over by the window there in 1917. The surgeons had run out of bits to cut off him.'

'They actually operated here in the big house?'

'Sure,' said Roddie. 'It had a fully equipped operating theatre that was always busy. As you well know, Davie, a lot of men had arms and legs removed at field hospitals near the front if it was a matter of life and death, but many others were bandaged up and sent back here to get mangled limbs amputated. I'll lend you a wee book called *The Vanishing Willows* which tells how they performed amputations here at Erskine. By the time the war ended in 1918, around three and a half thousand wounded men had been admitted. Many of them were eventually able to go home with artificial limbs, but others were so badly wounded that they had to stay here permanently.'

Davie nodded thoughtfully. 'Christ, it must have been like a conveyor belt wae aw the wounded comin through.'

'Absolutely. Sir William Macewen, the chief surgeon here, got skilled carpenters and engineers in a Glasgow shipyard to design artificial arms and legs from willow trees. Those craftsmen in turn taught disabled men at Erskine how to make them. They set up a big workshop here and within four years had made artificial limbs for nine and a half thousand wounded men.'

Downstairs, the freezing night air hit them when they opened the French window and went out to the gardens.

'It's like some kinda beautiful fairytale castle,' Davie enthused as he looked back at the hotel lit with chandeliers and sparkling Christmas lights.

Tom nodded. 'It sure is. To be honest, I never thought a place like this would be my style, but I love it here – and the people who work in it.'

'Aye, it certainly is magnificent. Even though the men were badly wounded, ah'll wager that a lot of them couldnae believe their luck at escapin the trenches alive an endin up somewhere like this back in Scotland. It sure beats the slums they'd been livin in.'

Davie eyed up the magnificent, white frosted canopy of the big cedar arching over them. 'And this'll be the tree you were telling me about, Tom.'

'Yup, this was one of Angus's favourite spots, and just over there behind it is where his life ended. Who knows, although it's not Samhuinn, maybe it's possible that his ghost is here right now. If you can hear us, Angus, we owe you.'

'Aye, we owe you and Johnny big time,' Roddie agreed. 'And the rest of the wounded lads who were in there with you.'

Tom nodded solemnly. 'But can we ever repay them?'

'Only wae the truth,' said Davie, immediately. 'Only wae the truth about why that war happened. Why did they have tae die so young and who was responsible? Ah certainly don't believe we repay them just by wearin a red poppy on our lapels for a few days in November. It's hypocrisy tae me.'

'The poppy should be worn with pride,' said Tom rather aggressively.

Roddie immediately put a calming hand on his shoulder. 'You're entitled to that view, Tom. Of course you are, but not everyone agrees. It's a deeply personal affair. For some it's a stark reminder of the heroism of soldiers, but for others the poppy's symbolism is corrupted and tainted by the hypocrisy of warmongers.'

'In Australia we always had a memorial service at school on ANZAC Day, and I remember watching the UK ceremony on TV with Gran.

We found it very emotional when millions of red poppies floated down inside the big hall.'

Roddie nodded. 'Aye, it's emotional all right, but I dislike the sense of militarism that goes with it. I hate to see politicians solemnly laying poppy wreaths in memory of the war dead, when it's those very bastards who lied and sent young men off to die needlessly. You'll remember seeing the photograph of Field Marshall Haig at the hospital here.'

'Yeah, inspecting the wounded men outside the big porch?'

'Aye, the very one. He was responsible for setting up the poppy fund in 1921.'

'Good onya, Field Marshall.'

'Haud on a minute, Tom,' said Davie. 'That was just a part of the British establishment's propaganda machine makin him out to be a great man. Haig didnae give a shit about ordinary workin men being slaughtered by the millions. "Butcher of the Somme" was what they called him.'

'Was he in charge during the Somme?'

Davie nodded. 'Aye, commander-in-chief. He was the millionaire son of a Scotch whisky magnate, and apparently of such limited talent that he bribed superior officers wae huge loans in order tae make his way up the military ladder.'

'According to some accounts I've read,' said Roddie, 'Haig never even went to see the ground on which the battles were fought, either before or during them. He was a stupid, humourless and conceited man who shamelessly toadied to Royalty.'

'But he was doing what everyone else thought was right, wasn't he?' said Tom, 'And he won.'

'Aye, accordin tae some historians,' said Davie. 'They've attempted tae revive his reputation by suggestin he was the architect of victory in 1918. Events at the Somme, they suggest, weakened an demoralized the German army an led tae their ultimate defeat. Ah don't think ah've ever heard so much fuckin crap in ma life. Haig was still livin in an age where he believed fine English stallions ridden by upper-class officers fae Sandhurst could win any war. Christ almighty, years after the slaughter ended he was still sayin that horses were the future in warfare.'

'I'm getting the odd vibe that you dislike this guy a tad, Davie.'

'Ah'm sorry tae keep on but it makes ma blood boil. At the end of the war his pals in high places handed him a £100,000 tax-free golden handshake and an earldom. Try tae imagine that, Tom. If ye compare the puchasin power of that amount back in 1918 wae today, it must be worth about £15 million. They gave that massive sum tae a man who was already a multi-millionaire.'

'Fuck sake. Bella Ramsey and the other war widows in Port Dundas could've done with just a tiny fraction of that to feed their kids.'

'Exactly! Those widows had tae depend on handouts from one of the very donkeys responsible for the deaths of their men. Ordinary soldiers were gettin paid less than £1 a week. That's why ah believe it's hypocrisy.'

'Yeah, I take your point, mate.' Tom looked thoughtfully at the big cedar, imagining Angus sitting there listening. 'You, Roddie and Julie have encouraged me to look at things differently. And you've given me enough reason to believe that I wasn't fighting on the side of right in Iraq, but can you appreciate how difficult it is for me to come to terms with that?'

'We do, Tom. Please believe me,' said Roddie. 'I would never for a second decry the memory of ordinary soldiers like you who obeyed orders and went out to Iraq and died there. But I find it difficult to know how to honour men lost in an illegal war founded on the lies and deceit of politicians. Politicians who aren't fit to lace the boots of the young men they send out to face the bombs and bullets.'

'Aye,' Davie agreed. 'It makes me livid tae see those lyin bastard politicians raise their snouts from the trough, then go an lay wreaths at war memorials in memory of aw the brave young men whose totally unnecessary deaths they are personally responsible for. Intelligent human beings should be able tae solve problems in ways that don't involve smashin each other o'er the heid.'

Tom shrugged. 'Laudable ambitions, Davie, but I can't believe you'll ever succeed in stopping war.'

'Much as ah hate tae say it, with madmen like Bush and Blair in control of the world, you're probably right. But Angus an Johnny, an the fifteen million other young men who were mutilated an slaughtered alongside them, suggest tae me that we should never stop tryin.'

'It's the scale of the slaughter I can't get my head round. Everyone in our regiment was gutted when two of our lads were killed in Afghanistan. Compare that to 1915 when our Aussie and New Zealand boys were put ashore on the coves at Gallipoli. Ten thousand of them were killed there. Ten thousand! It's impossible for a modern soldier to imagine that carnage.'

'The casualty figures for most battles in that war were mind-bogglin,' Davie confirmed. 'Over eight hundred thousand British soldiers never came back fae France, an many of them didnae even have a proper burial. The Menin Gate in Ypres names fifty-five thousand British soldiers whose remains were never found.'

Roddie shook his head. 'Dear God, it's hard to take that in. Fifty-five thousand young lads lost into the mud and gore of Flanders! That's a massive football crowd. The entire stadium.'

'Aye, it's a capacity crowd at Hampden, plus another three thousand on top. The Somme was worse. Lutyens memorial at Thiepval lists over seventy-three thousand British an Commonwealth soldiers missin at the Somme. They were either blown tae smithereens or sucked intae the mud and never seen again. The memorial at Paschendale lists the names of another thirty-five thousand missin men.'

A cold shiver ran up and down Tom's spine. 'Fuck sake. And that's not counting the many hundreds of thousands who had proper burials. It really is fuckin unbelievable. I've seen how war utterly devastated the lives of Angus and Johnny's families. It's almost beyond the human mind to comprehend that that same tragedy was repeated in millions of homes. And all for what?'

'Exactly. Aw for what?' echoed Davie.

'A soldier asking that might not strike you two as surprising, but it goes against everything we're taught. During my years in the army we were quietly, but constantly, reminded of our oath of allegiance – our sworn duty to unquestioning loyalty. Ours but to do and die.'

'Man's inhumanity to man,' said Roddie, putting his arms round Tom's and Davie's shoulders. 'Come on lads, I'm frozen. Let's go back in for a hot brew. We can continue this discussion another night over a few beers round the fire.'

'Yeah, that sounds good to me,' said Tom. 'And thank you, Roddie. I've now got a different grasp on what wars are all about.'

'Good, Tom, that's good. Always remember the words of Mahatma Gandhi: "Non-violence is not a garment to be put on and off at will. Its seat is in the heart, and it must be an inseparable part of our very being."'

CHAPTER TWENTY-THREE

A WEEK AFTER DAVIE'S TOUR of the hotel, Tom and Roddie helped tidy up after a big private party in the function suite. Then, in the wee small hours of Christmas morning, they sat down with a cup of tea and sandwiches.

'The joys of Christmas. Roll on the third of January.'

'And why's that Roddie?'

''Cause that's when a semblance of sanity returns to Scotland.'

'You're not a big fan of Christmas then.'

'Got it in one. Commercialized bloody nonsense.'

'What about your beautiful daughter?'

'Oh yes, she loves it. You know what she's like for presents.'

'And have I got a beaut for her.'

'What's that then?'

'Ahaa,' said Tom, tapping his nose. 'A trip to sunny parts is all I'm telling you, mate. Julie should know first.'

'Fair enough. Sounds good.'

'It was actually Dr McKenzie who suggested it a month or so back. I went to see him at Julie's insistence when I was a bit down, and he thought my body was missing all the Aussie sunshine it's used to. He said I should head off somewhere warm and sunny for a holiday.'

'Did you tell him about the iboga?'

'No. I didn't. He knows about the heroin, but I didn't feel it appropriate to tell him I was taking another illegal substance.'

'For what it's worth, Tom, iboga could be the source of the problem. You've had some pretty horrendous experiences under the influence of that stuff. Either that or a mild recurrence of PTSD.'

'Yeah, well, maybe you're right.' Tom stood up and walked to the French windows. 'Don't get me wrong, Roddie, I've never been happier anywhere else in my life than I am here. Overall I'm a helluva lot better, but it's strange how I can be feeling calm and relaxed one minute, then something happens and I'm anxious and down the next. It's like a light switch suddenly being flicked. It happened a lot in Iraq after the road-block disaster – every day if truth be told.'

'It must have been a nightmare for you.'

'Total fuckin nightmare, mate, and it took me very close to the edge of insanity. I thought I was completely over it, but you could be right. Dr Nimmo warned me that the PTSD could flare up from time to time.'

'Maybe it's not too late for you to see a psychologist.'

'No thanks. Whatever it is, my body feels as though it's crawling at one mile an hour, but my brain's racing at a thousand. Julie knows how to deal with it better than any psychologist. I can be feeling depressed and want to stay in kip, but she spends hours talking me out of it.'

'Yes, I recall the night you were supposed to come over to the lodge, but couldn't because you were feeling so bad. Julie told Susan and me you were talking about going home to Melbourne.'

'Yeah, but only because I was feeling like shit. I would never leave her, Roddie. Another day she took me away to see her ancestors' old farm ruin in Perthshire. By the time we got home, and you showed me the photographs, I was as right as rain. That's what I mean about flicking a switch.'

'I'm sure we all get short-term mood swings. It's not like clinical depression which tends to come in intense and prolonged episodes. I know. Wouldn't wish it on my worst enemy.'

'When Rachel died.'

'Aye, and for a long time after.'

'Dr McKenzie suggested I should get a sunlamp as well as a holiday.'

'SAD syndrome is certainly common at this time of the year in Scotland. Rachel was prone to it in the winter months and she used a lamp. A break somewhere warm and sunny will do you good, but you should have told him about the iboga. He's good, but he can't be expected to come up with the correct diagnosis if you don't tell him about it and the effect it had on you.'

'Yeah, maybe I should. SAD syndrome, eh? Something else to add to my growing list. PTSD, MAD, BAD and now SAD. Hopefully the sun will cure me of something.'

'I can safely say that you're neither bad nor mad, Tom, though I gather you're a little too quick with your fists at times.'

Tom raised his eyebrows. It had to be the incident with the poacher. 'Has Julie been telling tales out of school?'

'Not her style. Andy gets the local gossip via the Golf Inn grapevine. Violence begets violence. Some of the local hard-men were in boasting that they were gonnae pay the new, gun-busting security man at Mar Hall a little visit. Andy told them it would only be safe for them if they could raise a battallion.'

Tom laughed. 'Excellent. That would make it a wee bit of a challenge.'

At 7 a.m. Tom checked the hotel, showered, and drove to South Lodge to waken Julie for her Christmas morning shift on reception.

'Happy Christmas, sweetheart'

'Morning lover,' she murmured, still half asleep. The meaning of his words suddenly struck her and her eyes opened wide. 'It's Christmas!' She sat up and looked to the end of the bed for her stocking. For the first time in her life there was nothing there and her face fell.

Tom handed her an envelope. 'A prezzie with all my love.'

She looked disappointed that it wasn't a huge box covered in crackly wrapping paper and flowing with curly ribbons.

'Go on, open it.'

She unstuck the flap and out fell an airline ticket folder. She took out a sheaf of tickets and glanced through them, her eyes sparkling and a smile blossoming on her face.

'And now I'll explain. On the 25th of January I'm taking three weeks leave – yes, it's all arranged with Frank Osborne. We'll spend three days in the Ritz in Kuala Lumpur, then a few days with the orang-utans at Kota Kinabalu reserve. Then, after a week on the golden beach at Shangri-la resort, we'll head down to Melbourne to visit my grandparents.'

'Wow! That sounds fantastic, really amazing, but I hate to put a damper on your plans, handsome. I'll be back at uni by then.'

'All contingencies covered. I had a word with Davie about the advisability of you taking time off. "Nae bother, big man" he said. He's gonna look out relevant notes for the lectures you'll miss, and said it'll be cool if you use the time on the long-hauls to keep up to speed. Says he'll help you with revision if need be before the exams in May. Sun, sea and sand, sweetheart, just how good does that sound?'

'I've seen programmes on the telly about orang-utans and they're amazing animals.' Julie flung her arms around him and smothered his face with kisses. 'And sun, sea, and sand … and surf-boarding and sex. You can't go wrong.'

'It'll be good for you to see the big house I'm gonna inherit. It's a beaut. Perfect for raising those four ankle biters.'

'What if I insist that they grow up in Scotland?'

'And have the poor kids wearing bloody oilskins all their days?'

Julie laughed. 'Okay, we'll spend winters in Melbourne, and Scottish summers here in the lodge.'

'Would they be Australian or British citizens?'

'Neither. We'll have passports from an independent Scotland by then.'

'Okay, Two Scots and two Aussies.'

'It's a deal.'

An hour later, Julie dressed for work and left wearing a huge smile.

Cheerfully, Tom phoned his grandparents in Melbourne to wish them Happy Christmas and confirm that he would be over soon with Julie. His grandfather's opening words shocked and deflated him: 'Donna Mulhearty's father phoned from Sydney and wants to speak to you. I was going to let you get Christmas over first, but your gran thinks you should know now.'

Anger and confusion heralded the despair he thought had gone.

'Where in the name of hell did he get your phone number from?' Tom blurted, but he knew there should have been no need for his grandfather to explain. Donna Mulhearty had been a journalist and her colleagues would have contacts.

'You should arrange to speak to him when you're over, Tom. You know it's the right thing to do.'

Tom put the phone down and went upstairs to bed. He heard his grandfather's words, and knew the advice was well considered, but old fears had been unleashed by the very idea. Why would the Mulhearty demons not leave him alone?

The joy and excitement he had just shared with Julie evaporated. The switch had been flicked and such panic took hold of him that he began seriously thinking about cancelling the trip. Julie would be hugely disappointed, but he'd have just enough time to organise somewhere different.

For the first time in months, he lay brooding about Donna Mulhearty and events on the Amman Road. How had the military passed it off? What had been said in the press afterwards?

He drifted into a troubled sleep and dreamt about Iraq. He was standing on the Amman road with a car coming to a halt in front of him. The Iraqi driver slowly and carefully stepped from the car as instructed. The passenger door suddenly opened and a young western woman began to walk towards him with a smile. Amidst the sound of gunfire and sight of bullets ripping into her body, Tom leapt from the bed in horror yelling, 'No, Elvis!' when he saw that it was Julie. 'No, not Julie. Not Julie.'

Gasping for breath, bathed in sweat and confusion, he went downstairs and made coffee, all the while fighting the irrational desire to phone the hotel and check she was alright. Crippled by the horrors of his nightmare he crawled into the shower, but even the hot blast could not cleanse it from his mind. He dressed, climbed into the car and, on auto-pilot, found himself heading out along the motorway.

Tom parked at the spot he estimated the entrance to 34 Colinton Street had once been. This Christmas morning Port Dundas was deserted and devoid of all the warmth of earlier visits. No well-dressed children were learning to sail their expensive dinghies on the canal basin; no children were playing in snow and sledging down Colinton Street on battered old trays; no children were shrieking with laughter as an irate boatman jumped down onto the towpath and landed on his 'bahooky'.

He stepped from the car, made his way to the Bascule bridge, and steadied himself with both hands on the rail. As he stood there staring down at the canal, his thoughts were as black as the water below. He shuddered when it struck him like a sledgehammer that Julie may well have been Donna Mulhearty. Both had the same abhorrence of war and what was being done to Iraq. It could easily have been her out there as a human shield with Elvis's bullets ripping into her body. Given the same circumstances, he knew for certain that Roddie would walk to the end of the earth and back to discover the truth about her death. Mr Mulhearty was no different. As he stood there in the grey light of that Christmas morning, he understood for the first time what he had to do.

He walked down from the canal, imagining the street as it had once been, but everything, and everyone, had gone. The tenements with their reeking chimneys, Angus and Mary, Thomas and little Marion, the children and their brothers and sisters, mothers and fathers – all gone. The hooters and sirens of the big Port Dundas factories, and a thousand men pouring over the bridge onto Colinton Street on their way home from work had gone. Every last one of them was dead. There was nothing. Donna Mulhearty was dead. Tom Cahill, Giuseppe Del Buon and an honest, decent, hard-working Iraqi taxi driver were dead. Where did life begin, where did it end? He walked past the modern industrial units and stopped where Jeannie Spittal's shop had stood. What once had been the heart of the vibrant community was now a skip hire yard.

'It's a right wee Aladdin's cave that shop,' he recalled Mary saying. 'Jeannie's got the patience ae a saint the time she takes servin the weans.'

'Ah've got plenty sweeties fur us aw, Granny, but Mammy says ye've no tae eat too many cause you'll die a beeties.'

'Jeannie Spittal's got enough doon there tae kill the whole street.'

'Jeannie said ah looked like a wounded sodjer jist back fae France.'

'An ah love you too, Daddy. Tell me a story before ah go tae bed.'

'Night, night, ma wee wounded sodjer.'

'Night, night, Daddy. Can ah go tae France wae you tae keep ye safe?'

Tom thought of little Thomas sitting on the potty laughing and shouting 'more sweeties, more sweeties'. What happened to that delightful little Colinton Street boy? Why had Angus and Mary's hopes for their beloved son ended with him being knifed in the guts and thrown into Melbourne harbour?

Tom shuddered at the thought of his grandfather's death and walked back up to the car. With rain beginning to patter on the soft top, he sat there imagining a sash and case window rattling open above the close at 34.

'Thomas! C'mon up, son. Yer tea's ready.'

'Ohhhpen. Ohhhpen.'

'Ye should come sledgin wae me, Granny. It's rer fun.'

'Ah hope you've no been standin oan the ice oan the canaul. There's many a wee boy fell through an got drooned. Their mammies never, ever saw them again.'

'They're good boys. It's no their fault. We're aw trying tae gie Bella as much support as we can. She'll pick up. It's only two months since she got the telegram.'

'Thank God ah've got you two tae look after me if somethin bad happened tae Angus.'

'Ah wonder where ma big sodjer is the night. Whit if it's snowin like this in France an he's lyin oot in the open?'

Tom recalled following Mary the night she walked home in the lashing rain from Central Station to find nothing in the house to feed Thomas and Marion.

'Wiz it busy the day again, hen?'

'Busy! Ah think there must be three bloody world wars goin on.'

'Aye, ah think there's a big push on tae get it aw o'er by Christmas.'

'It wiz ma fault he went.'

'It wiz you! It wisnae they wimmin wae their white feathers.'

'Ah'm sorry, Michael. Ah'm sorry ah didnae come tae visit him. He died believin ah didnae love him. Ah couldnae bear tae see him in such pain and misery.'

'He loved you, Mary. Right to the minute he died.'

Fuck sake, how many millions of other loving couples like Mary and Angus had been torn apart? War had changed all their lives irrevocably – a cataclysmic explosion of violence whose aftershocks were still being felt all these generations later. How, as Angus had asked Michael, might life have panned out for the McCartneys and the McVeighs – for the whole world – without that war? Would he himself even have been born? Would he have become a soldier? And if he hadn't, would he ever have met Julie? According to Davie, and he trusted Davie implicitly, the war had been deliberately caused by massively wealthy and powerful individuals. Many millions of decent, ordinary young men like Johnny and Angus had been sacrificed solely so those fuckers could gain even greater wealth and power. He would have to read more about it himself, but he now understood Julie's and Roddie's anger at war. So much heartache, pain and despair for his own family. They didn't deserve it. They'd been decent, honest, loving folk and Angus might have lived to a ripe old age without that war – might even have been alive to see this new century. He felt ashamed that he had made derogatory remarks about him to Brigadier Nimmo without knowing a thing about him or what he'd been through. A deep sorrow now filled his brooding soul.

He fired up the car, but sat staring out at the empty street. Troubled by what he knew, he was even more confused by what he did not. He removed a little polythene bag from his wallet and rolled an iboga capsule between his thumb and fingers. Within half an hour he was slumped back in the driver's seat, willing himself back in time to the same spot outside the close at number 34.

It was a cold and miserable morning with several children running down Colinton Street spinning large metal barrel hoops with sticks. Thomas and Wullie, and Wullie's young brother George, walked up from the Boatmen's Institute on Dobbies Loan and stopped to look longingly into Jeannie Spittal's shop window. Its display comprised glass jars of sweeties, small toys, and an unlit Christmas tree sparsely decorated with silver tinsel and a knitted fairy. Moments later a large black motor car with gleaming chrome headlamps drove into Colinton Street from Port Dundas Road and the three boys automatically chased after it. Thomas went down on one knee to fire imaginary bullets at the car from a roughly carved, wooden toy rifle.

'It's ma Daddy's pal,' Thomas shouted excitedly. 'He's goin up tae oor hoose. He's a mullionaire.'

Tom admired the beautiful machine when the driver took it up to the top of the street, swung it round on the open ground beside the canal, and came back down to stop outside 34. Michael said a few words to the chauffeur before he stepped down from the passenger seat and was immediately besieged by a crowd of excited children. Faces appeared at virtually every window in the street.

'Yer goin tae ma hoose, mister. Sure ye are,' Thomas exclaimed excitedly and proudly to Michael and everyone within earshot. 'Ma mammy's waitin fur ye.'

Taking Thomas's hand, Michael limped up the close with a dozen or so children following behind. Tom empathized when he held a handkerchief to his nose on passing the stinking dunny on the half landing.

'Ohhhpen Ohhhpen,' Thomas shouted as they cleared the second flight, but his mother was already standing at the open door with a warm smile. Michael kissed her cheek and went through to the kitchen.

'It's very nice tae see ye again, sir,' said Thomas's grandfather, standing up to offer Michael the chair by the fire.

'It's Michael. Please do call me Michael,' he replied, shaking William's hand.

Mary handed him a cup of tea. 'Ah'll be ready in five minutes, Michael. Ah suppose ye had a big audience at the windows when ye drove up the street. A thousand tongues were waggin when ye left the other night. Never mind, ah suppose if they're talkin aboot me they're leavin somebody else alone.'

Michael laughed, adjusted his artificial leg, and sat down by the fire. 'Yes indeed. Sticks and stones, as the saying goes.'

'Sticks an stones'll brek yer bones, but names'll never hurt ye,' Thomas chimed in.

'Very good young man, very good indeed. You are one very clever chap. Just like y…' Michael suddenly halted, realising what he was about to say would be insensitive.

'Aye, very clever just like yer daddy.' William completed the sentence. 'It's nae bother, Michael, we've no stopped talkin tae him aboot his daddy aw week. Ye know yer daddy's away tae heaven noo, son, don't ye?'

'Aye, Granda. Wullie says his daddy an ma daddy are best pals in heaven. But can ye talk tae each other when yer in heaven, Granda?'

'Ye can talk aw right, pal. Yer Granny Cartney and yer daddy'll be talkin tae each other aboot ye right noo. They'll be lookin doon at ye an sayin how much they love ye an whit a right clever wee boy ye are.'

'Ma Granny Cartney's deid, but she still loves me?'

'Aye. Of course she still loves ye. She loves us aw son. She still loves us aw.'

'Will they still be able tae look doon at me when we go tae Australia?'

'Of course they will, pal. They'll love ye an be watchin o'er ye wherever ye go, so don't you worry aboot that.' William's eyes moistened and his voice choked. He excused himself and left the room. Michael looked questioningly at Mary.

'He's okay; he's just upset talkin aboot Lizzie. Yes, we're goin, Michael,' she said with a smile. 'Ah've decided we're definitely goin. Me an the auld yin sat an spoke aboot it fur oors after ye left the other night. The atmosphere's been bad here since he told me about encouragin Angus tae enlist. Ah know deep doon its no his fault that he wiz blown tae bits, but ah just cannae hide the bitterness. He agrees Australia will offer the weans a much better chance. He's happy for us. Says it'll be best for them if we start a new life o'er there.'

Michael crossed over to Mary and took her hand. 'I agree completely that it would be best for Thomas and Marion – offer the prospect of a better life, but what about you? What do you really feel deep down?'

'Empty, Michael. Ah feel a constant, terrible, gnawin emptiness in the pit of ma stomach. Ah feel empty an guilty. Ah should have been there fur him on oor anniversary; been there wae him when he died. Nobody will ever know jist how deeply ah loved Angus, an him me. Ah betrayed that. We always dreamed that one day we would go tae Australia wae the weans. Takin them oot there is the only part of oor dream that's left.'

'Angus told me all about that dream and he desperately wanted you to go. There is nothing I can say or do to ease your terrible heartache, so I won't even try to. But the guilt! That is different, Mary. You must not attempt to begin a new life in Australia carrying this totally unwarranted burden of guilt on your shoulders. Angus knew just how much it pained you to see him suffering. He knew you loved him deeply. You might not believe this, but guilt is what he felt.

'Perhaps it's all too soon,' Michael continued, 'but Father discussed it with trusted friends and there is what might be the perfect opportunity for you. A large liner, currently used as a troopship bringing ANZACs over, is due in to the Govan dry dock in the New Year. Following some work to her hull, she's scheduled to head back out to Australia on the 25th of January. The owner assures Father he would be delighted to have the widow and children of a Scottish war hero as guests aboard one of his ships. The only problem I can envisage is that she'll be returning to Sydney empty apart from some wounded men. Perhaps that might be too upsetting for you, but there will be plenty of free cabin space, and excellent cooks and stewards eager to please their wounded war heroes returning home.'

Mary's eyes filled with tears and she hugged Michael. 'Yer the nicest man and the kindest friend Angus an I could ever have had, Michael Farquhar. Thank you. Thank you so much.'

'Right, come on then,' said Michael cheerfully, trying to disguise his embarrassment at the compliments. 'Let's discuss it further on the way over there. I've got two beautiful, fresh holly wreaths for the graves.'

'Aye, we'd better no keep yer man doon there waitin any longer.'

'Can ah go wae ye, Mammy?' asked Thomas.

'Naw son. You stay an look efter Marion an yer Granda. A cemetery isnae the place for wee boys.'

Thomas's face crumpled, but he accepted the decision without protest.

Mary relented when Michael immediately indicated to her with a silent 'okay,' and gentle nod of the head, that it would be fine for him to join them.

'Awright, but ye'll need tae get well happed up.'

'Thanks, Mammy. Ah just want tae see ma daddy tae tell him Happy Christmas an that we're goin on a big boat wae wounded sodjers.'

Tom followed them downstairs and watched Michael help Thomas up into the back of the big car. Michael then took time to shake hands and speak to the excited children gathered round it. Tom suspected he was unobtrusively slipping pennies into their hands. He felt a tremendous surge of affection for Michael. He was indeed, as Mary said, a good man.

A mangy mongrel with raised hackles and a back leg missing barked and growled incessantly at Tom. The puzzled children looked on when, for no apparent reason, the crazed, snarling dog continually circled an empty spot on the street next to them.

A pang of sorrow gripped Tom as Michael's car drove off down Colinton Street. Young Thomas stood at the back window firing his toy rifle at his friends. Tom knew his grandfather couldn't see him, but he waved goodbye.

Colinton Street began to fade, but the dog's barking and growling grew louder and fiercer. Opening his eyes, Tom was startled to see the fangs of a bull terrier at the driver's door window of his car, inches from his face. Two gaunt, sallow-faced men in their twenties were standing beside the car. 'Whit the fuck's up wae you, pal?' said one of them as he stared in the window, his dog straining on its leash. 'Looks like yer due a wee top up the way yer sweatin there. Hey Malkie, ah think we've found a fellow smack-heid.'

'Is that right, Geordie, wee man? Gie's a look.'

Tom glanced at his watch, pulled himself up in the seat, and opened the car window. 'Sorry mate, I didn't catch that.'

'Ah said, that's a nice watch ye've got there. How come ye need a fancy watch when ye've already got a time piece there in yer flashy motor?' As Geordie distracted Tom, Malkie moved round to the other side of the car in a pincer movement. Before Tom had shaken off the effects of the iboga and gathered his wits, Malkie plunged a long blade through the passenger side of the car's soft top and slashed it open. The instant Tom's attention was diverted, Geordie put his hand through the open window and grabbed the key from the ignition.

'Tell ye whit, pal,' he said confidently, producing a Stanley knife from his well-stained shell suit jacket pocket, 'we'll dae a wee deal that's fair aw round. Ah'll gie you the key tae the nice motor if you gie me that watch. A fair deal. You'll be safely away fae here in ten seconds.' Geordie flashed a dog-breath smile at Tom, car key in one hand, knife in the other. Malkie leaned through the slashed soft top, blade in hand, his confidence fuelled by the image of himself as a would-be assassin.

Tom nodded in agreement and made to take his wrist-watch off as he stepped from the car. Geordie spun once in the air before his face was driven down hard into the road. His nose, lips and lower jaw exploded in a shower of blood and nicotine-stained teeth. The bull terrier, which Tom now saw was a harmless little Staffordshire, bolted in the direction of the motorway.

Tom leapt over the bonnet of the car to face a stunned Malkie and his waving blade. 'Come near me an yer fuckin dead meat, mister.' Malkie shouted with no conviction. His face was spared, but he screamed in agony when Tom forced the knife hand up his back, almost dislocating his right shoulder and elbow joint. 'Ah cannae swim! Ah cannae swim!' he squealed as he was frog-marched to the side of the canal.

'Well ye'd better fuckin learn fast,' Tom responded with his best impersonation of a Glasgow accent.

Malkie sank out of sight and the turbulence on the surface settled. Tom heard a warning, 'There's many a wee boy got drooned in there, an their mammies never, ever saw them again', and instantly regretted his action. Malkie broke the surface once and never understood why Tom effortlessly lifted him on to the canal bank.

He was remorseful and apologetic when Tom fired some questions, and insisted they would never have used the knives on him, or anyone else. He was consumed with self pity until he staggered down the street and saw the state of his partner-in-crime, Geordie, sitting stunned on the road. 'Is this wan ae yours, wee man?' Malkie asked, as he picked up a broken, stained tooth from the muddied verge.

CHAPTER TWENTY-FOUR

RETURNING FROM HIS EVENTFUL visit to Port Dundas, Tom showered and went on duty.

'Christmas night in the work house,' groaned Roddie, as they moved chairs and heavy tables in the fuction suite. 'You okay, you're very quiet? I was expecting you to be all excited about the holiday. Julie phoned to tell us and she's a high as a kite.'

'I'm excited about it okay, but I ran into a wee bit of trouble in Glasgow today and it upset me.'

'What happened?'

'I couldn't sleep this morning and went out for a drive. I ended up in Port Dundas, and wandered round the canal basins reminiscing about family. When I went back to the car I surprised two blokes vandalising it. They had slashed the canvas roof open and were trying to get the CD player out.'

'They had blades?'

'Yeah, but they ran away when I appeared.'

'Your insurance should cover it.'

'I imagine so. It's no big deal. Just a pain in the arse getting it replaced.'

'Knife crime in this country is out of control. Some of these young guys know nothing but a life of violence. Christ knows where it's all gonnae end. The important thing is you didn't get hurt'

'That's right. Nobody got hurt.'

Roddie changed the subject. 'I'm intrigued by this amazing trip to see the orang-utans. Julie wouldn't offend me by saying so, but it's the best Christmas present she's ever had.'

'She would never say anything to upset you, mate.'

'Your grandparents will be looking forward to seeing you.'

'Yeah, and me them. I've never given much thought to them getting old, but they are both very frail now and it's beginning to look as if they won't be around much longer. I'm gonna try and spend a bit more time with them before they go.'

'Do they have other family around?'

'Unfortunately no. Mum was their only child and I'm their only grandchild. I've been neglectful and want to try and make amends.'

'They'll appreciate that, Tom.'

'Yeah, I know they will. They live in that big house and find it a real struggle because all the bedrooms are upstairs.'

'They should move.'

'I'm forever telling them that, but it's a bit late now. Last time I was home I suggested they downsize to a small house all on the level, but they refused. Said they're not selling my inheritance, but I think it's because mum lived there most of her days and it holds all their happy memories of her growing up.'

'That's the main reason I couldn't sell the lodge. Julie will have it long after I'm gone. She'll inherit a nice house here, and you'll inherit one in Australia. Christ, you'll be bloody loaded the pair of you.'

Tom laughed. 'And so will your grandchildren. The big house in Mt Eliza is in a stunning position overlooking the bay.'

'Sounds lovely.'

'You'll see it someday soon and you'll love it, mate. When Gran and Grandpa are gone, we'll convert part of it to a granny flat for you and Susan. You can both come out and help us plan a new garden. It's massive, but quite drab because they've got it low maintenance. The only thing missing is a swimming pool, and that'll be first on my list.'

'You'd better start saving.'

'Gran took me aside one day and told me I'd be more than okay for money after they'd gone. Grandpa was a chartered accountant with a big income. His lifelong hobby and passion is numisantics, or whatever you call it.'

'Numismatics, coin collecting?'

'Yeah, that's it. Over the last fifty years he's built up a big collection of rare coins and gold sovereigns. God knows what it must be worth now. Dear old grandpa's loaded, but never spends a cent on anything other than coins.'

'He must get some enjoyment from them, surely?'

'Oh yeah, it wasn't simply an investment. When I was a kid he would take me down to the safety deposit boxes in the bank and sit for hours studying just a few of his thousands of coins. He tried to get me involved, but my only interest was getting the hell out of there and down the bay with the boogie.'

'And they'll all be yours some day?'

Tom grinned. 'Yeah, I'm afraid I'm gonna have to take on the terrible burden of their ownership.'

In the morning, Tom went to South Lodge and climbed into bed beside Julie. They kissed and cuddled, but he felt far from his usual passionate, randy self and couldn't get an erection.

'What's up, handsome?'

'Sorry. The old fella doesn't seem interested this morning. Truth is, sweetheart, I'm shattered. He'll be rarin to go after a decent kip.'

Julie left for work and Tom spread himself out on the bed. Although he hadn't slept for two days, the much needed 'decent kip' didn't materialise and he lay mulling over events of the past twenty-four hours. It was now clear that the rumour spread down through generations of McCartneys had no foundation. Mary had neither betrayed Angus with an affair, nor been involved in any way with his death. He had experienced a feeling of calm – of closure during this latest vision of Colinton Street, but his peace of mind had immediately been violated by the knife-wielding men. Is that why he overreacted? Undoubtedly the incident would have terrified most people, but never at any point did he fear the wretched pair. With absolute certainty he knew he could have disarmed them and chased them off. After pulling Malkie from the canal and questioning him, it was clear that both men had major drug addiction problems. According to Malkie, they had no intention of harming him and only wanted to frighten him into handing over his watch. Acquiring money to buy heroin had become their sole motivation in life. There but for the grace of God.

For the first time in his life he was troubled by the notion of resolving violence with violence. Why did he have to smash one man's face to pulp and almost drown the other? He would doubtless be portrayed in American movies as a macho, ass-kicking hero cleaning up the streets, but he was disgusted with himself. Fuck sake, he was so ashamed of his own gratuitous violence that he'd lied to Roddie. What was it Roddie had said about non-violence? It had to be an inseparable part of your very being. Not simply a lack of desire to inflict physical harm, but a lack of ill-will or hatred towards people. He was beginning to understand that.

Surely there must be a way that people could respond other than with corroding hatred or violence such as he had inflicted on Geordie and Malkie in Port Dundas, or on the three men outside the Glasgow nightclub back in May? Geordie's face would require considerable reconstruction, and while that might well be to his benefit, it would be left to Walter Nimmo, or one of his surgeon colleagues in the Royal Infirmary, to sort out the pieces. What if he had erred by a few inches and smashed him down onto his skull rather than his face? What if Malkie hadn't surfaced? Within the space of a minute he could have killed two men, and all for the sake of a cheap fake watch he'd bought years earlier in Hong Kong.

He recalled numerous events where he had inflicted injury and pain on human beings without the slightest sliver of remorse. Could he search his heart now and truthfully say he no longer wished harm on anyone? Was he any different from his grandfather, Thomas McCartney, who became a vicious bully? What exactly did that gentle little boy suffer when the love and affection lavished on him by his parents and grandparents in a Glasgow slum, were replaced by beatings from a cruel step-father in Australia? Lying brooding about the reasons for his grandfather's violence, he recognized there was no excuse for his own. Sure, being orphaned might have been traumatic, but he was raised by kindly grandparents who abhorred bloodshed or cruelty of any kind. Contemplating the distress Angus would have felt had he known what his beloved wee boy would become, a thought suddenly struck him. What could be a more fitting way for him to repay Angus for his sacrifice than to renounce violence? If he spoke out against it, committed himself to a peaceful world, Angus and Mary, yeah and Lizzie too, would surely smile down on him for restoring values of decency, kindness and compassion to their McCartney line.

He gave up on sleep, dressed, and set off for a walk through the Big Wood towards Lord Blantyre's seat. Within a short distance, however, an irresistible force pulled him in a different direction. Retracing his steps back past the lodge, he walked along the road and into the old cemetery. Approaching the graves under the big sycamore, the hairs prickled on the back of his neck and he froze. Beautiful fresh holly wreaths had been placed against Angus and Johnny's headstones.

Frosted grass revealed various footprints around the graves: two adults, he judged, and a child. What in the name of fuck was happening? Mary, Michael and Thomas had been here. Those very holly wreaths had been sitting in the back of Michael's car when they left

Port Dundas to come here. Was it yesterday? Was it ninety years ago? Dear God, at what point in time was he standing right now?

Confused and bewildered, his entire body chilled and shivering, he made it back to the lodge. Sitting with a hot chocolate drink, he attempted to conjure happy images of baby orang-utans in Malaysia. He pictured himself with Julie on a beautiful beach at Kota Kinabalu before being greeted by his grandparents at Melbourne airport. In his mind's eye they walked into the big house in Melbourne and he cheerfully described the many photographs of his mother on the walls there. When he imagined the lounge with its fantastic view of the bay, his comfort zone was smashed. A stranger was present. Donna Mulhearty's angry father stood there waiting to question the psychopath who had killed his beloved daughter. Oh fuck no! Would he be running away from the spectre of her, and now her father, for the rest of his life?

'I've been thinking over what you said yesterday,' said Tom to Grandpa Shaw on the phone. 'Speaking to Mr Mulhearty is the right thing to do. I'd be grateful if you'd phone him back on my behalf and tee up a meeting in Sydney or wherever best suits him. I'll get back to you tonight with possible dates. Assure him I'll honestly and openly tell him everything I know about Donna's death. The problem is I've turned the whole thing over so many times in my head that my recall of it becomes less and less clear each time. So much spin was put on it by the army and the press that I'm now having trouble separating fact from fiction.'

'Just tell him the truth, Tom. That's all the man wants.'

Tom went back upstairs to bed. Although he felt calmer after finally facing that demon, sleep remained elusive. 'Just tell him the truth, Tom.' Fuck sake, how could he when he no longer knew it himself? What happened that goddamn awful day almost two years ago? What went wrong? Whose fault was it? Could he have handled it differently? What if it had never happened? Questions! Why always fuckin questions, never answers?

He replayed the incident over and over in slow-motion in his head, trying to analyse every step taken, every word spoken, but, as ever, the sequence of events just became more jumbled. Would he ever really know? Would he ever be able to truthfully recount it to Donna Mulhearty's father? Mentally and physically exhausted, he lay on the bed concluding the answer had to be 'no'.

As often happens when one's addled brain gives up trying to remember a name or solve a problem, a solution comes. Iboga! Could he use it to revisit the one specific event that continued to define his life? If he took another capsule, just one more, could he will himself back to the Amman Road in order to see exactly what happened? Could he, indeed, influence the event? There was a risk of making the PTSD worse but, fuck it, he was 'Chancer McCartney' after all. Before he could change his mind, he took the little package from his wallet, swallowed an iboga, and settled back on the bed. He deliberately concentrated on the Amman Road and the sight of Donna Mulhearty being gunned down – the very image he had repeatedly tried to exorcise from his mind.

Nothing happened. Half an hour later he was still wide awake. Perhaps it would all prove too painful, too damaging to his psyche, for his brain to allow him to go back there? Maybe the drug's effectiveness had decreased or his tolerance to it increased? Was he addicted to it?

Taking another capsule from his wallet he hesitated. It was, he knew, both a stupid and very dangerous thing to do. A tide of nausea soon washed over him and he staggered to the toilet and retched repeatedly. Reeling under the effect of the additional iboga, he just made it back to Julie's bed. A profound icy coldness, the last thing that registered, was soon replaced by blistering heat. He blinked repeatedly until his eyes grew accustomed to the glaring rays of the sun directly overhead.

The men of Kilo 6 were standing beside the long-range patrol vehicle. He 'tuned' himself in to the familiar voice of trooper Brannigan who was talking about US marines being blown to bits at a nearby roadblock the day before. Tom felt a bizarre sense of dislocation looking on at himself as he was nearly two years earlier, before his life changed for ever. This was the pivotal moment. What exactly did happen? Could he actually turn it in a different direction? He had no idea, but he was going to try his damnedest.

'I hear what you're saying, Shortarse, but the Yanks just got unlucky, or fuckin careless,' said Sergeant McCartney. 'We stick squarely to our training and the rules of combat. We remain constantly in control of the situation and we all go home to shag another day, another woman.' He looked directly at Trooper Presley. 'You follow my orders to the letter, Elvis, because that's a dangerous bit of gear in your sweaty little paws there. Friendly fire's killing as many of us out here as the fuckin towel heads, and none of us fancies getting one of your bullets up our arse. You do not open fire unless I give you a direct order to fire. Understood?'

'Understood, Sarge.'

'If I do give that order, you do not hesitate for a second, you carry it out. Understood?'

'Understood, Sarge.'

'Are you okay? You're sweatin like a pig.'

Elvis nervously glanced around at the other troopers. 'I'm okay, Sarge.'

Sergeant McCartney walked some distance away from the group, stood in the middle of the road, and called Elvis over. 'What the fuck's wrong with you? And don't give me any bullshit?

The young trooper simply shook his head.

'I called you over here to give us some privacy, so shoot.'

Elvis looked at the ground, tears welling in his eyes. 'I'm scared, Sarge. I'm scared.'

'I've told you, we'll all be fine provided we stay alert.'

'Yeah, but some blokes in the bar last night were talking about the American patrol. It was one of the best and they were always alert. I don't want bits of me being sent home in a bag to my mum and dad.'

Sergeant McCartney laughed, but immediately regretted it when the young soldier turned to walk away. He pulled him back. 'I'm sorry, I wasn't laughing at you. I promise. We're all fuckin nervous. Each and every one of us. We're just that bit more experienced at hiding it than you. Calm down for fuck sake. You'll soon be home to a hero's welcome from your mum and dad.'

Elvis shook his head. 'My dad says we shouldn't be here. Says it's one big mistake like Vietnam.'

'For fuck sake,' said Sergeant McCartney angrily. 'We're here in Iraq with a job to do and that's it. We do it. I don't give a monkey's fuck what your dad says or thinks. If you had any doubts you shouldn't have enlisted. You listen up good to me, mister. The six of us here this morning don't have the fuckin luxury of deciding what's right or wrong. We wear the uniform, we pick up the cheque at the end of the month, we do what we are fuckin well told to do. Got it?'

'Got it, Sarge,'

'Well I'm telling you,' he snarled, prodding Elvis's chest with his finger, 'get your fuckin head sorted out right now. Carrying passengers is another luxury we're not allowed.'

'Vehicle approaching at speed!' shouted one of the soldiers, as a car appeared in the shimmering distance.

A feeling of impending doom numbed Tom as the familiar scene began to unfold before him like a much-repeated horror movie. He gathered all his willpower and attempted to make a mental connection with his other self, exposed in the merciless Iraqi sun.

'Take up your positions, I've got the road!' barked Sergeant McCartney, resetting the sand-coloured beret on his blond hair. If there's the slightest whiff of danger, let the fucker have it!' His hands clenched with annoyance on his M4 machine-gun when Presley remained on the road beside him as if rooted to the spot. 'Elvis!' he yelled practically in his ear, 'move your arse, these motherfuckers are dangerous.' It had the desired effect. Presley started as though he'd been kicked, and ran to take up his position in a shallow ditch alongside the road.

Troopers Mark Binnie and Mick Hare jumped up onto the back of the long-range patrol vehicle. Binnie swung the heavy machine gun round on its tripod to face the oncoming car while Hare covered the road behind the vehicle. Troopers Brannigan and Stevens took up their positions at strategic points along the road in a state of readiness as the car approached, raising a cloud of dust on the dry desert road.

In order to get exactly the same view Elvis had of the incident, Tom positioned himself immediately beside him as he crouched nervously in the ditch with his M4 at the ready on short burst mode. He could see sweat lashing down Elvis's forehead into his eyes and that it, or was it tears, must be blurring his vision.

McCartney stood in the centre of the road, gesturing to the driver to stop. The driver did everything by the book, approaching the road block slowly and pulling up at the precise point indicated by the soldier when he yelled, 'Get out of the car!'

As the driver walked slowly forward toward Sergeant McCartney, the front passenger door suddenly opened directly in front of Tom and Elvis. The woman made to step from the front passenger seat, but the man sitting behind grabbed her arm. 'No! Don't be so fuckin stupid.'

She turned with a look of annoyance and swatted his hand away.

'It's cool, Elvis. Relax, it's cool,' said Tom, frantically attempting to connect with the young trooper and change the course of events. He could hear Elvis's rasping breaths over his own, smell his fear. 'Please, Elvis. Please, it's okay mate, it's okay. Oh fuck no.' The woman walked directly away from them towards Sergeant McCartney. Her right hand reached inside her white canvas bag.

Tom thrashed uncontrollably on Julie's bed in South Lodge. 'No, Elvis!' he screamed in the instant before the devastating scene unfolded yet again before his eyes.

Downstairs, hands trembling, he helped himself to a large glass of expensive Ardbeg from Roddie's whisky collection. He went out to the store for logs, kindled a fire in the living room and sat staring into the flames.

'I don't give a monkey's fuck what your dad says or thinks,' echoed over and over in his head. Dear God, what a terrible thing to say to the boy. A young soldier in his charge had been man enough to express perfectly rational fears to him, and for that he had treated him like like a piece of shit. What a fuckin, nasty horrible scumbag you were McCartney, he berated himself. Elvis had been one of his men – okay it was only for a few days, but never once had he asked him how he was feeling or offered him support or encouragement of any kind. Then, at no time after the incident, had he considered the profound and terrible impact killing Donna Mulhearty would forever have on the young lad's life. Fuck sake, just what sort of person were you? He had served under some hard bastards in his days in the Australian army, but at no time had any of them treated him the way he'd treated Elvis. 'I'm sorry, Elvis. Truly sorry.'

And, besides the rookie, what was the aftermath of the road-block deaths on others? Never in the weeks and months after it had he given a solitary thought to the terrible impact it would have on anyone but himself. Did Hashim Abdallah have a wife and children totally dependent on his taxi income for survival? Was their cupboard now completely bare like Mary's had been? How did Donna Mulhearty's fiancé cope with the loss of his Julie? Did Tom Cahill and Giuseppi Del Buon leave grieving wives, children and adoring grandchildren?

He phoned Mar Hall to tell Julie he'd meet her there when her shift finished. Putting the phone down, he hesitated for a moment then picked it up again and dialled his grandparents' number in Melbourne.

'Sorry for phoning you at this unearthly hour, Grandpa. I'm not able to give you dates for the meeting with Mr Mulhearty yet, but I promise I will do asap. Could you do me a big favour? Ask him to ask his journalist friends if they could get me a contact number for Pete Presley. I think he's from Brizzie, but possibly the poor kid's had to move away. He's another one I need to meet up with when I'm over.'

'I'll do that, Tom. Your gran and I are very pleased you're going to see the Mulheartys. It'll help them to a closure. We know only too well the pain of losing a daughter.' Tom could hear the emotion in his grandfather's shaky voice.

'You know, Grandpa, I've never really thought about the pain you and gran suffered when mum died.'

'No.'

'No, and I know you're too polite to say this so I'll say it for you. It's time I grew up and started thinking about others rather than me, me, me.'

'Why are you being so hard on yourself? You're a good boy, Tom. Always were. Never at any time did your gran or I think you were selfish. We would never say anything like that about you.'

'Yeah, I know you wouldn't. Thanks, Grandpa.'

'Phone us back as soon as you've got dates.'

'I'll do that after I've spoken to Julie. You're gonna love her. I just know you are. Speak to you later.'

'Speak to you later, Tom.'

'And Grandpa.'

'Yes.'

'I've never said this to you before. I love you.'

Grandpa Shaw's voice choked off.

Tom put on warm clothing and slowly walked along the path through the Big Wood to Mar Hall. This had been Angus's last journey. He took the little polythene bag from his wallet and rolled the two remaining capsules around in his hand. Iboga had given him both terrific and terrifying experiences, but had it given him the fabled rite-of-passage to manhood? Yeah, he liked to think it had. Through it, he had exorcised his demons and, as of this very day, he was renouncing the violent instincts of his father and grandfather. Through iboga, he had hope for the future.

He kissed the little capsules before throwing them deep into the undergrowth. 'Thank you, iboga. Thank you so much.'

Julie looked up from her desk with a big smile when he walked into reception. 'Hiya handsome, I'm very much hoping you got that decent kip. How's the "old fella"?'

He leaned over to kiss her. 'Great kip, sweetheart. The old fella and I are rarin to go.'

Julie handed over at reception and they walked along the avenue to South Lodge. 'Davie phoned this morning,' Julie beamed. 'And you'll never guess what. He and Sandra are back together.'

'You little ripper. Good onya, cobber.'

'He says you've made such a big impact on him that he's told her and Callum all about you.'

'Really? That's nice to know. Hope I get to meet them both soon.'

'You missed them yesterday. They were down at Greenock with presents for Sandra's parents and called in at the lodge on the way home. Davie says he rattled the letterbox, but you must've been out for the count. He's got a wee gardening sideline selling holly wreaths at Christmas, and brought two over to put on Angus's and Johnny's graves.'

Tom burst into a fit of laughter.

'What's so funny about that?'

'I was along there this morning and convinced myself that Mary's and Thomas's ghosts had put the wreaths there. I thought I'd finally lost the plot.'

Both of them were laughing heartily when they reached the lodge.

'Three whole days off together before the New Year madness descends,' said Julie, as they cuddled up on the sofa in front of the fire.

'Magic. Pure pure bloody magic,' said Tom, before becoming serious. 'I've got one or two things I need to talk to you about over the next few days, sweetheart.'

'Is something wrong?' she asked with a concerned look on her face.

'The four little bambinos we talked about having.'

'Yes.'

'I feel I'm a fit person to be a father now.'

'I don't have the slightest doubt about that, Tom McCartney. And do you know what?'

'Tell me.'

'You'll make a terrific dad.'